ALSO BY SOPHIE LARK

Brutal Birthright

Brutal Prince

Stolen Heir

Savage Lover

Bloody Heart

Broken Vow

Heavy Crown

Sinners Duet

There Are No Saints

There Is No Devil

BLOODY HEART

SOPHIE LARK

Bloom books

Copyright © 2022, 2023 by Sophie Lark
Cover and internal design © 2023 by Sourcebooks
Cover design by Emily Wittig
Cover images © kues/Depositphotos
Cover and internal illustrations © Line Maria Eriksen

Published by Bloom Books, an imprint of Sourcebooks
P.O. Box 4410, Naperville, Illinois 60567-4410
(630) 961-3900
sourcebooks.com

Originally self-published in 2022 by Sophie Lark.

Cataloging-in-Publication Data is on file with the Library of Congress.

Printed and bound in Canada.
MBP 10 9 8 7 6 5 4 3 2

Dedicated to Keeana, who painted me a picture of the perfect strong and sexy woman for Dante.

XOXO

Sophie Lark

SOUNDTRACK

1. "Zombie"—The Cranberries
2. "Ring of Fire"—Lera Lynn
3. "July"—Noah Cyrus
4. "The Vampire Masquerade"—Peter Gundry
5. "Waltz for Dreamers"—Matt Stewart-Evans
6. "STUPID"—Ashnikko
7. "Back to Black"—Amy Winehouse
8. "Hurt"—Johnny Cash
9. "Don't Speak"—No Doubt
10. "Yesterday"—The Beatles
11. "When You're Gone"—The Cranberries
12. "The Chain"—Fleetwood Mac
13. "Hell or High Water"—The Neighbourhood
14. "Holy"—Justin Bieber

Music is a big part of my writing process. If you start a song when you see a 🎵 while reading, the song matches the scene like a movie score.

Spotify   Apple Music

1

SIMONE SOLOMON

"Simone! Why aren't you ready?"

My mother stands in the doorway, already dressed for the party.

By contrast, I'm wearing sweat shorts and a Wonder Woman T-shirt because I was curled up in my window seat, lost in a book.

"What time is it?" I ask.

"What time do you think it is?" Mama says, smiling slightly.

I would have said two or three in the afternoon, but the fact she's already put on her evening gown clues me in that it must be later.

"Uh…six?" I guess.

"Try seven thirty."

"Sorry!" I jump up from the window, knocking my copy of *Wuthering Heights* onto the carpet.

No wonder I'm starving. I missed lunch—and apparently dinner too.

"You'd better hurry," Mama says. "Your father already called for the car."

"The car is waiting, actually," my father says.

He stands next to Mama. They're the most elegant pair imaginable—both tall, slim, impeccably dressed. His rich dark coloring next to her fairness is the only contrast between them. Otherwise, they're perfectly matched.

Sometimes my father wears bright kente cloth on formal

occasions. Tonight he's dressed in a black tuxedo with a velvet lapel. The lavender calla lily in his boutonniere is the exact shade of my mother's gown.

Next to their sleek perfection, I feel like I'm all elbows and knees. Too awkward to even be seen with them.

"Maybe you should go on without me…" I say.

"Nice try," Mama says. "Hurry and get dressed."

I stifle my groan. At first, I was excited to be home from boarding school. Chicago seemed like a whirlwind of parties, galas, and events. Now, only a few months later, they're all starting to blur together. I'm tired of champagne and canapés, polite conversation, and even politer dancing. Plus, I wish my sister came along more often.

"Is Serwa coming?" I ask Mama.

"No." A small line forms between her eyebrows. "She's not having a very good day."

My parents leave me alone to dress.

I have a whole closet of gowns to choose from, most of them bought this year. I run my fingertips down the rainbow of fabric, trying to choose quickly.

I could spend an hour like this. I'm a bit of a daydreamer, and I love beautiful things. Especially clothes.

An interest in fashion can be perceived as frivolous. In my mind, clothes are wearable art. They're the statement that precedes you into every room. They're the tools that shape people's perception before you've spoken a word.

That's how I would describe it to anybody else.

To me, they mean so much more than that.

I have an intense reaction to color and texture. They create a mood inside me. I don't like to admit it to anyone because I know it's…strange. Most people don't feel physically repulsed by an unattractive shade of puce. And they don't feel an irresistible desire to touch silk or velvet.

I've always been that way for as long as I can remember. I've just learned how to hide it.

I force myself to grab a dress without poring over them for ages.

I take one of my favorites, a pale rose gown with fluttering chiffon down the back that reminds me of a butterfly's wings.

I dust on a little pink blush and lip gloss in the same shade. Not too much—my father doesn't like me to dress overly "mature." I only just turned eighteen.

When I hurry downstairs, my parents are already waiting in the limo. There's an odd tension in the air. My father is sitting stiffly upright in his seat. My mother glances at me, then looks out the window.

"Go," Tata barks to the driver.

"I got ready as quickly as I could…" I say tentatively.

My father ignores that entirely. "Would you like to tell me why I just found an acceptance letter from Parsons in the mail?" he demands.

I flush, looking down at my fingernails.

I'd hoped to intercept that particular envelope, but it's difficult to do in our house, where several different staff members check for mail twice a day.

I can tell my father is furious. Yet, at the same time, I feel a wild swoop of elation at his words…

I was accepted.

I hide my happiness. My father is not happy at all. I feel his displeasure radiating outward like a cold fog. It freezes me down to my bones.

I can't meet his eyes. Even in his best moods, my father has sharp features and an intense stare. When he's angry, he looks like the carved mask of some deity—epic and vengeful.

"Explain," he orders.

There's no point in lying. "I applied to school there."

"Why did you do that?" he says coldly.

"I…I wanted to see if I'd get in."

"What does it matter if you get in, since you'll be attending Cambridge?"

That's my father's alma mater. Cambridge is responsible for his posh manners, his European connections, and the slight British accent of which he's so proud.

My father, poor but brilliant, went to Cambridge on scholarship. He studied much more than economics—he studied the behavior and attitudes of his wealthy classmates: how they spoke, how they walked, how they dressed, and most of all, how they made money. He learned the language of international finance—hedge funds, leveraged capital, offshore tax havens…

He always said Cambridge was the making of him. It was understood that I would go to school there, just like Serwa did before me.

"I just…" I twist my hands helplessly in my lap. "I just like fashion…" I say lamely.

"That is not a serious area of study."

"Yafeu…" Mama says softly.

He turns to look at her. My mother is the only person my father listens to. But I already know she won't oppose him—not in something like this, where his opinion is already so rigidly set. She's just reminding him to be gentle. While he shatters my dream.

"Please, Tata." I try to keep my voice steady. My father won't listen if I become too emotional. I have to reason with him the best I can. "Some of the most prestigious designers in the country graduated from Parsons. Donna Karan, Marc Jacobs, Tom Ford…"

My father steeples his hands together in front of him. He has long, elegant fingers with manicured nails.

He speaks slowly and clearly, like a judge laying down the law. "When you were born, my parents said how unfortunate it was that I only had daughters. I disagreed. I told them daughters will always be loyal to their parents. Daughters are obedient and wise. Daughters bring honor to their families. A son may become prideful and think he knows better than his father. A daughter would never make that mistake."

My father puts his hand on my shoulder, looking into my eyes. "You are a good daughter, Simone."

We're pulling up to the Drake Hotel. My father takes a clean handkerchief from his pocket. He passes it to me. "Clean your face before you come inside."

I hadn't realized I was crying.

Mama rests her palm on my head for a moment, stroking my hair. "See you inside, *ma chérie*," she says.

Then they leave me alone in the back seat of the car.

Well, not really alone—our driver is sitting up front, patiently waiting for me to compose myself.

"Wilson?" I say in a strangled tone.

"Yes, Miss Solomon?"

"Could you give me a minute alone, possibly?"

"Of course," he says. "Let me pull to the side."

He pulls the town car up to the curb, out of the way of everyone else being dropped off at the front doors. Then he steps away from the vehicle, kindly leaving the engine running so I'll still have air-conditioning. He strikes up a conversation with one of the other chauffeurs. They go around the corner of the hotel, probably to share a cigarette.

Once I'm alone, I give myself over to crying. For five solid minutes, I wallow in my disappointment.

It's so stupid. It's not like I ever expected my parents to let me go to Parsons. It was just a fantasy that got me through my last year of school at Tremont and the endless soul-crushing exams that I was expected to pass with top marks. And I did—every one of them. No doubt I'll be receiving a similar acceptance letter from Cambridge any day now because I did apply there, as required.

I sent a portfolio of my designs to Parsons on a whim. I guess I thought it would be good to receive a rejection—to show me that my father was right, that my dream was a delusion that could never actually come to pass.

To hear I was accepted...

It's a sweet kind of torture. Maybe worse than never knowing at all. It's a bright, shimmering prize, put right within reach...then yanked away again.

I allow myself to be childish and miserable for those five minutes.

Then I take a deep breath and pull myself together.

My parents still expect me inside the grand ballroom of the Drake. I'm supposed to smile, make conversation, and let them introduce me to the important people of the night. I can't do that with a blotchy, swollen face.

I dab my face dry, reapplying a little lip gloss and mascara from my purse.

Right when I'm about to reach for the door handle, the driver's door is wrenched open instead, and someone slides into the front seat.

It's a man—a huge man, practically a giant. Broad-shouldered, dark-haired, and definitely not wearing a uniform like Wilson.

Before I can say a word, he slams his foot on the gas pedal and speeds away from the curb.

2
DANTE GALLO

Security at the Drake is stiff, thanks to all the hoity-toity political types coming in for the gala. Rich people will take any excuse to celebrate themselves. Awards banquets, fundraisers, charity auctions—it's all just an excuse for them to slap one another's backs publicly.

Papa's restaurant La Mer is providing the king crab legs, scarlet prawns, and oysters on the half shell that will make up the gargantuan seafood tower in the center of the buffet. We bid cheap on this job because we won't be making our profit on shrimp tonight.

I pull my van up to the service doors and help the kitchen staff unload the crates of iced shellfish. A security guard pokes his head into the kitchen, watching us crack open the crates.

"What do you even call that?" he says, staring at the scarlet prawns with a horrified expression.

"It's the best shrimp you can't afford," I tell him, grinning.

"Oh yeah? What's that cost?"

"Hundred and nineteen a pound."

"Get the fuck outta town!" He shakes his head in disbelief. "You better pull me a full-size mermaid with D-cup titties out of the ocean for that price."

Once we've got all the product safely stowed in the walk-in refrigerator, I nod to Vinny. We set the last chest under a room service cart.

Vinny works at the Drake, sometimes as a bellhop, and sometimes as a dishwasher. His real job is procuring items for guests—stuff a little more difficult to come by than fresh towels and extra ice.

I've known him since we were running around Old Town in Spider-Man sneakers. I got a whole hell of a lot bigger, while Vinny stayed the same—skinny, freckled, with terrible teeth but a great smile.

We take the service elevator up to the fourth floor. The elevator lurches alarmingly under our combined weight. The Drake is one of Chicago's roaring twenties hotels—renovated since then, but not much. It's all brass doorknobs, crystal chandeliers, tufted chairs, and that musty smell of carpets and drapery that haven't really been cleaned in the past fifty years.

I bet Dukuly is pissed at being shoved into some common suite on the fourth floor. He's got a lakeside view, but it's a far cry from the Presidential Suite. Unfortunately for him, he's not the most important person in town for the gala, not even close. At this particular event, he barely ranks in the top half.

That's probably why he's still sulking in his room while the gala's about to begin. I can smell the cigar smoke seeping from under his door.

"You want me to go in with you?" Vinny asks.

"Nah. You can get back downstairs."

It's gonna be all-hands-on-deck in the kitchen. I don't want Vinny getting into trouble or anybody coming to look for him. Plus, I've done business with Dukuly twice before. So I don't anticipate any trouble.

Vinny leaves me with the room service cart.

I knock on the door—three taps, as agreed.

Dukuly's bodyguard cracks it open. He's your typical burly-n'-surly type, dressed in a nice suit but looking like he lives at the top of a beanstalk.

He lets me into the suite, which consists of two bedrooms with a sitting room in between. After a quick pat-down to make sure I came unarmed, he grunts. "Have a seat."

I settle into the chintz sofa, while the ogre takes an armchair opposite. A second bodyguard leans against the wall, his arms crossed over his chest. This guy is a little leaner than his friend, with long hair pulled back in a ponytail at the nape of his neck. I want to tell him that the henchman ponytail went out of style with the last of the Steven Seagal movies. Before I get the chance, Dukuly comes out of his room, puffing furiously on his cigar.

He's already dressed in his formal tux, which strains around his belly. He's one of those men who practically look pregnant because his weight is solely concentrated around the middle, between spindly arms and legs. His closely trimmed beard is speckled with gray, and his thick eyebrows form a heavy shelf over his eyes.

"Dante," he says, by way of greeting.

"Edwin." I nod.

"Cigar?" He holds out a premium Cuban cigar, heavy and fragrant.

"Thanks." I stand to take it from him.

"Come by the window," he says. "We had a complaint from the front desk. Apparently, there's no smoking in any of the rooms anymore. What is this country coming to?"

He nods to Ponytail, who hastily unlatches the window and forces up the sash. No easy task, since the old windowpane is practically welded in place by time and stiffness. There's no screen—just a straight four-story drop to the awning below.

I can see limos and town cars pulling up to the curb, with party-goers streaming out of their doors, the women in bright jewel tones, the men in shades of black, gray, and navy.

Beyond that, I see cyclists riding along the lakeshore and sparkling blue water punctuated by white sails.

"Nice view," I say to Dukuly as he lights my cigar.

"The lake?" He scoffs. "I've stayed in the Royal Suite of the Burj Al Arab. This is nothing."

I puff my cigar to hide my smile. I knew he'd be salty about the room.

Edwin Dukuly is the minister of lands, mines, and energy for Liberia. But blood diamonds are what pay for his Vacheron watch and hefty cigars. Like a modern Marco Polo, he brings little baggies of diamonds with him everywhere he goes to trade for whatever local luxuries he's craving.

I've got those luxuries with me right now. Under six inches of ice in my seafood chest.

"Shall we?" He motions to the seating area once more. I stub out my cigar on the windowsill and follow him over.

We make an amusing tableau—four large men stuffed into pink-and-white-striped chairs.

I haul the chest onto the coffee table, cracking the lid. I lift out the liner that contains the ice and a camouflaging layer of shrimp, revealing the guns beneath.

I've brought him everything he asked for: three Kalashnikovs, four Glocks, a Ruger, and one handheld RPG-7 grenade launcher, typically used for taking down tanks. I have no fucking clue what he plans to do with that—I suspect he saw it in a movie once and thought it looked cool.

There's also a tightly wrapped kilo of cocaine. Nice powdery Colombian stuff. Dukuly's eyes light up when he sees that. He takes a little silver knife out of the breast pocket of his tuxedo and cuts through the wrapping. He scoops up a mound of the powder on the tip of his knife, pressing it to his nostril and snorting hard. Then he rubs the residue on his tongue and gums.

"Ah!" he sighs, setting the knife back down on the table. "I can always count on you, Dante."

To his men he says, "Put all that away, someplace the maids won't find it."

I clear my throat, reminding him of the small matter of payment.

He takes a little velvet bag out of that same breast pocket, passing it over to me. I pour the diamonds out on my palm.

I have a jeweler's loupe in my pocket, but I don't need to use it to see that Dukuly thinks I'm an idiot.

The diamonds are cloudy and small. The size and quantity are less than half the value we agreed upon.

"What's this?" I say.

"What?" Dukuly feigns ignorance. He's not a very good actor.

"These are shit," I say.

Dukuly's face flushes. His heavy brows fall so low that I can barely see the glitter of his eyes underneath. "You'd better watch your words, Dante."

"You're right." I lean forward in my seat. "Let me phrase this in the politest way possible. *Pay me what you owe me, you fucking reprobate.*"

The burly bodyguard snatches up one of the Glocks and points it directly at my face. I ignore him.

To Dukuly I say, "Are you serious? You're gonna shoot me in the middle of the Drake Hotel?"

Dukuly chuckles. "I have diplomatic immunity, my friend. I could shoot you on the front steps of the police station."

"You don't have immunity from the outfit. My father is the don of Chicago. Or did you forget?"

"Oh yes, Enzo Gallo." Dukuly nods his head, a slow smile spreading across his face. "A very powerful man. Or at least he was...I heard he lost his balls when he lost his wife. Was that your mother, or did he father you on some other whore?"

My mother is five years in the ground. But there's not an hour of the day when I don't think of her.

Rage floods my veins.

In one movement, I snatch the little silver knife off the table and bury it in the side of Dukuly's neck, jamming it in so deep that half the hilt disappears along with the blade.

Dukuly claps his hand over the wound, his eyes bulging and his mouth silently opening and closing like a fish out of water.

I hear the *click, click, click* as the burly bodyguard tries to shoot me in the back. The Glock fires impotently. I'm not stupid enough to bring loaded weapons to an arms deal.

However, I have no doubt that there are plenty of bullets in the guns inside their jackets.

I spin Dukuly around, using his body as a meat shield. I have to crouch—he's not as tall as I am.

Sure enough, Ponytail already has his gun out. He fires six shots in rapid succession, riddling the chest and bulging belly of his boss. He knows Dukuly is already dead—he's motivated by revenge now.

Well, so am I.

These fuckers tried to steal from me. They insulted my family.

Just as the boss is responsible for the actions of his soldiers, so the soldiers will pay for their boss's words. I'm going to rip their heads off their fucking shoulders.

But I don't like my odds at the moment—two against one, and I'm the only one without a gun.

So I sprint toward the window, dragging Dukuly's limp body along as my shield. I dive through the open frame, turning my shoulders sideways so I'll fit. It's a tight squeeze—I barely make it through sheer force of momentum.

I fall four stories through the air, watching the sky and the pavement swap positions.

Then I crash into the awning.

The canvas frame wasn't meant to support 220 lbs. of plummeting mass. The fabric tears and the struts collapse, encasing me in a cocoon of wreckage.

I hit the ground hard. Hard enough to knock the air out of me, but with a whole fuck of a lot less impact than I deserve.

Still, I'm dazed. It takes me a minute to clear my head. I flail my arms, trying to extricate myself from the mess.

When I look up at the window, I see the burly bodyguard glaring down at me. I'm sure he'd like to fire a few shots in my direction. He's only holding back because his diplomatic immunity expired with his boss.

That's when I see Ponytail barreling around the side of the building. He sprinted down those four flights of stairs like an Olympian. I watch him hurtling toward me, debating whether I should strangle him with my bare hands or pound his face into pulp.

Then I see the dozen hotel employees and gala guests swarming toward me, and I remember that I made a hell of a lot of noise falling. I'm sure somebody's already called the cops.

So I hunt for the closest vehicle with its engine running. I see a sleek black Benz pulled up to the curb. The driver's seat is empty, but the headlights are beaming.

Perfect.

I wrench open the door and jump into the front seat.

As I put the car in drive, I get one perfect glimpse of Ponytail's enraged face through the passenger window. He's so mad, he doesn't give a damn who's watching—he reaches for his gun.

I give him a little salute as I floor the gas.

The engine roars, and the car jerks away from the curb like a racehorse let out of its stall. The Benz may look like a boat, but it's got a decent engine under the hood.

My brother Nero would love this. He's obsessed with cars of all kinds. He'd appreciate the handling and this cushy leather seat that seems to re-form itself around my body.

The car smells of leather, and whiskey, and something else... something sweet and warm. Like sandalwood and saffron.

I'm speeding down Oak Street when a face pops up in the rearview mirror. It startles me so much that I jerk the wheel to the left, almost plowing into a bus headed in the opposite direction. I swerve right to compensate, so the car fishtails back and forth several times before smoothing out again.

I think I let out a yell, and the person in the back gives a little shriek in return—betraying her as a girl.

I want to pull over, but I've got to make sure no one's following me first. So I keep driving west toward the river, trying to catch another glimpse of my surprise passenger.

She's hunkered down in the back seat again, obviously terrified.

"It's all right," I say. "I'm not going to hurt you."

I try to make my voice sound as gentle as possible, but it comes out in a rough growl as usual. I don't know how to be charming to women in the best of circumstances, let alone when I've accidentally kidnapped one.

There's silence for a minute. Then she squeaks, "Could you please... let me out?"

"I will," I say. "In a minute."

I hear a little gulp and rustling.

"What's that noise?" I bark.

"Just...just my dress," she whispers.

"Why is it so loud?"

"It's quite puffy..."

Right, of course. She was probably about to go inside the gala. Though I don't know why her car was pulled to the side with no chauffeur in sight.

"Where was your driver?"

She hesitates, like she's scared to answer me. But she's more afraid not to. "I asked him to step out for a minute," she says. "I was...upset."

She's sitting up a little straighter now, so I can see her face again. In fact, it's almost perfectly framed in the rectangle of the rearview mirror. It's the most beautiful face I've ever seen.

There should be a better word than *beautiful*. Maybe there is, and I'm just not educated enough to know it.

What do you call it when you can't tear your eyes away from a face? When you think you're looking at the loveliest angle, then the raise of an eyebrow or an exhale through the lips rearranges the features, and you're freshly stunned all over again?

What do you call it when your heart is thudding faster than it did when there was a gun pointed at your face? And you're sweating, yet your mouth is dry. And all you can think is, *What the fuck is happening to me? Did I hit my head harder than I thought?*

Her face is square with a pointed chin. Her eyes are wide set, almond shaped, and golden brown in color like a little tigress. Her cheekbones and jawline are painfully sharp, while her wide full mouth looks soft as rose petals. Her hair is pulled up in a sleek chignon, showing off her bare shoulders and the slender stalk of her neck. Her skin is polished bronze—the smoothest skin I've ever seen.

Finding a girl like that in the back of the car is alarming. Like putting a quarter in a gumball machine and the Hope Diamond tumbles out.

This can't end well.

"Who are you?" I say.

"Simone Solomon. My father is Yafeu Solomon."

She says those two sentences together, as if she's used to introducing herself by way of her father. Which means he must be someone important, though I've never heard his name before.

I don't give a fuck about him at the moment.

I want to know why she was crying alone in her car when she was supposed to be sipping champagne with the rest of the fat cats.

"Why were you upset?" I ask her.

"Oh. Well…"

I watch the color spread across her cheeks, pink suffusing the brown like a chameleon changing colors. I can't take my eyes off her in the rear-view, barely stealing glances at the road.

"I got accepted to a design school. But my father… There's a different university I'm meant to attend."

"What's design school?"

"Fashion design…" She blushes harder. "You know, clothes and accessories and all that…"

"Did you make that dress?"

As soon as I say it, I know it's a stupid question. Rich people don't make their own clothes.

Simone doesn't laugh at me, though. She smooths her hands over the pink tulle skirt, saying, "I wish I did! It's Elie Saab Couture—similar to one that Fan Bingbing wore to the Cannes Film Festival in 2012. Hers had a cape, but the tulle and the beading in this sort of botanical shape—"

She breaks off. Maybe she saw that she might as well be speaking Mandarin for all I understood. I know fuck all about fashion. I own a dozen white T-shirts and the same amount in black.

But I wish she wouldn't stop. I like the way she speaks. Her voice is soft, elegant, cultured…the exact opposite of mine. Besides, people are always interesting when they talk about something they love.

"You don't care about dresses." She laughs softly at herself.

"Not really. I like listening to you, though."

"To me?" She laughs again. She forgot to be scared when she was talking about the dress.

"Is that surprising?"

"Well…" she says. "Everything about this is a little surprising."

Now that I'm sure no one followed me, I've turned north, and I'm driving almost aimlessly. I should get rid of the car—it's probably been reported stolen. I should get rid of the girl, too, for similar reasons. I could drop her off on any corner. And yet I don't.

"Do you have an accent?" I think she does, but I can't tell from where.

"I don't know," she says. "I've lived a lot of places."

"Where?"

"Well, I was born in Paris—that's where my mother's family lives. Then we moved to Hamburg, then Accra…after that, I think it was Vienna, Barcelona, Montreal for a while—god, that was cold. Then to DC, which wasn't much better. After that I went to boarding school in Maisons-Laffitte."

"Why were you always moving?"

"My father's an ambassador. And a businessman."

"What about your mom?"

"She was a chocolate heiress." Simone smiles proudly. "Her maiden name was Le Roux. You know Le Roux truffles?"

I shake my head. I feel ignorant and uncultured next to Simone. Even though she's so young, it sounds like she's been everywhere in the world.

"How old are you?" I ask her.

"Eighteen."

"Oh. You look younger."

"How old are you?"

"Twenty-one."

She laughs. "You look older."

"I know."

Our eyes are locked in that rearview mirror, and we're smiling at each other. Smiling much more than I usually do. I don't know why we're both so amused. There's a sort of energy between us, where the conversation flows easily, and nothing we say seems out of place. Even though we're strangers in this ass-backward situation.

"Are you staying at the Drake?" I ask her.

"No—we rented a house in Chicago for the summer."

"Where?"

"Lincoln Park."

"I'm in Old Town."

The neighborhoods are right next to each other.

I shouldn't have told her that—if she talks to the cops afterward, if she gives them a description of me, I won't be that hard to find. There are only so many Italian men the size of a draft horse in Old Town. Plus, the Gallos are hardly unknown to the Chicago PD.

"I better get going," I say to her.

My mouth says the words. My body's not quite in agreement. I've pulled the car into the nearest parking lot, but I'm not getting out.

I see those tawny-colored eyes watching me in the mirror. She blinks slowly, like a cat would do. Mesmerizing me.

"I'm going to leave you at the history museum," I tell her. "Do you have a phone?"

"Yes," she says.

That was sloppy, too. She could have called the police while we were driving, without me noticing.

What the fuck am I doing? I'm never this reckless.

Quickly, I wipe down the steering wheel and paddle shifters with the front of my shirt, making sure to remove any prints. I do the door handle, too.

"I'm getting out," I tell her. "Do me a favor and wait a couple of minutes before you call anyone."

"Wait!" Simone cries.

I turn around, facing her fully for the first time.

The sight of her in the flesh, not just reflected, takes my breath away. I literally can't breathe.

She darts forward across the seats and kisses me.

It only lasts a second, her delicate lips pressed against mine. Then she sits back again, looking almost as startled as I am.

"Goodbye," she says.

I stumble out of the car into the park.

3

SIMONE

I press my face against the window, watching the man jog off into Lincoln Park. He moves quickly for someone so massive.

Then I sink back in my seat, feeling like the whole car is spinning.

What on earth just happened?

I can't believe I kissed him.

That was my very first kiss.

I went to an all-girls boarding school. And while that didn't stop any of my classmates from finding romantic partners—male or female—I never met anybody I liked enough to date. I never had the time or the interest.

In all my wildest imaginations, I never thought my first kiss would be with a criminal. A kidnapper. A carjacker. And who knows what else!

I don't even know his name. I didn't ask him because I didn't think he'd tell me. I didn't want him to lie.

My heart is slamming against my ribs. My dress feels too tight around my chest, and I keep breathing faster and faster.

Those ten minutes together in the car seemed like hours. And yet I can hardly believe they happened at all. No one else would believe it if I told them.

I can't tell anyone about this. For one thing, my father would be furious. Also, as foolish as this sounds, I don't want to get that man in trouble. He stole the car, yes, but he didn't hurt me. He didn't even take the Benz with him.

Actually…he was quite a gentleman. Not in manners—he was rough and abrupt, especially at first. His voice sent shivers down my spine. It was deep and gravelly, definitely the voice of a villain.

He didn't look like a gentleman either. He was huge—both tall and broad, barely able to fit in the car. His arms looked as thick as my whole body. He had ink-black hair, rough stubble all over his face, and black hair on his arms and even the backs of his hands. And his eyes were ferocious. Every time he looked at me in the mirror, I felt pinned in place against the seat.

Still, I believed him when he said he wasn't going to hurt me. Actually, I believed all the things he said. The way he talked was so blunt that it seemed like he had to be honest.

I press my palms against my cheeks to cool them. I feel flustered and hot. My hands are hot, too—they're not helping.

I can't stop thinking about his eyes looking back at me, that rough voice, and those insanely broad shoulders. His huge hands gripping the steering wheel…

I've never seen a man like that. Not in any country I've visited.

I feel my phone vibrating in my little clutch, and I pull it out. I see a dozen missed calls and many more messages.

I pick up the call, saying, "Tata?"

"Simone!" My father's voice is thick with relief. "Are you all right? Where are you? What's happening?"

"I'm fine, Tata! I'm okay. I'm at the history museum, at the corner of Lincoln Park."

"Thank god. Stay right where you are, the police are on their way."

I couldn't leave unless it was on foot. I never got a driver's license.

It only takes minutes for the police to arrive. They pull me out of the car and surround me, putting a blanket around my shoulders, asking me a hundred questions at once.

All I say is, "I don't know, I don't know," over and over.

They take me directly back home, on my father's insistence, I'm sure. He's already waiting on the front porch. He pulls me away from the police, telling them not to ask me any more questions.

Mama keeps kissing me and holding my face between her hands like she can't believe it's really me.

Even Serwa is awake and down from her room, wrapped in her favorite fuzzy robe. She hugs me, too—not as hard as Mama. I hug her back just as gently. My sister is ten years older than me but a head shorter. I rest my chin on her hair, smelling her familiar scent of jasmine soap.

Once the police are gone, the real interrogation begins.

My father sits me down in the formal living room, demanding to know what happened.

"A man stole the car, Tata. I was in the back seat. He told me to get down and cover my eyes. Then he dropped me off."

The lie comes out of me with remarkable ease.

I'm not used to lying—especially not to my parents. But there's no way I could explain to them what really happened. I don't even understand it myself.

"Tell me the truth, Simone," my father says sternly. "Did he touch you? Did he hurt you?"

"Yafeu—" Mama says.

He holds up a hand to silence her. "Answer me."

"No," I say firmly. "He never touched me."

It was me who touched him.

"Good," my father says with immeasurable relief.

Now he hugs me, wrapping his strong arms around my shoulders and squeezing me tight.

I wonder if he would have done that if I *had* been "touched"?

"You missed your party," I say to Mama.

"It doesn't matter." She tucks a lock of shimmering pale hair behind her ear. "*Mon Dieu*, what a city! I knew this would happen. Everyone said it's all criminals and thieves here, shootings every day."

She looks at my father with reproach. It's always his choice which appointments he takes, where we go. Only twice has my mother put down her foot with him—when she was pregnant with my sister and then with me. She insisted on going home to Paris both times so we would be born on French soil.

My father's personality is so strong that I've never seen anyone win an argument with him. I've certainly never done it. He's like a glacier—cool and immovable. Nothing can stand before him. He could crush an entire city in his path, given enough time.

It took an immense amount of will to escape the poverty of his birth. Nobody else in his family made it out. He had three older sisters—all three died or disappeared while he was still a boy. His parents are gone, too. He's a world unto himself. He's Jupiter, spinning around the sun, and Mama, Serwa, and I are tiny satellites, pulled along in his orbit.

I don't think Mama minds, generally—she told me she'd fallen in love with my father the moment she'd laid eyes on him. She's been devoted to him since. He was incredibly handsome—tall, lean, as sharp as if he were carved out of obsidian. But I know it was more than that. She was an heiress, born in luxury. It was his obsessive drive that she loved. She'd never seen anything like it among all the children of privilege.

On their wedding day, she handed him control of her trust fund. In one year, he grew it to three times its original size.

I wonder if there really is such a thing as love at first sight.

What does it feel like?

Does it feel like an arrow shooting into your chest every time a pair of coal-black eyes fix on yours?

My face flushes all over again, just remembering.

"What is it?" Mama asks me. "You look strange. Do you need water? Food?"

"I'm fine, Mama," I assure her.

My father is getting up from the couch.

"Where are you going?" she asks him.

"I've got to talk to Jessica."

Jessica Thompson is his assistant.

"Right now?" Mama says, that line between her eyebrows appearing again.

"Immediately. She's going to have to issue a press release. There's no covering up the fact our daughter was abducted. Not with all the commotion at the hotel."

This is my father's way—as soon as one problem is solved, he's on to the next. I'm safe, so the next task at hand is damage control.

"It's fine, Mama," I say. "I'll just go to bed."

"I'll go up with you," Serwa says.

I know my sister means it kindly, but honestly, she's probably the one who needs help up the stairs. She's currently in the throes of a lung infection, and her antibiotics aren't working.

As we climb the wide curving staircase, I slip my arm around her waist to help her up. I can hear her wheezing breaths.

My bedroom is the first on the left. Serwa follows me in, sitting on the edge of my bed.

I turn around so she can unzip my dress for me. I'm not embarrassed to be naked in front of her—Serwa is so much older that she's always taken care of me, from the time I was little.

I step out of the dress, hanging it up carefully again in the closet. I only wore it for a short time, and I never danced in it—there's no need to send it to the cleaners.

As I hunt around for my favorite pajamas, Serwa says, "So tell me what really happened."

I use the excuse of the pajamas to avoid looking at her. "What do you mean?"

"I know you didn't tell Tata and Mama everything."

I find my pajamas with the little ice cream cones all over them and pull them on. "Well," I say, from inside the comforting darkness of the pajama top, "he was very handsome."

"The thief?" Serwa cries.

"Yes—*shh*! Mama will hear you."

"What did he look like?" Serwa whispers, her eyes bright with curiosity.

"He was huge—like one of those Russian powerlifters. Like he eats a dozen eggs and two chickens every meal."

Serwa giggles. "That doesn't sound handsome."

"No, he was. He had this brutal face, broad jaw, dark eyes…but I could see he was intelligent. Not just a thug."

"You could tell that just by looking at him?" Serwa says skeptically.

"Well…we talked a little, too."

"*What?* About what?" she says, forgetting to be quiet again.

"*Shh!*" I remind her, though this house is massive, and it's unlikely anyone could hear us unless they were standing right outside the door. "Just…about everything. He asked where I was from, where I lived, and why I was crying before the party."

"Why were you crying?" Serwa frowns.

"Tata found out about Parsons."

"Oh." She knew I was applying. She was too kind to tell me it was a terrible idea. "Was he angry?"

"Of course."

"I'm sorry." She hugs me. "Cambridge is lovely, though. You'll like it there."

Serwa went just like she was supposed to. She graduated with distinction, with a master's in macroeconomics. She was offered an analyst position with Lloyd's of London, but before she could start, she caught pneumonia three times in a row.

My sister has cystic fibrosis. My parents have paid for every type of treatment under the sun. Often, she gets better for months at a time. Or at least she's well enough to attend school or travel. But always, right when she's on the cusp of her next achievement, it brings her low again.

It's been the shadow hanging over our family all along. The

knowledge that Serwa's life is likely to be shorter than ours. That we only have her for so long.

That would be tragic in itself. What's worse is that my sister happens to be the kindest person I've ever known. She's gentle. She's warm. She never has a bad word to say about anyone. And she's always been there to help me and support me, even when her lungs are drowning and she's weak from coughing.

She's still so pretty, despite her illness. She reminds me of a doll, with her round face, dark eyes, flushed cheeks, and hair pulled back from a straight center part. She's petite and delicate. I wish I could hold her like a doll and protect her from anything awful happening to her.

I don't tell Serwa about the kiss. It's too bizarre and embarrassing. I've never behaved like that before. She'd be shocked. I'm shocked at myself, quite honestly.

"Well, I'm glad you're safe." Serwa squeezes my hand. My hand is bigger than hers. All of me is bigger—I grew taller than her when I was only ten years old.

"I love you, *onuabaa*."

"I love you, too."

Serwa goes back to her own room. After a moment I can hear her vibrating vest whirring away, knocking the mucus out of her airways.

I put on headphones because that sound makes me sad.

I lie in my bed listening to my apocalypse playlist. I never listen to peaceful music to sleep.

I squirm under the covers, remembering the moment my lips met the lips of the thief... Heat flooded my body like a match thrown into dry grass. The flame spread in all directions, consuming everything in its path.

It was over in an instant, but it keeps repeating again and again in my brain...

I drift off to the sounds of "Zombie" by the Cranberries.

♫ *"Zombie"—The Cranberries*

4

DANTE

I can't stop thinking about Simone.

Her elegance, her beauty, her composure even when I was speeding across the city with her trapped in the back of the car...

I know it's insane.

I looked up her father. He's some fancy diplomat from Ghana who also happens to be as rich as a Pharaoh. He's got a string of hotels from Madrid to Vienna.

My family is far from poor. But there's a big difference between Mafia money and international hotelier money. Both in volume and legitimacy.

Not to mention the fact Simone and I met under less-than-ideal circumstances. I have no idea what she told the cops. I can only assume it wasn't much, since nobody's come banging on my door yet. Still, it would be idiotic to start poking around her neighborhood, just begging to be spotted.

Yet, three nights later, that's exactly what I'm doing.

I found the massive Lincoln Park mansion that Solomon rented at the start of the summer. It wasn't difficult—the thing takes up almost an entire city block when you include the grounds. It looks like the fucking Palace of Versailles. Endless expanses of white limestone and pillars and ornate balconies. Gardens all around, plenty of trees, and three separate swimming pools.

Solomon has a security staff, but they're not exactly on high alert. It's pretty fucking easy to sneak onto the grounds and watch the house from the outside.

I came around dinnertime. I can't see the family—I don't know whether they're eating in one of the interior rooms or taking their meals separately. But I can see two of the security guards dicking around in the kitchen with a maid and some girl who's probably a personal assistant. They're all eating sandwiches and drinking beers, oblivious to me standing right outside the window.

I don't give a shit about any of them. There's just one person I'm here to see.

That person comes walking out into the back garden only twenty minutes later. She's wearing a short robe and flip-flops, her hair pulled up in a tight bun on top of her head.

Simone strips off the robe, revealing a modest one-piece swimsuit underneath. Even the dowdiest suit can't obscure the body underneath. I think my jaw is hanging open.

Simone is a fucking goddess. I didn't see it in the car because she was sitting down with that puffy pink skirt all fluffed up around her. But her body is insane.

Legs a mile long. Full natural breasts. Slim waist flaring out into Venus-like hips. All encased in that rich, smooth skin that gleams under the strings of outdoor lights.

She raises her hands over her head, her palms together, and dives into the pool like an arrow plunging down. She breaks through the water with barely a ripple, then swims underwater almost the full length of the pool. She kicks off the opposite wall, then lies on her back, stroking in the opposite direction.

Her breasts poke up above the water, her nipples stiffening in the cool air. The modest suit clings to her skin, showing every curve beneath now that it's soaked through.

My cock is so hard that I have to press down on it with my hand. It's jammed against the zipper of my jeans, trying to rip right through the fabric.

Simone keeps swimming back and forth. When she does the breaststroke, I see her strong round ass cheeks turning left and right in the water, the swimsuit riding up between them. And when she does the backstroke, I see those gorgeous breasts again, the nipples perpetually hard from the cold water and the exercise.

I don't know how long I stand there behind a Japanese maple, watching her. It might be ten minutes or an hour.

I would have stayed for twenty years for the sight that follows. When Simone finally tires and swims to the ladder, my breath catches in my throat. She pulls herself up out of the pool, water streaming down her body.

She might as well be naked for all the suit covers now. I can see every inch of those impossible curves. I can even see the indent of her navel and the little cleft between her pussy lips.

I want her like a wolf wants a doe. I want to devour her, every last bit. My mouth is literally salivating. My cock has been throbbing so long that it's almost gone numb.

Simone grabs her towel and starts drying off. As she rubs the towel back and forth across her back, the motion shakes her breasts, making them sway and bounce.

Little droplets sparkle on her skin and in her hair. I want to be one of those droplets sliding down her body. I want to lick the water off her. I want to suck her nipples through that suit.

I think the sight of her has actually driven me mad.

Because when she goes back inside the house, I watch the upper floor with wild eyes, waiting for the lights to switch on. Sure enough, after the time it takes for a person to climb the stairs and cross a hallway, I see a light flick on in the northwest corner of the house.

I should wait until it's dark.

I shouldn't do this at all.

But nothing short of a nuclear explosion could stop me now.

Watching out for security cameras, I run to the deck on that side of the house, and I climb onto the railing. Jumping from there, I can just grab hold of the balcony on the next level and haul myself up.

It's a Juliet-style balcony, tiny and connected only to the single room on the other side of double glass doors. It takes me less than a minute to pick the lock.

As I slip into the room, I see Simone hasn't changed out of her suit yet. She's been distracted by a little gray cat prowling around on her rug. She's crouched to scratch it behind the ears.

When she straightens again, I wrap my arm around her waist and put my other hand over her mouth.

She shrieks against my palm, the sound muffled to nothing. The little cat runs into her closet to hide.

Her wet bathing suit soaks the front of my shirt. Her heart beats wildly against my forearm.

"It's me," I growl in her ear. "Don't yell."

I let go of her, cautiously. She turns around inside my arms, looking up into my face with wide eyes.

"What are you *doing* here?" she whispers. "If anyone hears you—"

"They won't hear me. If you can be quiet."

"Are you crazy? How did you find me?"

"You told me where you lived."

"But why did you come?"

"I had to see you again."

We're still pressed tight together, and I feel her heart against my chest now, wild as a bird.

If I thought her face was beautiful before, it's nothing to how it looks from only a few inches away. I smell the chlorine on her skin and that sweet scent of sandalwood beneath that I noticed the moment I got into her car.

Her lips are parted. I want to shove my tongue between them.

Fuck it—that's why I came, isn't it?

I grab her face between my hands, and I kiss her like I should have in the car. I kiss her like she's a captive, like she's something I've stolen.

I force my tongue into her mouth, and I taste her sweetness. I bite her lips, and I suck them hard until they're swollen and throbbing.

For a moment she's stiff in my arms, shocked and probably terrified. But then she melts like chocolate, sinking into me, letting her hands cradle the back of my neck. Her fingers twine in my hair.

I pick her up and throw her on her bed. The bed is childish and feminine—covered by a pale pink canopy and stuffed with frilled pillows. I shove all that out of the way to make room for her slim body and my massive frame. The springs creak under my weight as I climb on top of her.

"Wait!" Simone gasps. "Tell me your name this time."

"Dante."

"Is that your real name?"

"Yes."

"You're not lying?"

I look into her eyes, deep amber in this light. "I'll never lie to you."

I kiss her harder than ever, grinding my body against hers. I'm fully clothed and she's almost naked.

I close my mouth around her breast, sucking her nipple through the material of the swimsuit, just like I imagined. I taste the pool water, and I feel the hard point of her nipple against my tongue.

Then I yank down the front of the swimsuit, baring that heavy teardrop-shaped breast. I close my warm mouth around her cold little nipple. She cries out so loudly that I clamp my hand over her mouth again. I suck hard on her breast, flick her nipple lightly with my tongue, then suck hard again.

Simone squirms underneath me. I grab her wrists, pinning them over her head. I move over to the other breast, ravenously sucking again. She squeals against my palm. I'm sure the stubble on my face is scratching the tender skin of her breasts.

Holding her wrists over her head with one of my hands, I reach down and hook my fingers under the elastic of her swimsuit. I pull the crotch to the side, baring her sweet little pussy.

Simone stiffens and lies very still. I slide my middle finger up and down the cleft of her pussy lips, feeling the velvet skin and the soft little tuft of hair. From the way her breathing slows and her heart rate quickens, I don't think anyone has ever touched her here before. Her legs tremble as I part her pussy lips.

I moisten my fingers with her wetness and slide them back and forth over the nub of her clit. Simone lets out a long groan. Her knees press together. I force them apart with my thigh, spreading them open so I have full access to every place I want to touch.

Her pussy is like a perfect tiny flower. The lips are the petals, and her wetness is the nectar within. I stroke my fingers through her folds and rub circles around her clit with the flat of my thumb. Her breath is coming faster and faster. She arches her back, trying to press against my hand, but I have her pinned against the mattress.

Her eyes are closed, her lips parted.

Slowly, very slowly, I slide my index finger inside her.

She bites her lip as if even that one finger is hard to take. She's definitely a virgin. I wouldn't be able to get my finger in at all if she weren't so wet.

I take my index finger out and put the middle finger in instead, which is a little thicker. She gasps again. Her pussy clenches around my finger. I feel the resistance of the parts of her that have never been breached before.

With my finger inside her, I slowly rub her clit again. She turns her face against my neck, her eyes closed and her lips pressed against my skin.

I rub a little harder, sliding my finger in and out of her.

She makes sounds like that little kitten in the closet—anxious and desperate. Her hands are still pinned. All she can do is move her hips half an inch, squeezing tight around my finger.

I feel her climax building. I see the flush sweeping over her skin. I hear her gasping against my neck. I see her legs starting to shake.

As she starts to come, she bites down hard on my shoulder, her sharp teeth almost breaking the skin. She lets out a cry only partially muffled by my flesh.

Her pussy grips me tight. My finger is as wet as if I dipped it in oil. That's the only reason I can still move it. Her whole body is trembling now, not just her legs.

At last she relaxes with a long sigh. I kiss her again, tasting the pheromones on her breath.

At that moment someone knocks on the door.

"Simone?" calls a feminine voice.

I jump up from the bed.

Before Simone can even reply, "Just a minute!" I'm already through the French doors, over the balcony railing, dropping to the deck below.

I sprint off across the grounds, the scent of Simone on my fingers, my lips, and my skin.

5
SIMONE

I'M IN SO MUCH TROUBLE.

When I first kissed Dante, it was a wild impulse at the end of a bizarre event that I thought would be nothing more than a bubble in time—effervescent and gone forever once the bubble popped.

Of course, I thought about him afterward. Constantly, in fact. But I never expected to see him again.

Then he broke into my room, and everything changed.

My universe swapped positions. Dante became the new reality. And everything else seemed as fragile as that bubble in the wind.

He consumed me entirely.

I lay awake all night, thinking about him.

I could smell his scent on my sheets—like cardamom and fir, spice and wood. I swear he left a dent in my mattress from his bulk.

I pressed my face into that dent, remembering.

His body on top of mine was overwhelming, the sheer size of him almost terrifying. Every time I touched a part of him—his boulder-like shoulder or his bicep bigger than a softball—I couldn't believe how thick and dense the muscles were.

His stubble was rough. It scratched my face and chest. He kissed me like an animal, thrusting his tongue into every part of my mouth. But he was gentle when he put his fingers inside me. Like he knew no one had ever done that before.

And that orgasm…oh my god.

I tried to replicate it two or three more times later that night when I couldn't sleep. I nuzzled into the pillow, smelling his scent, and I tried to remember exactly how he'd touched me. But my soft little hand was nothing like his huge calloused one, each of his fingers thicker than two or three of mine together.

It was maddening.

I had to have more of him.

I felt like I'd die if I didn't get it.

But I was totally powerless. I had no way of finding him again.

Then, today, someone sent fifty pink roses to the house. There was no card. No name on the delivery.

I knew it was for me. The roses were almost exactly the color of my dress the night of the gala. I knew they were from Dante. I knew he'd come find me again.

Tonight I'm supposed to go to a dinner for the Young Ambassadors. Mama asks me if I'm feeling well enough to go. When she heard me cry out in my room, I told her I fell asleep and had a nightmare. Of course, she assumes I'm traumatized from my brief kidnapping.

"I'm fine, Mama," I promise her. "I really want to go."

She looks at me skeptically. "Are you sure? You look…feverish."

"I'm sure! Please, Mama. I hate being cooped up at the house."

She hesitates, then nods. "I'll have the car ready for you at eight."

"Thank you."

I get dressed almost an hour early. Even though there's no real reason to think this, I'm certain I'll see Dante tonight. Maybe not until after the party—actually, maybe I shouldn't go at all. He might be planning to climb up to my room again.

No, I've got to go. Especially after I made such a fuss about it with Mama. I'll go to the party, but I won't stay long.

I really am feverish, my brain bouncing around like a pinball machine. It's hard to focus long enough to get dressed.

This dinner is a little less formal than the gala. I'm about to grab one of my pretty pastel party dresses, but then a wicked spirit seizes me, and I grab a different dress from the closet instead.

This is one, I've never worn before—emerald green, near backless, with a slit up the thigh. Material thin enough that you could crumple the whole thing and stuff it in a clutch. I slip on a light jacket over the top so my parents won't notice.

I line my eyes a little darker than usual, and I wear my hair loose around my shoulders. I have wavy hair—dark, with just a hint of red in it if the light hits it right. My father always tells me I look best with my hair up, but I suspect that's because I look a little wilder when it's down.

That's all right. I feel a little bit wild tonight.

I don't get this way very often. Actually, I can't think of a single night when I left the house in a spirit of rebelliousness.

Tonight I'm thrumming with energy. The evening air feels crisp against my face. Even the exhaust from the waiting car smells sharp and exciting.

Wilson is driving me. He's being extra nice—I think he feels guilty that I was "kidnapped" on his watch. Even though I told him a dozen times that it wasn't his fault.

He takes me over to the Pritzker Pavilion in Millennium Park. The pavilion looks like a vast chrome spaceship touched down in the middle of the park. It's bizarre and futuristic and, to my eyes, quite beautiful.

Because the pavilion is used for outdoor concerts, it includes a huge oval trellis stretching over the grass to create the perfect acoustics for outdoor listening. The trellis is strung with golden lights, and indeed, it's reflecting the sounds of the string quartet playing on the stage.

The open lawn is already crowded with partygoers. The Young Ambassadors is a youth organization for young people interested in a career in foreign service. In practice, it's stuffed with the kids of diplomats and politicians, looking to pad their résumés for college applications.

I've been a part of it for five years, first in France and now here. Plenty of the kids have attended international events, so I see at least a dozen people I recognize.

One of them is Jules, a boy from Stockholm whose father is a Swiss councillor. As soon as he sees me, he comes over with an extra glass of sparkling apple juice in hand.

"*Bonsoir*, Simone!" He hands me the drink. "Fancy meeting you here."

I already knew he was in Chicago. Mama made sure to tell me. Jules is exactly the kind of boy I'm allowed to date—when I'm allowed to date at all. He's polite, respectful, from a good family.

He's actually pretty cute, too. He's got dirty-blond hair, green eyes, a smattering of freckles, and the kind of perfect teeth you only get from early and expensive orthodontic intervention.

I had a crush on him a couple of years back, after we both attended a fundraiser in Prague.

But tonight, I notice how I'm actually an inch taller than him in heels. He looks childish in general compared to Dante. That applies to everyone here. Dante makes even grown men look like boys.

Still, I smile back at Jules and thank him for the drink. I always remember my manners.

"You look…wow," Jules says, letting his eyes flit over the revealing green dress. I took off the jacket and left it in the car with Wilson.

"Thanks."

Usually, I'd be blushing, regretting my choice in the sea of girls dressed like they stepped out of a Lilly Pulitzer catalog. But tonight I'm feeling myself. I'm remembering the way Dante attacked me with his hands and mouth, like my body was the most luscious one he'd ever laid eyes on.

He made me feel sensual. Desirable.

And I liked it.

"Fernand and Emily are here, too. Would you like to sit at our table during the dinner?" Jules asks me.

He gestures over by the stage, where two or three dozen white-linen-covered tables have been erected, with formal place settings and covered bread baskets all ready to go.

"I—Oh!"

I was about to say yes. Until I caught sight of a hulking figure at the edge of the field, standing away from the lights. Though I can't see his face, I recognize those Goliath proportions immediately.

"What it is?" Jules asks.

"I've got to go to the ladies' room," I say abruptly.

"Of course. It's over by the—"

"I can find it!"

I hurry away from Jules, leaving him standing there with a baffled expression.

I don't go directly over to Dante. I walk as if I'm headed to the portable toilets, and then I cut back the opposite direction, slipping away from the amphitheater and into the trees of Millennium Park.

This is the first time I've directly broken the rules.

When Dante stole the car with me in the back seat, that wasn't really my fault. The same as when he broke into my room. I couldn't be blamed for either of those things.

But now I'm making a conscious choice to leave the party and go meet a criminal in the woods. This is so unlike me that I hardly know myself. I should be sitting at a table with Jules, sipping sparkling apple juice like a good girl.

But that's not what I want at all.

What I want is stalking me through the shadows under the trees. I can hear his heavy tread behind me.

"Are you lost, miss?" he growls.

"I might be," I say, turning around.

Even though I came over here to find him, I still feel my heart rising in my throat at the sight of him.

I didn't realize he was standing so close. In heels, I'm almost six feet tall. Dante still towers over me. In width, he's at least double my size. That stern, brutal face is terrifying in the darkness. His black eyes glitter.

I'm trembling. I can't help it. I feel naked with his eyes roaming over me.

"Did you get the flowers I sent you?"

"Yes," I squeak.

He steps even closer to me, so I can feel the heat of his broad chest, just inches from my face.

"Did you wear that dress for me?"

"Yes," I whisper.

"Take it off."

"W—what?" I stammer.

We're only a hundred feet from the party. I can still hear the music—Brahms, I think. I can even hear the murmur of conversation and the clink of glasses.

"I said 'take it off.'"

I'm an obedient girl. I usually do what I'm told. Especially when the order comes from an authority.

Before I can think, I slip the spaghetti straps of the dress down my shoulders, baring my breasts to the cool night air. My nipples tighten. Their tautness feels like someone is touching them, though Dante hasn't lifted a hand. Yet.

I drop the dress all the way to the grass and fallen leaves. Then I step out of it.

"Panties, too," Dante orders.

My heart is racing. I've never been completely naked in front of a man.

I hook my thumbs in the waistband of my underwear and pull that down, too.

Now I'm standing nude except for a pair of heels in a copse of trees in a public park. Anyone could walk by at any time. I resist the urge to cross my arms over my breasts.

A slight breeze slides over my skin, like human breath. When the air touches between my legs, I can tell I'm very wet.

Dante looks over my body silently. His face is so impassive that I can't tell what he thinks. But his eyes are burning like two black coals. "Turn around."

Slowly, I turn until he's behind me once more.

"Bend over," he says.

I don't understand why he's doing this. I don't know what he wants. This isn't what I expected when I came to meet him. I thought we'd talk, or he might kiss me again.

Instead, I'm bending over to touch my toes, which is difficult to do in stilettos on the uneven ground.

It's humiliating, exposing myself like this. What is he planning? What if he took a picture of me like this? I'd die of shame.

I can hear him move behind me, and I almost straighten. I only hold this awful position because I'm more afraid to disobey him.

Dante kneels behind me.

He puts his face between my legs.

From behind, his warm, wet tongue slides up the length of my pussy.

It feels so good that my knees almost buckle. I only stay upright because his massive hands are gripping my hips.

Dante eats my pussy like he's starving. He licks and sucks and shoves his tongue inside me. He licks me absolutely everywhere. It's wet and intense and absolutely fucking outrageous.

The vulnerability of my position and the intimacy of the places he's putting his tongue are insane. I can't believe I'm allowing it. But it feels too good to stop. I feel filthy and naughty, and I fucking love it.

As he's fucking me with his tongue, he reaches around and rubs my clit with his hand.

Oh my god, I feel like I've been waiting years for him to do that again. I've been so pent up thinking about him that in seconds, I feel the climax building, the relentless headlong rush into that release I feared I might never experience again.

Dante buries his face even deeper in my most delicate parts. He uses those thick, rough fingers to rub and press and coax me exactly where he wants me to go.

Bent over like this, my head is down by my ankles, and all the blood is rushing to my brain. As I start to come, I feel like I might be having an aneurysm. Fireworks are bursting behind my closed eyelids, and I have no idea if I'm crying out as loud as I did in my bedroom. God, I hope not.

The orgasm rips through me, even stronger than before. I collapse, only saved from tumbling onto the ground by Dante's huge arms wrapped around me.

He holds me against his chest. I'm limp, and he's as solid as an oak tree.

When I can see again, he helps me step into my dress. My underwear is gone, impossible to see in the dark.

"Did you like that?" he asks me.

"Yes," I say, in my most proper tone. "It was very nice."

Dante laughs. It's the first time I've heard him laugh—a deep rumble that vibrates in his chest.

"Do you want to go for a drive?" he asks.

"I would love that."

6
DANTE

I take Simone over to my car. It's just an old Bronco, battered and gunmetal gray. It's not good to drive a flashy car in my business. Not good to draw too much attention. Besides, I wouldn't fit in some tiny sports car.

Simone doesn't seem to mind. She waits by her door for a second, not touching the handle. I realize she expects me to open it.

I lean forward to grab it right at the same second that she does. We bump into each other, which does nothing to me but almost knocks her off her feet. She blushes and says, "Sorry, that was—"

"No, I've got it."

I've never opened a door for a girl before. I wouldn't have thought about it.

I'm not exactly the "dating" type. More the "get drunk at a bar, and if someone's giving me the eye, I guess I'll take them home" type.

I like women the same way I like burgers—if I'm hungry, and there's one available, then I'll eat.

Simone is no burger.

She's a ten-course meal, if I'd been starving for fifty years.

She could bring me back to life if I were almost dead.

She climbs into the passenger side, looking around at the cracked leather seats, the worn steering wheel, and the little woven band hanging from the rearview mirror.

"What's that?" Simone asks, pointing.

"It's a friendship bracelet. My little sister made it for me. But she made it the size of her wrist, so it doesn't fit." I chuckle.

"You have a sister?" Simone asks, surprised. Like she thought I was raised by mountain trolls.

"Yeah." I put the car in reverse. "I've got one baby sister and two brothers."

"Oh," Simone sighs. "I always wished I came from a big family."

"There's no family like an Italian family. I've got so many uncles, cousins, and people who think we're related because our great-great-grandparents came from the same town in Piemonte that you could fill the whole damn city with them."

"You've always lived here?" Simone says.

"All my life."

"I *am* jealous."

"What are you talking about? You've been everywhere."

"Visitor everywhere, citizen nowhere," Simone says. "Do you know we've never owned a house? We rent these palaces…but they're always temporary."

"You should come to my house. It's so old, it's probably put down roots."

"I'd like to see it," she says, with real excitement. Then she asks, "Where are we going now?"

"Where would you like to go?"

"I don't know." She hesitates. "Are you afraid to be seen with me?"

"No. Are you?"

"A little," she says honestly. "My parents have an itinerary for me. Wilson drives me everywhere I go."

"I'll take you somewhere nobody will see us," I promise. "Or at least nobody you know."

I drive us over to Lakeview, to an old brick building with a nondescript door halfway down its alley. Simone looks like she barely wants to get out of the car once I've parked. Still, she follows me out, slipping her hand in the crook of my arm as we walk, holding on to me for protection. Nobody around here would fuck with us, but I like the feel of her clinging to my arm.

I knock twice on the door. After a moment it cracks just wide enough for the bouncer to give me a once-over. Tony breaks into a grin at the sight of me.

"There he is," he says. "Where've you been, Dante?"

"Places where they don't skimp on olives, ya cheap fuckers." I clap him on the shoulder.

"You're not supposed to eat a whole jar with your drink." Tony grins. "Guess they never taught you that in finishing school."

Tony cocks an eyebrow at Simone, who's hiding behind my arm.

"Dante," he says. "What are you doing with a pretty girl like that? Are you so tall, she can't see your face? Come on, love—you know you can do better than this guy."

Simone looks mildly alarmed, but her years of social training haven't deserted her. She looks up at me as if really examining my features for the first time.

"He's not so bad," she says. "Not if you squint."

Tony laughs. "Squint a lot in there—you won't notice the holes in the carpet either."

He lets us pass into the speakeasy.

The Room is a private club with only three hundred members. Papa and I are two of them. The rest are some of the most old-school Italian, Irish, and Russian gangsters in the city. And by old-school, I mean very old—I'm probably the youngest member by ten years at least.

That's why I'm not worried about bringing Simone here. She's more likely to witness a coronary than a shoot-out.

Plus, I figured she'd dig the vibe. It's a tiny space, dark as night since we're underground, except for the low light of the shaded lamps on the table, and the green neon sign over the bar. There are plush crimson chairs, faded carpets, ancient wallpaper, and a solid wall of dark, dusty liquor bottles that really might have been here since Prohibition.

The waiters are about a hundred years old, too. They shuffle around in their white dress shirts and long black aprons, never spilling a drop of a drink.

Carmine comes to our table, giving me a friendly nod and Simone a little bow. "What can I get you?" he rasps.

"Let's do the sampler," I say before Simone can answer.

"Thanks," she says, as Carmine totters back to the bar. "I didn't have a clue what to say. I've mostly only drunk champagne or wine. Plus a few mimosas. My parents aren't big drinkers, but you know wine is hardly considered alcohol in Europe."

"It's mother's milk for Italians."

Carmine comes back a few minutes later carrying a tray loaded with eight miniature cocktails, plus a wooden board bearing marinated olives, house-made pickles, nuts, dried fruit, and several kinds of cheese.

"Is all that for us?" Simone squeaks.

"These are historic-era cocktails," Carmine explains patiently. "Just a little sample of each. Here you got the Bee's Knees—a little honey and lemon in your gin. Then the Mary Pickford—that's Cuban rum, pineapple, and a touch of grenadine to give you that lovely pink color. I'm sure you've had a sidecar before—brandy sour with cognac, orange liqueur, and lemon. And finally, the classic Chicago Fizz—a little dark rum, ruby port, egg white, lemon, and club soda."

He sets the miniature cocktails in a row in front of Simone as he names each one.

"Cheers." I pick up the Chicago Fizz. Simone gingerly holds up the same. We clink glasses, and she takes a sip.

"Not bad," she says.

She has a foam mustache above her lip. It makes her look even more like a little cat. I can't help smiling.

"What?" She smiles back at me.

"Nothing," I say.

She starts to giggle.

"Why are you laughing?" I ask her.

"Nothing." She shakes her head.

I catch sight of myself in the mirror over the bar. I've got a mustache, too.

We're both laughing so much that the men at the other tables give us disapproving looks.

I wipe my face with a napkin, then wipe hers, gently.

"You were never gonna tell me, were you?"

"No." Simone snorts.

I put my hand over hers on the tabletop. Her hand is slim and perfectly shaped. It makes mine look like a baseball mitt by comparison.

The jukebox in the corner switches records. Even though it's a '20s style speakeasy, most of the music that plays is actually from the '60s or '70s, since that's the "good old days" for most of the patrons.

"Ring of Fire" by Johnny Cash begins to play.

"Dance with me," I say to Simone.

"Nobody's dancing," she says.

"We are." I pull her up from the table.

I'm a shit dancer, I already know that.

It doesn't matter. I just want to hold Simone against my chest. Nobody cares that we're dancing. They give us a glance, then return to their conversations.

I can smell the sweet, clean scent of Simone's hair. She knows exactly how to move.

♫ *"Ring of Fire"—Johnny Cash*

After a few more songs, we sit at our little table again. We try all the drinks as well as the food. Simone is flushed from the liquor. Her cheeks turn pink, and she gets more talkative than ever. She asks me all kinds of questions.

I haven't drunk much, but I feel intoxicated by the sight of her. By the color in her face and the brightness of her eyes. They alter, depending on the light. Sometimes they're clear and golden like honey. Here, in low light, they look as orange as amber.

"Are you…a mafioso?" Simone whispers, not wanting anyone else to hear.

"I guess." I shrug. "It's not like a gang you join. It's a family business."

"What do you mean?" Simone looks genuinely curious, not judgmental.

"Well…" I try to think of how to explain it. "Like all businesses, there are the deals you run aboveboard and the ones that exploit the loopholes. There are the laws you follow and the ones you don't because fuck the people who made those laws—they're just as dirty, and they exploit them just the same for money and power."

I try to phrase this without insulting her. "Your father—he makes deals, he calls in favors. He has his friends and his enemies. My father's the same."

"I suppose," Simone says, toying with the glass of her sidecar. "It's not only backdoor business deals, though, is it?"

She looks up at me, clearly not wanting to offend me with the question but wanting to know the truth.

"No," I say. "It isn't."

Nero and I knocked over two armored trucks in Canaryville just last month. I'm not above any kind of crime, not really.

I don't give a fuck about stealing from a bank. Banks, governments, businesses—you show me one that's truly clean. It's all a system to shuffle money around, and I have as much right to siphon off a few thousand as any fat cat banker.

I wouldn't hurt somebody for fun. But when there's a reason…I don't hesitate.

"Have you ever killed anyone?" Simone asks so quietly that I can barely hear her over the music.

My jaw clenches involuntarily. I killed someone the night we met. And that wasn't the first time. "What do you think?"

She bites her lip, unable to answer. Or unwilling.

"Come on," I say. "Let's get out of here."

We get back into the Bronco. I drive east, over to Lake Shore Drive. I've got the windows down, and the cool night air streams through.

Simone looks a little sleepy, either because it's getting late or because she's not used to the drinks. I pull her head down onto my lap so she's closer and she can rest.

She lies there with her hand on my thigh.

The warmth of her cheek against my crotch, and the friction whenever she moves her head even a little, starts to excite me. I can smell her light perfume. I know she can feel my cock swelling under my pants, and that turns me on more.

When I'm too hard for her not to notice, she lifts her head a little. But she doesn't sit up. She starts unbuttoning my jeans instead.

She slides down the zipper, reaching into my boxers with her slim hand. She pulls my cock out.

It looks as thick as her wrist, the head flopping heavily into her palm. She startles but squeezes it tentatively. A little clear fluid beads at the tip.

She licks her lips to moisten them. Then she licks the head of my cock, tasting it.

The idea that my cum is the first she's ever tasted turns me on more than ever. I want to look down and watch her, but I have to keep my eyes on the road.

I feel those full soft lips close around the head of my cock. She's licking, tasting, exploring. She doesn't know what she's doing. But that's more erotic than any porn-star blow job. I'm taking her mouth for the first time, feeling my cock bang around against her cheeks and tongue as she tries to figure it out…

I'm so hard that I groan from every touch.

I want to be gentle with her, but it's so fucking hard to wait. I put my heavy palm on the back of her hair and push her head down so my cock slides farther into her throat.

Simone gags, her saliva running down my shaft. I hold her head there, thrusting my cock in and out of her mouth. I can feel the head pushing into the back of her throat, unable to get any farther. The squeezing around my cock is tight and hot and wet.

I let her up so she can breathe. Simone gasps for air, tears running down from the corners of her eyes. Not because she's upset, just from the gagging.

After she gets her breath, she tries again. She holds the base of my cock in her hand and tries to get as much of the head into her mouth as she can.

Her technique is shit, but her effort is A+. I'm torn between my desire to protect her, to be gentle with her, and the rabid lust that makes me want to fuck her face as hard as I can within the confines of the seat belt and the steering wheel.

Simone is delicate and cultured. It brings out the animal in me. I want to rip her clothes off, throw her down, use her body. Her natural gentleness and sweetness make me want to dominate her all the more. She's a good girl—I want to make her *my* good girl. My obedient little kitten.

I've never felt desire like this: crazed, furious, and extreme. I feel like I'm barely holding on to my last shreds of self-control.

If I didn't have to keep the car on the road, I probably wouldn't be able to contain myself at all. That's the only thing that keeps me patient enough to let her work, to let her slide her lips and tongue around my cock until I finally explode.

Hot cum boils up into her mouth. I can tell she wasn't expecting it. Some drips out onto my jeans, and some, she swallows.

She sits up, gasping and wiping her mouth.

I'm so dazed, I can barely drive. The orgasm was wild, wrenching. It jerked the wheel. I really should have pulled over.

My heart is thudding like a sledgehammer.

"Was that okay?" Simone asks.

I pull her back over and kiss her roughly. Tasting myself on her lips. "You're perfect. Fucking perfect."

7
SIMONE

It's not easy sneaking out to see Dante.

Especially not after that first night, when I got back so late.

My parents were furious. Wilson had been waiting for me at Millennium Park for over an hour. Luckily, the staff was still cleaning up from the dinner, so I could pretend I'd been sick in the bathrooms after Dante dropped me off again.

Mama sniffed suspiciously, probably smelling the liquor on my breath. And maybe something else, too—the lingering scent of sex on my skin.

I didn't care. Within a couple of days, I was finding ways to meet up with Dante again. I told Mama I was going out with Emily from Young Ambassadors. I had Wilson drop me at neutral places like the mall or movie theater.

Mama is actually pleased to see me socializing on my own, outside of mandated events. She keeps telling me to bring my "friends" over for dinner or to use the pool.

Instead, Dante comes to pick me up from my phony friend dates. He spirits me away to where we can be alone. Sometimes we do see a movie or go out to eat, though he tries to pick places away from the trendy restaurants where I might be recognized.

Really, I just want to be alone with him.

We go to distant beaches, lookout points, corners of parks, his house, or even hotels. Then he undresses me and puts his massive hands all over my body. He kisses me and touches me for hours, always finishing with his face buried between my legs, making me come over and over.

We haven't had sex yet. But I feel us edging closer.

Dante knows he'd be my first. He's trying to be patient. I can tell that every time he touches me, it awakens that part of him that has no patience and very little gentleness. It's terrifying because I know he could snap me in half if he truly lost control. But at the same time, I want him as badly as he wants me.

It's not only physical either.

We spend hours talking. About books, movies, music, our best and our worst memories, the things we want to do, and the things we're afraid of trying.

The only thing we don't talk about is our future together.

We skirt around the issue of my family. I've told Dante all about Mama and Tata and Serwa. He knows what they're like.

So he must know how violently they would oppose the two of us being together. I don't care about Dante's past—but they won't be so forgiving.

My father is rigid. He demands everything of himself and the people around him. He's had a path laid out for me since birth. It doesn't include a relationship with the son of a Mafia boss.

Plus, Dante has no intention of abandoning the "family business." I don't think I could ask him to.

Especially after I meet his family.

I meet Aida first, the baby sister. She's not really a baby—eleven years old, skinny, dressed in torn-up jeans and a baseball shirt. Her fingernails are broken and filthy, and her hair is wildly tangled. I can see scabs on both her knees through the holes in her jeans.

She's pretty, despite that. Or she will be when she grows into her face. Her eyes aren't dark like Dante's—they're a silvery gray, bright with curiosity.

"Oh!" she says. "You look different than I expected."

"What did you think I'd look like?"

"I dunno." She laughs. "I guess I thought you'd be big like Dante."

"When did you ever see a girl as big as me?" Dante rumbles.

"I'm going to be! I'm going to be bigger and stronger than all of you," Aida says.

"You have to eat something other than ice cream and Popsicles if you want that to happen," Dante says.

We're actually eating ice cream during this conversation, down by Lane Beach.

"I said I wanted a cone, not a cup," Aida reminds Dante.

"You're dirty enough without ice cream melting all over you," Dante says.

"I had a bath," Aida says.

"When?"

"This week."

"Liar."

"I went swimming. That counts."

"If there wasn't any soap involved, it doesn't count."

It's fascinating seeing this eighty-pound girl interact with Dante without a shred of fear. Actually, it's clear that she adores him. She tells me how he took her to Six Flags and rode the looping Demon four times.

"Weren't you scared?" I ask her.

"I was more scared," Dante says. "I don't think those little cars were engineered with me in mind."

"I did throw up," Aida says cheerfully. "But not on anything important."

I meet Dante's brothers, too—Sebastian and Nero. Sebastian is only a little older than Aida but already taller than me. He looks like a puppy with his big brown eyes and his feet too large for his body. He's shy and mostly leaves it to his brothers to answer any questions I ask him.

Nero's a different creature entirely. He's sixteen years old and frankly the most terrifying of the bunch. He's beautiful in a way that would be shocking on a grown man, let alone a teenager. But he's fierce and moody and deeply suspicious of me.

"Dante talks about you all the time," I tell him.

"Really?" he says rudely. "Because I haven't seen him in a month."

"Take it easy," Dante tells him gruffly.

"It's okay," I say. "I have been monopolizing you."

"You live in that mansion on Burling Street?" Nero says.

"Yes."

"Fancy. Does Dante wear a tux to visit you?" His cool-gray eyes are narrowed at me. I'm sure he knows Dante hasn't openly visited me there, ever.

Meanwhile, I've been to his house several times. I love it. It's stuffed full of history and memories. Every scuff on the woodwork is from one of the Gallo siblings or an uncle or aunt who came before. It's warm and personal and just as lovely as the Burling Street mansion, in its own way.

Dante took me up to the roof, where the fox grapes hung heavy and fragrant from the pergola. He picked a few for me, and I ate them, sun warmed and bursting with juice.

I even met Enzo Gallo, Dante's father. I don't know what I expected—a thug, I guess. I couldn't have been more wrong. Enzo is cultured, polite. I can see he used to be strong like Dante before age and sadness wore him down. Dante told me how Gianna Gallo died. I'm sure to a powerful man like Enzo, an unexpected illness must seem like the cruelest twist of fate—something completely outside his control.

Like Nero, Enzo is wary of me. I doubt I'm what he wants for his son any more than Dante fits my father's expectations. We're from two different worlds. Enzo seems to avoid the spotlight just as my father craves it.

One night, after I eat dinner with the whole family, Enzo

pulls Dante into another room, and they're gone for almost twenty minutes. I hear the angry rumble of Dante's voice but not what he's saying to his father. When he emerges a few minutes later, Dante is flushed.

"Let's go," he says to me.

As we drive away from the house, I ask him, "What happened?"

"Nothing." He shakes his head.

I lay my hand over his, feeling his pulse thudding through the raised veins on the back of his hand. "You can tell me."

Dante looks over at me, his eyes burning. "No one's ever going to take you away from me," he says.

I see that anger bubbling up that he tries to keep locked below the surface. Dante is so strong that I'm sure he learned early that he had to control his temper, or he'd destroy everything in his path. But he's still young, even if he doesn't look it. I don't know how long that control lasts.

"No one will," I whisper.

He turns his hand over and squeezes mine, our fingers interlocked. "Good."

The next night, Dante texts to ask if I can meet him.

I tell him that Mama's making me go to a masquerade ball. It's some fundraiser for Chicago charter schools.

He doesn't text back, probably annoyed that it's the third event this week that's kept us apart.

I was already sick to death of fancy parties when the summer started. Now that I have Dante to distract me, they feel like pure torture. Every minute of the events, I feel like a magnet pulled and pulled toward wherever I think Dante might be. The impulse to go to him is overwhelming.

I'm especially irritated when the doorbell rings. Or at least I become irritated when Mama calls me down and I see Jules standing there. He's peering up the staircase, smiling shyly and holding a bouquet of yellow lilies.

"I asked Jules to pick you up," Mama says. "Since Wilson has the night off."

I'm sure it's no coincidence that she gave Wilson tonight off. It's the perfect opportunity to shove me into a date.

There's not really any way for me to refuse. Not now.

"Great," I mutter. "I'll finish getting ready."

"I'll wait down here!" Jules calls up to me.

He's wearing a pale gray suit with a silver mask pushed up on his head.

At least two or three galas a year are masquerade balls. Rich people love wearing masks. It's a tradition that goes back to Carnival in the Middle Ages. The reasons are obvious—in a strict society, a mask provides freedom. Your identity, your actions, even your facial expressions are free from the endless scrutiny that we usually endure. You don't have to worry that you'll be the subject of gossip the next morning or an unflattering picture on social media. For once, you can do whatever you like.

I've never taken advantage of the mask before.

But even I feel a sense of relief slipping the *gatto* down over my face. It's a traditional Italian mask, with a cat's ears and eyes, painted gold and black.

My full skirt swishes around me as I walk. It's more costume than gown, black with gold gems scattered across it like stars.

Jules swallows hard when he sees me. "Wow!" he says.

I can't help teasing him. "You only ever see me in dresses, Jules. I would think you'd be more surprised by a pair of sweatpants."

Jules shrugs, laughing nervously. "I guess so."

"Don't get into too much trouble, you two," Mama says lightly.

Fat chance of that happening.

"Definitely not, Mrs. Solomon," Jules assures her.

I follow him out to his car. It's a Corvette, so low to the ground that I have a hard time getting into it with my huge puffy skirt. I kind of have to fall down into the passenger seat.

Jules closes the door behind me, careful of my dress.

I can tell he's nervous, driving us over to the history museum. We're never really alone together, always meeting at social events, in public places. I want to tell him he can relax because this isn't really a date, but of course there's no way to do that.

"Where did you go the other night?" he asks me.

"Hmm?" I was looking out the window, thinking about something else.

"You disappeared from the Young Ambassadors dinner. I thought you were going to sit at my table."

"Oh. Sorry. I left early. I wasn't feeling well."

"Okay, good. I mean, not good you were sick. But I'm glad it wasn't because you didn't want to sit with me."

There's a little color in his pale cheeks, under the freckles.

I feel a pang of guilt. Jules is a nice guy and not bad looking. He's fit, well-mannered, smart. An excellent skier and violinist, from what I've heard. But the little sparks I felt for him in the past are nothing compared to the inferno Dante can light inside me with a single glance.

We pull up to the museum. I feel a thrill at the sight of the long brick facade. This is where Dante dropped me off the day he stole the car with me in the back seat. I wish he were taking me to the ball instead of Jules.

Since the party's already in full swing, we have to wait in a line of a dozen limos and sports cars. Jules hands the valet the keys, then takes my arm to help me up the long carpeted steps to the entrance.

In the grand hall, there's so much chattering and clinking of glasses that I can hardly hear the music playing. I can't deny that the array of brilliant masks and gowns is absolutely lovely. I see peacocks and butterflies, harlequins and fairies. Some people have gone with

Italian-style gowns with bustles and lace sleeves, others with strapless princess styles.

The men are mostly dressed in suits or tuxes. Some wear the classic *columbina* half mask. Others wear the slightly disturbing *volto* full-face mask, the angular *bauta*, or the sinister *scaramouche* with the long nose.

"Would you like a drink?" Jules asks.

"Thank you."

As he heads off toward the bar, someone sidles up next to me in a plague doctor costume.

"Simone…" a low voice whispers.

"Yes?" I say hesitantly.

"It's me!" Emily giggles. She pulls her mask down just a little so I can see her bright blue eyes.

I laugh. "What are you doing in that?"

"Spying," she says. "Sneaking around. Listening in on conversations."

"What have you learned so far?"

"Oh, only that Jean VanCliffe brought his mistress to the party, not his wife—you can see her over there in the burgundy gown. And that Angela Price is high as a kite, which is why she's been dancing all by herself for the past half hour."

"Riveting stuff," I tell her. "You should write a book."

"Don't tempt me. I'd love to write a tell-all novel about the rich and famous of Chicago."

"I don't know if they're actually that interesting—except to themselves."

Jules comes back to join us, handing me a flute of champagne.

"Oh, sorry." Emily grins. "I didn't mean to interrupt your *date*."

"It's not—" I start.

"That's okay," Jules says, smiling under his mask. "We came to socialize after all."

"Oh!" Emily says sarcastically. "I thought we came to support poor little babes who need new computers."

"Right. Of course," Jules says uncomfortably.

"She's just teasing you," I tell him.

"Right," Jules says again.

That's always been his weak point—no sense of humor.

"Should we dance?" he asks me.

He pulls me out onto the dance floor among the endless rotation of couples swirling around us. The band is playing "The Vampire Masquerade," fittingly enough. Jules is a much more practiced dancer than Dante. But he's almost flamboyant—he whirls me around, spinning me, even dipping me a little. It's clear he wants as many people as possible to see us.

I do like dancing. I love all the rich colors, beading, and brocade all around me. The way the dresses swish and rustle, the way the fabrics shine, bending the light that glitters down from several chandeliers overhead. I like the sweet scent of champagne and a dozen perfumes, over the more mellow scent of pomade and after-shave and the lower notes of shoe polish and leather.

The band switches to "Midnight Waltz."

"Do you want to keep dancing?" Jules asks me.

"Sure."

I'd rather dance than talk.

We whirl around the floor fast enough that I'm breathing hard. Jules asks me a few questions about how my parents are doing and if I've chosen my college yet.

"I'll be going to Harvard," he says proudly.

"That's great." I smile.

Just then my back fetches up against something hard and immovable. "Oh, sorry!"

I turn around.

I have to look up to meet the eyes of the man towering over me.

He's dressed all in black. His hair is combed straight back. He's wearing a black silk mask that covers the whole of his face, only his dark eyes glittering down at me.

Before I can say a word, he grabs my waist, enclosing my hand in his.

"Excuse me—" Jules protests.

"You don't mind if I take her," the man growls.

It's not a question. He sweeps me away without another glance at Jules.

I knew it was Dante from the moment I saw his bulk. There isn't another man in the room with shoulders that wide. If I hadn't already guessed, that rough voice and the intoxicating scent of his cologne would have given it away.

I'm only surprised he managed to get in the room at all—I doubt he's on the donor list for KIPP. And I didn't expect him to own a perfectly fitted suit.

"What are you doing here?"

Behind the mask, his eyes are more ferocious than ever. "Watching you dance with another man," he growls.

The edge in his voice sends a shiver down my spine. His hand swallows mine. I feel the heat coming off his body.

I can't read his expression, but I can feel his muscles tense with fury. "Are you jealous?" I whisper.

"Extremely."

I don't know why that sends a frisson of pleasure through me. "Why?"

In answer, Dante only pulls me tighter.

I feel eyes turning to look at us. It's impossible not to notice the tallest man in the room. The other dancers create space for us, no one wanting to be flattened by Dante as he spins me around to "Waltz for Dreamers."

Usually, I dislike when people stare at me, but right now I couldn't care less. They can whisper all they like. All I care about are Dante's fingers locked around my waist, the impossible strength he uses to whip me around, and the way he doesn't take his eyes off my face for an instant.

"Why am I jealous?" he says.

"Yes."

He presses me tightly against him. "Because I don't care if the richest, fanciest fuckers in the world are in this room. You belong to me."

8
DANTE

I CAME TO THE BALL TO SURPRISE SIMONE.

I bought a ticket, at an outrageous price, from someone who had actually been invited. Then I got out the one and only suit I own and even found a mask.

I did all that to see her smile when she realized I'd infiltrated the one party we could attend together without anyone seeing my face.

But then I showed up. I drank in the wealth and power in the room. Every rich and influential person in Chicago and from cities all around. I scanned the room full of beautiful people, looking for the most stunning woman of all.

And I saw her dancing with another man.

I recognized Simone immediately. No one has skin that glows like hers or a figure that outshines even the most ostentatious gown. She makes every man in the room drool with envy. The lucky fuck she was dancing with knew she was miles out of his league.

But I was jealous anyway. So fucking jealous, I could barely breathe.

I could tell the kid was rich just by his watch and his suit. In fact, I was pretty sure he was the same little shit she was talking to at the Young Ambassadors Dinner.

I wanted to break his fucking legs for dancing with her.

He knew how to dance. He looked like he'd been doing it all

his life—and he probably had. He had style, bearing, manners—everything I don't. And he had Simone in his arms.

So I ripped her away from him. Literally pulled her right out of his hands and took her. I spun her around that floor until she was dizzy, showing every stiff shirt in that room that she was mine, and I'd take her whenever I wanted.

But it wasn't enough. Not even close to enough.

So now I'm pulling her off the dance floor, out of the ballroom, all the way out of the party entirely.

Some idiot in a security guard uniform tries to stop us.

"Excuse me, sir—sir!" he calls.

I grab a wad of bills out of my pocket and stuff it into his hand. "Shut the fuck up, and show me which way we can go to be alone," I tell him.

He stares at the money for a second, then mutters, "That way. Just don't touch anything, okay?"

I pull Simone away through the empty galleries of the museum. I'm dragging her along, my hand locked around her wrist.

She's hurrying after me, stumbling a little in her high heels, with the heavy, cumbersome skirt of her gown slowing her down.

"What are you doing?" She gasps. "Where are we going?"

I have no idea.

I'm just looking for a place. A place where no one can see us or hear us. Where I can take possession of Simone once and for all.

Finally, we come to the Napoleon exhibit. Most of the lights are dimmed. I see a pale plaster death mask, military medals, handwritten letters under glass, a diamond-encrusted sword, and a row of cologne bottles. Plus portraits of the emperor, muskets, and a battered bicorne hat.

And then what I was looking for: a long velvet chaise, emerald green, with four carved legs and pillows at one end. It's roped off but otherwise unprotected.

I pick Simone up, and I throw her down on that chaise.

"What are you doing?" she says, terrified. "We're going to get in so much trouble—"

I shove the mask off my face and silence her with my mouth crashing down on hers. I kiss her voraciously. I taste the champagne on her tongue. I'm going to wipe every memory of that other man off her flesh. Everywhere he touched her, I'm going to touch her harder.

The chaise groans under my weight. I don't care. I'll splinter the whole damn thing with Simone underneath me. I'll bring this whole museum, and every artifact inside it, crashing down around us.

There's only one thing of value in here: Simone.

She belongs to me. Only to me.

I try to free her chest from the heavy bodice of her gown. The material resists me, but I rip it open. Her breasts spill out. I grope them hard, pinching her nipples until Simone gasps and moans.

I pull up the skirt, too.

She's wearing thigh-high stockings and lace panties underneath. I rip those off. Then I push my fingers inside her. She's soaking wet, as I knew she would be.

I've already waited too long for this.

I'm done waiting.

I set my cock free from my trousers.

It's raging hard, dying to sink into her warmth and wetness for the very first time. I tell myself to be gentle, to go slow. But my body isn't taking orders from my brain anymore.

I put the head of my cock at her entrance.

And I plunge inside.

9

SIMONE

Dante's lost his mind.

He throws me down on the chaise, not caring that this chair is over two hundred years old and never built for someone his size, let alone both of us.

He pushes up his mask so I can see his face, but that's hardly any better.

He looks crazed. His eyes are blazing. His jaw is an iron bar of tension.

His lips attack mine. He bites my lips, and he shoves his tongue in my mouth, sucking the breath from my lungs. His hands are all over me. I hear fabric tearing, and I don't care in the slightest. I want his hands on my body, on my bare flesh.

He grabs my breasts and squeezes them.

Any boy who touched me before did it gently, hesitantly, always asking for permission.

Dante takes what he wants. He takes money, guns, and most of all, me. There's no law on this earth he won't break. And he sure as hell doesn't care about social convention.

So I'm not surprised by how he acts.

I'm surprised by how I respond to it.

My body longs for it. It wants more and more and more. It doesn't matter how roughly his hands grope and grab and squeeze.

My flesh throbs, but the pleasure is so much more intense than the pain.

I'm grinding against him, feeling his rock-hard cock trapped between his belly and my thigh.

I'm terrified of that cock. I probably should have practiced with one that was smaller, softer, more reasonable...

It's too late now. Practicing and waiting are at an end. Dante is taking what he wants tonight. And I want to give it to him.

He rips my panties, tearing them off my waist. He shoves his fingers inside me. Even that is hard to take. I'm wet and I'm eager, but every muscle in my body is tight, anxious, desperate.

He lets his cock loose, and it hits my hip, heavy and hot.

He grabs it, lining it up with my pussy instead.

Then he pushes the head between my lips. It feels impossibly thick and extremely warm. Much warmer than his fingers or even his tongue.

I'm trembling with nerves. I would say something, but he's still kissing me, filling my mouth with his tongue. All I can do is wrap my arms around his neck, close my eyes, and hope it doesn't hurt too much.

Dante grabs my hips in his hands and pulls me toward him. His cock pushes inside me, an inch at a time.

It does hurt. It hurts a whole fucking lot, actually. And it seems to get worse the deeper he goes.

Even though his cock is smooth, it's scraping me raw inside. Shoving and burrowing all the way up. I cry out into his mouth, biting down hard on his lip.

Still, he keeps going. With shallow thrusts, he keeps pushing it all the way inside, until our bodies are tight together, no space between us anymore.

It's too much. I really can't stand it.

And yet...it feels good, too.

His body heat fills me inside and out. The heavy head of his cock rubs against a spot deep inside me, a spot I didn't even know existed. That little bit of flesh is a button of pleasure, similar to my clit. It throbs and swells at the slightest touch,

Dante is barely moving. His cock slides in and out only an inch. The head rubs against that spot, teasing it.

I'm getting wetter and wetter. That helps his cock slide. I don't know if the wetness is blood or just lubrication. I don't care. It allows Dante to pull his cock in and out a little more, so I can rock my hips against him, and he can flex the huge slabs of muscle on his back and ass, driving into me even deeper.

Our mouths are locked together. I'm clinging to him. I've never been entwined with another person like this.

We're hot from dancing. Hot with emotion and desire. He's sweating a little. It makes him smell intensely good. I stop kissing him for a second so I can lick the side of his neck, tasting salt and his own personal scent.

I grip the lobe of his ear between my teeth, and I bite down. Dante growls, turning his head to suck on the side of my neck.

I've never seen a man like Dante. Never felt this raw strength and power.

Some primal part of my brain tells me that I *need* him. I need him in me, even deeper than this.

"Harder," I moan in his ear.

Dante buries his cock all the way inside me. I feel his back flexing, his muscles working. It drives me insane with arousal.

"Harder," I groan.

His thick arms are wrapped all the way around me. He's squeezing me so tight that I'm afraid he's going to crack my ribs, snap my spine. Still, I want more.

"Harder, Dante, please!"

With a beastly roar, he erupts inside me. I feel pulse after pulse of that thing I was craving—that thick, hot fluid.

I'm coming, too. I didn't even know I was going to. But the

psychological arousal of him coming inside me has pushed me over the edge. The orgasm comes from deep, deep inside—from that little sensitive spot that can feel the twitching of his cock, the fluid spurting out of him.

I'm squeezing and grinding and coming just as he is, my eyes closed and my face buried in his neck.

Then it's over, and he's pulling out of me, warm liquid running down the inside of my thigh.

Without his cock filling that space, I feel empty and raw. I don't dare look at the mess we made. I just pull down my skirt and try to hold my top together with my arm.

Dante is panting, not looking quite as wild now but not quite sane again either.

He kisses me again, slowly and deeply this time. "Are you all right?"

"Yes," I say, panting, too.

"Did it hurt too much?"

"A little. Not too much."

I kiss him, tasting the arousal in his breath. Each exhale is moist and warm, still faster than normal.

"I love you, Simone," he says, his dark eyes boring into mine. "I know it's only been a month—"

"I love you, too," I tell him quickly. "I don't care how long it's been. This thing between us—"

"It's not normal," Dante says. "I love you like…like I'd destroy anything that tried to come between us. Like I'd burn the whole world down if I had to."

His eyes keep hold of mine. I can't look away. I don't want to look away. I only want to nod.

"I know," I say.

"I want you. Nothing else," he says.

"You have me. All of me."

"Promise me, Simone."

"I'm yours. Till the day I die."

He smiles and presses his heavy lips on mine. "I want you longer than that," he growls.

I was never raised to fall in love like this. Without reason or choice. Only wild, intense obsession.

I never meant for this to happen.

But now that it has, there's no escaping.

I belong to Dante. And he belongs to me.

10
DANTE

THIS SUMMER HAS BEEN THE BEST OF MY LIFE. I'M IN LOVE FOR THE first time. The only time.

Simone is perfection in my eyes.

She's a beautiful dreamer. I've never been able to see things like she can. She's always pointing out the colors of things, the textures, the shapes.

"Look at those swirls running through those clouds over there—it reminds me of wood grain, don't you think?"

"Look how the buildings are lit from the side. The glass looks like gold."

"Do you smell that? Those are damask roses. Some people think they smell like tea leaves…"

"Oh, feel this stone, Dante! If you closed your eyes, you'd think it was soap…"

We get more and more bold, going all over the city together, because I want to show Simone my favorite places. She hasn't been here as long as me.

I take her to Promontory Point, to Chicago Botanic Garden, and to Wabash Arts Corridor to see all the murals painted along the walls.

I even take her to an exhibit of 1930s and '40s Old Hollywood costumes. Simone loves that more than anything. She loses her mind over the green dress from *Gone with the Wind*, apparently sewn out of curtains—I never saw the film. I do recognize the ruby slippers from *The Wizard of Oz*—one of several pairs made for the movie, according to the little placard next to the display.

Watching her excitement over the clothes, I tell her, "You should accept the offer from Parsons. You should go there."

Simone pauses next to a display of outerwear from *Casablanca*.

"What if I did?" she says, not looking at me. "What would happen with us?"

I'm standing right behind her, almost close enough to touch the curve of her hip. I see the edge of her face, her lashes lying against her cheek as she looks down at the floor.

"I could visit you," I say. "Or I could come to New York…plenty of Italians in Manhattan. I've got cousins there, uncles…"

Simone turns around, her face lit up. "Would you?"

"I'd rather go to New York than the fucking UK."

The truth is, I'd go anywhere to see Simone while she's at school. But I know it's Parsons she wants, not Cambridge.

"My parents are already annoyed at me that I delayed my acceptance." She sighs. "I said I'd go for the winter semester…"

"It's not their life."

"I know. I'm the only one they've got, though. Serwa…"

"It's not your responsibility to make up for all the things your sister can't do."

"She's actually been doing much better lately," Simone says happily. "She's on a new medication. She's been applying for jobs in London. At least we'll be close by each other, if I do go to Cambridge…"

I haven't met Serwa or any of Simone's family.

Simone thinks they won't accept me.

She's probably right. I know what I am. I look like a thug and have the manners of one. My father can be dignified when he wants to be. He can hobnob with politicians and CEOs. I never learned to do that. Papa turned over the uglier parts of our business to me, and that's all I know.

I tell Simone that she doesn't have to bend to her father's demands. But I have my own responsibilities to my family. What would they do if I went to New York? Nero isn't old enough to handle things on his own. And there's truth to what Edwin Dukuly said right before I killed him. Papa is still powerful, but he hasn't had the same focus since Mama died. He tells me what needs doing; I'm the one who has to do it.

Simone isn't the right wife for me in my family's eyes either. I should marry a girl from a Mafia family—someone who understands our world. It would form an alliance. Help keep our children safe.

Plus there's the issue of the scrutiny it would bring, to marry someone like Simone. The Gallos stay out of the spotlight. We always have. It's called the *underworld* for a reason—because we don't get our picture in the society section of the *Tribune*.

That was what happened at the masquerade ball. Someone took our picture, and the next day, the *Times* published a center spread photo of Simone and me waltzing around the museum ballroom. Luckily, I was wearing a mask, but Papa was far from impressed to see the caption: *Simone Solomon, daughter of Yafeu Solomon, dances with an unknown guest.*

Papa gets all the newspapers. He slapped it down in front of me, right across my breakfast plate.

"I didn't know you were a patron of the arts," he said.

He had already met Simone. But I'd promised him that she and I would keep a low profile.

"You can't see my face," I told him.

"This infatuation is going too far. Her father isn't stupid—he cultivates his daughter like one of his hotel properties. She's an asset. One that you're devaluing, publicly."

"Don't talk about her like that," I snarled, looking up into my father's face.

I could see his anger rising to meet mine. "You're young, Dante. There are many beautiful women in the world."

"Not for you, there wasn't."

Papa flinched. He's not a sentimental man, not a man who shows weakness. When my mother was ripped away from him, his attachment to her created a hole. Because he can't talk about her without emotion, he doesn't talk about her at all.

"Your mother wasn't from our world. That was hard on her. A woman shouldn't marry a man like me, or you, unless she's raised to accept certain realities."

"Mama accepted them."

"Not wholly. It was the only point of conflict in our marriage."

I stood from the breakfast table so abruptly that my movement shoved the heavy table, slopping fresh-squeezed orange juice over the rim of the carafe.

"I'm not going to stop seeing her," I told my father.

Now I'm telling Simone that she needs to make her choice as well. She's delayed school by a few months, but eventually she'll have to decide.

Parsons or Cambridge?

Me or the man her father would pick out for her?

I have to take Simone back earlier than I'd like.

I drop her off at the library, her excuse for where she said she was going today.

I see her chauffeur, Wilson, already parked down the street, waiting to pick her up.

I don't like the subterfuge. I hate feeling like her dirty secret.

Since I've got time to kill, I swing over to Seb's school and pick him up.

He comes out the front doors as soon as the bell rings, his

basketball tucked under his arm. It's as much a part of him these days as his shaggy haircut or the silver chain with the medallion of Saint Eustachius that he always wears. Our uncle Francesco used to wear it, until he was killed by the *Bratva*.

Seb smiles when he sees me. "I didn't know you were coming."

"Thought you might want to go to the park." I knock his ball out of his hand and steal it from him.

Seb says, "Let's see if you can do that on the court."

I take him over to Oz Park, where there are plenty of open basketball courts. I've got a pair of shorts in my trunk, sneakers, too. No shirt, though, so I don't bother with that at all. Seb shucks his off, too. He's skinny but starting to get ropey with muscle. He's almost as tall as Nero now, even though he's only thirteen.

We play half-court "make it, take it." I let Seb take possession first. He tries to get around me, and he's fast as fuck, but I'm still faster, at least with my hands. I strip the ball off him, take it back to the line, then shoot a three-pointer right over his head.

It swishes through the hoop, not even glancing the rim.

"Yeah, yeah," Seb says, as I *tsk* at him.

I'm the one who taught Seb to play. I'm the one who took him to the courts every day after our mother died, when he was so low that I didn't see him smile for a year. It was hardest on him and Aida— or at least that's what I thought at the time. They were only six and eight, just babies still.

But now I wonder if it didn't hit Nero worst of all. Seb and Aida are okay. They've pulled out of it, recovered their happiness again, while Nero just seems so…angry. He gets in fight after fight, each one nastier than the one before. I think he's going to kill somebody. To distract him, I've been taking him along on the armored truck hits. And he's good at it—good at boosting the getaway cars, good at following instructions, even good at planning the hits himself. He's smart as hell, though you'd never know it from his grades.

I couldn't go to New York. Not full-time. I said it to Simone in the heat of the moment, but I can't leave my siblings here alone. Aida's getting prettier and more troublesome by the day. Seb needs to practice with me so he can make the high school team. Nero needs me to keep him out of jail or from getting himself killed. He thinks he's invincible. Or he doesn't care that he's not.

I can still visit Simone, though. If she goes to Parsons.

Seb does some tricky little fake and steals the ball off me mid-drive toward the hoop. When he tries to bring it back down to score, I block his shot, knocking it right back down.

"You're not gettin' that bitch-ass little shot over my head."

"You've got like eight inches on me," Seb complains.

"There's always gonna be somebody taller than you. You've got to be faster, stronger, more devious, more accurate."

I drive toward the hoop again, easily knocking him aside with my superior weight.

After I've made the shot, I hold out my hand, helping to pick him up off the concrete.

Seb gets up again, wincing.

He's skinny, smaller than me, with big brown eyes that break my heart. I want to go easy on him. But how would that help him? It wouldn't. Nobody else is ever gonna go easy.

"Try again," I say, tossing him the ball.

11
SIMONE

Serwa got a job with Barclays in London. She'll be leaving in a couple of weeks.

"Are you excited?" I say, sitting on her bed and watching her pack her books into boxes.

"Very."

She's looking better than I've seen in months. The antibiotics cleared out the infection in her lungs, and she's barely been coughing with the new medications. Tata says she could even get a lung transplant in another year or two. She'll never entirely be cured, but a transplant could add decades onto her life.

Serwa is so much smaller than the rest of us—as petite and delicate as an American Girl doll. It's almost like her illness is a curse preserving her in time. She doesn't look any older than me, though there are ten years between us.

I'm so used to seeing her in her a housecoat lately that it's a thrill just to see her in a dress. It's a pretty yellow sundress made of eyelet lace.

"I'm going to miss you," she says.

"I might be in London, too," I remind her.

She cocks her head to the side, examining me with her wide-set eyes. "Really? I thought you might stay in Chicago."

Heat rises in my cheeks. "Why did you think that?"

"Oh, because of whoever you've been sneaking out to see."

I blush even harder. "I'm not—"

Serwa shakes her head at me. "You're a terrible liar, Simone. I've seen you smiling, texting on your phone. And when did you ever want to go shopping five times in a week?"

"Well…"

"Is it the thief?"

My mouth goes dry. "What makes you say that?"

"I saw the picture in the *Tribune*. Not many guests at the masquerade ball are 'unknown.' Not to mention he was the size of a house. I think I remember you saying that the man who stole our car was big…"

"You can't tell Tata," I beg her.

"Of course not." Serwa's expression is serious. "But I don't know how you think you can keep this a secret. And a criminal, Simone? It was funny to talk about after he took the car. But you can't seriously be dating him."

"He's not what you think," I snap.

I don't mean to have such a harsh tone, but I can't stand Serwa calling Dante a *criminal*. I know what she's picturing. Dante's not like that.

"You don't have much experience with men," Serwa says. "You're trusting, Simone, and you're sheltered. You don't know what's out there in the rest of the world."

That's ironic, coming from my sister, who's spent months at a time locked up in our house. She hasn't seen much more of the world than I have.

"I know Dante."

"Is he a criminal or not?"

"He's…he's not… It's different. He's from an Italian family…"

"*Mafia?*" Serwa says with a horrified expression.

"You don't know him." My stomach is churning.

"This isn't what you want for yourself," Serwa says.

I've always listened to my sister. Unlike my parents, she supported my dreams. She told me I should apply to Parsons. To have her turn on me now is upsetting. It makes me question my judgment.

I feel like I'm going to throw up.

"Dante and I have a connection," I whisper. "The way I feel about him…I can't even explain it to you, Serwa. Do you know how you meet people, people who are beautiful, or charming, or funny, and you like them? But there are dozens of people like that. They don't mean anything to you, not really. Then, every once in a while, you meet someone who has a kind of glow. It lights you up inside, makes you burn like you never burned before. All of a sudden, you have to be around them. You need that light. Everything without them is darker, colder, lonelier. Even your own thoughts. They become the thing that sparks your brain, that makes the future look bright."

Serwa says, "I've had a crush or two."

"A crush is candlelight. Dante's the sun, right inside my chest. It could burn for a million years and not go out."

Serwa is staring at me, her mouth open. This is not what she expected. "What are you saying…?"

"I love him."

"Love him! But, Simone—"

"I know what you're going to say. You think I don't even know what that means yet. But I do, Serwa. I love him."

Serwa slowly shakes her head. She doesn't know how to convince me. How furious our parents will be. How crazy it is to fall in love with the first boy you've ever kissed…

"Do you have a picture of him?" she says at last.

I open the hidden folder on my phone where I keep the one and only picture I have of Dante.

It's a shot I took the night we went to the speakeasy. He was sitting across from me at the table, listening to the music.

I lifted my phone to snap a picture of him, and he turned his head right at that moment, looking directly at me. Stern and unsmiling.

It was so dim in the speakeasy that the photo looks almost black-and-white, robbed of all saturation. Dante's hair melts into the shadows around his face, and his skin looks paler than it actually is. His eyes are like onyx under the heavy slashes of his brows. His jaw is so darkly shadowed with stubble that it almost looks like a bruise.

Serwa presses her lips together tightly.

I know what she sees: A gangster. A thug.

She doesn't know that Dante is so much more than that.

"How old is he?"

"Twenty-one."

"He looks older."

"I know."

She hands my phone back. Her eyes are worried. "I hope you know what you're doing, Simone."

I don't. Not at all. Not even a little bit.

I walk back to my own room. I'm supposed to be going out to see Dante in an hour. I told Mama I was meeting Emily at a restaurant.

My stomach is still rolling from my conversation with Serwa. I hate conflict. I hate disapproval. When it's from the people I love most, it's unbearable.

I run to my en suite bathroom and throw up in the sink. Then I rinse my mouth out with water and glance at my face in the mirror.

My eyes look just as worried as Serwa's.

12
DANTE

It's almost a week since I saw Simone. I'm on edge, craving her like a substance I can't get out of my system.

She texts me that her parents have been suspicious—asking questions every time she tries to leave the house.

I text her back:

We should stop sneaking around.

There's a long pause where I see her start responding, then stop, then start again. Finally, she says, I know. I hate it, too.

I scowl, typing quickly.

Then tell them about me.

Another long pause. Then she responds.

I want to. I'm afraid.

I understand her position. I know how important her family is to her. I know she thrives on their approval, their acceptance.

I understand it because my family is important to me, too. They're a part of me, as much as my height or the color of my eyes.

For Simone, it's probably stronger. When you move around all the time, your family is the one constant. They're the center of your world. I have sympathy for her position.

In fact, I even understand how her parents feel. Simone is a hothouse orchid, rare and beautiful, pruned and protected. She's been painstakingly raised all this time so she can be the showpiece of her family. Because of her sister's illness, her parents transferred all their hopes and dreams onto Simone.

Simone was never meant for me. They probably thought they'd pair her up with some duke or earl for fuck's sake. She's certainly gorgeous enough. Not to mention well-read, well-spoken, and well-mannered.

Then there's me. The opposite of what they'd want in every way. Simone is a stained glass window, and I'm the stone gargoyle outside the cathedral.

High school education. Criminal record. My family's got money and power, but from all the wrong sources. The Gallo name is as dark as our hair.

None of that will pass unnoticed by Simone's father. As soon as she tells him about me, he'll put his people to work, digging up every skeleton I've buried—figuratively speaking, I hope. Though it could be done literally, too.

It's dangerous, putting myself in his crosshairs.

And I plan to do a fuck of a lot more than just draw his attention. I'm going to make myself his enemy—the would-be thief of his baby girl.

I know as well as Simone that Yafeu Solomon won't accept that. Not for a second.

But there's no way around it.

Not if I want to be with her for real, forever.

So I pick up my phone and send my message to her:

No more hiding. I want to meet them.

I wait for her response, my mouth dry and my jaw tense. Finally, she replies:

I'll tell them tonight.

I set the phone down, letting out a long sigh. I hope I'm not making a huge mistake.

Papa tells me to meet him at Stella's so we can have dinner with Vincenzo Bianchi, the head of one of the other Italian families. His son got himself in trouble, driving drunk with two sixteen-year-old girls in his car. He went off the road in Calumet Heights, and one of the girls went through the windshield. Bianchi is trying to keep his son out of prison.

"It's this fuckin' DA," Bianchi says, shoveling up a mouthful of ravioli. "He's on a fuckin' witch hunt here. My Bosco is a good boy. Never been in trouble once in his life. And just because this is his second DUI—"

Bosco is not a "good boy." Actually, he's a piece of shit. Thirty-two years old, making a fucking mess of his father's businesses, roaring around the city with jailbait in his passenger seat, coked out of his mind. We'd all be better off if the prosecutor locked him up and threw away the key before Bosco could bring down any more heat on the rest of us.

But because Papa is the don, he has to do his best to help Bianchi—whether he deserves it or not.

"I've got some pull with the district attorney's office," Papa says. "But you have to understand, Vincenzo, he may do some time over this. If we'd been able to get there first—put one of the girls behind the wheel... It's not good that the cops found him in the car. They did the drug test and the Breathalyzer..."

"Fuck the drug test! Bosco doesn't do any fuckin' drugs."

"Maybe we get some of the evidence to go missing," Papa says. "There's always some cop willing to 'misplace' the paperwork for a couple grand."

Papa looks over at me, swirling his wine in his glass.

This is where I'm supposed to chime in with suggestions or some encouragement for Bianchi. Let him know we'll help him out with the usual threats, bribes, intimidation of witnesses…

I haven't been paying attention, though. I'm distracted, agitated. Thinking about Simone. Wondering if she told her father about me yet. Maybe she doesn't want to. Maybe she's embarrassed of me. My chest burns at that thought—burns with shame and anger.

"What do you think, Dante?" Papa prods me.

"Is the girl dead?" I say abruptly.

"What?" Bianchi looks offended.

"The girl who went through the windshield. Is she dead?"

"She's in a coma." Bianchi grunts. "I'd pull the plug if it were me. Why keep a fuckin' vegetable hooked up like that?"

"You should be glad her parents don't share your opinion. Or Bosco would be looking at a murder charge."

My father throws me a warning glare.

"Her parents should have kept their daughter at home," Bianchi sneers. "You should have seen how she was dressed. Like a ten-dollar whore."

My fists are balled like two rocks under the table. I want to smash Bianchi right across the jaw. He's a fucking hypocrite, acting like a father of the year when his own son is worth less than spit on the sidewalk.

This is exactly the kind of dirty work Simone's family would most look down on. Right in this moment, I'm exactly what they disdain.

I push away from the table before I say something I'll regret.

"I'm gonna go find Nero," I say.

As I stalk away, I hear Papa smoothing things over with Bianchi. "We'll take care of it, Vincenzo. Don't worry."

I head back to the kitchen, where I nod to Zalewski, the Polack who owns the restaurant.

"You going down to the game?" he asks me.

"Is Nero playing?"

He nods.

"I'll go watch, then."

I push through the narrow door that looks like it leads to a storage closet. Instead, it gives way to a steep dark staircase that descends into the bowels of the building.

This is where Zalewski runs his illegal poker game.

It's not the biggest or the fanciest game in the city, but it's the one with the most cache. While the ringers and the grinders like to play the bigger games where they're assured at least a couple of fish they can strip for chips, only the best of the best play at Zalewski's game. You win there, and you can win anywhere.

I'm guessing this is what Nero's been saving his money for when I give him his cut of the armored-truck jobs. He thinks he's going to take down Siberia, the Russian ringer.

They call him *Siberia* because he always gets the cooler—the hand that kills your hand, even when you played it perfectly.

Sure enough, when I get down to the dim, smoky table, I see Siberia sitting at one end, flanked by two fellow *Bratva*, and then Nero sitting opposite with a hefty stack of chips in front of him. The other three players are the Matador, Action Jack, and Maggie the Mouth.

"Hey, Dante!" Maggie shouts as soon as she sees me. "Where you been, big boy? I haven't seen you in a month!"

Nero spares me a glance, his gray eyes flashing up at me before he turns them right back to his stack of chips again. I see him counting his stack and Siberia's, which takes him all of two seconds. My brother is brilliant, much as I hate to admit it. But he's also reckless and eager to make a name for himself. I don't like that he's playing, especially against Siberia, who's as cold and humorless as his name would suggest.

Siberia looks more like a Viking than a Russian, with a full red beard and a barrel chest. He's tattooed all the way down to his fingernails.

It looks like he's got about fifteen thousand dollars in front of him, though I can't count it at a glance like Nero did. Nero has about two-thirds as much—maybe ten thousand dollars in chips, which, as far as I know, is about all the money he owns.

I'd like to grab him by his collar and haul him out of here, but you don't leave midgame.

So I just have to watch as the dealer lays out the cards.

Siberia's on the small blind. He throws in a ten-dollar chip. The Russian on his left folds, then the Matador does the same. Maggie thinks about it for a minute before laying down her cards. Nero opens the betting with a hundred-dollar chip.

Siberia snorts. He's seen plenty of young and hungry players in his time.

Not wanting to match that aggressive bet, the Matador and the other Russian fold. It's just Siberia and Nero in the hand now.

Siberia isn't going to be bullied by any kid. He re-raises to three hundred dollars. Nero calls.

The dealer lays out the flop: ace, ten, ten.

Nero has position. Siberia fires half the pot—another three hundred dollars. Nero raises to one thousand dollars, taking control of the hand. Siberia calls.

Nero's betting hard, but I know my brother. I know how aggressive he is and how much he wants to prove himself. I don't believe he's got anything yet. He's probably chasing a straight.

The turn card is a six of diamonds. Unlikely to help either player.

For the first time, Siberia hesitates. He's probably worried that Nero has a ten. Which means Siberia must not have one himself—I put him on ace/king. That would mean he has two pair, which would lose to three of a kind.

Siberia checks, not wanting to bet out of position.

Nero smiles. Thinking he can take the pot down, he bets another thousand.

Siberia grunts and shakes his head. He's changed his mind—he thinks Nero's full of shit, and he's not gonna let him buy the pot. He reraises to three thousand dollars.

Nero's gotten himself in trouble, I'm sure of it. He doesn't have that ten, and Siberia knows it.

Nero calls anyway—now there's almost nine thousand dollars in the pot.

The river is another dead card—three of clubs.

Siberia, trying to control the pot size, simply checks.

Without a flicker of hesitation, Nero shoves in his entire stack.

The table is dead silent.

Siberia sits and stews, his eyes darting back and forth from the mound of chips to Nero's calm triumphant expression. The Russian knows he's supposed to call. But his pride is at stake—if Nero has a ten after all, Siberia will look stupid. He's only into the pot forty-three hundred dollars. He can't bet his whole stack without knowing for sure. Nobody tries to bluff him—they know it's impossible.

I can see how angry Siberia is, though he doesn't want to show it. He hates to admit he wasted all those chips.

After a full two minutes of tanking, he mucks his cards, refusing to show them.

It doesn't matter. Nero knows exactly what he had.

Nero flips over his own cards: a jack and a queen. No tens in sight.

"Fucking hell!" Maggie shouts.

Nero laughs. "You gave up too easy," he says to Siberia.

The man's face turns as red as his beard. His pale blue eyes are bloodshot and bulging. He's too furious to speak. I don't know if he's ever been successfully bluffed before.

Nero doesn't even have the decency to hide his glee. If anything, he's trying to make Siberia angrier.

"Beginner's luck," Nero says in his most mocking tone.

I want to tell Nero it's time to go, but leaving right after a hit like that would only make the Russians angrier. I stuff my hands in my pockets to hide my agitation.

Nero stacks his winnings, preparing for the next hand. He refuses to look at me. He knows this is a very bad idea.

I see him glance at Siberia's stack again. Now Nero has the bigger war chest—fourteen thousand dollars to the Russian's eleven thousand dollars. More importantly, he has Siberia right where he wants him: tilted.

When someone's on tilt, it doesn't matter what the next hand is. They're in. Siberia's blood is boiling—he wants to battle. He takes a swig from the bottle of gin next to him and gets ready to play.

The button moves over to Siberia. He has position on Nero. Sure enough, he places a blind bet on the button—a hundred-dollar chip on the straddle—before a single card has been dealt. It's a silent challenge to Nero.

The dealer lays the cards. Everyone else at the table knows Siberia is out for blood. They want to get out of his way—he's not after them, just Nero. The Russian on the small blind folds, as do the Matador and Maggie the Mouth. Action goes to Nero.

I hold my breath, hoping he's got nothing and will lay his cards down.

Instead, Nero raises to five hundred dollars.

"You want to dance with the devil again, boy?" Siberia growls.

"Abso-fuckin'-lutely," Nero says. "As long as you found your courage in the bottom of that bottle, comrade."

Nobody at the table wants to touch this hand. Action Jack folds, and the other Russian after him.

Siberia and Nero face off.

Siberia hasn't even looked at his cards yet. He bends up the corners, taking a glance. The red in his face fades just a little. Fuck. He's got something good, on the button, in position. Sure enough, he smooth calls. He doesn't want to give away that he's got a monster hand. He wants to trap Nero into bluffing him again.

And Nero's in just the right spot to be tricked. Because Siberia's tilted, and because of his straddle, Nero probably assumes he's got a shit hand.

The flop comes out queen, queen, ten.

Nero is the first to act. Insouciantly, he says, "I'm gonna bet here. I hope it won't scare you away, Siberia."

He bets the pot—a thousand dollars.

Siberia throws in the thousand without hesitation. "Dig your own fuckin' grave, boy."

He thinks Nero is chasing a straight again.

The turn is another king.

I'm watching Siberia's face as the card comes out. And I think I see the smallest twitch of one red eyebrow. He just made his hand. I'm pretty sure he's got a full house.

Nero's so fucking cocky, he's not even paying attention. He wasn't looking at Siberia, so he didn't see the twitch. He's looking down at his own chips, preparing to bet again. I wish I could shout for him to stop.

The pot is three thousand dollars now. Nero bets another two thousand.

Siberia raises Nero on the turn, just like he did the hand before. This time he won't be bluffed off for anything. He raises to five thousand.

Nero calls, smooth as butter.

Even the dealer looks nervous at the obvious tension in the room. He flips over the river card: two of spades. No good to anybody.

Siberia smiles. He's sure Nero chased the straight, just like last hand. And he didn't get it.

Pretending like he did, Nero says, "I'm all in."

Siberia grins, showing all his yellow teeth. He snap calls Nero before the words *all in* have even left his lips.

Siberia flips over pocket kings—he's got the nut boat, kings over queens.

Nero lets out a small sigh. Then he turns over pocket queens. He had quads from the very beginning.

Siberia stares blankly at the table, like he can't even comprehend what he's seeing. The friend on his right mutters, "*Etot grebanyy chiter!*"

Reality hits. Siberia lets out an inhuman roar. He leaps up, and his two compatriots jump up, too. If they hadn't been frisked for weapons on their way down, I don't think the whole Red Army could have prevented them from riddling my brother with bullets. As it is, they look like they want to tear him apart with their bare hands.

Nero sits tense and still, not foolish enough to scoop up his winnings.

"*Sit down*," I bark, my voice cutting across the room.

Siberia looks over at me, his shoulders shaking with rage. "Your brother is a *cheater*."

"He outplayed you," I say bluntly. "I watched the whole thing."

I've taken a couple of steps closer, so I'm right behind Nero. The other players are rooted to their seats, not wanting to make a sound in case the Russian turns his rage on them. Even Maggie the Mouth keeps her yap shut for once.

"He's too young to play," one of the other *Bratva* spits.

"You didn't care about that when you took his buy-in," I say.

"What's done is done." The dealer raises his hands. "Let's just pay out and shut down the game for the night."

It's the wrong thing to say—he'd be better off offering Siberia another buy-in. Still, with my bulk blocking the doorway, the Russians have to let it go.

Not without one last dig, however.

"Shit play wins today," Siberia sneers.

Nero narrows his eyes. He doesn't care if they call him a cheater—but unskilled? That's too much.

In a thick KGB accent, Nero scoffs, "You want a cookie, fat baby?"

The *Bratva* rush at him.

I flip the whole table over, flinging it aside like it's cardboard. Chips scatter in every direction, rolling across the floor. I jump between Nero and the Russians, grabbing the first one and throwing him onto the upended table.

Behind me, I hear the *snick* of Nero's switchblade opening. Whoever frisked him didn't do a very good job. Or more accurately, they'd have to use a full-body MRI to find something Nero wants to keep hidden.

Siberia and the other Russian hesitate.

Footsteps thunder down the stairs, and Zalewski bawls out, "Knock it off, all of you!"

He heard the ruckus of the table flipping over and the Russian flying across the room. Now he's down in the basement, red-faced and furious.

"No fucking fighting at my game!" he howls. "Get out, all of you!"

"Not without my chips," Nero says stubbornly.

I'd like to strangle my brother myself at this point.

Instead, I jerk my head at the dealer, to tell him to pick up the chips.

When he's scooped up what looks like twenty thousand dollars, I say, "Cash him out."

The dealer looks at Zalewski. He nods curtly.

Then the dealer opens the lockbox and counts out the bills. He hands them to me, and I stuff them in my pocket.

All the while, the Russians are watching with their furious pale eyes.

"We'll meet again across the table," Siberia says to Nero.

"No, you fucking won't," I tell him.

And with that, I haul Nero back up the stairs.

13
SIMONE

EVEN THOUGH I'M DREADING TELLING MY PARENTS ABOUT DANTE, I sit them down that same night as soon as we're done eating. I would have liked Serwa to be there, too, but she was tired and went to bed early.

"Mama, Tata," I say, "I have something to tell you."

My mother looks expectant. My father is frowning—he doesn't like surprises.

I take a deep breath. "I met someone. We've been dating a couple of months now."

Mama smiles. She looks pleased, like she already expected this. "It's Jules, isn't it?" she says. "I saw his mother at brunch last week, and she said—"

"It's not Jules," I interrupt.

"Oh." Her smile fades but not all the way. She thinks it must be some other boy from Young Ambassadors or a friend of Emily's.

"His name is Dante Gallo," I say. "He's from here. From Chicago."

"Who is he?" my father asks at once.

"He's, well, uh…his family works in construction. And the restaurant business…" I say. I'm trying to list the least offensive of their professions.

My father isn't fooled for a minute. "Is that who you've been sneaking out to see?" he barks.

"Yafeu, why are you—" Mama says.

"Don't think Wilson hasn't told me," my father says, not taking his eyes off me. "He drops you off at the library, and you call him six hours later. You disappear from dinners and parties…"

"I didn't realize I was under surveillance," I say coldly.

"Sneaking out?" Mama frowns. "I really don't see—"

"What are you hiding?" my father demands. "Who is this man you're seeing?"

I'm sweating, and my stomach is rolling over and over. I hate this. But I'm not going to cry or throw up—not this time. I have to stay calm. I have to explain.

"He's a good man," I say firmly. "I care about him…very much. I didn't want to tell you about him because I knew what you'd think."

"What?" my father says with deadly calm. "What would I think?"

"His family has…a criminal history."

My father swears in Twi.

My mother stares at me, wide-eyed. "You can't be serious, Simone…"

"I am. I'm very serious."

"You've become infatuated with some…some *malfaiteur?*"

"He's not like that."

I didn't want to lie anymore, but I don't know how to explain what Dante is, actually. He's strong, he's bold, he's intelligent, he's passionate…I hate to hear him described in the awful terms my parents are using. But at the same time, I can't exactly claim that he's innocent, that he's never broken the law…

"I want you to meet him," I say in the firmest tone I can muster.

"Out of the question!" my father scoffs.

"Wait, Yafeu," my mother says. "Maybe we should—"

"Absolutely not!" Turning to me, he orders, "You're not going to see this man again. You'll block him on your phone, you'll give his name and description to the staff, and from this moment on—"

"No!" I shout.

My parents fall silent, staring at me in shock.

I don't think I've ever told them no before. I've definitely never yelled at them.

Heart racing, I say, "I'm not going to stop seeing him. Not before you've even met him. You can't say anything about him now when he's a stranger. You don't know him like I do…"

My father looks like he wants to shout something back at me, but Mama puts her hand on his arm, steadying him. After a moment, he takes a breath and says, "Fine, Simone. You'll invite him here for dinner."

Even Mama looks surprised at that.

"Dinner?" I say.

He presses his lips together in a thin line. "We'll meet this man who's insinuated himself into my daughter's heart. And we'll see exactly what sort of person he is."

Blood is thundering in my ears. I can't believe he's agreeing. It seems like a trick. Like the other shoe is about to drop.

But my father doesn't say anything else. He waits for my response.

"Thank you," I say quietly. "I'll invite him tomorrow night."

"Good," Tata says. "I can't wait."

———————

The dinner is a disaster.

From the moment my father opens the door, I know that's how it's going to be.

He's put on one of his best suits—the navy Brioni. This isn't as a gesture of welcome or respect. He wants to appear as intimidating as possible.

He greets Dante coldly. My father can be horribly stern when he wants to be.

The problem is that Dante is equally stern in return. He's wearing a button-up shirt and a pair of slacks. His hair is nicely combed, and his dress shoes are polished. But he doesn't look refined like Tata. With the sleeves of Dante's shirt rolled up, his meaty forearms are displayed, dusted with dark hair and thick with veins and muscle. His massive hand closes around my father's, and it looks like a brutal hand, with its swollen knuckles and the gold family ring Dante wears on his pinky.

By contrast, my father's hands are slim, refined, manicured. My father's watch and cuff links look like the jewelry of a gentleman.

Dante looks like he hasn't shaved, even though I know he has. It's just the darkness of his facial hair that marks his cheeks in a perpetual five-o'clock shadow.

When he greets my mother and sister, I know he's using his gentlest tone, but it comes out like a grunt. They're not used to his voice. Mama actually jumps a little. They don't know how to differentiate between his softer tone and his truly terrifying growl. To them, he sounds rude and uncouth in everything he says, even when he tries to compliment them.

"You have a beautiful home," he tells Mama.

That sounds wrong, too, like he's never been in a nice house before, when I know the Gallo mansion is lovely and venerable in its own way. Much more than this rented place.

I'm already sick with dread, and the dinner's barely begun.

We all sit around the formal dining table.

Tata is at the head. Mama's at the foot. Serwa sits on one side; Dante and I, on the other. At least we're right next to each other.

One of the housemaids brings out the soup.

It's gazpacho, with a sheen of olive oil glimmering on its surface. Dante eyes the chilled soup warily.

He picks up his spoon. It looks comically small in his huge hand. My father, mother, and sister are all staring at him like he's an animal in a zoo. I'm so angry at them that I want to cry. I know they don't mean it, but it hurts me to see their stiff expressions, the veneer of politeness with distaste underneath.

Dante can feel it, too. He's trying to be calm. Trying to be warm to them. But it's impossible under the bright lights, the tense scrutiny, the silence that blankets the table. Every clink of our spoons is magnified in the formal dining space.

Dante takes a few polite bites of the soup before laying down his spoon. It's too much to eat with so many people watching you.

"The soup doesn't agree with you?" my father says with chilly politeness. "I can order something else from the kitchen. What do *you* like to eat?"

He says it like he thinks Dante lives on a diet of pizza and french fries. Like normal human food is beyond Dante's appreciation.

"The soup is excellent," Dante growls. He picks up his spoon again and takes five or six hasty bites. In his hurry, a little of the red soup splashes on the snow-white tablecloth. Dante flushes and tries to dab the spot with his napkin, making it worse.

"Oh, don't bother about that," Mama says.

She means it kindly, but it sounds condescending, like Dante is a Great Dane sitting at the table, from which nothing better could be expected.

I can't eat a bite. The soup smells awful to me, like it has iron filings in it. I'm holding back tears.

"Dante." My father's voice is as calm and deliberate as ever. "What do you do for a living?"

"My family owns several businesses." To his credit, Dante's voice is as calm as Tata's, and he has no trouble meeting my father's eyes.

"What sort of businesses?"

"Construction. Real estate. Fine dining."

"Indeed," my father says. "Also several laundromats and a strip club, isn't that right?"

A muscle jumps in Dante's jaw. My father is making it clear that he's done his research on the Gallo family.

Dante says, "That's right."

"Your family has a long history in Chicago, don't they?"

"Yes."

"That house on Meyer Avenue is simply…charming. Your family must have had it a hundred years."

"Since 1902," Dante says stiffly.

My father lays down his spoon and folds his slim, shapely hands on the table in front of him. "What I'm wondering," he says, "is why you think I would ever allow my daughter to align herself with the Italian Mafia?"

A frigid silence falls over the table. We all seem frozen in place, my mother stiff and wide-eyed in her chair, Serwa holding her spoon to her mouth but not taking a sip of her soup, and me digging my nails into my palm so hard, I might be drawing blood. My father staring at Dante, and Dante staring right back at him.

"All families have their secrets," Dante says, his harsh voice in direct opposition to my father's cultured tones. "You, for instance, growing up in Accra…I doubt you'd have to look far to find a relative who cut someone's throat for a few cedi."

My father doesn't flinch, but I see the outrage in his eyes. I don't know if Dante is aware how accurate that statement was. My father had two uncles who worked for a local gangster. One day they offered his sisters positions as housemaids in the wealthy part of the city. The girls packed their bags, planning to come home on the weekends. But they never came back—my father never saw them again.

Tata's hand twitches on the tabletop. I think he's about to respond, but Dante isn't finished yet.

"That's normal in Africa, I guess," Dante growls. "What about after you came to London? That's where the real money is. Hedge funds, mergers and acquisitions, large-scale real estate transactions… the Outfit is good with money. Very good. But we've got nothing on international financiers…that's crime on a whole other scale."

My father makes a *tsk* sound, his top lip drawn up in a sneer. "I'm sure you'd like that to be true. My hands may be black, but yours are bloody. Those hands will never touch my daughter. Not after tonight."

Dante's eyes get so dark that they're darker even than my father's—no iris at all, only black pupil.

I'm afraid he's going to tell Tata that he's already touched me. In every way possible. I'm not Daddy's pure little princess anymore. Not even close.

But Dante would never betray me like that.

Instead, he says, "That's not your decision."

"Yes, it is," Tata says. "I am Simone's father. She will obey me."

Dante looks over at me. It's the first time our eyes have met since this awful dinner began. And it's the first time I see a crack in Dante's armor. He walked in here like a dark knight, stern and unyielding. Now in his eyes, I see the first hint of vulnerability. A question: Is my father speaking the truth?

My mouth is too dry to speak. My tongue darts out to moisten my cracked lips, but it's not enough. I can't form any words.

That muscle jumps in Dante's jaw again. His brows lower in disappointment. He turns to my mother.

"Thank you for your hospitality."

With that, he stands and walks out of the room.

I should jump up.

I should chase after him.

Instead, I vomit directly into my soup bowl. All over the untouched gazpacho.

14
DANTE

I SHOULDN'T HAVE STORMED OUT OF SIMONE'S HOUSE.

I knew her father was going to challenge me. I just thought Simone would be on my side. I thought we'd face her parents together.

There isn't a person in this world who could rip me away from her. I thought she felt the same.

So, when I turned and looked at her and saw that doubt in her eyes…it put a tear in my heart. I could feel the flesh ripping inside my chest.

I would go through anything for her. As long as we're in it together.

She was embarrassed of me. I could tell. I dressed so carefully. But it wasn't enough. I can't change what I look like, who I am.

I felt like a bear lumbering around in an art gallery. Everything I did was clumsy and wrong.

And then I left in a rage—proving I was exactly as uncivilized as they thought.

I try to call Simone after. Twenty or thirty times. She never answers. I can't tell if she's ignoring me or if her father took her phone.

I lurk around their house for days. I don't see Simone leaving in the chauffeured car. Only her father every day and once her mother.

It's driving me insane.

The more time passes, the more I think the dinner was my fault. It was too much to expect Simone to back me up when I was acting like an animal. I antagonized her father right from the start—what did I expect her to do?

I have to see her.

I wait until night, and I sneak onto the grounds again.

But this time, the security team isn't just fucking around. They're on high alert. They've put up sensors, and they've got a fucking Doberman prowling around. The thing starts barking before I'm ten feet onto the grounds.

I hadn't planned for any of that. I was too anxious to see Simone. I didn't think it through.

They chase me off immediately, and I hear one of the guards calling the cops. I slink off, humiliated all over again.

I look up at Simone's window, which hangs like a bright, glowing frame against the dark house.

I see a figure standing there, her hand pressed to the window. I see her slim silhouette and her spread fingers on the glass. But I can't see her face. I don't know if she wants me to leave or to try again.

I have no idea what she's thinking.

15

SIMONE

The fight with my parents after dinner is terrible. We shout for hours—or, I should say, my father and I shout. My mother sits there, silent and pale, shocked at the both of us.

"How could you do this to us?" my father demands. "After everything we've done for you, Simone! What have you ever needed or wanted that we have not provided? Parties, clothes, vacations, the finest education money can buy! You're spoiled. Horribly spoiled. To think that you'd disgrace us like this! That you'd disgrace yourself! A thug, a criminal, a *mafioso*! It's disgusting. I thought we raised you better than that. I thought you had morals. This is what you want for yourself? To be the wife of a gangster? Until he kills you or one of his associates does. Is that what you want? To be obliterated by a car bomb? Or maybe you'd like to sit alone in a house bought with blood money while your husband rots in jail!"

His words are like razor blades, slashing at me over and over from every direction. No single cut is enough to kill, but I feel weakened by the bleeding.

The problem is that he's shouting my own thoughts back at me. My own worst fears.

"Even if you don't care about your future, how could you do this to us? After everything your mother and I have worked for. You'd put this stain on our name and reputation? And what about your sister? You think she'll keep her job in the banking industry when they know she's connected to the Italian Mafia? Selfish! You're completely selfish."

I have to sit down on the couch as his words hammer me down, over and over.

Finally, Mama speaks. "Simone, I know you think you love this man—"

"I do, Mama. I love him."

"You don't know what love is yet, *ma chérie*. You are so young. You'll fall in love so many times…"

"No, Mama. Not like this…"

I can't explain it to them. I can't explain that love may come and go, but my bond with Dante is forever. I'm sewn to him down every inch of my skin. My heart is in his chest, and his is in mine. I see inside him. And he sees me.

I know I'm young and foolish. But if I've ever been sure of anything in my life it's this: What I feel for Dante will never come again. Not in any other person. He's my first, last, and only.

Now I really am a prisoner. They take my phone, my laptop. I'm not allowed to leave the house for any reason.

I'm in agony knowing Dante must be trying to text and call me. I'm terrified of what my father will do if Dante persists.

I cry in my room until I'm as dry as desert sand. No tears left in my head. Nothing but aching sobs.

Mama brings up trays of food, and I ignore them.

Only Serwa is allowed in my room. She sits next to me on the bed and strokes my back.

"It was very brave of him to come to the house," she says. Serwa, at least, formed a gentle opinion of Dante upon meeting him.

"I don't want you to leave." I sob. She's supposed to go to London in a few more days to start her new job.

"I'll stay if you want," she says.

I do want that. Badly. But I shake my head. "No," I say. "You should go. Maybe Tata will let you call me…"

"Of course he will," Serwa says.

I sleep for hours and hours every day. I don't know why I'm so tired. It must be the thick black misery choking me.

I try to eat some of the food Mama brings up so I won't be so sick and dizzy, but as often as not, I end up throwing it up again.

One of the nights, I hear a commotion in the yard—shouting and scuffling. I can't see anything out my window, but I'm sure it's Dante, trying to break in to see me. My father has increased our security detail. Dante doesn't get through. I assume they don't catch him either, since my father would surely rub it in my face.

Does Dante know I'm a prisoner in here? Does he know how badly I want to speak to him, even just for a minute?

Or does he think I'm caving to my parents? That I'm going to give him up like they want?

I'm not giving up.

And yet…

If I'm honest with myself…

I'm not exactly trying to escape the house either.

It's not just because I'm ill and miserable. I feel like I'm balancing on the blade of a knife—on either side of me, a ten-thousand-foot drop into nothingness.

It's an impossible choice between Dante and my family. Either way, I lose something precious to me. A part of myself.

I don't know what to do. The longer I balance on the blade, the more it bites into my flesh, cutting me in half.

In the end, it becomes a completely different choice.

Serwa brings a bowl of ice cream up to my room. It's seven o'clock at night, eight days after the disastrous dinner.

She sets the ice cream in my lap. Mint chocolate chip—my favorite.

"You have to eat something, *onuabaa*," she says.

I stir the ice cream around in the bowl. It's already starting to melt. The green looks garish.

I take a bite, then set it down. "It doesn't taste right."

Serwa frowns. She's always sensitive to signs of illness in other people because she herself has always been unwell. She's always the first one to bring me a hot pad when I have period cramps or to lend me her nebulizer when I have a cold.

"You look pale," she says to me.

"I've barely been out of the room in a week. No sunshine in here."

I know I'm being sulky. Serwa is supposed to leave tomorrow for London. I should ask her if she wants to cuddle and watch a movie or if she needs any help packing her suitcase.

Before I can offer, Serwa stands abruptly.

"I've got to run over to the pharmacy," she says. "I'll be back soon."

"Send Wilson, why don't you?"

"I'll be back," Serwa repeats.

I lie down on the bed again, too tired to care much about why she needs to run to the pharmacy right this minute. Actually, I'm a bit jealous that she can run errands whenever she likes while I'm stuck here under full-scale surveillance.

She returns an hour later, carrying a plastic bag from CVS.

"Simone," she says hesitantly. "I think you should use this."

She holds out a rectangular box.

It's a pregnancy test. I stare at it blankly, then scowl at her. "I don't need that."

Dante and I only had unprotected sex one time. It would be very unlikely that I got pregnant from one single time.

"Please," Serwa says quietly. "For my peace of mind."

I take the box from her hand. I don't want to take the test. It's humiliating, and I'm stressed enough as it is. But the sight of the test has put a kernel of doubt in my mind.

I've been tired, headachy, nauseated...

I try to think back to the last time I bled. The past few weeks

seem like a blur. I can't exactly remember if I had a period this month or the one before. I'm not very regular.

I'll pee on the stick just to be sure. To show Serwa there's nothing to worry about—other than the thousand other things I'm already worried about.

I stalk over to my en suite bathroom, which isn't nearly as tidy and sparkling clean as usual. I haven't been letting the maid in to clean. Damp towels litter the floor, and toothpaste flecks the mirror. My cosmetics are scattered across the countertop, and the waste bin is overflowing.

I sit down on the toilet to read the instructions. It's simple enough—I take the cap off the indicator, pee on the end of the stick, and let it sit for ninety seconds.

I follow the steps, trying not to consider what would happen if I were pregnant. What a disaster that would be.

Even the smell of my own urine turns my stomach. I can barely stand to put the cap back on the test and set it on the counter next to the mess of bobby pins and half-used lipstick.

I look at myself in the mirror, pulling up my oversize T-shirt to examine my body.

I look the same as ever. No bulge on my belly. No change in my shape.

Even my breasts look the same. I squeeze them in my hands to see if they feel any fuller. They seem normal—though a little sore.

It hasn't been ninety seconds yet. I don't care. I snatch up the stick to prove to myself that this whole thing is ridiculous.

I see one vertical pink line. Negative.

Then, right before my eyes, a second horizontal line rises into existence. Like invisible ink held up to the light, it blooms out of pure-white cotton, growing thicker and darker by the moment.

The two pink lines form a cross. A plus sign. Positive.

The test falls from my numb fingers into the sink.

Serwa hears it fall. She comes to the doorway.

Her big dark eyes look down at the test, then up to my face. "What are you going to do?" she says.

I shake my head silently. I have no idea.

"We have to tell Mama," Serwa says.

"No!" I say, a little too sharply.

If we tell Mama, she'll tell Tata. And he'll be furious. I can't even imagine that level of anger.

No, there's only one person I want to turn to right now: Dante.

"You have to get my phone," I beg Serwa. "I have to talk to him."

She presses her lips together nervously. "I know where it is."

Serwa goes off to steal back my phone. As soon as I'm alone in my room, reality comes crashing down on me.

Pregnant. I'm pregnant. Right this moment, there's a bundle of cells growing and dividing inside me.

It seems impossible, and yet it's the most real and immediate thing in the world.

The walls of my bedroom seem to rush toward me like a collapsing box and then speed away again. I sink to the carpet, sweating and shaking. I'm breathing too hard, too fast. My heart is seizing in my chest. I think I might be dying...

What am I going to do?

What am I going to do?

What am I going to do?

"Simone!" Serwa cries, dropping next to me. She puts her arm around my shoulders, pulling my head against her chest.

I'm crying again. My reserve of tears has replenished enough for my face to be soaking wet once more.

Serwa pushes the phone into my hand. The screen is cracked. I don't know if my father dropped it or threw it in anger.

Luckily, it still switches on. I see fifty-seven missed calls and a dozen messages from Dante.

I was planning to call him right now, but I'm crying too hard.

I type a message instead:

I have to talk to you. Come meet me at midnight, at the gazebo in the park.

He'll know the one I mean. We've gone for walks together in Lincoln Park. We sat in that gazebo and kissed and talked for hours. It's only a moment until Dante replies, as if he'd been holding his phone in his hand, staring at the screen.

Simone! I tried to call you. I tried to come see you.

I know, I reply.

Are you all right?

My hands are shaking so hard, I can hardly type.

Yes. Come to the gazebo. Midnight. It's important. I have to see you.

I'll be there, he says. I promise.

I hand the phone back to Serwa so she can return it to its hiding place, wherever my father had it stashed away.

"How are you going to get out?" Serwa asks me.

"I need your help."

16
DANTE

I'M LIMP WITH RELIEF AFTER FINALLY HEARING FROM SIMONE.

I was going insane with her locked up in that house. I had half a mind to take Nero, Seb, and six of our men, then storm the castle. The only reason I didn't is because I couldn't risk anyone getting hurt. It is Simone's family keeping her hostage after all.

Still, I hardly feel any better after reading her messages. She sounds awful—keyed up about something.

I want to see her now. I don't want to wait until midnight.

The relief is already leeching away, replaced with dread.

She said she has to talk to me.

Is she going to tell me she can't see me anymore?

Her father's had an entire week to work on her. To guilt and shame her and prey on her fears. I'm sure he's found out everything he can about me. I'm sure he's told her all my darkest secrets and worse. He might have told her anything, true or untrue.

No, that can't be it.

If she didn't want to see me anymore, she'd just tell me. Her father would let her call if that were the reason. He'd stand right next to her while she did it.

No, she wants to sneak out to see me. That means she loves me still. She wants us to be together.

I tell myself that over and over so darker thoughts don't creep in.

Simone and I are meant to be together. I know it.

It wasn't an accident that I met her that day.

It was fate that threw me out that window. Fate that pulled me into that car. Fate that I drove away with her in the back seat. And fate the moment our eyes met in the mirror.

I'm not a romantic; I never have been. But I have instinct. I know when something's right.

Simone is mine. All the years before we knew each other, we were two asteroids in space, on two separate paths with a single trajectory. We were always destined to collide.

I check my watch again and again. It's nine o'clock. Then ten. Then almost eleven. I grab my jacket and my car keys—I can't risk being late.

My Bronco is parked below street level, in our underground garage.

When I head down there, I hear Nero blasting rap music and the clink of his tools. He's always working on one or another of our vehicles. We have the ones we use for work, then his own personal projects, the vintage motorcycles and cars he painstakingly restores from rusted hulks to shining works of art. It's the only time I see him focused and patient. I wish he could apply that consistency to anything else in his life.

"I need the Bronco," I tell him over the din of the music.

"It's up on the lift," Nero says without looking up. "I'm putting on new tires."

"How long will that take?"

"I dunno. An hour."

"What about the Beamer?"

"Papa's got that one." He sits up, wiping his forehead with the back of his hand. It leaves a long streak of grease across his skin. "You can take my Camaro. It's low on gas, though."

"Don't we have any?"

We usually keep a couple of canisters on hand.

"No," Nero says.

"Why not?"

He shrugs. "Haven't refilled lately."

I swallow my irritation. I've got plenty of time to stop at a gas station. And it's my fault I didn't check the cars earlier.

I climb into the red Camaro, not bothering to say goodbye to Nero because he's already back tinkering around under the Mustang.

As I pull up to street level, I think I see the flare of headlights behind me, but they disappear a moment later. Probably a car turning the corner.

I drive over to the gas station on Wells Street.

When I get there, the pumps are dark. It closed at 10:30.

"Fuck!" I shout.

I'm anxious, keyed up. I wanted to get to the park early. I don't like the idea of Simone being there alone in the dark, waiting for me.

I drive over to Orleans instead, looking for another gas station. The dial is so low that it's not even on empty—it's a few millimeters below. Definitely not enough to get to Lincoln Park without filling up.

The streets are dark and mostly empty. Not many other cars around.

Which is why I notice the black SUV following me. I take a left on Superior, and the SUV does, too. I can't see who's driving, except that there are definitely two figures in the front seats. Two large figures.

To test my theory, I turn right on Franklin, then slow down.

Sure enough, the SUV turns as well. When they see me creeping along, they take a quick detour on Chicago Avenue. I floor the gas, speeding up the road. I want to lose the other car while we're out of each other's sight. I roar down Chestnut, then back along Orleans, keeping an eye on my rearview mirror the whole time to see if I've lost them.

The gas gauge is as empty as it goes now. I'm running on fumes.

Speeding around isn't helping—I've got to find a place to fill up right now, whether I've lost the other car or not.

I pull into the gas station, climbing out warily and glancing around on all sides as I swipe my credit card and open the tank.

I fit the nozzle into the side of the Camaro, still sweeping the dark empty lot with my eyes, jumpy as a cat.

The tank seems to take ages to fill. I can hear the cold gasoline pouring out, fast but not fast enough. I feel tense and nervy. When I think there's probably enough gas in the tank, I stop the flow and pull the nozzle free.

Too late.

The black SUV screeches into the lot, pulling right in front of my car so I'll have to reverse to get out. I'm about to drop the nozzle, but before I can move, before the SUV has even stopped all the way, four Russians fling the doors open and jump out. The two in the front, I don't recognize. Siberia and his friend from the poker game come out the back. They surround me, closing in like a noose.

Gripping the gas nozzle in my right hand, I slip my left into my jeans pocket, feeling for metal.

"Dante Gallo," Siberia says. He's wearing a canvas jacket with the collar turned up. The thin material strains across the bulk of his chest and shoulders.

He's the biggest of the Russians, but the other three aren't exactly small. One has a darker complexion—probably Armenian. One has tattoos down the sides of his face along the hairline. And one is wearing brass knuckles on both fists. They glint dully in the dim light. When he smiles, he's got a gold tooth in the front, almost exactly the same shade as the brass.

"I was hoping it was Nero," Siberia says, nodding toward my car.

"You're lucky it wasn't," I growl. "You so much as look at my brother, and I'll rip your spine out like a fucking ragweed."

"Oh, you think so?" Siberia says softly. "I'm not so sure. You think you're some kind of big man? We have a lot of big men in Russia.

Brutal, too. I met a lot of big men in prison. You know my nickname is not from poker. It comes from the Gulag where I served eight years. Sometimes the guards staged matches between the biggest men. Boxing matches, bare-knuckle. The prize was food. I ate very well off the broken bones of those big men."

"Then tell your friends to back the fuck off and face me yourself."

Even while I'm speaking, the two on my left are drawing closer, trying to flank me.

"You want a fair fight?" Siberia scoffs. "Fair like your brother's hand?"

Before he's even finished his taunt, the two on the left rush me. It's what I expected.

I depress the handle of the nozzle and fling gasoline right in their faces. At the same time, I'm already flicking open the lid of my Zippo and lighting the flame. I throw the Zippo at Brass Knuckles, hitting him square in the chest. He ignites like a torch. Within half a second, Tattoos is likewise aflame.

They scream in shock and pain, flailing, forgetting to drop and roll. You don't often hear a man scream. It's worse than a woman.

The Armenian and Siberia don't help their friends. They rush at me instead.

Some of the liquid flame splashed onto the arm of my jacket. I can't even feel the heat. My whole body is burning with adrenaline. I ball my fists and swing my arms upward at the Armenian's jaw. The force of the blow knocks him sideways into Siberia.

It doesn't slow him down any. He shoves his friend aside and comes at me, his fists raised in front of his face like a proper pugilist. He throws tight punches right at my face. I block my jaw, and he attacks my body instead, hitting me in the gut and ribs with full force.

Each blow is like a hammer. His fists are massive and rock-hard. They slam into me, rapid-fire. Keeping my hands up, I crack him across the jaw with an elbow, followed by a left cross. It barely phases him.

Meanwhile, the Armenian dives at my legs. He takes me down. We roll over on the concrete. I hear the unmistakable sound of a switchblade opening. With no time to look up, I grab the Armenian by the front of his shirt and lift him, throwing him in the direction of Siberia. Siberia's blade sinks into his friend's arm, but he jerks it free again and runs at me, swinging the knife at my face.

I put my arm up. The blade cuts through my leather jacket like linen. It bites through the flesh of my forearm, leaving a long gash down to the bone. I feel the blood flowing down, dripping off my fingers.

Meanwhile, Brass Knuckles and Tattoo are screaming and rolling around, trying to extinguish the flames. But all they're doing is rolling into the pooled gasoline, splashing it around and spreading the fire.

The Armenian has doubled over. I knee him in the face and smash my fists on the back of his skull. Siberia swings his blade at my face again, and I jerk back, the tip of the knife cutting down my right cheek. I dive at Siberia, grabbing his knife hand by the wrist. My hand is slippery with blood, and it's hard to hold on. I hit him again and again with my left fist, and he does the same, while straining to force the blade forward into my chest.

I hear a whooshing behind me. It sounds like a high wind rushing down a very small tube. I'm afraid I know what that means.

Releasing Siberia's hand, I let him stab the switchblade into my right shoulder. Meanwhile, I hit him hard in the throat with the heel of my hand. He stumbles backward, choking.

With the blade still embedded in my shoulder, I crouch low and run as fast as I can away from the gas pumps. I've only taken a dozen steps before the pump explodes. The heat hits me first, like a wall of liquid heat, shoving me from behind. The sound comes a split second later—loud, booming, and metallic. I hear it as I fly, crashing hard on the concrete. My head slams against the curb.

I'm dazed and deafened.

It takes me a minute to even raise my head. I look back at the brilliant remains of the fireball and the flaming hulk of metal that used to be Nero's car. The Russians' SUV is likewise on fire, as are two of the bodies next to the pump. The other two figures were thrown farther out, including Siberia, who's still alive. I hear him groaning.

I pull myself onto the curb. Then I grab the handle of the knife jutting out of my deltoid, and I yank the blade out. It hurts worse coming out than it did going in.

My hand looks like a bloody glove. The whole arm is stiff and useless.

I can feel blood leaking from my nose and ears. Several of my ribs feel cracked, if not broken. I don't know if that's from Siberia, the explosion, or landing on the cement.

I pull my phone out of my pocket. The screen is shattered. My watch is broken, too. I have no idea what time it is—all I know is that I'm late. My car is out of commission, and I hear the distant wail of sirens headed for me.

I haul myself up to my knees, and then I stand, hunched over.

I've got to get to Simone.

I can't hail a cab—nobody's going to pick me up in this state. I could steal a car, but that would only draw more attention.

There's only one thing left to do. I've got to run.

I limp in the direction of Lincoln Park. After a few yards, I break into a shuffling kind of jog. My head is throbbing with every step. My ribs are agony, stabbing me with each breath.

But I have to get to Simone.

I can't stop even for a second.

17
SIMONE

Serwa helps me sneak out of the house. It's not terribly difficult because we're not actually in a prison. My main concern is that I don't want to be followed because I want to speak to Dante uninterrupted, without my father hearing or calling the police.

Serwa carries a huge load of recycling out to the bins in the backyard, then drops it all over the patio, with a whole lot of shattering glass, bouncing milk jugs, and rolling cans. When the two security guards run over to help her pick it all up, I sneak out the back gate.

I hear that nasty dog growling as I run across the lawn, but the guards have him on a leash, so he can't chase me. Thank god for that—I've never seen a meaner animal.

Dressed in jeans and a gray sweatshirt, with the hood pulled up, I feel like a criminal. I never go out at night alone. Lincoln Park is a safe neighborhood, relatively speaking, but I'm still in downtown Chicago. I flinch away from anybody walking in the opposite direction down the sidewalk. I feel like everybody's looking at me, even though nobody is.

I walk about six blocks over to the park. I wanted to meet here for symbolic reasons; Dante and I sat under the wisteria vines and talked and kissed for hours, and it was a beautiful afternoon, one of the best of my life.

The sun was shining then, and the bees were droning, and I had the man I love next to me. Now I'm all alone. It's chilly and dark. The season has changed—the wisteria has lost its thick green leaves and clusters of purple blooms. It's just dry brown vines now. The gazebo isn't a sheltered alcove anymore—it's exposed to the wind and the eyes of anyone else who might be roaming the park.

I huddle in the corner of the gazebo, trying to keep watch in all directions at once.

I should have worn a coat, not a sweater. It's windier and colder than I expected.

With each gust of air, the dry branches of the trees scratch together. I hear rustling sounds that might be a squirrel or a cat. I jump every time and stare around in all directions.

It was stupid to come here. I should have had Dante meet me at a café—somewhere warm and bright and safe.

I should have brought my phone. I was afraid Tata would notice it missing.

The dark and the cold and the fear are preying on my mind. If Dante appeared right now, I would throw myself into his arms unhesitatingly. I've missed him so, so, so badly, it feels like an organ was torn out of my body. I would blurt out the news about the pregnancy—those would be the first words out of my mouth.

But the longer I wait, the more I become confused and upset that he hasn't come. He promised to meet me at midnight. He said he would be here. I was sure I could count on him—sure he wouldn't keep me waiting even a moment. It's past midnight now, past 12:30. What could possibly be keeping him away?

Then I start to wonder if this is how it's always going to be.

That's what my father said, and my mother. They told me if I stayed with Dante, I'd have a life of perpetual danger and fear. They said there could be no happy ending with a man like that. That he would bring violence and crime into my life, no matter how hard he tried to hide it away from me.

And now I'm starting to realize this pregnancy changes everything...

If I keep this baby...what kind of life will they have?

What kind of father?

I might be willing to risk my own safety to be with Dante...but would I risk the safety of my child?

I have visions of criminals breaking into our house in the middle of the night, bent on revenge.

Or what about a SWAT team? It only takes one stray bullet to snuff out a life...especially if that life is particularly small and vulnerable.

My heart is racing, faster and faster.

I need to vomit again. I'm continually sick, dizzy, aching. Shivering with cold.

How could Dante fail me like this? He promised me...

Maybe his promises don't mean much.

We've only known each other for a few months. I thought we were soul mates. I thought I knew him.

But the man I know wouldn't leave me waiting for an hour in a dark park, all alone. Not when I begged him to come.

I should leave. What if someone mugs me? I don't just have myself to think about anymore. I haven't decided whether to keep this baby or not, not entirely, but right now it seems like the most important thing in the world. Like I walked into this deserted place carrying something unbearably precious and fragile.

I'm just at the point of fleeing from the gazebo when I hear a sound—much louder than any cat or squirrel. Crashing through the bushes, headed right for me.

My body stiffens like petrified wood, and I clutch my hands over my mouth, trying not to scream.

A hulking figure leaps into the gazebo—soot blackened and covered in blood. Wild eyes stare out of his face, eyes and teeth horribly white against his filthy skin.

I scream so loudly that it tears my throat.

"Simone!" he cries, reaching for me with his massive hands.

I understand that it's Dante, but I back away from him, still shrieking.

His hands are covered in blood, every inch of them. His knuckles are swollen, cut, bleeding, and the whole of his hands are drenched—not from those cuts but from something else. From someone else.

"Don't touch me!" I scream, staring at those awful hands.

Those are the hands of a criminal. A killer.

"I'm so sorry…" he says.

"Don't touch me! I…I…"

Everything I planned to say to him has flown out of my head. All I can see is his battered face, his bloodied hands, the snarl still baring his teeth. I see the unmistakable evidence of violence. Evidence of the life he leads.

A life that can't include a child.

"I'm going away tomorrow," I say, through numb lips. "I don't want to see you anymore."

Dante stands perfectly still, his hands falling to his sides. "You don't mean that."

I don't. I don't mean it. But I have to do it. "This is over between us," I tell him. "We're done."

He looks stunned. Dazed, even. "Please, Simone…"

I shake my head, silent tears coursing down my cheeks. "I'm leaving. Don't follow me."

He swallows hard, his lip split and swollen. "I love you," he says.

For once, the one and only time, his voice sounds gentle. It tears my heart in half like paper. Tears it again and again.

I could stay. I would stay if it were just me.

But it's not just me anymore.

I turn and run away from him.

18
DANTE

I don't believe she'll actually go.

I think she loves me. So I think she'll stay.

But I'm wrong.

She flies to London the next morning.

And she doesn't come back again.

19

SIMONE

MAYBE IF I WEREN'T SO COLD AND SCARED THAT NIGHT, I WOULD have made a different choice.

Maybe if I weren't so sick in London…

I had hyperemesis gravidarum throughout the pregnancy. Vomiting twenty, thirty times a day. I got so skinny, I was nothing but bones. The doctors put a permanent IV line into me so I wouldn't die of dehydration.

I was hospitalized in the second trimester.

The baby was born early in the third, at thirty-four weeks. He was tiny. God, so very, very tiny, only 5 lbs. 2 oz. He didn't cry as he came out. He looked blue and wizened. Barely alive.

The birth was nightmarish. They gave me nitrous gas for the pain, but I had a poor reaction to it. I started to hallucinate—I thought the nurses were demons trying to tear me apart. I thought the doctor was a monster wearing the mask of a human.

I thought Dante came to the hospital, but he only stood in the doorway, glaring at me. I begged him to forgive me for leaving. For not telling him about the baby. He wouldn't speak to me—he only stared at me with a cold, furious expression.

After the birth, when I'm in my right mind again, I believe that was the one thing I saw that was actually true: Dante won't forgive me for this, if he ever finds out. Never ever.

My parents come to the hospital. They hadn't known I was pregnant—I made Serwa swear not to tell them. Mama cries and asks why I kept such an awful secret. Tata scowls and demands to know if Dante is aware of what he did to me.

"No," I whisper. "I haven't spoken to him. He doesn't know."

Because the baby is small and has trouble breathing, they put him in the NICU, in an incubator. I've barely seen him or held him at all. All I know is that he has a lot of curly black hair and a tiny limp body.

The nurses keep giving me drugs. I'm sleeping all the time. When I wake up, the baby's never in the room.

On the third day, I wake, and my parents are sitting next to the bed. There's nobody else in the room—no nurses or Serwa.

"Where's the baby?" I ask them.

Mama glances over at my father. Her face looks pale and drawn. They're both dressed nicely—Mama in a blazer and skirt set, Tata in a suit. Not exactly formal, but the closest thing to it. As if they have an event to attend. Or maybe this is the event.

I feel disgusting by comparison—unwashed and unkempt in the cheap cotton hospital smock.

I wonder if other people feel this way by comparison to their own family—unworthy.

"We need to discuss what you plan to do," Mama says.

"About what?"

"About your future."

The word *future* used to have such a bright sparkle to me. Now it sounds hollow and terrifying. Like a long dark hallway to nowhere.

I'm silent. I don't know what to say.

"It's time to get your life back on track," Tata tells me. His voice is measured, but his face is stiff and stern. He looks at me not with anger…just disappointment. "You've made some very poor decisions, Simone. It's time to right the ship."

I swallow, my mouth dry. "What do you mean?"

"Here's what's going to happen," my father says. "Your sister is going to adopt the baby, privately and discreetly. She will present the child as her own. She will raise it as her own. You are going to Cambridge for the winter semester. You'll get your degree. You'll get a job afterward. You won't tell anyone about your indiscretion in Chicago. This whole ugly chapter will be put behind us."

I lie there silently, while those bizarre statements wash over me.

"I want to see my son," I say at last.

"That's not happening," Tata says.

"Where is he?"

"You don't need to concern yourself with that."

"*WHERE IS HE?*" I shriek.

"He's already at home with Serwa," Mama says, trying to calm me. "He's being very well cared for. You know how good your sister is with children."

That's true. Serwa loves children. She practically raised *me*.

But it doesn't make me feel better in the slightest. I want to see my baby. I want to see his face.

"I'm not giving him away," I hiss at my father.

He looks right back at me, his dark eyes matching mine in anger. "You think you can take care of a child? You don't have a cent to your name that I don't give you. How will you feed it? Where will you live? I'm not supporting you in throwing your life away. And what kind of a mother would you be anyway? You're a child. Look at you. You can barely get out of that bed."

More gently, Mama says, "Simone…I know you care for this baby. More than your own selfish desires. You are not at a time in your life to have a child. Later, yes, but now…you're not ready for that. It wouldn't be in his best interest. And think of your sister…"

"What about her?"

"Serwa will never have another chance to have a baby."

This is the first thing they say that hits at my heart. All their words up until then were nothing but dust that I planned to brush aside. But that statement…it cuts me.

Mama looks at me with her gentle blue eyes. "She loves him already."

"You must give her this," Tata says. "Let her raise the baby. Let her have that one thing. You have the rest of your life ahead of you. Serwa doesn't. This is her only chance."

Of all the angles they used to attack me, this is the one that hits my most vulnerable spot.

Maybe I could have withstood the threats of disowning or the fear of raising my son alone in poverty.

"Look," Mama says.

She holds up her phone.

On the screen is a picture of my sister sitting in a rocking chair, with a little bundle in her lap. I can't see the baby's face—he's wrapped in a blanket and a knitted cap, his head turned toward her.

But I can see Serwa's face.

I see her looking down at my son with kindness, love…and pure joy. It's the happiest I've ever seen her look.

And I'm the most miserable I've ever been.

In that moment of weakness, still stitched and bleeding from the birth, my head still swimming with drugs…I agree.

I sign the papers.

I give my son away.

And I fall down, down, down into a dark well. A depression so deep that I think I'll never climb out of it again.

The sadness lasts for years.

20
DANTE

NINE YEARS LATER

WE'VE STARTED PHASE ONE OF DEVELOPMENT DOWN ON THE South Shore.

This will be a two-billion-dollar project spread out over the next six years, in four phases.

Phase one is commercial real estate. Gallo construction is just finishing our first skyscraper, right on the waterfront. The tallest part of the tower block reaches 1,191 feet in the air. Which means that when it's completed, it'll be the third-tallest building in Chicago.

To my eyes, it's the most beautiful. And not just 'cause I built it. The twisting, spiral shape is covered with a smooth facade of glass, shading from deep violet at the base, up to pure blue, and then sea green at the top. Or at least that's how it will look when fully completed.

At the moment, the top ten floors are a bare skeleton of steel, open to the wide air and the thousand-foot drop to the ground.

To the east of the building, you can see the flat expanse of the lake. To the west, the view is blocked by a massive rooftop billboard. The images on the billboard rotate—right now it's showing a Coca-Cola ad with a soda bottle the size of an Olympic swimming pool.

We've purchased that building, too, so the first thing I'm gonna do is rip down the billboard. Then I'll have a clear view over to Russell Square Park instead.

"There you are," a feminine voice says.

I turn around.

Abigail Green is standing behind me, holding her clipboard and a pen. She's looking at me in her usual way—sly and smiling, like we've got a secret.

We don't. I'm using Ms. Green to lease the offices in this building because her commercial real estate firm is the largest and most prestigious in Chicago. I don't give a fuck that she's five-ten, blond, and built like a porn star—though I'm sure that helped her build her client base when she started.

Abigail is smart. We've gone over all the numbers for what types of businesses I want in the building, the ideal lease lengths, and how much we should charge. Even though we're a few months out from completion, we're already at 78 percent occupancy. So she's done a great job. It's the…extra attention I could live without.

She wanted to meet here today instead of at her office. She said she wanted to see the building in person now that it's getting close to being done.

"So what do you think?" I nod toward the floor-to-ceiling, wall-to-wall view of the lake. I'm standing right at the edge. There's nothing stopping me from stepping out into clear, empty space.

"It's gorgeous!" Abigail says. She shivers, though, seeing how I lean against the bare metal struts. "I take it you're not afraid of heights."

I'm not afraid of heights.

Though sometimes they're a temptation.

She walks a little closer to me—though not too close. She bites her lip, looking me up and down. "I guess a guy your size isn't afraid of much of anything."

"No," I say flatly. "But it doesn't have anything to do with size."

Fear preys on people who have something to lose.

I don't give a fuck about much these days. I put all this time and effort into this complex—but the truth is, it was Nero's idea. He wants the Gallos to be the richest family in Chicago.

I threw myself into the work because that's what I do. I steer this family. I execute the plans. I make sure everything goes off perfectly—no mistakes, no failures. I keep everyone safe, happy, and successful.

When each task is done, I feel exactly the same as I did before... empty.

"I've got two more lease agreements for you to sign," Abigail says.

I cross the bare, empty floor to take her clipboard. These office suites will be plush and luxurious once we get the windows, the drywall, and the carpeting in place. For now it's an open box, with streaks of plaster and dust across the floor, plus a few scattered screws.

I scan the agreements, then sign at the bottom.

Abigail is watching my face the whole time, while she toys with the bangle on her left wrist. "It's not often I look up to a man. Especially not when I'm wearing heels."

She's got on sky-high stilettos, nylons, a knee-length skirt with a tasteful slit up the back, a silk blouse, and expensive-looking earrings. I can smell her floral perfume and the slightly waxy scent of her red lipstick. She's standing very close to me.

There's nothing unattractive about Abigail.

At least not to a normal person.

The problem is I have a narrow and specific definition of what I find attractive. It was formed a long time ago, and it hasn't changed since. Abigail doesn't fit it. Almost no one does.

I hand the clipboard back to her. Abigail takes it, but she doesn't move from where she's standing. She trails her index finger, with its perfectly manicured red fingernail, down the outside of my arm. Then she lightly grips my bicep.

"Is that the kind of muscle you get swinging a hammer?" she purrs. "Or do you get your workout some other way..."

It's obvious what Abigail wants.

I could give it to her—I've done it before, plenty of times, with other women. I could turn her around, yank up her skirt, rip open her nylons, bend her over, and fuck her until I blow. It would be over in five minutes, and it would end this little game.

If I had the urge, I'd do it. But I don't feel it today. I feel less than nothing.

So I ignore her comment.

"Thanks for bringing those papers by. I'll walk you back to the elevator."

Abigail frowns, seriously irritated. "I don't get you. You're not married. And I'm pretty sure you're not gay…"

"I guess you've never encountered 'not interested' before."

"No, I haven't." Abigail is unabashed. "I don't think I've ever been turned down by a man. What is it—you don't like successful women?"

"If I didn't, I wouldn't have hired you."

"What then?"

Now I'm the one who's annoyed. I pay Abigail to find tenants for my buildings, not to interrogate me. I frown and take a step toward her. She stumbles backward on her stilettos, her expression turning to fright.

"None of your *fucking* business," I growl.

"S-sorry," she stammers.

She drops her pen, stoops to pick it up, then tucks a piece of hair behind her ear without looking me in the eye. "I'll scan these and email a copy to you," she mutters.

"Thanks."

Abigail hurries back toward the elevators. I stay exactly where I am.

Once she's gone, I walk back over to the window again. Or at least the place where the windows will be eventually.

I'm standing on the west side of the building, looking out over that billboard.

The image flips over again. Now, instead of soda, it's showing a seventy-foot-long perfume ad. It's a woman's face, in extreme close-up—the most famous face in the world.

Wide-set eyes slightly tilted up at the outer edges, honey brown with dark rings around the iris. Thick black lashes and straight dark brows. Smooth cheeks like polished bronze. A square face, delicate chin, full mouth. Those lovely lips are curved up in a smile. But the eyes are sad…terribly sad.

Or at least that's how they look to me.

But what do I know?

She's probably the happiest person in the world—why wouldn't she be? She's a fucking supermodel. Rich, successful, famous, traveling the world, hobnobbing with celebrities…what could she possibly be missing?

It's me who's fucking miserable.

I stare at that face for a long time, even though every moment of it feels like pure torture. It feels like a vise tightening around my chest, squeezing and squeezing until my breastbone is about to crack.

Then, finally, the image flips over to cola again.

I turn away, my face still burning.

21
SIMONE

"Simone, put that right hand on your hip. A little lower. Yes, that's perfect. Ivory, tilt your chin up just a touch… That's it, perfect. Somebody move that fan—I want the skirt blowing the other way. No, the *other* other way! Good. Now tilt that reflector…"

The camera clicks again and again. With each click, I shift my position slightly. First looking directly at the lens, then down at the ground, then over my right shoulder. Then I shift my weight to my opposite hip, and then I lean back against Ivory, and then I rest my arm on her shoulder.

I move through positions automatically, without even thinking. I always keep my face to the light, and I remember to hold my jacket open like Hugo wanted.

We're shooting a campaign for Prada. It's my third this year. They always pair me with Ivory because we make such a nice contrast to each other—her so light, and me so dark. Hugo sings that old "Ebony and Ivory" song at us when he's in a silly mood.

He's not silly today. We're shooting at the sand dunes in Algodones, and it's been a bit of a disaster from the start. First it was windy. The sand was blowing in our eyes and teeth and fucking with Ivory's hair. Her hair is fine as candy floss and white as a cloud.

Ivory's not just blond—she's albino. Her skin is pure milk, and her eyes are violet, more red than blue in the right light. Of course, that means she has to be slathered in sunscreen to shoot outdoors like this, and the direct sunlight is murder on her eyes. When we did the first set of outfits with the oversize retro Duple sunglasses, she was just fine. But now that she's changed into a long, flowing maxi dress and no shades, her eyes are tearing up, and she can't stop blinking. It doesn't help that Hugo has that damn reflector pointed right at her face.

Worst of all was the giraffe. Hugo had the bright idea that we should shoot with actual animals—first an ostrich, then a Masai giraffe on loan from the zoo. The handler came along to make sure he behaved. But the giraffe didn't like Hugo's shouting one bit, or the flashes from the light boxes. He ended up galloping off, one massive hoof the size of a dinner plate barely missing Ivory's face. After that she didn't want to stand anywhere near the animals. It took over an hour for the handler to get the giraffe back, chasing after him in our dune buggy.

Anyway, we're behind schedule now. Hugo has decided we better get through a couple of outfits with just Ivory and me and the sand dunes before we run out of light.

"Lift that handbag, Simone," Hugo says. "No, not that high—this isn't *The Price is Right*. Do it casual. Natural."

There's nothing natural about contorting myself into the perfect position to showcase both the jacket and the bag just the way Hugo wants, but I don't even bother to roll my eyes at him. I'd like to wrap this up as well.

"All right," Hugo says, once he's got a few hundred images of this set. "Who's gonna hold my snake?"

"I really hope that's not a euphemism." Ivory wrinkles her nose.

"Ha ha, very funny." Hugo sniffs. He's short and lean, with a salt-and-pepper goatee, a long nose, and a penchant for baseball caps. Ivory says it's because he's balding and doesn't want anyone to know.

He opens a large chest with suspicious-looking air holes in the side. "I mean an actual snake. A Burmese python, to be exact. Why don't you drape him 'round your neck, Ivory—he's an albino, too. You two should get along perfectly."

"Fucking hell no." Ivory takes a step backward. It's difficult to tell, but I think she went about three shades paler at the sight of Hugo lifting the massive snake out of the crate.

The thing must be twelve feet long. It looks heavy from the way Hugo is struggling to heft it out.

"Let me help," the handler says, grabbing the snake's lower half. The handler still looks sweaty and dirty from his romp across the sand to recover the giraffe.

The snake flops around at first, then perks up once it realizes it's out in the open air.

It's quite lovely—cream colored with yellow patches. It reminds me a little bit of buttered popcorn. Its skin looks smooth and dry.

"I'll do it," I say.

"Switch to the white prairie skirt," Hugo says.

He's not talking to me—he's instructing Danielle, the wardrobe specialist.

She runs to retrieve the skirt in question, along with a different pair of sandals. She helps me remove my current outfit so I can change. I do it right out in the open, stripping to a nude-colored thong. Nobody pays any attention to my nakedness. Nudity is as common as vape pens and Instagram posts in the modeling world.

"Which top?" Danielle asks.

"None," Hugo says. "You don't care, do you, Simone?"

I shake my head. I don't give a damn about going topless.

Hugo drapes the snake around my shoulders. It really is heavy—over a hundred pounds, I'd guess. The handler helps support the tail while I get into position between two sand dunes.

The snake's tail hangs down over my bare breast. Its body runs across my shoulders, then down my left arm. He's wrapped himself around my forearm, his head resting on my open palm. I cover my other breast with my free hand.

"Oh, that's perfect," Hugo sighs. "Okay, stand straight on like that... All right, now turn a little to your left and look over your shoulder at me. Yeah. Extend that arm and see if the snake will look right at you..."

Modeling can be peaceful. You become almost a human statue, poseable and moveable, but not feeling much. You know you're making something beautiful. It's always fun to see the images later, after cropping and editing. You get to see what you were that day: A goddess. An angel. A diva. A party girl. A CEO. An explorer...

But the real reason I started modeling was for money. After my blowup with my parents, I realized how much they owned me. Without money, you have no independence. So I took the first job I could find that would give me that freedom.

I started with runway work in Paris. I was just one of the hundreds of models flown in for Fashion Week. I strutted up and down like a walking coat hanger for hours at a time, cycling through dozens of outfits. Then I started booking commercial work, too. Just small campaigns for shampoo and nylon brands at first, getting paid a couple of hundred dollars a pop.

A year later I got my first big job—the cover of *Sports Illustrated*'s swimsuit edition. Technically, I wasn't wearing a swimsuit at all—just a lot of strategically placed body paint in the shape of a cheetah-print bikini. After that they started calling me *the Body*.

I suppose I have Henry to thank for that nickname. My figure never quite went back to the way it was after he was born. I got slim again, but my breasts and hips were fuller than before. And that coincided with the end of an era in modeling. Heroin chic was out, and the J.Lo butt came in. Everybody wanted curves, curves, curves. And that was me—I was part of the new wave of sexy super-models. Kate Upton, Charlotte McKinney, Chrissy Teigen, Emily Ratajkowski, and Simone Solomon...plus a Kardashian or two.

Everybody wanted that exotic, ethnically ambiguous look and

that "real woman" hourglass figure. I don't know how "real" any of us were, but the money we made was solid enough.

The work flowed in fast. More jobs than I could handle. I flew to every corner of the globe.

It helped keep me busy and keep my mind off how fucking miserable I was.

I tried not to think about Dante—how I'd left and how I'd lied to him. Lied by omission. The biggest fucking omission there is.

But I didn't forget about my son.

Between each job, I flew back to London to see him. I let Serwa raise Henry—but he was still mine, in my heart. I held him, I played with him, I fed him. And my heart bled all over again every time I handed him back to my sister.

Serwa loved him, too—I could see that. She centered her world around him. Quit her job at Barclays, spent all day long taking him to the park, the river, the Eye.

My parents were funding it. They were fine paying for her to raise the baby, but not for me to do so.

I was bitter. So fucking bitter.

I saved every penny I made from modeling. I planned to take Henry back, when I had enough.

But Serwa was so attached to him, too.

And she was sick. After a year or two of recovery, she started to get weaker again. I thought if I took my son away from her, it would kill her.

So we shared him. She took care of him while I was working, and he was mine when I came home. He called us both *Mama* when he started to speak.

It wasn't a terrible system. In fact, it worked surprisingly well. I missed them both so badly when I was gone. But modeling years are short—it's an industry of youth. I had to work while I could. And I saved, saved, saved the money.

Serwa and I were closer than ever. I didn't speak to my parents at all. I cut them off when they took my baby away without even asking. I told Serwa to make sure they never visited when I was home. She was careful to keep that promise—to keep them separate from me.

I did let them visit Henry when I wasn't home. He has so little family, I didn't want to deny him his grandparents. When I'd come home, he'd tell me all about how Grandma taught him to make crepes and Grandpa gave him a Rubik's Cube.

My parents tried to make amends many times. I wouldn't answer their calls or their letters.

Until Serwa died. She passed away three years ago. She was only thirty-four.

We were all there at the hospital together. It was the first time I'd seen my parents in years. My mother looked older. My father looked almost exactly the same—just a few threads of silver in his close-cropped hair.

I looked at them both, and I felt this hatred well up inside me. I was so, so angry at them. The anger hadn't faded at all. If anything, it was stronger. I saw them standing there with my son between them, and I wanted to tear Henry away from them, like they tried to tear him away from me, and never let them see him again.

But I swallowed my rage because we were there for Serwa, not for me. We sat and talked with her and told her everything was going to be all right, that she was going to recover again, like she always had before. She was on a short list for a lung transplant. We thought that would fix everything.

Instead, she died that night.

When the doctor told us, my father broke down in tears. I'd never seen him cry before, never in my life. He grabbed me and pulled me into his arms and sobbed, saying, "Simone, forgive me. You're all we have left."

I felt so alone without Serwa. I wanted my mother and father back just as badly as they wanted me. I hugged Tata, and my mother hugged us both, and we all cried together.

I don't know if I forgave them, though. I never answered about that.

And even now, three years later, I'm not sure if I have.

We see each other often. From the outside, we look like the same close-knit family we used to be—minus Serwa and with the addition of Henry.

But, of course, what you see from the outside never tells the story of a family. It's a ripe red apple. When you cut it open, there could be anything inside. Crisp healthy flesh…or rot and worms.

Henry lives with me now, full-time. I can afford a nanny-tutor for him. Her name is Carly. The three of us travel all over the world together.

The gossip rags wrote that I'd adopted my nephew. I didn't correct them. I don't talk about my son publicly, not ever. I don't allow photos of him. It was my choice to plaster my face on billboards and magazines. I keep him hidden the best I can so he can choose for himself someday if he wants a public life or a private one.

Also, I'm afraid…

Afraid of what might happen if Dante ever saw a picture of Henry.

Because when I search Henry's face, I see my features…but I also see Dante.

I stole his son from him.

My worst fear is that he might someday steal him back.

The shoot is over. Hugo has carefully laid the snake back down in its nest inside the trunk. Ivory shakes her head at me.

"Don't hug me after you touched that thing," she says.

I grin at her. "But you look so cute in that sweater. So snuggly and cuddly…"

"Don't even think about it!"

"Will you at least share a car back to the city with me?"

"Yes," she says loftily. "That would be acceptable."

Ivory and I have been friends for four years now. It's hard to stay close to anybody in the modeling world—we all travel around so much. But you do tend to work with the same people over time, as certain photographers or casting agents recommend you for jobs.

I'm probably the only person who knows that Ivory's real name is Jennifer Parker, and she didn't grow up in France like she likes to tell people. Actually, she's Canadian—from a little town in Quebec called Mille-Isles.

Ivory says she has to craft mystique around herself. *Nobody ever would have given a fig about Marilyn Monroe if she kept calling herself Norma Jean.*

I understand secrets.

I understand that the truth can be painful, that it's much easier to live a make-believe life, where any questions that people ask you can't hurt you at all because they're all just part of the narrative. It's so easy to talk about yourself when nothing you say is real.

That's how I do interviews.

What's your favorite color?

Red.

What's your favorite food?

Pasta.

Who would you most like to eat lunch with?

Chris Evans, of course.

It's all just nonsense. The interviewers don't care what I say. Neither do the people who read glossy magazines. Simone the Supermodel is just a character. She's "the Body." Nobody cares if I have a brain.

Ivory and I share a cab back to the city center. She drops me off at the Ritz-Carlton.

I take the elevator straight up to my room. As soon as he hears my key in the lock, Henry comes over to the door. He tries to scare me, but it doesn't work because I was already looking for him as soon as I opened the door.

"Hey, you." I wrap my arms around him and pull him against my chest.

Henry is so damn tall. He's only nine years old, and he's already up past my shoulder. I have to buy him clothes for sizes twelve to fourteen, and even then, the waist is baggy, while the pants are barely long enough.

"I took pictures with a snake today. Do you want to see?" I show him the snaps I took on my phone.

"It's a Burmese python!" he says. "'D'you know they can grow up to twenty feet?"

"Luckily, this guy wasn't that big."

"They've got two lungs. Most snakes only have one."

Henry loves to read. He remembers everything he reads and everything he watches on TV. I've had to cut down his YouTube time because he was following his curiosity down all sorts of rabbit holes—some that I wouldn't want him learning about even five or six years from now.

He's got long arms and legs now, and his face is leaning out. It's hard to see the chubby little boy he used to be. Some things are the same, though—he's still a gentle giant: helpful, kind, and careful of others' feelings.

"What should we do tonight?" I ask him.

"I dunno."

"Did you finish all your schoolwork?"

"Yeah."

"Let me see it."

He takes me over to the little hotel desk where he's got his papers and textbooks all spread out. He shows me the chapters he was reading with his tutor.

Sometimes, when I know we'll be in the same place for a while, I enroll Henry in one of the international schools, just so he can experience classrooms and friends in a somewhat normal manner. He seems to like it when he's there. But he seems to like anyplace we go. He's so easygoing that I can never be sure if he's genuinely happy or if this is all he knows.

I have a lot of money saved now. Enough that I could stop working or slow down. We could live almost anywhere.

The question is, where?

I've been to every city in the world, it feels like. But none of them are home.

Most recently, my parents were living in DC. After Serwa died, my father launched himself into humanitarian work. He's brokering some big international antitrafficking coalition. In fact, he's doing a cross-country media blitz right now.

Well, speak of the devil.

My phone buzzes with my father's number.

"Hold on," I say to Henry.

I answer the call.

"Simone." My father's deep smooth voice cuts through the airwaves between us as if he's right in the room with me. "How was your shoot today?"

"Good. I think they got everything they wanted, so that was probably the last day."

"Excellent. And what do you have booked next?"

"Well…" My stomach gives a little squirm. Even after all this time. "I'm actually supposed to do a shoot for Balenciaga next week."

"In Chicago?"

I pause. "Yes."

"That's what your assistant said. I'm glad to hear it—because your mother and I will be there at the same time."

"Oh, great," I say weakly.

I was already dreading going back to Chicago. I haven't been there in almost a decade. The idea of meeting up with my parents there… it doesn't exactly thrill me. Too many old memories dredged up.

"I'm holding a rally," Tata says. "In support of the Freedom Foundation. The mayor of Chicago will be speaking, as well as one of the city aldermen. I'd like you to be there."

I fidget in place, shifting from foot to foot. "I don't know, Tata...I'm not very political..."

"It's a good cause, little one. You could lend your support to something meaningful..."

There's that note of disapproval again. He doesn't think my career is meaningful. I'm one of the top-paid models in the world, and he still sees this as a frivolous hobby.

"Just sit on the podium with me. You don't have to speak. You can do that, can't you?" my father says in his most reasonable tone. It's framed as a request, but I know he expects me to say yes. I bristle against that pressure. I've been on my own for a long time now. I don't actually have to do what he says.

But, at the same time, my parents are all I have now that Serwa is gone. Other than Henry, of course. I don't want to tear down the truce between us. Not over something as petty as this.

Chicago is a big city. I can go there without running into Dante.

"All right, Tata," I hear myself say. "I'll go to your rally."

After I hang up, I pull out my phone and find the picture of Dante I've saved all these years. I try not to look at it because he looks so fierce and angry. Like he's staring into my soul and doesn't like what he sees.

I'm addicted. Sometimes I resist for months. But I always come back to it again. I've never had the strength to delete it.

I look at his black eyes. That ferocious jaw. The firm lines of his mouth.

The ache I feel is as strong as ever.

I shut off my phone and shove it away from me.

22
DANTE

I drive over to Riona's law firm to drop off the documents she needs for our new business credit line. Riona is the eldest daughter of the Griffins. Her family and mine have partnered for the South Shore development, and she's handling the legal aspects of our new joint business entity.

It's not the sort of law she usually does. In fact, she started as a defense attorney, keeping the Griffins' soldiers out of trouble as they handled some of the less savory aspects of Irish Mafia business.

She got me out of hot water when I was arrested on a bullshit murder charge.

It was pretty fucking ironic, sitting in Cook County Jail for a crime I actually didn't commit. After all the things I've gotten away with over the years…I didn't expect to be framed for shooting some two-bit nobody.

Anyway, Riona helped me out, and I haven't forgotten it. I owe her a favor. A couple of favors, probably.

Her brother is married to my baby sister, so we were already in-laws. Now we've become friends. I meet her for lunch sometimes when I'm close to her office. Every once in a while, when she's really pissed off about something, we go for a run together. She needs it—generally speaking, Riona is wound tighter than a two-dollar watch.

Today is no different. She comes hustling out of her office with two bright spots of color on her cheeks in an otherwise pale face. She's got her red hair pulled back in a sleek bun, and she's wearing her typical ball-busting attorney outfit of a dark navy pantsuit and a cream silk blouse.

"Hey!" she says when she spots me. "I'm grabbing a coffee from the café downstairs—you want to come?"

"Sure. I brought these." I hand her the documents.

"Oh, thanks." Riona looks them over quickly to make sure I didn't forget anything. That doesn't offend me—I know it's her way to check everything twice because she doesn't trust anyone to be as meticulous as she is. "I'll drop these off at my office first."

I follow her down the hall to her private corner office. I've been in here a couple of times before. It looks more like a fancy Manhattan living room than an office—pewter-colored walls, modern art prints, some weird sculpture that looks like a solar model. I mean, it's super stylish, but it's cold and intense, a bit like Riona herself.

She puts the documents down on her desk. I notice she lines the edge of the folder up with the corner of her desk, even though she's gonna move it again as soon as she comes back.

"Did you get those lease agreements from Abigail Green?" she asks me.

"Yeah."

Riona gives me a quick glance. "She's very…persistent, isn't she?"

"She's good at her job," I say shortly.

"I bet she's good at a lot of things…" Riona turns her cool-green eyes on me.

"I'm not fucking her." I grunt.

"That's too bad," Riona says. "I probably could have gotten her to knock down her commission a point."

"Nope. You'll just have to use your usual lawyer tricks—a relentless onslaught of argument until you beat her into submission."

Riona smiles. "You know me so well."

"I guess so. 'Cause I can tell you came out of that meeting pretty fuckin' hot."

"Oh, that." Riona scowls. "It's this case I've been working on—the other attorney filed a bunch of bullshit motions. He's trying to annoy me into giving up."

He definitely doesn't know Riona, then.

"Do you want me to murder him for you?" I say.

Riona snorts. "If he keeps irritating me, then maybe...and by the way, thank you for not putting that in a text message this time."

"No paper trail. I'm learning," I say, tapping my temple with my index finger. "I can just see you getting your phone records subpoenaed for some case. They pull you up on the stand and say, 'Ms. Griffin, can you read for the court your conversation of September twenty-eighth with Mr. Gallo?'"

Riona laughs, playing along. "Well, Your Honor, he said, 'Do you want me to murder him for you?' and I said, 'Yes, please—slowly, with a pickax.' But it was all in good fun, Your Honor. The fact he slipped and fell on a pickax later that night was completely coincidental..."

We head down to the café on the ground floor of her building. It's a clean, bright space, with pastries delivered fresh three times a day. They get the orders out in minutes—an absolute must for all the lawyers on the clock. Riona's firm shares the building with several other law groups, so everybody in here looks busy, grumpy, and ready to file an injunction if they didn't get the right amount of foam on their latte.

I order a sandwich; Riona, a coffee and croissant. When I try to pay for both orders, she cuts across me with her credit card at the ready.

"I've got to treat you," she says matter-of-factly, "because I'm trying to butter you up."

"That doesn't sound good."

"It's nothing terrible..."

"I bet."

I follow her over to the nearest open table. She sits across from me, folding her hands in front of her in the way I know means she's about to make her pitch.

"My brother's speaking at a rally," Riona says. "It's for the Freedom Foundation. I want you to handle security for the event. You'd be working with the mayor's team."

"Okay…" I'm wondering what the favor is, exactly. "I'm not some kind of security expert, though…"

"I know. I just want someone from our own family there. The team they hired is going to be focused on the mayor, primarily, and the speaker as well. I want somebody keeping an eye on Callum."

Callum is her big brother, the one married to Aida. I've got almost as much motivation to keep him safe as Riona does. Which is why I'm still waiting for the other shoe to drop.

The barista comes over with Riona's croissant and my sandwich. I take a big bite of my BLT. Riona leaves her food untouched, wanting to finish our conversation before she eats.

"It's on Saturday," she says. "You'd be overseeing the setup and supervising the event. The mayor wants to make sure we're careful because the speaker has received several death threats over the past few months."

"Who is it?" I ask bluntly.

Riona doesn't beat around the bush. "Yafeu Solomon."

I set down my sandwich. "I don't think that's a good idea."

"You don't have to talk to him. He probably won't even see you."

Riona is aware of my former interactions with the Solomon family. Other than my siblings, she's one of the only people who know.

I sit silently, thinking.

If it were anybody else asking me, I'd just tell them no. I have no interest in being around Yafeu Solomon, especially not in protecting him. In fact, if I saw some assassin rushing him with a knife, I'd be tempted to simply step aside.

But I do owe Riona a favor.

That's why she's asking. A good lawyer never asks a question where they don't already know the answer.

I sigh. "Who do I contact from the mayor's office?"

Riona lets herself smile just for a second, pleased that she successfully roped me in. "His name's John Peterson," she says, texting me his number. "He's already expecting your call."

I almost want to laugh. "Of course he is."

"You know I like to have my ducks lined up." Riona checks her watch. "I better get back upstairs."

"You didn't eat."

"I'll take it with me." She picks up the croissant in a napkin, keeping her fingers clean, then takes a quick sip of her coffee.

"Thank you, Dante," she says.

"How many more favors do I owe you till we're square?"

She laughs. "I don't know—what's twenty-five years to life worth?"

"I guess at least one or two more."

She gives me a little wave and heads back toward the elevators.

I stay put so I can finish my sandwich. No sense letting good food go to waste.

23

SIMONE

DRIVING AROUND DOWNTOWN CHICAGO SETS MY NERVES ON EDGE.

I don't know if the city changed or if my memories are off. In my mind, the city had a kind of late-afternoon golden glow—all the glass in the high-rises illuminated like a sunset. I remembered the lake and the river, clean and blue, and the gorgeous Art Deco architecture in between.

Now a bunch of the luxury shops along the Magnificent Mile have been boarded up, probably because of the riots and protests over the summer, and the whole city looks dingier and dirtier than I remember.

But that's probably just the difference in my own head.

I was in love last time I was here. Everything looked beautiful to me then. I didn't notice the ugly parts.

Now that I'm older, I see things realistically.

"What's wrong, Mom?" Henry asks me. He's sitting next to me in the cab, reading one of the Diary of a Wimpy Kid books. He's read them all a dozen times, but he likes to look through his favorite ones again and show me the best cartoon panels.

"Nothing," I say. "Why would anything be wrong?"

"Your face looks mad."

"No, not mad."

"Are you sad?"

"Maybe a little tired, baby."

"I was tired on the plane. So I went to sleep for a while."

"I should have done that, too."

I pull Henry against my shoulder and rest my chin on the top of his head. His curls are so soft. He's a beautiful boy—big dark eyes. Lashes that any girl would envy. A long narrow face. His hands and feet are already as big as mine, and they're still growing. Like a puppy, it just shows how tall he'll be once he grows into them.

"When are we gonna see Grandma and Grandpa?"

"Right now. We're meeting them for dinner."

"Good. I can show them my book."

As we drive, we pass the Drake hotel. I didn't book my room there, for obvious reasons. But there's no avoiding the places I saw on my first stay in Chicago.

I can see exactly the spot where the chauffeured car was parked when I was sobbing in the back and Dante wrenched open the driver's side door and jumped in.

It's funny to think about how I cried over Parsons. How childish of me. My biggest problem then was not attending the school I wanted. I had no idea how much worse things were about to get.

I lost the love of my life.

I lost my child.

Then I lost my sister.

At least I got Henry back. The rest of it is like dust in the wind... scattered too far for me to ever gather it up again.

The cab pulls up in front of the restaurant. I pay the driver while Henry hops out onto the curb, eager to see my parents. He loves them. And they adore him. My father takes Henry to the zoo and teaches him how to make jollof rice. My mother plays cribbage with him and shows him how to paint with watercolor.

I appreciate their relationship with my son. I really do. But if I ever saw them trying to crush his dream like they did to mine... I'd cut them out of our lives without a moment's hesitation. I will never let my son be bent to someone else's will. I'm going to do for him what I couldn't do for myself. I'm going to let him choose his own path.

The hostess leads us to the table where my parents are already sitting, sipping a glass of wine each. They stand as we approach so they can kiss us on both cheeks.

"You're looking strong," my father says to Henry.

"I was playing basketball at the international school in Madrid."

"You should play golf. That's the sport of finance and business."

"He likes basketball," I say, a little too sharply.

"Well, he'll have the height for it," my father says. "He's tall like his grandfather."

Tall like his father, too. But we never mention that.

Perhaps in the silence that follows, my parents are thinking of Dante. I doubt they ever do under normal circumstances, but it's impossible to miss that particular elephant in the room on our first night back in Chicago.

Tata quickly switches to something else. "How's your school-work going, Henry?"

While Henry tells Tata all about it, Mama asks me about his tutor.

"She's back at the hotel right now," I say. "She didn't want to come to dinner with us."

"She must enjoy flying all over the world with you two."

"Probably. Though I'm sure it gets lonely. She starts grad school in the fall, so I'll have to find someone new. There's no rush, though—Henry is ahead in school. He could easily take a year off without falling behind."

"He's very bright," Mama says, looking over at him proudly. "Does he like seafood? We could order the clams to start…"

The meal is pleasant. I'm happy to see my parents again. But that old anger is simmering inside me, deep below the surface. It was a mistake to come back here, even for a week. I should have turned down the job and refused my parents' invitation.

"What days are you working?" my father asks.

"Tomorrow and the next day."

"We could pick up Henry in the morning and take him to Navy Pier while you're at your shoot."

"I'm sure he'd enjoy that."

"Just don't book anything Saturday night," my father says. "There's an evening event, after the rally."

My lips tighten, but I nod. "That sounds nice."

"It's so lovely to be together again," Mama says, smiling.

All of us but Serwa.

I blink back tears, taking a sip of my wine.

I don't think you ever stop missing the people you've lost.

Maybe someday it hurts less. But that hasn't happened yet.

24
DANTE

Saturday morning I get up early so I can watch the setup for the rally. It hasn't been too bad working with Peterson, the head of the mayor's security team. He's former military like me, so there was a shared language in place from the start. We agreed that he'd handle most of the crowd security, while I'd be in charge of exterior threats like explosives, drones, or long-range attacks.

When I arrive at Grant Park, the podium and the perimeter are already in place. The politicians are going to be making their speeches on one end of Hutchinson Field, while the attendees spread out across the lawn. On the west side of the field, you've got the lakeshore, and on the east, a bank of high-rise buildings. The closest buildings are about 1700 yards away from the podium, so they shouldn't be an issue. Even so, I've got a mirror shield on hand, at the base of the podium.

I'm more concerned with the people on the field. Everybody attending the rally is supposed to come through the metal detectors, but the park is a huge open space. We don't really have enough guards to be absolutely certain someone hasn't snuck over the barricades with a gun hidden in their jacket.

For that reason, I keep telling the setup crew to move the crowd barriers back in front of the podium.

"Nobody should be within fifty yards of the stage," I tell them.

"But it looks weird with such a big gap in front of the podium…" Jessica complains. She's the event coordinator. I can tell she thinks I'm way overdoing it on the security front. Which is probably true—this isn't my area of expertise. I'm not used to balancing the needs of safety and security against the needs of the press photographers to get a photogenic angle.

"That's half a football field," she says. "Come on, I'm sure we can handle a little more intimacy…"

"You have the barriers ten yards out," I tell her. "That's well within range for even an untrained shooter with a cheap pistol."

Peterson comes ambling over. He's a little over six feet tall, with the build of a powerlifter and the beard of a lumberjack. "What's going on?"

"Dante wants to move the barriers back," Jessica says, barely hiding her annoyance. "*Again.*"

"Better do it, then," Peterson says.

"*Fifty yards?*" Jessica hisses.

"Well…maybe half that." Peterson cocks an eyebrow at me to see if I'm all right with that compromise.

"Yeah," I say. "All right."

It's the first of ten or twelve conflicts we have as setup continues. I make Jessica move the floral arrangements that block egress from the stage, and I tell her that everybody in the meet-and-greet area needs to be screened, even the ones with press passes.

By the time we're an hour out from the rally, she's looking teary and frustrated, like I've ruined everything. Maybe I have. I know I'm being paranoid, but Riona asked me to do a job, and I'm going to do it to the best of my abilities.

Callum is the first speaker to arrive. He's got Aida with him. They're walking slower than usual because Aida is about eight months along in her pregnancy. She's carrying the joint heir of the Gallos and the Griffins—the tie that will bind our families together in perpetuity.

The first half of her pregnancy, she was barely showing. Now she's in full bloom.

As she walks toward me across the grass, the sun shines down on her head, and she looks like a goddess—like Demeter or Aphrodite. Her curly dark hair is longer than I've ever seen it, loose around her shoulders. Her slim figure has filled out, and her expression is happy in a way I've never seen before. Not amused or mischievous…just genuinely joyful. Her eyes are bright, her cheeks are full of color, and her skin and hair look healthy and vibrant.

She's the first of my siblings to have children. Looking at her, I feel so proud and happy.

But also, it gives me a little pain. I see Callum at her side, carefully holding her elbow so she can walk over the uneven ground safely in her high heels. He's helping her, protecting her, hovering around her more than ever. He's about to become a father, and I can tell that means much more to him than this rally or anything else in the world.

I envy him.

I don't care about anything as much as he cares about my sister and their child.

"You look beautiful," I tell Aida, kissing her on the cheek.

"Oh god." She laughs. "You know you must be the size of a walrus if your brother starts giving you compliments to cheer you up."

"Have you been sick?" I ask her.

"No," Callum says, giving her a stern look. "She's just got swollen feet because she's working too much."

"It's fine." Aida winks at him. "You can rub them for me later."

"Did you pick a name yet?" I ask her.

"I was thinking we could name him after Cal's great-grandfather," she says, grinning. "Don't you think Ruaidhri just rolls off the tongue?"

"Absolutely not," Cal says.

"It means 'great king.'"

"You can't be a king if nobody can pronounce your name," Cal says. "Didn't you have a grandpa named 'Clemente'?"

"That sounds like a pope." Aida makes a face.

"I think you're supposed to name babies after objects now," I tell her. "Apple, and Blue, and Fox, and stuff like that."

"Oh, perfect!" Aida says cheerfully. "I'll name him after where he was conceived. Sweet little Elevator Gallo…"

"I think you mean Elevator Griffin," Cal corrects her.

"Elevator Griffin-Gallo," Aida says. "Very presidential."

"You're going to be sitting up there, by the way," I tell her, pointing to the left side of the stage.

"Oooh, *padded* folding chairs!"

"Only the best for my sister." I nod toward the trailer stocked with snacks and drinks. "You can wait over there if you want. They're going to start letting people onto the field in a minute."

Aida squeezes my arm. "Thanks for babysitting us all today."

As she heads over to the trailer, Cal hangs back to talk to me for a minute.

"I don't think there's going to be any problem," he says. "Antitrafficking is maybe the one bipartisan issue we have left. Riona was just being paranoid."

"You're going to speak right after the mayor?"

"Yeah. We've gotten pretty close the past couple of months. He's going to endorse me when I run for his position."

"So he's passing the torch."

"Basically."

"How much is that going to cost us?" I say in a low tone.

Cal snorts. "About five hundred K. Paid via 'speaking fees' at future events."

It's crucial that Cal becomes mayor so we can get the rest of our South Shore development approved.

"And Yafeu Solomon gets up right after you?" I say.

"That's right." Callum gives me a careful look. "Aida said there was some kind of history between your families."

"I met him once," I say stiffly. "There's no connection between us."

"Okay," Cal says. I can't tell from his expression if Aida told him the whole story or not. But it's clear from *mine* that I don't want to talk about it. So Cal doesn't push it. He just claps me on the shoulder and says, "See you in a bit."

The rest of the hour passes in a blur of activity—getting the attendees situated on the open lawn, walking the perimeter once more, checking in with the far-flung members of the security team via our earpieces, and so forth. Peterson wrangles the speakers, organizing their positions on the stage so I don't have to talk to Yafeu. I haven't even seen him yet, since he was the last to arrive, while I was over on the south end of the lawn dealing with the officers on loan from the Chicago PD.

Finally, music starts pouring from the speakers as the organizers build the energy of the crowd. They're playing "Start Me Up" by the Rolling Stones. I don't know where they get their playlists, but the conjunction of rock stars and stodgy politicians has always seemed odd to me.

Though I guess there's nothing stodgy about Cal. He looks tall, fit, handsome, and powerful as he strides across the stage, waving to the crowd. When I first met him, I thought he seemed intelligent, but he had this arrogance and intensity that was off-putting. With those laser-focused blue eyes, he looked like the T-1000 Terminator.

Aida has brought out a better side of him. Given him a little humor and charm. I don't doubt he'll become mayor and whatever he sets his sights on after that.

I'd fucking hate it. The older I get, the less I like talking to people at all.

Still, it's interesting to see how the crowd responds to him, screaming and cheering as soon as he sets foot onstage. A whole lot of them seem to know Aida, too—they roar when she blows a kiss to the crowd. Seb told me the pair of them have some Instagram account that's gotten popular. I really am old—I don't even have Facebook, let alone Instagram.

The mayor follows them out onstage a minute later. He's not a tall man, but he has presence. He's got white hair, bald on top and too long on the sides, rimless glasses perched on a beak of a nose, and a big smile full of crooked teeth. Even though he's only five-seven, his impressive belly helps give him a sense of dignity. He waves to the crowd with both hands, his pudgy fingers reminding me of cartoon gloves.

Mayor Williams is as crooked as they come, but in a genial kind of way. He's always been willing to do business with the Irish and Italian Mafia families or anyone else who wants to keep the city running with bribes, favors, and exchanges.

Having him in place has been a good thing. Having Cal as mayor would be even better. What we don't want is some crusader or the head of a rival family.

As I'm thinking about who might run against Cal, Yafeu Solomon climbs the steps to the stage. I look up at him from my position in front of the barricades.

He looks almost exactly the same as when I saw him last—tall, slim, wearing a well-tailored dark suit. His face is just as regal as ever, with no new lines that I can see. Only the little threads of silver in his black hair show that any time has passed at all.

He's not looking down at me. He's gazing out over the large crowd with a satisfied expression on his face. It's an excellent turnout—a credit to his cause.

For a moment I assume the woman walking behind him is his wife. Then he steps to the side of her, and I see her face in full. And I realize it's Simone.

I'm frozen in place, staring up at her.

I prepared myself to see her father. I never imagined for a second that Simone would be with him.

I've tortured myself with glimpses of her in Ibiza, Paris, London, Miami…shots taken by paparazzi or on red carpets. As far as I know, she's never come back to Chicago. I never thought she would.

Now she's standing thirty feet away from me. If she were to look down, she'd see me. But she isn't looking at the crowd at all. She's taken her seat at the very corner of the stage, and she's staring down at her hands, obviously not liking the attention.

I can't fucking believe it. I can't take my eyes off her.

The mayor is getting up to make the first speech. I'm supposed to be scanning the crowd, checking in with the guards, making sure he's protected from all angles.

I'm doing none of it. I'm riveted by the sight of Simone.

Fucking hell, she's twice as beautiful as before. She's got to be the only supermodel in the world whose photos don't do her justice.

We were just kids when we met. She was lovely then, but barely an adult.

Now she's a woman in the fullest sense of the word. She's everything a woman can be: Soft yet strong. Slim yet curvy. Feminine and powerful. So powerful that I can't tear my eyes off her face. They're pulled back magnetically to Simone's eyes, her lips, her skin, her slender neck, her full breasts, her long legs crossed in front of her at the ankle, and her slim hands folded in her lap.

There's a new depth of emotion in her expression. Like her eyes contain an entire novel, if I only knew how to read them.

The mayor has given his whole speech, and I haven't looked away from her once. She hasn't raised her eyes to look at me.

I can't believe we're this close and she doesn't even feel it.

My desire for her has come roaring back, like a forest fire hit by wind.

I told myself that if I ever saw her again, I wouldn't do this. I wouldn't let myself feel what I felt before.

Well, now it's happening, and I realize I don't have a shred of control. I can't stop myself from wanting to jump on that stage, pick

her up, throw her over my shoulder, and carry her away. I want to tear that sundress off her and bury my face between those breasts… I want to take her back the one way I know how…by taking possession of her body again.

I want that, and I can't stop myself from wanting it.

I can barely stop myself from doing it.

I have to grit my teeth hard and clench my fists at my sides.

That's what I'm doing when Cal stands to speak. Simone watches him cross the stage. Finally, her eyes pass over me.

I can tell the moment she spots me. She goes rigid in her chair, her expression changing from mild interest to absolute shock.

She's looking right at me, our eyes locked.

I can feel myself glaring back at her, my jaw clenched and my whole body stiff with the struggle not to run up on that stage. I probably look cold and angry. But I don't know how else to look. I can't smile at her; that would be absurd.

I don't know what to do. And that frustrates me more. I hate that I'm here in this moment, without warning or preparation, forced to look at this woman I've loved for so long. I hate this. I hate that I can't read her expression. She looks upset—that much I can tell. Is it because she's afraid? Because she doesn't want to see me? There's no way to know.

Cal's getting a great response from the crowd. They cheer after almost every line.

The roar of the crowd is right behind me, but it seems distant and muted. Simone's face fills my whole view.

It's like the billboard all over again. But this time, she's so close that I could actually touch her…

I wrench my eyes away and try to focus on my actual job. I'm supposed to be making sure nobody's about to take a pop at Cal. He looks invincible up there behind the podium—just getting into the swing of his speech.

I scan the crowd like I'm supposed to be doing, even though

I know my brain isn't filing information in the usual way. I should be looking for people whose expressions don't match the rest of the crowd. Whose movements don't line up. People reaching into their jackets, or people who look antsy, like they're trying to psych themselves up.

Riona said Solomon has been getting death threats, but most threats mean nothing. Even the crazies who try to take action barely ever succeed. The last assassination of a politician on American soil was the mayor of Kirkwood, Missouri, way back in 2008.

So I don't actually think anything is going to happen today. But I've got to keep a lookout anyway. I promised Riona. I can't get distracted just because the woman who ripped my heart out happens to have appeared in front of me.

Cal is winding down. Yafeu Solomon will be getting up next.

I take another sweep of the crowd. Then I look at the stage, where Cal stands tall behind the podium. I see a banner of flags over the stage. The arrangement is odd—they're not hung level with one another. In fact, a couple of the flags are hung in a diagonal line, leading directly down to the podium.

From an aesthetic standpoint, it looks strange. I wonder if Jessica had to move them after I made her change the floral arrangements.

I see the flags kick up just a little with a change in wind. It's a still day, but the flags are light enough that they show the direction of even the tiniest breath of air.

In fact, they almost look like they were arranged to do exactly that…

Cal introduces Yafeu Solomon. Solomon strides forward, joining Cal at the podium and shaking his hand.

"Good afternoon, brothers and sisters," he says, in his deep calm voice. "I am so grateful to you all for coming out in support of our cause today. I don't think there is a greater tragedy taking place in the world today, spread out across the globe, affecting the people of every nation.

"Human trafficking is a crime against all people. It is a crime against humanity. All of us are born free—it is the most crucial characteristic of humans, that none of us should be a slave or a tool to another person. We must all be free to seek our happiness in this life.

"This monstrous scourge takes many forms—forced labor, sexual slavery, arranged marriages, and child trafficking. We must form coalitions with groups like the United Nations and…"

I'm not listening to Solomon. I'm trying to follow the line of the flags, to see why they've been arranged in this way. What line of sight they'd provide to someone in the right position.

The high-rises on the opposite side of the field are far away. A mile off. I didn't consider them a threat because only a tiny minority of snipers could make that shot.

At that distance, you're looking at a five- or six-second flight time for the bullet. You'd have to account for temperature, humidity, elevation, wind, and spindrift. Even the rotation of the earth becomes a factor. The mathematical calculations are convoluted—and some have to be done on the fly, if there's a change in wind or angle or if the target moves.

Snipers take headshots in case the target is wearing a vest.

They don't shoot the moment the speech begins. They wait for the speaker to go into full flow, when they've found their position and they're not shifting around as much.

Yafeu Solomon is ninety seconds into his speech. If someone is about to shoot him, it will happen very soon.

I'm staring across the road at the high-rises, looking for motion at any of the windows. A curtain moving, a face peering out.

Instead, I see a momentary flash. It's there and gone in a quarter second. Light reflecting off glass or metal.

I don't stop to think. I sprint toward the stage as fast as I can.

At first, Solomon doesn't notice. I'm almost right below the podium when he breaks off his sentence. I don't know if he recognizes me. He's just staring, frozen.

Grabbing the mirror shield in both hands, I lift it and angle it toward the sun, shouting, "GET DOWN!"

I point the mirror toward the high-rise.

The sun glances off the broad flat surface and beams back at the building. If there's someone in the window, it will send a blazing glare right at them. So bright, it will blind them.

I don't hear the shot. I just see the bullet embed itself in the stage.

Solomon barely has time to flinch, let alone duck behind the podium. He stares at the bullet hole, too shocked to move.

It's Simone who grabs him from behind and drags him away. Cal has already seized Aida and pulled her off the stage. The crowd is screaming, stampeding toward the far side of the field.

I keep angling the mirror toward the high-rise, knowing that any second, another bullet might come spinning down toward my skull.

But a second shot never comes. The sniper knows he's fucked—he missed his mark, and now he's got to get out of his perch before the cops storm the building.

I throw down the mirror and run around the side of the stage, looking for Simone.

I find her crouched with her father, both of them looking wildly around as the security team and the Chicago PD close a circle around us.

"Who was that?" Simone cries, her eyes wide.

"Who knows," Solomon says, shaking his head.

When I look at his face, I'm not sure I believe him.

25
SIMONE

Seeing Dante Gallo staring at me from the front of the crowd is one of the worst surprises of my life.

I almost don't recognize him—at twenty-one, he was already the biggest man I'd ever met. Now he barely looks human. He's grown at least another inch or two and filled out even more. Muscle on top of muscle, straining against the bounds of a T-shirt that must be an XXXL.

His jaw has broadened, and he has a few lines across his forehead and at the corners of his eyes—not smile lines. It looks like he's been squinting into the sun.

But the thing that transforms his face the most is his expression. He's glaring at me with pure, unadulterated hatred. He looks like he wants to leap up on this stage and tear my head off my shoulders.

Honestly, I can't blame him.

After I left Chicago, I thought about calling him a thousand times.

If I hadn't been so sick…

If I hadn't been so scared…

If I hadn't been so depressed…

It's hard to remember what my existence was like during those nine months of pregnancy.

All the color bleached out of the world. Everything looked like shades of pewter, steel, ash, and stone. I tried to watch movies I used to like, tried to listen to the songs I loved, and I just felt...nothing.

It was so hard just to drag myself across the little flat I was sharing with Serwa in Mayfair. So hard to go pee or get a glass of water. The idea of picking up the phone and dialing, trying to explain to Dante why I left...it was too much. I couldn't do it.

And then, after the baby was born, it got so much worse. I felt like my son was torn away from me but also like he might be better off with Serwa. I felt so angry at my parents for the position they'd put me in but also that I owed this to my sister—this one chance at happiness, the only chance she was likely to get.

I was so confused. And so alone.

I longed to reach out to Dante. I ached for him. But I knew he'd be furious with me. I hid the pregnancy from him. I made him miss the birth of his son.

And I was still terrified of what might happen if he knew. I wanted to keep Henry safe. I didn't want him pulled into a world of violence and crime. I kept remembering the blood dripping from Dante's hands, how terrifying and monstrous he'd looked that night in the park.

And I thought of how angry he'd be if he found out what I'd done.

Seeing him now in Grant Park, he already looks like he wants to kill me. How much angrier will he be if he ever finds out the truth?

I can't let that happen.

It was a mistake to come to Chicago. I finished my shoot for Balenciaga—I should leave as soon as the rally is over.

That's what I'm thinking when out of nowhere, Dante starts sprinting toward the stage.

I jump up from my seat, thinking he's running right at me.

Instead, he grabs some kind of big curved circular mirror and angles it across the field. While he's doing that, he bellows, "GET DOWN!"

I don't understand what's happening, but instinctively I crouch, and so does everybody else. Everyone except my father. He seems frozen in place, just as shocked as I am.

I see the sun flare off Dante's mirror, and then I hear a sharp whistling. A dent appears in the stage floor, like a tiny meteorite just came hurtling from the sky.

My brain says, *Bullet. That was a bullet.*

Everyone starts screaming and running.

Callum Griffin grabs his pregnant wife and drags her away. Callum's face is pale as chalk. They were sitting right behind where the bullet hit. A couple of feet higher, and it might have hit his wife right in the belly.

I don't run—not off the stage, anyway. I run over to Tata because I realize that bullet was meant for him, and there might be more coming. I grab his arm, and I yank as hard as I can, pulling him away from the podium.

For once my father doesn't seem in control of the situation. He seems confused and frightened. So am I, though apparently just a little bit less than him. I drag him off the stage so we can crouch behind it.

The problem is that I have no idea which direction the shooting is coming from. So I pull my father as far underneath the stage as I can, hoping that will protect us.

A moment later, Dante's huge frame drops beside us with a thud. He says, "Are you two all right?"

"Y-yes," I stammer.

They're the first words we've spoken to each other in almost ten years.

"Who was that?" I ask my father.

I can't understand who would want to kill him.

"Who knows." Tata shakes his head. He looks bewildered and dazed.

Security guards are closing in around us. I feel paranoid and edgy—how do we know some of these men weren't in on it, whatever *it* is?

Strange as it seems, I'm grateful Dante is next to us. Whatever our history might be, I saw him save my father from that bullet. I think he'd do it again, if one of these men tried to shoot us.

The police hustle us off to a SWAT van at the edge of the parking lot. They ask us dozens of questions, most of which we can't answer.

I don't see Dante—I think he went back toward the stage. Or maybe he left.

I'm shaking uncontrollably. The cops put a blanket around my shoulders and give me a glass of water to drink. Every time I try to lift the cup to my lips, ice water sloshes over the rim and douses my hands.

I finally manage to take a drink, right when a gorgeous redheaded woman comes pushing her way through the police cordon.

One of the security guards tries to stop her. "Just a minute, ma'am!"

"It's all right," Dante says, raising a hand.

He's come back from the stage. He's holding something in his hand.

The redhead throws her arms around him and gives him a hug.

"Oh my god, Dante!" she cries. "I know I asked you to keep a lookout, but I really wasn't expecting this…"

Dante hugs her back like he knows her well.

I feel a deep and ugly stab of jealousy.

I know I have no right. But this woman is just so beautiful…

If she weren't so tall or so well-dressed. If her hair weren't such a vibrant shade of red…maybe I could have swallowed it. But the sight of Dante's huge hands around her little waist is just too much to bear.

Dante lets go of her, turning to one of the police officers instead. "This is the bullet." He drops a piece of twisted metal into the officer's palm.

"You touched it?"

"You're not gonna get any prints off it." Dante grunts. "Look at the state of it. Not to mention there wouldn't be any in the first place. This shooter's a professional. Just the distance alone... Only a dozen people in the world could make that shot."

"How would you know?" the cop says suspiciously.

"Because he was a sniper himself," the redhead snaps. "And a damn good one, so you should listen to what he says. And thank him for his service, while you're at it."

"Right," the cop mumbles. "Of course."

Dante was a sniper?

He was in the military?

I never knew what he was doing all those years. I tried to look him up once or twice, but he didn't have any social media or any news articles about him. None that I found, anyway.

This woman obviously knows Dante better than I do. And she's quick to defend him.

I shiver miserably inside my blanket. She must be his girlfriend. I look at her left hand—I can't help myself. No ring. Not yet, at least.

It doesn't matter. None of this matters. Dante isn't mine anymore—he only was for a brief moment in time. He's allowed to have a girlfriend or even a wife. I have no right to be jealous.

And yet, if auras were visible, mine would be poison green. As bright green as the other woman's eyes.

"That's a handmade bullet," Dante says to the cop. "Bronze alloy. You're not gonna be able to trace the source, let alone get some nice, juicy thumbprint. Your best bet is to find the window he shot from and see if he left anything in the room. He probably cleared out in a hurry."

"What building was he in?" the cop asks.

"That one," Dante points to a tall high-rise with a white facade. It could be a hotel, though it's hard to tell from this distance. "I think he was five floors up, on the southeast corner."

The cop is writing it all down in his notebook.

A big, burly man with a beard comes over and claps Dante on the shoulder, shaking his head. "Fucking hell, man. I thought you were just being paranoid." He looks over at my father. "Somebody wanted you dead, my friend."

Tata doesn't have any blanket around him. He's sitting up straight and calm, having recovered from the shock a lot faster than I did.

"Apparently so." He gives a respectful nod to Dante. "You saved my life."

Dante shrugs his huge shoulders, a surly expression on his face. "He might have missed either way."

"I doubt it," Tata says. "Dante Gallo, isn't it?"

He holds out his hand to shake.

Dante looks at my father's hand with an expression of distaste, as if he'd rather not take it. I'm sure he doesn't appreciate my father's tone—as if when they met before, it was just at a cocktail party. Tata's acting like they're casual acquaintances. Like there's no bad blood between us.

He's certainly not offering any kind of apology. And he never will. I know my father well enough to know that.

Dante saving his life means nothing. My father's grateful, but it won't change his opinion on anything.

Not that it matters at this late date.

I'm thinking Dante won't shake hands, but my father keeps his extended, with calm persistence, and at last Dante gives it a quick grip, then drops it again.

"Will you be coming to the fundraiser tonight?" Tata asks him.

"Are you still planning on attending?" the redhead says, surprised.

"Of course," my father says. "Why wouldn't I?"

"Well, your would-be shooter is still roaming around, for one thing." She's watching my father with her cool-green eyes, examining him closely. She looks intelligent and almost predatory. Not someone to be trifled with.

"I'm sure they'll have plenty of security at the event," my father says. "I'll feel quite safe—especially if Dante is there. Will you attend? I'd like to thank you publicly."

The muscles flex along Dante's broad jaw. He opens his mouth to respond, and I'm pretty sure from the shape of his lips, he's about to say no.

The redhead interrupts him.

"He'll be there," she says smoothly. Then she turns those keen green eyes on me so abruptly that I almost jump. She looks me over head to toe in a glance. I'm certain she recognizes me.

"I'm Riona Griffin," she says, holding out her hand to me.

I shake it. Her fingers are cool, dry, and soft. She has a fresh French manicure and a firm grip.

"Nice to meet you. Simone Solomon." I wish my voice were as confident and professional as hers. Instead, it comes out in a little squeak, still shaky with nerves.

"I know." She smiles. "You're very famous."

I don't know how to reply. I'd like to know who she is, what she does, and how she knows Dante. But there's no way to ask those questions with any grace.

All I can do is sit there stupidly while she turns back to Dante. "What are you going to do now?"

"I wanna follow that officer up to the perch," Dante says. Seeing that none of us understands, he clarifies, "The place where the shooter was situated."

"Are you on the case, Inspector?" Riona says in a teasing tone.

"I am curious," Dante admits.

My father looks less curious, despite the fact he was the person being shot at. He's already scrolling through his phone, checking for news reports of the failed assassination attempt.

"I'll come with you," Riona says. She looks back at me. "Nice to meet you, Simone."

"Nice to meet you," I echo.

Dante doesn't say anything at all. He walks away from me without a word—without even a glance in my direction.

I watch his broad back stalking away.

When I turn around again, my father is watching me. He looks at me with his dark eyes, as if daring me to say something.

I keep my mouth firmly shut. I have no interest in hearing what my father has to say about Dante, for good or for ill. If his opinion hasn't changed, then I don't want to hear it. And if it has—well, it's too late for that. It can't do me any good now.

So I sit in silence, while my father goes back to scrolling through his news feed.

26
DANTE

Thanks to Riona's powers of persuasion, and a little pressure from Callum, the cops agree to let me in the hotel room they think the sniper used.

He was long gone by the time they arrived—with plenty of time to pack up his equipment. But *vacated* doesn't mean "empty." Nobody can sit in a room without leaving a trace.

For instance, he didn't bother to move the hotel-room table that he slid closer to the window. I can see the marks on the carpet where the table was originally situated. Now it's exactly in front of the east-facing window he must have used for his shot.

I assume he picked this hotel because it's old and the windows actually open. He left the sash up. I can see the square hole he cut in the screen and the piece of discarded mesh lying on the ground next to the radiator.

I can barely see Hutchinson Field from here, not with the naked eye. I've got better than twenty-twenty vision, but I can't make out anything besides the stage itself. Not the flags, the flowers, or the chairs still sitting on the stage, some of them tipped over when everyone scattered.

The sniper would have seen it all clearly through his scope, however.

According to the cops, he checked into the room using the hotel's app. The miracles of modern technology—he didn't even need to visit the front desk for a key. He could open the door automatically using his phone.

Of course, the name he registered under is fake. So is the credit card he used to pay. The Royal Arms will be out the $229 for the room.

"Did anybody see him going in or out?" I ask one of the cops. "Maybe one of the maids?"

"Nobody that we talked to," the cop says. "The maids only work in the morning. He checked into the room at one twenty p.m. Or at least that's what their computer says."

The cop is giving me the information but not cheerfully. He's annoyed that I'm looking over his shoulder. That has to be particularly galling, since this cop, like most cops in Chicago, knows exactly who I am. There's no love lost between the Gallos and the Chicago PD.

Riona has a slightly better relationship with them, though not by much. She's friends with a couple of the DAs. But she also keeps bad guys like me out of jail.

Right now, she's looking around the room with almost as much curiosity as I'm feeling. "Nothing in the trash," she says, peering into the bin.

I can see marks on top of the table. That's where the sniper had his rifle set up. I can't tell what type of rifle it was—not from a couple of scratches. But I assume he had the latest and greatest—something like the McMillan TAC-50 or the Barrett M82A1.

I'm leaning toward the TAC-50. The bullet I found looked like a .50 caliber. Tac-50s are made right in the good old US of A, in Phoenix. I saw plenty of them in Iraq. Used one myself, after my L115A3 got fucked up by a makeshift grenade.

It's also the gun that set the most recent long-distance records. It has the most confirmed kills over 1367 yards.

"Are you sure it was just one guy?" Riona says to the cops. "Don't snipers usually work in teams?"

She directs the second part of that question at me.

She knows I had a partner in Iraq—Raylan Boone, a kid from Kentucky.

"Sometimes they do. Sometimes not," I say. "Used to be that you needed somebody to take measurements and do calculations. Now you've got range finders, ballistic calculators, handheld meteorological equipment, ballistic-prediction software…"

Still, there's nothing quite like another person keeping an eye out. All those endless hours crouching in bombed-out buildings and tumbled-down towers…talking, waiting, keeping each other from catching a bullet to the back of the head. Raylan's a brother to me now, just about as much as my actual brothers.

I get the feeling this guy was alone, though.

There's no reason for it, no evidence. It's just the emptiness of the room, the precision with which he removed every trace of himself. This guy is a perfectionist. And perfectionists don't tolerate other people very well.

I look down his line of sight again. I can see the way the flags are lined up and other markers he set along the way—a white cloth tied to a power line. A string on the edge of a tree branch.

Wind direction and speed can vary dramatically along the path of the bullet. He was careful to set up markers along the way. Gauges, too, maybe. And the way the flags lined up on the stage…that was no coincidence. He must have been down there. Or had somebody on the inside.

We might have passed right by each other. I try to remember the faces of the setup crew and the security teams—thinking back if there was anybody who behaved strangely or seemed out of place.

If there was, I didn't notice it at the time.

I look down at the table. I can see the tiniest residue of gunpowder, much finer than sand. I see the sparkle of graphite,= and white grains of aconite. I put my nose right down on top of it and inhale. It definitely smells like nitrocellulose.

"It's not cocaine, you know," one of the cops sneers. "It won't give you a buzz."

"No, no, let the bloodhound work." His partner laughs.

I can tell Riona wants to lip them off, but I give her a shake of my head to show her that I don't care what those fuckheads think.

"Anything else, Inspector Clouseau?" a cop says sarcastically.

"No," I say. "Nothing else."

The cops keep dusting the room for prints—useless in a hotel—and combing the carpets and drapes for evidence. Riona and I head back down to ground level.

"So?" she says in an expectant tone.

"Wasn't much to see in the room." I shrug.

"No—I'm wondering if you're planning to go to the cocktail reception."

"Why would I?" I frown.

She lets out a snort. "You're going to pretend you don't care in the slightest? I saw your face when you saw her crossing that stage."

"Did you know she was going to be here?" I demand, rounding on Riona.

"No," she says calmly. "But I'm not sorry that she is. You two have unfinished business."

"No, we don't," I say, in the tone of voice that would usually scare the other person off saying anything else. But Riona argues for a living. Nothing short of complete removal of her vocal cords is going to stop her from talking.

"Right," she says. "That's why you're so cheerful and optimistic. Because you're emotionally healthy in every way."

"You're not my psychiatrist," I snap at her. We had to see a shrink sometimes in the army. I fucking hated it.

"I am your friend, though." Riona holds me in her steady gaze. "I think you should go."

"She left me nine years ago because her family thought I wasn't good enough for her. I doubt they changed their minds."

"Why not? You're a decorated veteran. A successful real estate developer. Plus, you just saved her dad's life for fuck's sake."

"I'm still a Gallo."

I didn't stop blowing people's heads off just because I came home from Iraq. I'm still the same gangster I was nine years ago. Worse, actually. The fact our legitimate business has grown along with our criminal organization...I doubt that's going to impress Yafeu Solomon. Not that I give a fuck what he thinks.

"I think you should go," Riona repeats. "Not to start anything up again. Just to get closure."

"Nobody gets closure by opening the door again."

"They don't get it by sulking either," Riona snaps.

Her patience has run out—she's done being nice to me.

"I'm heading over there in an hour," she says. "And I'm picking you up on the way."

"Don't bother."

"Put a suit on. A nice one."

"I don't own a suit," I lie.

"Come naked, then." Riona grins. "If that doesn't impress her, nothing will."

27
SIMONE

I'M SO NERVOUS GETTING READY THAT MY HANDS ARE SHAKING—almost as much as they did after that sniper's bullet missed my father's head by a matter of inches.

I wonder if Dante will actually come tonight.

I don't think he will. He certainly didn't seem very interested when Tata invited him.

I don't think he wants to see me again. He didn't speak to me at all after the shooting. Well—he asked if we were all right. But I think he would have asked that of a complete stranger. It doesn't mean anything.

He saved my father's life. I don't think that meant anything either. Dante was working security—he was just doing his job.

The redheaded woman was Riona Griffin. She's a sister of Callum Griffin, the alderman of the Forty-Third Ward. Dante must be connected to their family. That's why he was supervising the event.

They must be dating. That's the only explanation I can think of.

It's been nine years. I should have known he'd be taken now. I'm surprised he's not married already. A man like that, a walking specimen of masculinity…he must have women chasing after him everywhere he goes.

I saw it myself when we were dating. Everywhere we went, women couldn't help but stare at him.

Every woman wants to know what it's like to be with a man that big. To be lifted and then thrown on a bed like you're featherlight. When you get a look at those hands, twice the size of your own hands...you can't help but think how big the parts of him that you can't see must be...

I already know the answer to that question, and my mind is still racing.

Of course, Dante has been with other women since we split.

I've had other boyfriends myself. But none of them compared to him.

It's an awful thing, when the first man you ever sleep with is built like a Greek god. Everybody who comes after seems all too mortal.

I dated photographers, designers, other models; I dated an Israeli banker and a man who owned his own island on the coast of Spain. Some of them were kind, and some were witty. But none of them were Dante.

They were just men.

Dante is *the* man. The one who first formed my conception of what a man should be. The one who made me fall in love. Who took my virginity. And who gave me a son.

The others were barely acquaintances by comparison.

When I'd feel the tiniest flutter for one of those men, I'd ask myself, *Is this love? Could I be falling in love again?*

Then I'd look back through all the pain and misery of those years, to the months when Dante and I were together. They shone as bright as diamonds in my mind. As much as I tried to bury them in the mud and dirt of the devastation that followed, those memories were still there, as hard and sparkling as ever.

I look at myself in the mirror, wondering what Dante saw when he saw my face again. Did he think I looked different? Older? Sadder?

I was so damn young when we met.

I start making up my face, quickly and fiercely.

I don't think he's coming tonight, but if he is, I'm going to look as beautiful as possible. I know he doesn't want me anymore—he probably hates me. But I won't be pathetic.

I can hear Mama shouting in the next room. Well, not shouting exactly—but definitely using a more agitated tone than usual. She's not happy that Tata's still going to the party tonight.

"*Someone just tried to kill you!*" she cries. "If that doesn't justify a night off, then I don't know what does!"

Henry looks up from his Switch. He's lying on my bed playing *Cuphead*. "Did someone actually try to kill Grandpa?"

I know you're supposed to lie to your kids sometimes. But Henry was brought into the world with so much turmoil and secrecy that I didn't have energy for any more. From the time he was small, I've told him the truth about almost everything.

"Yes," I say. "Someone shot at him while he was giving his speech."

"Who?"

"I don't know."

"Did the police catch him?"

"Not yet."

"Hmm." Henry returns his attention to his game.

Kids don't understand death. They know adults make a big deal about it. But to them, it's like a video game. They think they'll always come back, even if they have to start the level over.

"Is Grandma gonna stay with me again?" Henry asks.

"She's coming with us. Carly will be here, though."

"Can I order room service?"

"Yes. You need to get chicken or salmon—not just fries this time."

Henry looks up at me, grinning. "Potatoes are a vegetable, you know."

"I don't think they are."

"What are they, then?"

"Uh…maybe a root?"

Henry sighs. "They're spuds, Mom. Spuds."

I can't tell if he's messing with me. Henry has an odd sense of humor, probably from spending too much time with adults and not enough with other kids. Plus, I'm pretty sure he's smarter than me, so I'm not ever fully confident when I'm arguing with him. He's always coming out with weird things he just read in some book. And when I google it afterward, he's usually right.

I run my fingers through his soft curls, kissing the top of his head. He reaches up briefly to give me a kind of half hug, with his attention still on his game.

"I'll see you in a couple of hours," I tell him.

I don't plan to be at the party late. I want to tuck Henry into bed myself when I get back to the hotel.

Mama's already dressed when I come out to the main room. She doesn't look very happy.

"I can't believe it," she says, giving me a quick hug. "I told your father we should skip the reception…"

"It's at an event center," I tell her. "Not out in the open."

"Even so…"

"We're going," my father says in his imperious way. "You can come along or not, Éloise."

My mother sighs, her lips thin and pale with stress. "I'm coming."

We take a cab over to the Heritage House event center. As soon as my father steps out of the car, he's surrounded by press and the flashes of a dozen cameras. Obviously, the news of the shooting got out. People are shouting questions at him from all sides.

"Do you have any idea who'd want to kill you, Mr. Solomon?"

"Was this the first time you've suffered an attack?"

"Is this related to your campaign for the Freedom Foundation?"

"Are you still going forward with your coalition?"

"Do you have a statement for the shooter?"

My father draws himself up to his full height, facing the semicircle of cameras and microphones.

"I do have a statement," he says. "To the man who shot at me today—you failed. I'm still standing. And even if you had succeeded in killing me, my cause will never die. This is a global coalition, a global movement. Humanity has decided that we will no longer endure the enslavement and abuse of our most vulnerable members. I will never stop fighting for the end of human trafficking, and neither will my allies here in Chicago and across the world."

I don't know if he had that speech prepared or if he thought it up on the fly. My father always delivers his lines with the precision of a professor and the fire of a preacher. His eyes are blazing, and he looks like a force of nature.

I find it terrifying. To me, it sounds like he's taunting the sniper. That man is still running around at large. If he was paid to do the job, he probably intends to try again. I don't like standing out here on the steps, open and unprotected.

I'm relieved when Tata finishes his statement to the press so we can all go inside.

Heritage House doesn't really look like a house at all—more like a giant renovated barn with cedar-paneled walls, iron chandeliers, string lights, and picture windows looking out onto a garden. It's rustic and picturesque, much prettier than your average hotel ballroom.

The band isn't the usual string quartet either. It consists of a blond girl in a white cotton dress and cowboy boots, with an acoustic guitar strung around her neck, and three men playing an upright bass, a fiddle, and a banjo. Their music isn't hokey at all—it's quite lovely. The girl has a low voice that starts raspy, then soars high, clear as a bell.

Waiters are carrying around trays of champagne and fizzy lemonade with striped straws. I realize I've barely eaten all day. I'm starving. I head over to the buffet, grateful to see there's real food, not just canapés. I start loading up a plate with grapes, strawberries, and shrimp, while the heavily pregnant woman next to me does the same.

As we reach for a chicken-salad sandwich at the same time, she turns to me and says, "Oh, hello again!"

I stare at her blankly, confused by how familiar she looks. Then I realize we were on the stage together earlier today—only she was seated on the opposite side, so I only caught a glimpse of her for a moment. "You're Callum Griffin's wife."

The woman laughs—loud and infectious. "You don't recognize me, Simone? Is it the belly?"

She turns sideways to show me her pregnant tummy in full glorious profile.

It's her face I'm staring at—those bright gray eyes, against the tan skin and the wide white smile.

"Aida!" I gasp.

"In the flesh. More flesh than usual." She grins.

She was such a skinny, wild, almost-feral child. I can't connect the image I have of her in my mind—skinned knees, tangled hair, filthy boy's clothes—with the glamorous woman standing in front of me.

"You're so beautiful!" I say before I can stop myself.

Aida only laughs harder. She seems to think this is the best joke in the world.

"Bet you didn't see that coming! Nobody thought I'd grow up to be hot when I was running around like Mowgli, terrorizing the neighbor kids. There was a whole summer when I didn't wear shoes or brush my teeth once."

I want to hug her. I always liked Aida and Sebastian, and even Nero. Enzo was warm to me, too. They were all kind—more than I deserved.

"I read your interview in *Vanity Fair*," Aida says. "I was checking to see if you'd give me a shout-out, but no such luck…"

"God, I hate doing those." I shake my head.

"Top-paid model of the year in 2019," Aida says. "I've been keeping tabs on you."

I feel myself blushing. I've never particularly liked the "fame" part of modeling. Luckily, even top models aren't nearly as famous as actors or musicians. Or as easy to recognize when we haven't had the benefit of a hair and makeup team. So I can still get around anonymously most of the time.

"Who's number one this year?" Aida teases me. "Do you hate her guts?"

"I really don't pay attention to any of that. I mean, I'm grateful for the work, but…"

"Oh, come on," Aida says. "I want the dirty details. Who's nice, and who's a total shit? Who's sleeping together but I'd never guess?"

I can't believe how much Aida's managed to retain the wild energy she had as a child. She's so animated and playful. She's got all the joie de vivre in the world, while I don't seem to have an ounce of it anymore.

I try to play along, to think of something that might amuse her. "Well," I say. "There was this one photographer—"

Before I can go any further, Callum Griffin joins us.

"Sorry we didn't have a chance to meet properly before," he says, shaking my hand.

"Yes," Aida says to him, in a pretend-posh tone. "How very remiss of you not to introduce yourself amidst the gunfire, my love."

"I see you've met my wife."

I can tell Callum is used to Aida's teasing.

"We actually go way back," Aida says.

"You do?" Callum raises one thick dark eyebrow.

"That's right. You had no idea that I'm BFFs with the most gorgeous woman in the world, did you?" Aida laughs.

"I'm *married* to the most gorgeous woman in the world." Callum smiles at her.

"Oh my god!" Aida squeezes his arm through his suit jacket. "What a charmer. No wonder you keep getting elected to things."

"Thank you for coming to the rally today," Callum says to me. "It's a good cause."

"Yes, thanks, Simone," Aida says solemnly. "I know most people are *pro* child trafficking, but not you. You're firmly against it, and I respect that."

"Yes, I am," I say, trying not to laugh. Aida hasn't changed a bit. She may have grown up to look the part of a politician's wife, but her blithe heart is just the same.

Glancing at her belly again, I say, "Congratulations, you two. Do you know what you're having?"

"A boy," Callum says proudly. I think he would have been proud either way, but I was with Dante long enough to know what a son means to these dynastic families.

"That's wonderful! I—" Without thinking, I was about to say that I have a son as well.

"What is it?" Aida's keen gray eyes scan my face. I remember all too well how intelligent she is, and how perceptive.

"I was just going to say how happy I am for you. I'm sure your… whole family must be so excited."

It's the first time I've mentioned Dante, even obliquely.

Aida is still watching me closely, her head tilted to the side. "They are," she says softly. "All of them."

Knowing Aida's curiosity, I'm surprised she hasn't asked me about Dante yet. Her restraint probably isn't a good sign. It means she knows things between us are still in an ugly place.

"Oh," Callum says. "There's Ree."

I follow his gaze to see Riona Griffin walking into the room dressed in a stunning cobalt gown. The dress is modest, with long sleeves, but it hugs her figure to perfection. That rich blue against her creamy skin and vibrant hair is far more eye-catching than any amount of bare flesh could be.

Sure enough, Dante follows a dozen feet behind her. My heart goes flying upward, like a quail startled out of the brush. Just as quickly, an arrow pierces through it when Dante's stern gaze passes over me like I'm not even here.

I wonder if he and Riona came together. They must have, arriving at the same time.

I feel Aida watching me, observing my reaction to her brother. I wish I could keep my face as still and stony as Dante's.

"Come on!" Aida says abruptly, grabbing my arm. "Let's go say hi!"

I don't have a choice. She drags me over to Dante, with a surprisingly strong grip for someone who is smaller than me and already carrying another human along everywhere she goes.

She practically shoves me right into him, saying, "Hey, Brother! It's me—your one and only sister. Just wanted to show you I'm alive, since you forgot to check on me."

"I saw Cal pull you off the stage," Dante says gruffly.

He's not looking at me. But I feel the tension between us, thick and electric. It makes the hair stand up on the back of my neck. I'm terrified for him to turn and face me. And yet I can't stand being ignored by him.

"You remember our friend Simone, don't you?" Aida says.

"*Aida*," Dante says in a growl so low that it's more like a vibration. "Quit fucking around."

Aida ignores him. "Simone was just saying how much she loved this song and how she wanted to dance. Why don't you take her out for a spin, big brother?"

I don't know how she has the balls to say it, blocking him from getting away while Dante looks angry enough to swat her out of his path with one swipe of his arm.

He turns his glare on me, like I might have actually said I wanted a dance partner.

I try to stammer out a denial while Aida talks right over me. "Go on! I know you remember how to dance, Dante."

To my surprise, and without my agreement, Dante puts one huge hand around my waist and pulls me onto the dance floor. It's the first time he's touched me in nine years. I can feel the heat of his hand through the thin material of my dress. I can feel the calluses on his palm.

I remember how strong he is. How easy it is for him to pull me into position.

But he never used to be this stiff. I might as well be dancing with a statue. No part of us is touching, besides my hand in his and his other hand on my waist. He's looking straight ahead, over my shoulder. His mouth looks grim and angry.

It's torture being this close to him, yet with so much space between us.

I can't stand this. I can't stand being hated by him.

I try to think of something to say—something, anything. Everything I think of seems ridiculous.

How have you been?

What are you up to these days?

How's your family?

Dante seems equally stumped. Or he prefers silence. The song plays on, melancholy and slow.

I don't think he's going to speak to me—we'll finish out this dance in silence, then part ways.

Then, as if the words pain him to get out, Dante says, "Do you actually love this song?"

"I don't know it," I whisper.

I've been too tense to even pay attention. I look up at the stage now.

The girl is singing softly into the microphone. The song is simple, with a slight country flavor. Her voice is low and clear above the acoustic guitar. She whistles the bridge, pursing her lips and making a sound like a wood lark.

♫ *"July"—Noah Cyrus*

"It's called 'July,'" Dante says.

We met in July. I don't know if he means to remind me of that or if he's just making small talk because he doesn't want to say anything else to me.

My chest is burning like I've been running miles instead of slowly dancing.

I can smell Dante's scent, powerfully masculine. He's not wearing the same cologne he used to, but the smell of his skin is the same—heady and raw. I can see his slabs of muscle shifting beneath his heavy suit jacket. He's a better dancer now. But there's no enjoyment in his body or on his face.

God, that face…

The dark shadow all along his jaw, visible even when he's cleanly shaved. The deep cleft in his chin. His black eyes, the darkest and fiercest I've ever seen. His thick dark hair that looks wet even when it isn't, combed straight back from his brow.

I want him. Just as badly as ever. Even more…

It's like that desire was growing and spreading inside me all this time, without me even knowing. All the time that I thought I was getting over him…I never let go at all.

Hot tears prick my eyes. I blink rapidly to get rid of them. I can't let him see me like this.

Dante clears his throat. Still not looking at me, he says, "I read about your sister. I'm sorry."

I make a strangled sound that's supposed to be something like, "Thank you."

"They said you adopted her son."

Everything slows around us. The strings lights are a blur of gold. The wood-paneled walls slide by in slow motion. I can tell the song is about to end, but the last bars seem to be drawing out forever.

I could tell Dante the truth right now.

I could tell him that Henry is *his* son.

But two things are stopping me:

First, I have no idea if Dante is still embedded in the Italian Mafia. I'm guessing he probably is. No matter how his business might have grown in the past nine years, I doubt he's cut out every trace of his former employment or rid himself of his ties to the criminals of Chicago. He's as dangerous a man as ever—probably even more so.

And the second, more cowardly reason…

Dante will be furious when he finds out.

When I first left, I thought of the baby as mine alone. Mine to protect, mine to care for. I thought it was my right to take my child to another country, to a safer life.

But when Henry was ripped out of my arms at the hospital, I began to think differently. Every time I missed a moment of his life because I was working—a first step or an early word—I realized how much Dante was missing, too.

Hiding my pregnancy was awful.

Hiding my son was unforgivable.

So I can't tell the truth about Henry because I'm scared. Scared of Dante.

I find myself nodding stupidly. Behaving as if Henry really is my nephew. Continuing my lie because I don't know what else to do.

The song comes to an end, and Dante releases my hand.

He gives me a little nod, almost a bow.

Then he walks away from me without another word.

And I'm standing there, miserable and alone, every cell of my body yearning for the man disappearing into the crowd.

28
DANTE

WHY DID I DANCE WITH HER?

God damn Aida for sticking her nose in where it doesn't belong.

I'm used to my sister's complete disregard for other people's boundaries, but this time she went too far. She knows Simone is off-limits in every conceivable way. I don't talk about her. I don't even think about her.

But that's not really true, is it?

I think about her every fucking day, one way or another.

Why hasn't that ever gone away?

After she left, I think I went mad for a while. I saw Simone everywhere—on street corners, in restaurants, in cars that passed. Every time, I'd turn my head, thinking it was really her, only to realize it was a stranger. Someone who didn't actually look like her at all.

And then the real mindfuck started. Her face began appearing on the covers of magazines, in retail shops, and cosmetic aisles. Her new career seemed like a cruel joke designed to torment me. Once I fell asleep watching TV, and I woke up to the sound of her laugh— she was on *The Late Show* being interviewed by Stephen Colbert.

So what's it like being the most beautiful woman in the world, Simone? As the most beautiful man, I have some thoughts... (Cue audience laughter.)

I couldn't get away from her. There was nowhere I could hide.

I hated Chicago. I hated my work. I even hated my family, though it wasn't their fault. I hated all the things that made Simone leave me. The things that made me unworthy.

I didn't want to be myself anymore—the man who loved her and wasn't loved in return.

So I joined the military.

I flew across the world to the godforsaken desert, just to find a place where I wouldn't have to see her face.

I still did, though. I saw her face in barracks, in sand dunes, in empty starry nights. It floated behind my closed eyelids at night when I tried to sleep.

I would have said that I remembered every detail of it.

And yet she took my breath away at the rally. I hadn't remembered even a quarter of how beautiful she can be.

She looks even more stunning tonight. She's wearing a simple white gown, one-shouldered with a tasteful slit up her left thigh. Every time she moved, I got a glimpse of that long leg, her deep-bronze skin against the glowing white.

Her waist felt tight and lean under my palm. But her figure was fuller than it used to be. That's why they call her *the Body*—because there's never been a body like that in all of creation. Every other woman in the world is just a pale imitation of her. Like they were all made in her image but with none of the same skill. She's the Picasso, and the rest are just postcards.

Why did she leave me?

I know why. I know I failed her that night, leaving her alone and scared in the park. I know I terrified her when I showed up, crazed and dripping blood. And I know she was teetering on the edge of leaving me even before that because I wasn't the man she'd planned to love, the one her family wanted for her.

So I guess the questions I really want to know the answers to are, *Why didn't she love me anyway? Why didn't she love me as much as I loved her?*

I thought she did. I looked into her eyes, and I thought I saw my own feelings reflected at me. I thought I could see inside her and knew exactly what she felt.

I've never been so wrong.

Now she's back here, like an angel that only visits the earth once every decade. I'm the fool who wants to fall at her feet and beg her to take me back up to heaven with her.

A man like me doesn't deserve heaven.

I can see the musicians finishing their set. The event organizer is messing with the microphones, probably about to bring Yafeu Solomon up onstage to speak.

I remember what he said about wanting to thank me in public. I've got zero interest in that. I don't want his thanks or anybody's attention.

So I head toward the exit.

It was stupid to come here in the first place. I don't know why I let Riona rope me into it. What did I think was going to happen? That Simone would apologize? That she'd beg me to take her back?

She didn't do it at the rally, so why would she do it tonight?

I wouldn't want that anyway.

She didn't want me then, and she certainly doesn't now. Her status has risen like a rocket. I'm the same gangster I was before—shined up a little, but still with bruised, battered knuckles if you look closely enough.

I'm almost at the door when Riona intercepts me.

"Where are you going?"

"I don't want to hear Solomon's speech."

Riona brushes back a strand of her bright red hair. She looks nice tonight—she always looks nice. But I'm not fooled by the dress or the heels. She's a pit bull at her core. And I can see she's debating how hard to push me after she already strong-armed me into coming here tonight. "I saw you dancing with Simone."

"Yeah."

"What did she say?"

"Nothing. We barely spoke."

Riona sighs. "You know she's only here for a couple of days…"

"Good," I say roughly. "Then I probably won't see her again."

I push past Riona, leaving Heritage House.

After the heat and press of the dance floor, the cool night air is a relief. Riona picked me up on her way over, so she won't care if I leave without her.

As I cross the parking lot, I see Mikolaj Wilk and Nessa Griffin pull up in Nessa's Jeep. Miko's driving, and Nessa is leaning over to rest her head on his shoulder. Nessa's laughing about something, and even Miko has a smile on his lean pale face. His pale hair is ghostly in the dim interior of the car, and the tattoos rising up his neck look like a dark collar.

I raise my hand to wave at them, but they don't see me, too wrapped up in each other.

Fucking hell. I don't want to be jealous, but it's hard not to feel bitter when even the unlikeliest couple can make it work, while Simone and I couldn't.

Mikolaj hated the Griffins with every fiber of his being. He kidnapped Nessa, their youngest child. He murdered Jack Du Pont, Callum's bodyguard and best friend. Yet somehow, after all that, he and Nessa fell in love, were married, and even made peace with the Griffin family.

I guess there's something missing in me.

Some core component required for happiness.

Because the only time I've felt it were those few short months with Simone. And she obviously didn't feel the same.

I take an Uber back to my house. The lights are mostly out—Papa goes to bed early now, and Nero's probably out with his girlfriend, Camille. Only Seb's bedroom light is on. I can see it high up on the third floor, like a lighthouse above the dark sea of the lawn.

I jog up the front walk. The pavement is cracked. The yard is full of dead leaves. The old oak trees have grown so tall and thick that the house is too shady—perpetually dim, even in the daytime.

It's still a beautiful old mansion, but it won't last forever.

Aida's son will probably never live here.

Maybe if Nero or Seb have a kid, there will be one more generation giving life to these old walls.

I don't see myself ever having children. Even though I'm barely over thirty, I feel old. Like life already passed me by.

As I climb the steps to the front door, I see a package on the porch. It's small, about the size of a ring box, wrapped in brown paper.

In my world, you don't pick up unmarked packages. But this is too small to be a bomb. It could be full of anthrax, I suppose.

At this moment, I don't really care. I pick it up and strip off the wrapping.

Something rattles around inside the box. It sounds small and hard. Too heavy to be a ring.

I open the lid.

It's a .50-caliber bullet—hand turned on a lathe. Bronze alloy. Smelling of oil and gunpowder.

I lift it out of the box, turning the cool, slippery cylinder between my fingers.

There's a note nested in cotton. Small, square, and handwritten.

It says, *I know who you are.*

29
SIMONE

I'M EATING BREAKFAST WITH MY PARENTS IN THEIR ROOM. WE GOT adjoining suites, so it's easy enough to go through the door between them while still wearing my pajamas and sit down at the table filled with room service trays.

Mama always orders too much food. She hates the idea that anybody might go hungry, even though she eats like a bird herself. She's got platters of fresh fruit, bacon, eggs, ham, and pastries, as well as coffee, tea, and orange juice.

"I've got a plate of waffles here for Henry, too," she tells me as I sit down.

"He's still sleeping."

After the fundraiser, Henry and I cuddled and watched a movie until way too late at night. I was stressed and upset from my dance with Dante. The only thing that calmed me down was the feeling of my son's head lying on my shoulder and his peaceful, slow breathing after he fell asleep.

"What were you watching?" Mama asks me. "I heard explosions."

"Sorry," I say. "I should have turned it down."

"Oh, it's fine." Mama shakes her head. "Your father wears earplugs, and I was awake reading anyway."

"It was *Spider-Man: Into the Spider-Verse*," I tell her. "That's Henry's favorite movie."

I love it, too, actually. Miles Morales reminds me of Henry—smart, kindhearted, determined. Sometimes messing up but always trying again.

Who would I be in the movie?

Peter B. Parker, I guess. Fucked up his own life but can still be a good mentor at least.

That's what I'm hanging on to. I've made so many mistakes, but I'll do whatever I can to give Henry a good life. I want to give him the world and the freedom to find his way in it.

"How did you sleep, Tata?" I ask my father.

"Well," he says, drinking his coffee. "You know I can sleep anywhere."

My father seems to accomplish things by pure force of will. He would never allow something as mundane as a lumpy mattress or street noise to keep him awake.

"What should we do with Henry today?" Mama says.

"Oh…" I hesitate. I was planning to leave Chicago today. I have another job booked in New York next week—I thought I'd take Henry there early, go see a few Broadway shows together.

"You're not leaving already, are you?" Mama asks plaintively. "We barely got to see you."

"You don't have another job until next week," my father says. "What's the rush?"

I hate when he contacts my assistant. I'm going to tell her not to give him my schedule anymore.

"I guess I could stay another day or two," I admit.

Right then, there's a knock on the door.

"Who's that?" Mama says.

"Probably Carly."

Carly's room is down the hall. We all slept late, past the time when she usually starts Henry's schoolwork.

My father is already striding over to open the door. Instead of Carly's petite frame, I'm shocked to see Dante's broad shoulders filling the doorway.

"Good morning," he says politely.

"Good morning. Come in," my father says at once.

Dante steps inside. His eyes find mine, and my hand clenches tightly around my coffee mug. I wish I had combed my hair and washed my face. And I wish I weren't wearing pajamas with little pineapples all over them.

"Come join us for breakfast," Mama says.

"I already ate," Dante replies gruffly. Then, to smooth the rejection, he adds, "Thank you, though."

"Have some coffee at least," Tata says.

"All right."

Mama pours him a mug. Before she can add any sugar, I say, "Just cream."

Dante's eyes flash over to me again, maybe surprised that I remember how he likes his coffee.

Screwing up my courage, I pick up the mug and hand it to him. His thick fingers brush over the back of my hand as he takes it. The brief touch lingers on my skin.

"Thank you," Dante says. He's saying it to me, looking in my eyes. It's the first time he's looked at me without anger on his face. He's still not friendly, but it's an improvement.

"So, what can we do for you, Dante?" my father asks.

Dante is still standing. He looks awkwardly around for somewhere to set down his mug, settling for the windowsill.

"I want to know who shot at you yesterday," he says bluntly.

"I'd like to know as well," Tata replies.

"Do you have any ideas?"

"I'm afraid I've made a lot of enemies with this new coalition. You would think this would be a topic that anyone could agree upon, but in fact, it's ruffled the feathers of a lot of important people. We've called for extreme sanctions against countries like Saudi Arabia, who have permitted de facto slavery within their borders."

"Is that where the death threats came from?" Dante asks. "Saudi Arabia?"

"Some," Tata says. "Some from Russia, China, Iran, Belarus, and Venezuela, too. We've pushed to have these countries downgraded to Tier Three status by the State Department—meaning they're considered countries that do not comply with the minimum standards of human rights in regard to trafficking."

Dante frowns, thinking. "What about domestic threats?"

"We've made plenty of enemies in America, too," Tata admits. "We're pushing for aggressive prosecution and harsher sentencing for people who facilitate sex trafficking on and off American soil. For instance, American citizens who charter private jets and offshore boats for such purposes. I'm sure you're familiar with the spate of accusations against politicians and celebrities who have attended those sorts of…parties."

"I've heard of it." Dante grunts. "Anyone in particular who might blame you for those accusations?"

"Maybe one person," Tata says. "But he got off scot-free, so I don't think he has much motivation for revenge."

"Who?" Dante says.

"His name is Roland Kenwood. He's a publisher. Heavily involved in politics, too. Wealthy as sin, of course. Which is why the case never went anywhere."

"Where does he live?" I ask.

"Here in Chicago," Dante interjects. "I know who he is."

"Yes, I'm sure Callum Griffin has crossed paths with him," Tata says.

"You think he'd risk hiring someone to kill you right in his own backyard?" I say.

My father shrugs. "The mental machinations of a man who would hire fifteen-year-old girls for his parties is beyond me. Maybe he wanted to watch it go down. Or maybe it wasn't him at all. I'm not a detective, just a diplomat."

Dante nods slowly. He seems to think that's a good lead.

The door between the two suites opens. Henry comes stumbling through, sleepy-eyed, with his hair a wild tangle of curls all around his head, and his striped pajama top misbuttoned so one side hangs lower than the other.

I freeze at the sight of him. As I see Dante looking right at his son, I can't even breathe.

I wonder if Dante realizes how silent the room just became.

Henry doesn't seem to notice. He gives Dante one quick curious look, then heads straight for the breakfast table. "Any pancakes?"

"Yes," Mama says hastily. "I mean, there's waffles..."

She pulls the lid off the tray.

I'm still watching Dante, my heart in my throat.

Is there a flicker of suspicion in his dark eyes? Or does he just see a boy like any other?

"I'll let you get back to your food," Dante says to us all.

He heads for the door.

I jump up and hurry after him, waiting until he's out in the hallway to say, "One moment!"

Dante stops, turning slowly.

"I want to come with you," I say.

"Where?"

"To talk to this Kenwood person. I know you're going to see him."

"I don't think that's a good idea."

"If he's trying to kill my father, I want to help stop him. You're not always going to be there to block any bullets headed our way."

"He'll know who you are," Dante says.

"So what? That might be a good thing. How else are you going to make him talk to you? He might be goaded into doing it, if he does know me."

Dante frowns. He doesn't like that idea at all. Whether because he thinks it will only cause more trouble or because he doesn't want to spend time with me, I can't tell.

"I'll think about it," he says at last.

He turns to leave again. I want to say something else, anything else, but I don't know what.

Finally, I blurt, "Thank you, Dante. For saving my father's life. And for looking into this."

"I'm not promising anything," Dante says. "But I want to know who that shooter is."

I feel a warm spread of hope in my chest.

I know Dante isn't doing this for me.

Still, if anyone can figure this out, it's him.

30
DANTE

I can't be certain whether the sniper is local or not, but I believe he is.

It's not easy to transport that kind of equipment internationally. Better to use a local shooter—if you can find anyone with the skills to handle a job like that.

And I do think an arrogant fuck like Kenwood would order the hit somewhere he could see it. What's the fun of having an enemy murdered if you can't watch the fallout?

I'm pretty sure that gunpowder was a nitrocellulose propellant. Du Pont manufactures it in a plant in Delaware. That type of powder is less common than it used to be, when Du Pont was the main supplier for the military.

That makes me think the sniper is either old, or they have some attachment to that particular mix. I wonder if the propellant was supplied to any other group, besides the army?

Other than that, I don't have any leads.

Except the note.

I know who you are.

What does it mean? It was obviously left for me by the shooter. I'm sure he was pissed that I fucked up his job. He won't get paid since Solomon didn't go down.

But why the note? If he found my house and he wanted revenge, he could have just hidden in the bushes and taken a shot at me.

I know who you are.

Was he just letting me know he tracked me down? It wouldn't have been all that hard to do—the botched assassination attempt was all over the news. Against my preferences, Yafeu Solomon openly identified me as the person who'd intervened. Finding my house would have been simple.

No, the message means more than that.

I know who you are.

He's talking about my time in the military. I was part of the second wave of soldiers sent back overseas after the Islamic State seized swaths of Iraq and Syria. We worked with the Iraqi forces to retake Mosul, Anbar, and Fallujah.

Snipers were crucial, since most of the fighting took place in urban environments. We covered the ground troops while they surged through the cities, clearing building after building.

Sometimes rival snipers had their own perches, and we had to triangulate, set up smoke screens, and try to flush them out. If we were the forward guard, the sniper battles lasted for days.

I had 162 confirmed kills. The army gave me a Silver Star and three Bronze Stars.

None of that means a fuckin' thing to me. But it means something to other people. Maybe to this other sniper.

He's decided we're antagonists. Rivals.

I take his bullet out of my pocket and roll it between my fingers again. He left that for me as a warning.

I try to think what his next move will be. Attacking Solomon again? Attacking me?

I'm seething with frustration. I don't know this man—so I can't guess how he thinks.

The only way to find his identity is to figure out who hired him. So, for that reason, I do need to visit Roland Kenwood.

We don't exactly move in the same circles. While there's some overlap with Callum Griffin and the politicians Kenwood keeps in his pocket, the rest of his connections are among the famous faces of Chicago. Kenwood is a star fucker, for lack of a better term. He's known for throwing glitzy and glamorous parties stuffed with musicians, athletes, models, and, of course, writers.

Kenwood's publishing house specializes in memoirs. He's put out several of the bestselling autobiographies of the past decade, including those of the last two presidents.

That's why I think I might actually need Simone after all.

I'm not famous—not even close. But she is.

Even if Kenwood hates Yafeu Solomon with every fiber of his being, Simone could get into one of his parties. She'd be the crown jewel of the event—one of the most famous faces on the planet.

I don't like the idea. First, because every second I spend around her is pure torture. And second, because Kenwood is dangerous. I already hate the fact Simone is spending time with her father while he's got a target painted on his back. The thought of bringing her right into the lion's den makes me sick.

But I don't see any way around it.

I text her because I don't think I can stomach hearing her voice over the phone.

Roland Kenwood is throwing a party tomorrow night. You want to come with me?

Simone responds immediately:

I'm in.

We pull up to the gates of Kenwood's estate in River North. I can already hear the thumping dance music coming from the house, though I can't see anything through the thick stands of trees.

The security guards scan the list, unimpressed by the Ferrari I rented for the night. I was hoping they'd just wave me through if they saw me in a four-hundred-thousand-dollar car.

No such luck. They peer in the window at me, scowling.

"You're not on the list." One of them grunts.

Simone leans forward. She's looking stunning in a silver minidress that clings to her frame. Her hair is a cloud of curls around her face. It makes her features look particularly soft, young, and feminine.

"Are you sure?" she says, in her gentle, cultured voice. "I think Mr. Kenwood was particularly looking forward to meeting me. You know who I am, don't you?"

"*I* do," the second guard says quickly. "I still have my *Sports Illustrated* with you on the cover."

Simone gives him her most charming smile. I know she's just getting us through the gates, but it makes me burn with jealousy to see her looking up at him with those catlike eyes, her thick lashes fluttering.

"That's so sweet!" she says. "I wish you had it here. I'd sign it for you."

"I'll let Mr. Kenwood know you're on your way up," the guard says politely.

"Thank you!" Simone blows him a kiss.

I put the car in drive, barely waiting for the gates to part before I roar through. I feel the back of my neck burning. Simone is even more gorgeous now than when I knew her. I wonder if I could stand being with her, the way men drool over her everywhere she goes. Those guards couldn't keep their jaws shut. It made me want to jump out of the car and beat the shit out of them. And Simone's not even mine.

Doesn't matter. That's not an option anymore.

Simone made it pretty clear nine years ago how she feels about me.

I'm not ever giving her another chance to rip my heart out and stomp on it. I barely survived the last time.

We speed up to the house. Simone lets out a little gasp when she sees it. I don't think she's impressed—the place is just outrageous. It's the most ostentatious mansion I've ever seen. It looks like it would be better suited to Bel Air than Chicago.

It's a white Greco-Roman monstrosity, like three mansions stacked on top of each other. A jumble of pillars and scrolls, archways and pass-throughs. The semicircular driveway centers around a gargantuan fountain, bigger than the Trevi Fountain in Rome. Water spurts from the mouths of dolphins, while several mermaids cling to the burly arms and legs of King Triton.

I pull up next to the fountain so the valet can take my keys.

"Oh my god," Simone whispers, getting out of the car.

"Welcome," the valet says. "Head through the main level. The party is throughout the house and on the back grounds."

More cars are pulling in behind us. Each one is a supercar worth two hundred and fifty thousand dollars or more. Some kid who looks all of twenty-one climbs out of a Lamborghini. He's dressed in a tropical-printed silk shirt and matching trousers, with about twenty gold chains slung around his neck. He's wearing mirrored sunglasses despite the fact it's ten o'clock at night.

"I don't think this is going to be my kind of party," I say to Simone.

"What's your kind of party?" she asks me, her eyebrow raised.

"Well…" Now that I think about it, I guess no kind of party.

"Maybe a pint of Guinness, an hour at the batting cages, and a drive along the lakeshore," Simone says, with a small smile.

That would be the perfect day for me.

It disturbs me how easily Simone listed that off. Just like how she remembered my preferences in coffee. It makes me feel raw and exposed.

Sometimes I tell myself that the intense connection I felt to Simone was all in my mind. That it couldn't have been real, or she never would have left.

Then she proves that she really did understand me, and that fucks with my head. It fucks with the story I told myself to explain how she could cut me off so easy.

I know I'm glowering at her. I can tell by the way she shrinks back from me, the smile fading off her face.

"Let's go in the house," I say.

"Sure," Simone replies in a small voice.

I don't take her arm, but I stick close to her as we enter Kenwood's mansion. The lights are low, and I don't know who's going to be here.

The music is loud and thudding, shaking the walls and rattling the art on the walls. While the exterior of the house is faux antique, the interior is all fluorescent pop art, Lucite furniture, pinball machines, and gaudy sculptures that look like giant red lips, glittery guitars, and chrome balloon animals.

The guests are equally garish. Half the outfits would look more at home at a circus than a party, but I see enough brand names to know it's all expensive.

"Is this what's fashionable now?" I mutter to Simone.

"I guess, if you've got the money for it." She nods toward a young woman wearing a skintight minidress and a pair of thigh-high blue fur boots. "Those boots are four thousand dollars. They're from the Versace fall line that hasn't even been released yet."

"Huh. I thought she skinned a Muppet."

Simone laughs. "Well, 'expensive' doesn't always mean attractive."

I remember that Simone wanted to design her own clothes, once upon a time. "Did you ever end up going to Parsons?" I ask her.

She shakes her head. "No. I never did."

"Why not?"

"Oh…" she sighs. "Work and…other things got in the way."

Other things meaning her parents, probably.

"I do make sketches of designs sometimes…" Simone says. "I have a whole notebook full of them."

Without thinking, I say, "I'd like to see them."

"You would?"

She's looking up at me with the most heartbreaking expression on her face. Why, why, why the *fuck* does she care what I think? I don't understand her. How can she be so callous with me and yet so vulnerable?

"We better get going," I say roughly. "In case those guards really do call Kenwood."

"Right." Simone drops her eyes. "Of course."

The house is packed with partygoers, especially on the main level. Looking out into the backyard, we can see dozens of people lounging around the pool, swimming, or soaking in the hot tub. Some look like they fell in the pool with their clothes on, while others are half or fully naked.

The whole place reeks of alcohol. There's liquor absolutely everywhere, plus a cornucopia of party drugs, right out in the open. I see a group of young women mixing up a bowlful of pills, then taking a handful each and washing it down with cognac.

Some of the girls look extremely young. Especially the ones hired to work the party. They're dressed like guests, in minidresses, crop tops, booty shorts, and heels, but it's clear from the way they prowl the party, finding older men and sitting down in their laps, that they've been hired as entertainment.

Simone watches them, frowning.

"How old do you think they are?" she says, looking at one particularly youthful redhead with her hair in pigtails.

"I have no idea," I say. "Kenwood definitely has a reputation. I'm guessing he wouldn't be stupid enough to bring in anybody under eighteen here in the city. But they say when he flies guests out to his boat…he brings in girls as young as twelve."

"That makes me want to throw up," Simone says coldly.

"I agree."

"I had three aunts," she says quietly. "My father's older sisters. They thought they were getting jobs as maids. Then they disappeared. Tata thinks they might have been trafficked. He looked for them for years but never found them. That's why he started the Freedom Foundation."

I didn't know that. I assumed Yafeu was using charity work like most wealthy people do—to enhance his status and connections. I didn't realize he had such a personal connection to the issue. It actually makes me feel sorry for him. For a moment, at least.

Simone looks around the party with renewed focus. "What now? What do we do?"

"Well…" I haven't seen Kenwood anywhere yet. "I guess I want to snoop around his house. Try to find his office, or a laptop or iPad. See if I can access it or steal it and have somebody smarter hack into it."

"All right," Simone says nervously. I know she wants to help me, but this is where we cross the line from party crashers to criminals. She's probably never broken the law in her life.

We climb the wide curving staircase to the upper floor. All the lights are off here, probably to dissuade partygoers from coming up. I have to yank Simone into the nearest room, to avoid a guard prowling past.

There are guards all over this place. Unless Kenwood hired extra security for the party, he's pretty fucking paranoid. Which means he has something to hide.

Simone and I search the rooms. She keeps watch outside the door, while I look through each space in turn.

Kenwood has all kinds of weird stuff up here.

First, we find a massive billiards room with fifty or more taxidermy heads on the wall. They're all exotic animals, some that I couldn't even name. Their glass eyes look down blankly over cheetah-printed chairs and zebra-striped chaises.

Next to that, a room that appears to be an exact replica of the Star Trek *Enterprise* bridge. I don't know what purpose it serves for Kenwood. I can only assume he comes in here and sits in the captain's chair, then stares at the wall painted to look like outer space.

"That's just creepy," Simone whispers, peering through the doorway.

"What?"

She points. There are hidden cameras in two corners of the room. In the next room as well. Probably all over the house.

"We better hurry up," I tell her. "He might have spotted us already."

Simone follows me farther down the hallway. We haven't seen anything that looks like an office yet. Just a guest room, a bathroom, and another guest room.

"Come on," I mutter to Simone. "Let's check the doors at the end of the hall."

She's right next to me, not touching me but walking so close that I can feel her body heat on my bare arm. It's colder on this upper level than it was downstairs. I can hear the air conditioner whirring. And I can see Simone's nipples poking through the shiny silver material of her dress. I look away quickly.

"Wait here," I say to her as we reach the double doors at the end of the hall. "If you hear anyone, come find me."

I slip inside what looks like Kenwood's main suite.

I walk across an acre of carpet. Kenwood's room looks like it was designed by Liberace. His bed is on a raised circular dais, bookended by hanging curtains and two massive vases of hothouse flowers. I can smell their heavy perfume from here. Everything is tasseled, gilded, or mirrored. The whole ceiling is a mirror, as well as several of the walls, which gives the room a creepy fun house feeling. I keep catching glimpses of my reflection from different angles, and it makes me jump every time, thinking there might be someone else in here.

I start searching Kenwood's nightstand and drawers, looking for an extra phone, tablet, or laptop. I look behind the paintings for a safe. I'm not as good at cracking locks as Nero, but I might be able to get a safe open, given enough time.

Over in the sitting area, I see a whole wall full of photos of

Kenwood shaking hands with famous people. He's got mayors, governors, senators, and presidents, all giving him that weird shoulder-clapping handshake they seem to love.

Then dozens more pictures of Kenwood with actors, singers, models, CEOs, and athletes. He's even got a shot with an astronaut, signed and everything. I doubt Kenwood is actually friends with all these people, but it's obvious he's a collector. Obsessed with shining bright by standing in other people's spotlights.

When I come to what I think is Kenwood's closet, I get a surprise. Behind the door is a little room with a single chair. The whole wall is stacked with monitors, and each monitor shows one of the camera feeds from the house. There are cameras in every room, except the one I'm occupying currently. That includes the half dozen guest rooms scattered throughout the house.

I'm assuming the guests aren't told. Because right now, I could watch several different couples fucking or the threesome currently taking place in the hot tub. If I were a lecherous fuck like Kenwood.

I'm guessing that's how he gets his jollies—sitting here watching the girls he hired servicing his wealthy friends. Or maybe he uses the footage for blackmail. That would explain how he managed to wiggle out of the charges brought against him by the Freedom Foundation and the Chicago PD.

The computer connected to the monitors is encrypted. But I could grab the hard drive. I know plenty of people who could break into that thing, given several hours and the right financial incentive. Hell, I bet Nero could do it.

I unplug the drive and tuck it in the front of my jeans, under my T-shirt. It's not a great hiding spot, but it'll do for now.

I head back to the doors, wondering if I should tell Simone I got what we came for or if we should keep snooping around.

But when I slip back out into the hallway, Simone is nowhere to be seen.

She's completely disappeared.

31
SIMONE

While Dante searches the main bedroom, I keep watch outside, making sure that guard doesn't circle back around.

Keeping guard is pretty boring. At first, I'm distracted by the fear of getting caught and the guilty sensation of sneaking around someplace you're not supposed to be. Once that fades, I'm just standing in the dark, listening to the distant thud of house music. I saw the DJ out in the backyard—I'm pretty sure he's the same one who played at Ryan Phillippe's birthday party in Los Angeles.

Sometimes I go to celebrity parties, when Ivory drags me along. She loves that kind of thing. That's why she got into modeling in the first place—she loves the attention, the feeling of being special.

For me, the attention only makes me feel lonelier. People think they love Simone Solomon, but they don't actually know me. All their compliments mean nothing because they're directed at the persona I created. That Simone is just a product. She doesn't really exist.

I know what it felt like to be loved by someone who actually understood me. Dante loved me, not like my parents do—because of what they want me to be. He loved me exactly the way I was.

Serwa did, too. But she's gone now.

And Dante, though he's only a few meters away on the other side of that door…he might as well be a thousand miles away. I lost his love forever when I ran from him.

At least I have Henry.

I'm afraid, though. Afraid that by making Henry the center of my world, I put too much pressure on him, just like my parents did to me. It's not right to put all my happiness on him. He shouldn't have to carry that burden.

I don't know what else to do, though.

Other than Henry, nothing in my life really makes me happy.

God, if only I hadn't ruined things with Dante…

I thought I caught him looking at me when we walked down the hallway. I thought his eyes had that same look in them that they used to—hungry and intent.

But then I blinked, and he was just staring down the hall again, refusing to meet my eyes.

As I wait, I hear voices down at the end of the hall. I'm about to duck inside the main bedroom to warn Dante, but I can hear that the two people are moving in the opposite direction, across to the far wing of the house.

My hallway and theirs form a T shape. As the figures cross the intersection of the two points, I see Roland Kenwood. I looked up his picture online before we came. He's medium height, lean, with a long tanned face, an aristocratic nose, and a shock of gray hair. In the photos for his publishing house, he's dressed in dark suits with monochromatic dress shirts beneath. Right now, he's wearing a lime-green shirt unbuttoned to the navel, pool shorts, and sandals. He's accompanied by a young woman. A very young woman—maybe even a girl. She barely comes up to his shoulder, and she's wearing a Shirley Temple dress, with her hair in two blond plaits over her shoulders, the ends tied with bows.

I can't see the girl's face because she's looking up at Kenwood as they pass. But I hear her childish giggle.

My skin crawls. They're walking quickly—if I don't move fast, they'll disappear into this warren of a house.

I poke my head into the main bedroom, looking for Dante. The suite is too big and too dark for me to see much of anything.

"Dante?" I whisper.

There's no answer.

I don't have time to find him. I run down the hall as quietly as I can, looking to see where Kenwood went.

As I turn left at the T, I can just see the hem of the girl's skirt disappearing into the last doorway on the right. I hurry after her, worried about what Kenwood plans to do once he gets her alone.

By the time I get to the end of the hall, the door is closed. I press my ear against the wood, unable to hear anything on the other side. I know I'm not going to be able to go inside without being spotted, but I don't have any choice. That girl could be Henry's age.

So I grab the knob and turn it, stepping into the brightly lit room.

It's completely empty.

I see a couple of couches, a big-screen TV, and a full bar stocked with liquor and snacks. But nothing else. No people.

I don't understand. This is the only door in and out of the room. I saw Kenwood go in with the little girl. And nobody came out.

Then, so quiet that I almost miss it, there's a giggle.

It's coming from the far wall.

I cross the carpet to what looks like a ten-foot-tall silkscreen of Andy Warhol's *Mao*. I listen closely. Silence. And then…that giggle again. Coming from behind the painting.

I grab the frame. The painting swings away from the wall on a hinge. Behind it is another room.

I step over the ledge into the space. The painting swings back in place, closing me in.

This room is much larger. The padded walls are upholstered in red velvet, as is the ceiling. The carpet is so thick, my feet sink into it. I can't help but think that all this is designed to block any sound from escaping.

The room is so dim that the furniture seems to loom up out of nowhere, like rock formations obscured by fog. It doesn't help that the furniture is all extraordinarily odd—even by Kenwood's standards. In fact, I can't tell what half of it is. I see a leather-covered bench with two wings on either side. Then something that looks like a table, with a soft padded top and metal rings fixed all around the edges. A giant birdcage, at least six feet tall, with a perch that looks like a playground swing. Then some kind of rig that looks like exercise equipment, with several different straps and loops and...

I blush as I realize I'm looking at fetish equipment. All the furniture serves a sexual purpose—some obvious, now that I realize the theme, and others still a mystery to me.

I hear a low murmur from the far side of the room. This time the voice is masculine—Kenwood.

I hurry over, not even trying to be quiet. Now that I know I'm in a sex dungeon, I'm definitely going to grab that girl and get out of here.

Kenwood is sitting on a couch set against the opposite wall. His arms are stretched out along the cushions, and his head is thrown back, his eyes closed.

The girl kneels between his spread legs, her head bobbing up and down.

Kenwood groans. He grabs the back of her neck and pushes her face down on his cock.

"Stop!" I scream, rushing forward.

Kenwood sits up, startled and annoyed.

The girl turns around, wiping her mouth on the back of her hand.

Even in the dim light, her face startles me. I see big innocent eyes thickly framed with false lashes. Bright spots of blush on her cheeks. But wrinkles line the corners of her eyes and the edges of her mouth, made more obvious by her thick makeup. She's not a child at all—just dressed like one. She's older than me, by quite a few years.

She stands. She must be less than five feet tall. Her expression is curious and malicious. With the bleached pigtails and the frilly dress, she looks like a demonic doll.

Kenwood is looking at me, too. Now that his surprise has passed, a little smirk turns up the corners of his mouth. Without breaking eye contact, he tucks his wet penis back into his shorts.

"Simone Solomon," he says. "How nice of you to join us. I assume you're not familiar with my assistant, Millie."

"Nice to meet you." Millie giggles.

Her voice is high-pitched and deliberately childish. It makes my stomach roll, as does the way she stands—her hands clasped behind her back and her head tilted to the side.

"Now, what can I do for you?" Kenwood says. "I assume you have a reason for crashing my party and snooping through my house?"

My eyes dart between Kenwood and his assistant. They're both smirking at me, well aware of what I thought I was witnessing when I interrupted them.

"I—I..."

"Spit it out," Kenwood says. Then, with a sly glance at Millie, he adds, "Or swallow. I like it better that way."

"Did you hire someone to kill my father?" I demand.

Kenwood snorts. "You think I hired that sniper?"

I did. Up until I saw the arrogant look on his face. Now I'm less sure.

"Yes..." I say hesitantly.

"Why is that?"

"Because the Freedom Foundation gathered all that information on your private parties. The FBI opened an investigation. You almost got arrested..."

Kenwood's face darkens. He doesn't like me mentioning any of that. It's obviously a hated memory for him.

"I *wasn't* arrested though, was I?" he hisses.

"No." I refuse to drop his gaze. "But you might be soon."

"Is that what he told you?" Kenwood jeers. "Your father?"

I'm confused. I don't understand what he's getting at. "He thinks you're the most likely person to want him dead."

"Why would I?" Kenwood spits. "I've kept up my end of the deal."

"What deal?"

Kenwood laughs, pushing up from the deep sofa. I take a step back now that he's standing.

But Kenwood isn't walking toward me. He goes over to the bar, next to a massive painting of Alexander the Great on horseback, and starts mixing himself a drink.

He pours bourbon over ice and swirls it before taking a drink. Millie skips over to him. He dips his index finger in the liquor, then holds it out to her. She sucks the alcohol off his finger, looking up at him the whole time. Then she licks her lips.

Kenwood fixes me with his cool stare again.

"Your father and I made a deal. I gave him the names of three of my suppliers, and a couple of 'friends' that I didn't mind throwing under the bus. In return, the video his little foundation made at one of *my* parties—which would have been thrown the fuck out in court anyway, by the way—went missing. Saved me a scandal, at the low price of a couple of disposable degenerates. In fact"—Kenwood laughs—"getting Phil Bernucci arrested was doing me a favor. That fucker tried to poach the movie rights to *The Hangman's Game*, which I owned for the next eight years, and he knew it. Watching him lose his beach house in Malibu to lawyer fees was fucking beautiful."

I shake my head. "I don't believe you."

My father would never destroy evidence of a crime like that. He built the Freedom Foundation to stop trafficking. To stop people like Kenwood.

"I don't care what you believe, you silly bitch," Kenwood snaps, throwing the rest of his drink down his throat.

At that moment, a man pushes open the painting of Alexander the Great and steps into the room. It's one of Kenwood's guards.

Kenwood sets down his glass next to a red button set in the smooth wooden surface of the bar. A call button. Kenwood pressed it while he was making his drink.

"Grab her," Kenwood says carelessly.

I try to turn and run, but the burly security guard is much faster than me, especially when I'm hobbled by a tight dress and high heels. He seizes my arms, pinning them behind my back. I scream when he grabs me, and the guard clamps his huge hand over my mouth. I keep screaming, squirming, and biting at his hand, but he's much stronger than me.

"Hold still, or I'll break your fuckin' arm," he growls, twisting my arm behind my back. Pain shoots up from my elbow to my shoulder. I stop squirming.

"That's better," Kenwood says. Jerking his head at Millie, he says, "Tell the guards to search the rest of the house. Find whoever she came with."

Millie pouts. "I want to stay and watch."

"Get going," Kenwood says coldly.

Turning back around, he looks me up and down.

"Strip her," he says to the guard.

I don't know if he simply intends to search me or something worse. The guard grabs the front of my dress and yanks it down, ripping the shoulder strap. As soon as his hand isn't covering my mouth anymore, I scream as loudly as I can, "DANTE!"

I hear a roar like a bear. Dante comes bursting through the Andy Warhol print on the far wall. He tears the canvas like it's not even there, barreling through into the room beyond.

Kenwood shrieks with rage, his fingernails digging into his cheeks. "*My Mao!*"

Dante takes one look at me, my arms still pinned behind my back, my dress torn so that one strap is dangling down, and my left breast bare. His face darkens with pure murderous rage.

He charges at the guard. The guy lets go of me, trying to get his fists up, but he might as well be trying to box a grizzly. Dante's massive fist comes crashing down on his jaw, and then his other fist goes swinging up like a hammer. He hits the guard again and again, driving him back. Each of his blows lands with a horrible thud. When he hits the guard in the mouth, blood spatters sideways, landing wetly on my arm and Kenwood's shoe.

Dante hits the guard twice more, then picks him up and throws him. The guard is a big man, but Dante flings him across the room like a discus. He crashes against the wall, then goes slumping down on the sofa, groaning and only half-conscious.

Kenwood looks terrified. He's madly punching the call button set into the bar, but it's too late. In three steps, Dante's picked him up by the throat, lifting his feet off the floor. Dante's thick fingers sink into Kenwood's throat. Kenwood's face turns red and then almost purple, his eyes bulging and spit flying from his lips as he tries to form words. He claws at Dante's hand and arm, but they might as well be made of stone for all Dante seems to feel it. Kenwood's feet kick helplessly in the air.

I think Dante's just releasing his aggression, but as Kenwood's eyes start to roll back, I realize Dante might actually kill him.

"Dante, stop!" I cry. "He didn't do anything to me!"

It's like he can't even hear me. Kenwood is going limp now as Dante's fingers sink deeper and deeper into his throat. I think he's going to break the man's neck.

"Dante!" I shriek. "*Stop!*"

My voice cuts through his rage. He turns to look at me, and maybe the terror on my face snaps him the rest of the way out of it. He lets go of Kenwood, who goes crashing to the floor, unable to catch himself. He's still alive, though—I can hear his rasping breaths.

"He hit his panic button," I tell Dante. "We've got to get out of here before the rest of his goons show up. Or the cops."

Dante still looks dazed, like his anger put him in an entirely different state. One that he can't come back from so easily.

But he does hear me. He grabs my hand. "Come on."

The feeling of his warm fingers enclosing mine sends a jolt of electricity up my arm. I let Dante pull me along, back through the painting he destroyed, back through the empty room, and then down the hallway.

Footfalls thud up the staircase—two or three men at least. Dante yanks me into the nearest doorway, pressing me against the wall with his bulk to keep me safe and out of sight. We're closer now than we were when we danced. My face is pressed against his huge chest, and his arms pin me against the wall. His body is hotter than a furnace, still inflamed by his anger at Kenwood. I can feel his heart thundering away by my cheek. His chest rises rapidly with each breath.

As we wait for the footsteps to go by, I look up at Dante's face.

For once, he's looking back down at me. His eyes are black and gleaming like wet stone. His expression is ferocious.

I open my mouth to say something. Instead, his lips come slamming down on mine. He crushes me in his arms, attacking me with his mouth. He kisses me like he's been waiting nine years to do it.

His stubble is rough. It scrapes my face. But his mouth…oh my god, he tastes so good. I've been starving for that taste. His scent makes me dizzy and weak.

I cling to him. I melt into him. I whimper from how badly I want him.

And then he stops.

"We better get out of here," he growls.

I completely forgot we were in the middle of escaping.

Dante pulls me out in the hallway. He pauses to listen. Then, hearing nothing but the pounding music from below, we sprint down the dark hall, all the way to the stairs, then down to the main level. Dante shoves through the press of guests—the party is more packed than ever now. He steals the Ferrari's keys from the valet stand, and soon we're roaring back toward the gates.

One of the guards steps forward, his hand outstretched like he's going to stop us. But Dante doesn't take his foot off the gas even a little. The gates are already open. The guard has to leap out of the way as we roar past him, missing him by an inch. We speed down the dark road, away from the gaudy mansion.

I let my breath out in a long sigh.

"My god. That was insane."

My heart is still racing. I've never actually witnessed a fistfight before. I'm not used to violence. I don't even watch it in movies. That's why it was so disturbing to me when I saw Dante covered in blood that night.

Now I've actually seen him in action—seen him throw another man across the room as if he weighed nothing. I watched him choke Kenwood until the life faded from his eyes.

It was horrifying. And yet…I know Dante did it for me. I saw the look on his face when he crashed into the room and saw me with my dress ripped, my arms pinned behind my back. He went into a rage *for me*. To protect me.

I want to look over at him. I want to say something. But I'm so afraid to break the silence between us. To shatter this brief moment in time when I know for certain that Dante still cares about me at least a little. I'm afraid if I say anything, the understanding between us will splinter like glass and fall apart, leaving me cut and bleeding all over again.

But I have to speak. I have to say something.

"Dante…"

His dark eyes meet mine. They look a thousand miles deep. I can see past the anger, down to the pain he's been hiding. I hurt this man. I hurt him badly.

"I'm sorry," I say.

Why was it so hard to get those words out?

Why didn't I say them to Dante a long, long time ago…?

The effect is instantaneous. Dante's huge hands tighten around the wheel, and he swerves hard to the right. The car screeches and almost spins, sliding onto the gravel shoulder before coming to a stop.

Dante turns and faces me.

He's frightening me, but I have to keep going.

"I'm sorry I left," I babble. "It was a mistake. A mistake I've paid for every day since."

"*You* paid for it?" he says, his tone dangerous.

"Yes." I'm trying not to cry, but I can't help the hot tears pricking at my eyes. "I've been so unhappy…I never stopped missing you. Not for a day. Not for an hour."

He's silent, his jaw clenching and working.

I see the battle on his face. Two forces warring inside him—the desire to rage and yell, against maybe, I hope, the desire to tell me that he missed me, too.

"You're sorry?" Those black eyes search my face.

"Yes."

"I want you to show me how sorry you are."

I don't understand what that means.

He pulls the car back out onto the road. I don't know where we're going, and I'm too afraid to ask. I'm nervous and confused. But there's also a grain of hope inside me…because he didn't reject me outright. I think there's the tiniest chance he might forgive me still.

We drive back into the city without speaking. Then Dante stops abruptly outside the Peninsula hotel. This isn't where I'm staying, so I'm confused.

"Go wait in the lobby," Dante orders.

I do what he says.

As always happens when I'm self-conscious, I feel like everyone is looking at me. I have to hold the left strap of my dress together because it's still torn. After a few minutes, Dante joins me with a room key in his hand.

"Upstairs," he says.

A shiver runs down my spine. I think I'm starting to understand, though I don't dare say a word. I follow Dante obediently into the elevator, my hands trembling and my knees shaking with nerves.

The elevator rises to the top floor. Dante leads me down the hallway to the Honeymoon Suite.

He unlocks the door and pushes it open.

I hesitate on the threshold. I know if I step over, something is about to happen.

I don't care what it is. In that moment, I finally understand that I'll do anything to have Dante again. Even just for a night.

I step into the hotel room. Dante closes the door behind me. I can feel his heat and bulk right behind my back. I feel him looming over me. I've never known a man who could make me feel so small and helpless just by standing next to me.

When he speaks, his voice is the deepest and harshest I've ever heard it.

"Do you know what those nine years did to me?" he says. "Do you know what I did to try to forget you? I abandoned my family. I joined the military. I flew halfway across the world and fought in a hellscape. I killed a hundred and sixty-two men, just to numb the pain of missing you. And none of it worked, not for a second. I never stopped hurting. I never stopped wondering how you could leave me, when I couldn't let go of you even for a second."

"I'm sor—" I try to say again.

Dante grabs my throat from behind, cutting off the words and pinning my back against his broad chest.

"I don't want to hear you say you're sorry," he hisses. "You need to show me here and now how sorry you are, if you want me to believe you."

He's not squeezing hard, but even the tiniest bit of pressure restricts the blood flow to my brain. My head is spinning.

"Nod if you understand."

I nod as much as I can with the collar of his hand around my throat.

"Say, 'Yes, Sir,'" he growls. He relaxes his grip enough for me to respond.

"Yes, Sir," I whisper.

"Turn around."

I turn to face him. I'm shaking so hard, I can't even look up at his face.

"Look at me," he orders.

Slowly, I raise my eyes to his. His eyes look like pure dark ink. His face is brutal, handsome, and terrifying.

"Take off your dress."

Without hesitation, I slip down the straps—the one that's already broken and the one that's whole. The thin silver material slides down my body, puddling on the floor at my feet.

Dante's eyes burn over my naked flesh. "Underwear, too."

I remember how he made me strip like this in the woods a long time ago. I don't think tonight is going to be like that night.

I slip down my lace thong and step out of it, still wearing my heels.

Dante lets his eyes roam over my fully naked body. I can see him taking in every inch of it, maybe comparing it with the memory he's had in his mind all these years.

Then he strides past me into the room. He sits down on the edge of the bed. I'm about to follow him, but he barks, "Stay there."

I stand there naked as he slowly unlaces his dress shoes and takes them off. Then he strips off his socks.

With his big, thick fingers, he unbuttons his dress shirt, baring the muscle of his chest. I can see he added several more tattoos since the last time I saw him shirtless.

He pulls the dress shirt off, revealing his monstrous shoulders and arms and torso.

Oh….my fucking god…his body is insane. He looks like he spent every minute since I last saw him torturing himself in the gym. I think he took every bit of his aggression out on his weight set.

I feel myself getting wet.

"Now…" Dante says. "Get down on your hands and knees, and crawl over here."

I don't hesitate.

I drop to my knees and crawl across the carpet. My face burns with humiliation, but at the same time, I don't give a fuck. I'll do whatever he asks.

When I reach his feet, I look up at him.

Dante is unzipping his dress pants, pulling out his cock. It's just as big as I remembered. It looks dark and swollen in this light. I can feel my mouth watering.

"Suck it," he orders.

I take his cock in my mouth. The second I do, I taste the thin salty fluid leaking from the tip, familiar and delicious to me. Saliva floods my mouth. I start sucking his cock ravenously.

I'm sucking it wildly, eagerly. I'm showing him how much I missed this cock, missed this body, and most of all missed *him*. I'm proving that I ached for him, longed for him, just as much as he did for me. Maybe even more.

I worship that cock. I use my hands, my lips, my tongue, my throat. It's wet and messy and without any dignity at all. And I don't give a fuck. All I care about is that it feels good for him. He can be my master, and I'll be his slave, if that's what it takes to get him back again.

I can tell it's working. Though he's trying not to, Dante groans and thrusts his hand in my hair, pushing my head down harder on his cock. He rolls his hips, fucking the back of my throat, and I take his cock deeper than I ever have before.

But before I can finish him off, he stops me.

He stands and pulls his leather belt free from his trouser loops. He loops one end around his hand and pulls it tight, making the leather snap like a whip.

I gulp.

"Put your hands on the bed and bend over," he orders.

I put my palms flat on the mattress. Because I'm tall and still wearing heels, I have to bend all the way over.

I hear Dante moving behind me. I close my eyes, knowing what's coming next.

The leather belt whistles through the air and comes down hard on my ass.

CRACK!

I jump and let out a yelp.

"Hold still," Dante barks.

I try to hold still. I try not to flinch away from the next blow.

CRACK!

The belt hits my other ass cheek. I can't help crying out again.

I know Dante isn't hitting me nearly as hard as he could, but it fucking stings. I'm sure he's raising welts on my bare ass.

CRACK!

CRACK!

CRACK!

He keeps spanking me with the belt. I yelp every time, unable to bite it back.

Dante pauses for a moment. He reaches between my legs and feels my pussy with his fingers. I'm soaking wet—it started as soon as I took off my clothes, and it's only gotten worse. Nothing he does makes it stop. I just keep getting wetter.

His fingers on my clit give me sweet relief, soothing the burning pain of my ass. But it only lasts a moment. I hear the whistle of leather, and the belt comes crashing down on my buttocks again.

CRACK!

CRACK!

CRACK!

"Are you sorry now?" Dante growls.

"Yes!" I sob.

CRACK!

CRACK!

CRACK!

"How about now?"

"Yes! I'm sorry!"

Dante grabs me by the hair and pulls me upright. He shoves me back down on my knees and wraps the belt around my neck. He uses the belt to pull my mouth back down on his cock, which is raging hard, jutting out from his body like solid steel.

He shoves his cock all the way to the back of my throat and holds me in place with the belt while he fucks my face. It's rough and aggressive, and I can't breathe. But I don't give a shit. The more Dante uses his superior size and strength on me, the more I love it. I love that he's using me like this. I love that I can't do anything about it.

He takes himself all the way to the edge again, but he doesn't blow. Instead, he pulls me up on the bed and makes me suck his cock some more. I'm lying on my side while he thrusts in and out of my mouth from a kneeling position. I've never given oral for so long before. My jaw is aching. But, at the same time, the feeling of the thick head of his cock banging against the back of my throat is oddly satisfying.

While he fucks my face, Dante reaches down and fingers me again. He rubs my clit and pushes his fingers inside me. I grind against his hand, my pussy swollen and aching for more.

His fingers wet with my juices, Dante starts to press against my ass as well.

I stiffen. I've never done anal before. Never even considered it.

"Keep sucking," Dante orders.

I suck his cock, gripping the base with my hand and working the head with my mouth.

Meanwhile, Dante slides his fingers in my pussy and ass.

At first, it's uncomfortable and way too intense. But he goes slowly, rubbing my clit at the same time, until I relax enough for him to finger me the way he wants.

"Are you going to do whatever I say?" he growls.

"Yes," I moan around his cock.

"Are you going to let me fuck you any way I want?"

"Yes…"

I can't refuse.

I can't say no.

I need him.

Dante mounts me from behind. He puts the head of his cock up against the entrance of my pussy, and he slams into me with one thrust. I cry out, louder than ever. He's fucking huge. And I've been waiting so long for this…

He grips my hips between his massive hands, and he thrusts into me again and again, so hard that his hips slam against my ass. He's fucking me like an animal, like a bull in heat, hard and rough and deep. I can't get enough of it. I've been wanting him so badly for so long that nothing less than the wildest and most aggressive sex could satisfy me.

He takes me in every position. He lifts me and fucks me against the wall. He bends me over the bed and fucks me while standing behind me. He makes me ride him in reverse so he can watch my ass and back flexing. And then he makes me ride him the other way, with my tits bouncing in his face.

It goes on for hours.

I come again and again. I come from his fingers and tongue and, most of all, from riding him.

The orgasms are intense and wrenching. They crash over me like waves, smashing me beneath their weight. And while I'm still recovering, still limp from pleasure, Dante flips me over and fucks me in a new position.

We're both drenched in sweat. Our bodies slide against each other, slick and flushed. We don't stop to drink water or to rest. We'll keep going until it kills us.

Finally, I'm done. I can't take anymore.

Dante climbs on top of me. He fucks me hard, droplets of his sweat pattering down on my bare chest. I can tell he's ready to let go

and finally come himself. He fucks me harder and harder, building to his climax. Then he grabs the base of his cock and pulls out of me.

He throws his head back, tendons standing out on his neck and shoulders. His muscles are pumped and swollen from hours of exertion. Veins run down both arms and down the back of the hand gripping his cock. He roars as the orgasm rips through him. Huge spurts of cum pour out of his cock, splashing down on my bare skin, heavy and hot. He paints my flesh with his cum, long ropes of it across my breasts and belly. It looks white and pearly against my skin.

Then he sits back on the bed, panting and flushed.

Our eyes meet.

I touch the cum on my belly. I bring my fingers to my lips and taste it to see if it's just like I remember.

Dante watches me, his eyes glittering. He lunges forward and kisses me. He presses me back down on the mattress with his bulk, kissing me long and deep with his hands thrust in my hair. He doesn't care how sweaty and messy we are. Neither do I.

Our bodies are wrung out and exhausted, but we're not done with each other. I don't know if we'll ever be satisfied. We were too long apart.

Dante pulls back just enough to look in my eyes. "I never stopped loving you. I never could."

I'm about to say the exact same thing.

But then I remember something. One awful fact that Dante doesn't yet know.

He doesn't know we have a son. He doesn't know I kept Henry a secret from him.

He says he could never stop loving me…but he doesn't know the reasons he might do exactly that.

I should tell him. I should tell him right now, I know that…

But I've waited so long to be in his arms again. Surely, I can enjoy it for one night before risking it all being ripped away from me again…

So I don't tell Dante that last secret. I just pull him close, and I kiss him again and again…

32
DANTE

I WAKE UP NEXT TO THE LOVE OF MY LIFE. THE SUN IS SHINING IN through a gap in the curtains, illuminating her glowing skin. Very gently, so I don't wake her, I inhale the scent of her hair, which still smells warm and sweet, like sandalwood. She hasn't changed. Not in any of the ways that matter.

Even though I'm trying not to wake her, her eyes flutter, and she nuzzles deeper into my arms, pressing her face against my chest. The feeling of her naked flesh against mine is too much to resist. My cock is already swelling between my legs, pressing against her belly. We only have to rearrange ourselves a little so it slides inside her.

I fuck her slowly and gently, knowing she might be sore from the night before.

I've never experienced sex like that. Raw, primal, animalistic, cathartic. I needed it. I needed it exactly like that. I had to take possession of Simone again. I had to make her mine in every possible way. I had to dominate her to know that she really belonged to me again, and me alone.

Maybe it's fucked up. But I know she understood it. She wanted it as badly as I did.

We both needed it. We needed to reconnect in a way that no one else could understand or endure. Simone and I are soul mates. Soul mates don't fuck like normal people. We unleash our darkest and wildest desires, without shame or judgment. We can fuck with violence or tenderness, aggression or care, and it's never misunderstood. It only brings us closer.

I've never felt closer to her than I do at this moment. She's the other part of me. I've been wandering around for nine years with only half my soul. I never thought I'd be whole again.

I kiss her, loving the way she tastes even right now, both of us still messy and sleepy. We haven't showered, but it doesn't matter. I love the smell of her sweat and her skin.

I fuck her slowly, my body pressed tight against hers. I can feel her clit rubbing against my lower belly, right above my cock. I spread her thighs and fuck her even deeper and tighter, until she starts to come. She clings to me, her pussy pulsing and squeezing around my cock.

I don't have to hold back this time. I can come whenever I want. So I let go, too, blowing right in that warm, wet pussy that squeezes me tighter than any glove. Tighter even than a hand wrapped around my shaft. I deposit my load deep inside her, and then I keep thrusting a few more times because I love the feel of that extra wetness.

I don't pull out. I want to stay connected to her like this for as long as possible.

We lie there in the sunshine and doze a while.

Then, finally, Simone gets up to pee.

I turn the shower on so we can clean ourselves up.

As soon as Simone steps under the stream, I start soaping her down, inch by inch. I wash her hair, massaging her scalp with my fingers. She leans against me, still limp from the night before.

"We never actually talked about what Kenwood said," I say.

"Right…" Simone lets out a long sigh, I think from how good the scalp massage feels, not anything to do with Kenwood. "He said he didn't hire anyone to kill my father."

"Do you believe him?"

"I don't know…He didn't sound like he was lying."

"Liars never do."

"Well…" Simone shifts uncomfortably. "He said he made a deal with my father. He said Tata destroyed evidence in return for Kenwood giving him a tip on a different sex ring."

"Hm." I think that over. "It's possible. But that doesn't mean Kenwood has no grudge against your father."

"Yeah, I guess," Simone says miserably.

"What's wrong?"

"It's just…my father is always so black-and-white. So rigid in his morals. The idea that he'd make a deal with a man like that…"

"Everyone does."

"You said that a long time ago. But I didn't believe you then."

"Look," I say, "everyone wishes they could get things done without compromises or ugliness. But sometimes you have to work with enemies as well as with friends."

Simone is quiet for a minute, while I rinse the soap out of her hair. Finally, she says, "Let's assume Kenwood was telling the truth. If he didn't hire the sniper, then who did?"

"I have no fucking clue. I stole one of Kenwood's hard drives, though. Maybe that has something on it."

After we've finished cleaning off, Simone orders breakfast up to the room, and I run downstairs to the hotel gift shop. Simone's dress is still torn, so she doesn't have anything to wear.

I buy her one of those *I Heart Chicago* T-shirts, plus a pair of sweat shorts and some flip-flops.

When I get back up to the room, Simone is already pouring our coffee, making mine with cream and no sugar, just the way I like. She changes out of her robe into the clothes. The shorts and the oversize T-shirt make her look almost like a teenager again, especially with her face clean of makeup and her damp hair twisted up in a bun, with little curls escaping all around. She sits like a teenager in her chair, with one knee tucked up by her chest and the other bare foot dangling.

It makes my heart squeeze in my chest, seeing her just the way she used to look.

I can't believe how happy I feel, sitting here with her, eating our toast together in the sunshine. It scares me. I'm afraid to get comfortable, to believe in this. I can't help thinking that something is going to happen to rip it all away again.

"I want you to stay," I say to Simone.

Her amber-colored eyes flit up to look at me, and I see the flare of excitement in them. But it only lasts a second, and then she's biting her lip, looking troubled. "I...I have some jobs booked."

"So what? Come back after."

"I want to..."

"What's the problem? Is it your family—"

"No!" she interrupts. "It's not them. I would never...I wouldn't let that stop me. I don't care what they think anymore."

Her face is dark and almost angry. I'm not sure where that bitterness comes from. Maybe it's just regret at how they influenced her before.

I don't care. I don't blame her for that anymore. She was young. We both were.

"What is it, then?"

Simone stares down at her plate, ripping her toast into fragments. "I have to talk to you about something," she says. "Tonight."

"Why tonight? Why not right now?"

"I have to do something else, first."

I don't like the mystery. I feel like Simone and I have no chance if we can't be completely open with each other. I don't want to be blindsided like I was before.

"Just promise me something," I say.

"Anything."

"Promise you won't run away again."

I don't say it out loud, but if she does...I'm just going to put a gun to my head and fucking kill myself. Because I won't survive it again.

Simone looks me right in the eye. Her face is somber and sad. "*I* won't leave *you*."

I think she's telling the truth. But the enunciation of the sentence is slightly off, like she's implying I might leave her instead.

That doesn't make sense, but it doesn't matter. I'm not going to fuck up our conversation this time around.

"Where do you want to meet tonight?" I ask her.

"Come to my hotel," she says. "Nine o'clock, after Henry goes to bed."

"Perfect. I'll be there."

Nothing could keep me away. Not this time.

I kiss Simone again, tasting the butter and coffee on her lips. Then I walk her down to the front entryway so she can take a cab back to her hotel. I'm sure she's anxious to get back to her nephew.

I've got my own plans for the day.

First, I'm supposed to meet Cal and Aida for lunch. And after that, I'm going to figure out what the fuck is going on with this shooter. I've got some contacts who track hired killers—if a contract was put out on Yafeu Solomon, they may have heard about it.

I'm meeting my sister at a restaurant on Randolph Street, close to city hall, where Cal has his alderman office. Aida's in there half the time as well, meeting with councilmen and aldermen, teamsters and business owners, helping Cal broker the hundred different deals that benefit our families.

Cal was instrumental in getting the first part of the South Shore development approved. Today we're going over the permits for phase two, which should start next year, after our current tower block is finished.

So I spend the morning down at South Shore, making sure nothing's getting fucked up past fixing. Then, right before noon, I drive over to the Rose Grille.

It's a large, busy restaurant, with dozens of white-cloth-covered tables, sparkling glassware, and baskets of fresh rolls with whipped honey butter. It's a favorite spot for political types, since city hall is right across the street. Almost all the diners have their phones out, tweeting or texting or whatever the fuck they do to try to stay relevant every minute of the day.

Cal and Aida are already seated when I get there. Aida's punctuality has improved about 10,000 percent since she married Cal. I can see she's already demolished half the rolls. My sister's appetite was legendary even before she was pregnant, so I'd hate to see her grocery bill in the third trimester.

We're sitting next to the large picture window at the front of the restaurant. The sun is glaring in my eyes. I try to lower the blinds.

"Why don't you just sit on the other side of the table?" Aida asks me.

"He doesn't want to sit with his back to the door," Cal says, without looking up from the stack of permit papers.

Cal knows. It's a commonality between gangsters and soldiers that you never sit with your back to the doorway.

The blinds are fixed in place and can't be lowered. I take my seat again, pushing my chair back a little.

"Sparkling or still water?" the waiter asks me.

"Still."

"Ice or no ice?"

"I don't give a fuck."

"He means no ice, thank you," Aida says to the waiter. Then, to me, she says, "You're a dick."

"I don't like fancy places," I grumble. "They have to make everything so damned complicated."

"This is not fancy," Aida says. "This is normal."

"Oh yeah?" I raise an eyebrow at her. "Now that you're a Griffin, a thirty-dollar salad is plebeian to you?"

Aida sets down the butter knife, glaring. "First of all, I'm still a Gallo," she tells me. Then she adds, "No offense," for Callum's benefit.

"None taken," he says, flipping to the next page of permit applications.

"And if you're planning on winning back your ex-girlfriend, who probably eats gold-leaf soufflé for a snack because she's a fucking world-famous supermodel, you better take her somewhere nicer than the Rose Grille."

I feel my face flushing. "Who says I'm trying to win her back?"

Aida rolls her eyes. "I know you're not stupid enough to let her get away again. Not after you spent nine whole years moping."

The waiter sets down our water glasses. He forgot and filled them all with ice. Not that I give a shit either way.

"Can I take your order?" he says nervously.

"Burger, medium," I say. "*Please.*"

"Same." Aida hands him her menu. "Thanks."

"Steak sandwich," Cal says, not looking up from his papers.

Once the waiter leaves, I point to the water glasses. "See? He wasn't listening to you anyway."

"That's probably toilet water in yours," Aida says sweetly.

Callum's reading the last page of applications. "What's this one?"

"Let me see…" I lean over for a closer look. Aida leans in, too. But she's not as coordinated as usual, since her proportions have changed. Her belly bumps the table, knocking Callum's ice water into his lap.

Cal jumps up from the table, shouting, ice cubes flying in every direction off his crotch. At that exact moment, the window shatters, a waterfall of glass raining down. Something whistles through the air, right where Cal's head was a millisecond before. A vase of peonies explodes over his shoulder. A hail of pottery shards hits my right arm, while shards of glass from the window cut my left.

Cal and I react almost at the same time. We grab the table, flip it on its side, and pull Aida behind it so it forms a barricade between us and the window.

Meanwhile, the rest of the diners have cottoned on to the fact that the window is broken, and we've hunkered down in a makeshift foxhole. After a moment of shocked silence, there's a stampede for the front doors.

"Go!" I say to Cal.

Taking advantage of the chaos, and staying low to the ground, we run in the opposite direction, toward the kitchens. The shooter is across the street—we need to go out the back.

We shove through the swinging double doors into the kitchen. The cooks are all standing around in confusion, having heard the commotion out in the dining room, but not knowing what the fuck is going on.

"Clear out!" Cal shouts at them.

They spook like deer, dashing into the alleyway behind the restaurant.

Cal pulls his gun out of his suit jacket, and I do the same with the one I'm wearing on a holster under my shirt. Cal's in a tactical stance, covering the entrance to the kitchen. I do the same with the exit.

"Do you want to stay in here?" Cal asks me.

"Let's get the fuck out before the cops come."

There's a chance that another shooter has the back covered, but I doubt it. I think we're dealing with the same motherfucker from the rally. A lone wolf.

To be sure, I pull on a white chef's coat and go out the back door, quickly scanning the rooftops on both sides of the alley to make sure we're clear. Then I cover the door from behind the trash bins while Cal and Aida come out.

We hustle down the alley to the restaurant's catering van. The keys are tucked under the sun visor, so it takes us all of five seconds to steal it. We roar down the alleyway, metal catering trays rattling around in the back.

"What the fuck was that!" Aida shouts, as we turn onto Franklin Street.

"That was a fucking sniper," Cal says through gritted teeth. He's

furious—and not because someone just tried to kill him. Because this is the second time a shooting has happened within ten feet of his pregnant wife. "You're going out of town until we find this asshole."

"No way!" Aida shouts. "I'm not—"

"This isn't up for debate!" Cal roars. His body is stiff with fury, his blue eyes like gas flame. "I'm not taking the chance of you getting hurt, or the baby."

"I'm staying with you," Aida tells him stubbornly.

Cal shakes his head "That's the worst place you could be."

That's when I understand the same thing Callum just realized. The sniper was never shooting at Yafeu Solomon—he was aiming for Cal all along. Cal was right behind Solomon on the stage. That bullet was meant for my brother-in-law.

"Who the fuck is this guy?" I mutter to Cal.

His face is ferocious. "That's exactly what I want to know."

I drive us east along the river, thinking.

I don't think it was a coincidence that the sniper waited for Cal and me to eat lunch together before he took another shot.

This guy has a grudge against us. Both of us.

But why...

I try to run through our list of mutual enemies. We definitely pissed the Russians off. After their last boss took a shot at Cal's little sister, Fergus Griffin plugged him with a full clip and left him to bleed out on the floor of the ballet.

On top of that, Nero stole a diamond from their safe deposit box at Alliance Bank—though I'm not sure if they know about that yet. The stone was a national treasure, stolen from the Hermitage Museum by the *Bratva* before we relieved them of it.

That diamond funded our South Shore project. We traded it to a Greek shipping magnate for cold, hard cash. I like to think that whole deal was done under the table, but the truth is that a forty-carat blue diamond is never going to remain entirely secret. It's too tempting to brag about and too easy to trace.

The *Bratva* are prideful and vicious. If they know what we did, they'll want revenge.

But a sniper isn't exactly their style. They like violent, bloody, graphic retribution. Something horrifying. Something that sends a message. Nothing as quick or painless as a .50-caliber bullet to the skull.

This hit was personal.

The bullet was aimed at Cal, but the message was for me. I stopped the first sniper shot because I saw his flags. This time, he didn't want me to see anything. He wanted my brother-in-law's head to explode right next to me, without me noticing anything at all. He wanted me to feel the guilt and shame of failure. He wanted to prove he's better than me.

But why?

That's what I'm wondering when I take Cal and Aida over to the Griffin mansion on the Gold Coast. Cal wants to talk to his father, and he thinks Aida will be safer there, surrounded by a full security team.

I want to use their computer.

I call Nero and tell him to meet us there. I'm not bad with research, but Nero's a fucking genius. He can break into places he has no business being—usually the databases that store blueprints and security schematics.

He pulls into the Griffins' drive at almost the same time as us, jumping out of his Mustang. His hair looks windblown and messy, though he didn't have the top down, and he's tucking his T-shirt back into his jeans.

"Did I interrupt something?" I ask him.

"Yes, you did," Nero says coolly. "So this better be important."

"It is," Aida tells him. "Someone's trying to kill Cal."

"Someone besides you?" Nero says.

"This isn't funny!" Aida snaps, her fists balled at her sides. I wouldn't believe it unless I saw it myself, but I think there might be tears in the corners of her bright gray eyes.

Nero looks similarly taken aback. If Aida can't see the humor in a situation, then it really must be serious.

We go into the Griffins' mansion, which is massive, ultramodern, and located right on the rim of the lake, with a widespread view of the water.

"What's going on?" Imogen Griffin says, watching us all pour into her kitchen.

While Cal explains the situation to his mother, Nero and I go upstairs to Callum's old office. He's still got a full computer rig up there but only one office chair.

"You take that one," Nero says, nodding toward the minuscule armchair on the other side of the desk. It looks like it was made for a twelve-year-old.

"I'm not gonna fit in that one."

"Well, you're gonna have to, because I need a decent chair to work."

"You need the right chair to type?"

Nero glowers at me. "That's why I'm doing it and you're not. If it were just typing, then you could sit right here and google away."

"Fine." I lean against the wall with my arms crossed.

"Quit sulking, or I'll send you to make a sandwich, too," Nero says.

"Try it, and see what happens," I growl.

Nero starts clicking away on the keys. It does look like fucking typing, but I get his point. It takes him about twenty minutes to access the military records I asked him to find.

"I want all the top snipers from the past ten years," I tell him.

Nero finds the data, printing it out on several sheets of paper.

While I scan down the lists of names, deployments, and commendations, Nero starts searching for recent sniper school graduates.

I'm not exactly sure what I'm looking for. Some of the names I recognize—guys I was deployed with in Iraq or that I knew by reputation. There's a certain level of competition between snipers in various units. If somebody was setting themselves apart, making a name for themselves, you were sure to hear about it, even if you weren't fighting in the same area or even deployed at the same time.

What doesn't make sense is that none of these people have any connection to Cal.

I feel certain this sniper is American and that he's got a beef with me. Call it a hunch, call it projection, but this motherfucker is trying to prove something to me.

I know who you are.

He left me that note, and not because he looked me up after he missed that shot at the rally. He *already* knew who I was, I'm sure of it. Which means he heard of the "Devil of Mosul." That's what the insurgents called me. And that's what some of the other soldiers started calling me, too. They thought it was funny—a badass nickname.

I never liked it. I preferred *Deuce*, which is what my own unit called me. Raylan gave me that nickname after I won a massive pot with pocket twos. I was thinking of my brother Nero back home when I bet—thinking how he would play the hand. I didn't expect to win. But for once I was lucky.

Maybe this other sniper knew me as the Devil, not Deuce.

Maybe he saw it as a challenge.

But why target Cal? Why not take a shot at me or someone close to me? Cal's my brother-in-law, but he's not the most obvious target...

That's when my eyes run over a name I recognize for a different reason.

Christian Du Pont.

And the puzzle piece clicks into place in my brain.

The Du Ponts are one of the wealthiest families in America. Pierre Samuel Du Pont started manufacturing gunpowder in the early 1800s. Their empire expanded into chemicals, automotives, agriculture, and more. They intermarried with the Astors, the Rockefellers, the Roosevelts, and the Vanderbilts. And they had children. So many children. More than four thousand descendants. Which meant that even their vast fortune was divided into too many pieces.

Callum went to a fancy private school with some of those descendants. In fact, his best friend and roommate was Jack Du Pont. Unfortunately for Jack, as a third cousin, twice removed, he inherited the name and nothing else. So he worked for the Griffins, as a driver and a bodyguard.

It was in that capacity that he smashed my little brother Sebastian's knee and ended his basketball career. So I can't say I was the biggest fan of the guy. But we put aside our differences when Cal married Aida. Part of the agreement was that we wouldn't seek revenge for Seb's knee.

While I never became friendly with Jack, I knew him. I even worked with him on a couple of jobs.

Until last year, when the Polish Mafia cut his throat.

Mikolaj Wilk kidnapped Cal's youngest sister, Nessa. He teamed up with the *Bratva* to try and shatter the alliance between the Griffins and the Gallos. They lured us to Graceland Cemetery.

Jack was there, helping Callum make the ransom drop. Nero and I scaled the cemetery wall, planning to flank the Russians and the Poles.

But Miko was too quick for us. He sent the Russians off with the ransom, and he fooled Callum with a decoy girl. When Jack chased after the money, one of Mikolaj's men crept up behind him and slit his throat. Jack bled out against a tombstone.

Ironically, Mikolaj and Nessa are married now. We've made a truce with the Polish Mafia and killed the head of the *Bratva*.

But that doesn't mean our feud had no casualties—there's no bringing poor Jack back from the dead.

I scan the entry for Christian Du Pont—graduated from the U.S. Army Sniper Course in Fort Benning, one year after me. Deployed to Iraq almost the exact same time that I was there.

He's got a decent record—a couple of commendations, three Bronze Stars awarded.

I never heard of him, though.

"Hey," I say to Nero, interrupting his search of the sniper school records. "See if you can find anything else on Christian Du Pont."

Nero starts searching that name. "I see his sniper school records. He beat your score on the Advanced Range Test."

"He did?"

I go over behind Nero so I can look over his shoulder at the screen. Sure enough, Christian beat me by just one point. He scored lower on Land Navigation, though.

"Is there a picture of him?" I say.

Nero pulls up a few shots of Christian in training, though he's hard to differentiate from the other soldiers in their helmets and gear. But then Nero finds his headshot, the one they use for military IDs.

"Holy shit," Nero says.

We stare silently. It's a bit like seeing a ghost. Christian and Jack Du Pont could be brothers—same strawberry-blond hair and narrow blue eyes. The only difference is that Christian is younger in his photo, and his hair is buzzed.

"What's their relation?" I ask Nero.

"Doesn't say here, obviously. But it lists his parents as Claire and Alexander Du Pont. And there's a picture of Alexander with his brother Horace on this Yale alumni site. So looks like Jack and Christian were cousins."

"So he blames us for getting his cousin killed. Why didn't he do anything about it until now?"

"He only just came home," Nero tells me. "Look at his discharge records—he was in Iraq until the start of the summer."

"Why'd he leave?"

"It says 'Chapter Five to Thirteen' dismissal."

"What the fuck does that mean?"

Nero types, then reads, "Separation because of personality disorder. A preexisting maladaptive pattern of behavior of long duration that interferes with a soldier's ability to perform his duties."

"That doesn't sound good."

"No, it does not. Especially because he was just about to break your one-day record in Mosul."

"You think he's in competition with me?"

"Yeah." Nero leans back in his computer chair, folding his arms across his chest. "I do."

"Show me his service record again."

Nero pulls it up, and I check the list of assignments, looking to see if Du Pont and I were ever in the same place at the same time. If we ever met without me remembering.

"We never served together," I mutter. "But look at this…"

I point to his last deployment.

"He was in the Forty-Eighth two years ago."

"So?" Nero says.

"That's the same unit as Raylan."

"Good," Nero grunts. "Call him up. See what he knows."

I do it right there and then, dialing my most recent contact number for my old friend, hoping it's still the right one.

The phone rings and rings, then switches to voicemail, without any confirmation that it's Raylan's number.

Taking a chance, I say, "Long Shot, it's me. I need your help. Call me as soon as you can."

I hang up the phone. Nero's still leaning back in his chair, thinking. "If this Christian guy knows what actually happened in the cemetery, he's not gonna be happy with Miko either."

"True. I'll call Mikolaj to warn him." I pull Kenwood's hard drive out of my bag, handing it to Nero. "I have another job for you—can you crack into this?"

"Probably," Nero says coolly.

"Let me know what you find."

"And what about Du Pont?"

I look at Christian Du Pont's picture on the screen: Cool-blue eyes. Intense stare.

"We can't wait for him to set up his next perch. We gotta find this fucker and flush him out."

33
SIMONE

When I get back to the hotel room, I'm hoping Henry will be working on his schoolwork with Carly. Alone.

No such luck—my parents are sitting right next to them in the little living room of the suite, my father reading, and my mother sketching in a leather-bound notebook.

They both look up as I enter the room wearing the *I Heart Chicago* T-shirt, sweat shorts, and flip-flops.

"Where have you been?" Mama asks, eyebrows raised. She obviously thinks I was abducted by a tour bus and forced to sightsee all morning long.

My father is more suspicious. His eyes flit to the high-heeled sandals I'm carrying. At least I had the sense to throw out the torn dress. Still, he knows a walk of shame when he sees one.

I'm not going to play their game, though. I'm a grown adult. I don't have to report back like I used to when I had a curfew. If I want to stay out all night long, that's my business.

Ignoring my mother's question, I say, "Carly, when you're finished with that paper, I'm going to take Henry out. So you can have the rest of the day off."

"Well, thank you." Carly grins. "I saw a sushi place down the road that was calling my name."

She's a lovely girl—freckled, friendly, always willing to accommodate my strange schedule. She's good to Henry, and I'll be forever grateful to her for that. But at the end of the day, I'm her boss, not her friend. Sometimes having her around just makes me miss Serwa.

"What should we do?" Mama muses. "We could all go to the park together!"

"Sorry," I tell her gently. "I need to spend some time alone with Henry today."

"Oh, of course."

"We could take him tomorrow, though," I say.

"Tomorrow would be perfect." She smiles.

I go into my own room to change my clothes.

My heart is beating rapidly. I've pictured having this conversation a hundred times, but it was always just theoretical—on some day in the distant future. Now that day is today.

Henry is already dressed. He's wearing basketball shorts and a T-shirt, with a Lakers cap crammed over his curls. He hates doing his hair, so he'll wear a hat instead any chance he gets. His clothes don't match exactly, but they're pretty close—he's getting better at picking outfits for himself.

I can't believe this autonomous human I made is already getting his own preferences in colors and patterns. He loathes the feeling of blue jeans and almost exclusively wears shorts or joggers. His feet look enormous in his sneakers. We already wear the same shoe size.

The sight of him hurts my heart. I love the way he slouches, the way he walks, his little sleepy half smile.

This is what I didn't know about having kids: it's like falling in love all over again. You love everything about that little person. They are more crucial to you than your own self.

I also didn't know that having Henry would bind me to Dante more than anything else. Every time I look at my son, I see parts of Dante: His height. His hands. His dark eyes. His intelligence. His focus. As Henry gets older, I have no doubt his voice will deepen like Dante's.

Henry is the greatest gift I've ever received. He's the best thing in my life. And it's Dante who gave him to me. We created this boy together—to my mind, the most perfect and beautiful human ever made.

This feeling is totally one-sided—Dante doesn't even know we have a son together. But I'll be grateful to him all my life for Henry.

I won't ever have a child with another man. I knew that as soon as Henry started to grow up. I saw how handsome and strong and determined he was. I felt this bizarre sense of destiny, that I'd created the most incredible son on the planet. The wonderfulness of Henry is proof that Dante and I are the perfect match. I could never have a baby with anyone else.

These are insane beliefs, I know that. But I can't help the way I feel. Dante is the one for me—the only one. And whether we'll ever be together again or not, nobody else will take his place.

How can I express this to Henry, in its simplest form?

He deserves to know his father. He deserved to know him all along. I was wrong to let it go on this long.

Still, after all this time, I'm not prepared. I don't know how to explain any of this to him. And I'm fucking terrified.

I take Henry down to the waterfront. We rent a couple of bicycles, and we cycle along the lakeshore for a few miles. The path is full of joggers, walkers, runners, cyclists, skateboarders, people with scooters, strollers, even Rollerblades.

I let Henry go ahead of me. The rented bikes are simple three-speeds, with wide handlebars and banana seats. It's hard to keep up with him while he's pedaling madly, the wind in his face. His hat flies off his head, and by some miracle, I manage to reach up and snatch it out of the air. Henry grins back at me, calling out, "Nice, Mom!"

When I see an ice cream stand up ahead, I tell him to stop. We order cones, then take them down on the sand to eat. Mine's strawberry cheesecake. Henry ordered vanilla, like he always does.

Henry licks his cone, which is already starting to melt. It's not warm out, but it's sunny.

"What did you want to talk to me about?" he says.

"How did you know I wanted to talk?"

"'Cause you wouldn't let Grandma come with us."

"Right." I take a deep breath. "Do you remember how I told you that your father lived in another country?"

"Yeah," Henry says calmly.

I told him that a few years ago. Henry had just started at the international school in Madrid. I assume the other kids asked him about his father because he came home and started asking questions, too.

"Well…he lives here. In Chicago."

Henry glances over at me, curious. He doesn't seem alarmed, but I can tell he's interested. "He's here now?"

"Yes. Actually…" My heart is hammering. "You saw him the other day. He was the man that came to our hotel room."

"That big guy? With black hair?"

"Yes."

"Oh."

Henry's still eating his ice cream. I'm watching his face, trying to interpret how he's taking this news.

He looks surprisingly unsurprised. Henry is extraordinarily calm. He doesn't often show strong emotion. I think he feels it, inside. But outside he's still water.

"Who is he?" Henry asks at last.

"His name is Dante Gallo."

"Did he come to the hotel to visit me?"

"No. He doesn't know about you yet. I guess…I guess I wanted to talk to you first."

Henry finishes the ice cream on top of his cone and starts chomping the cone itself. Our conversation isn't dampening his hunger any.

I ask, "Would you like to meet him?"

"I already met him."

"I mean, do you want to talk to him?"

Henry considers for a minute, chewing. "Yes," he says, nodding.

"It might change things." I bite the edge of my thumbnail. I haven't touched my ice cream at all, and it's melting out of the cone, dripping on the sand. I shouldn't have bought one for myself—I'm too anxious to eat.

"Change what?" Henry asks.

"Just…you might go to visit him sometimes. Or stay with him."

I know that concept might seem intimidating, and I don't want that to influence Henry's choice. But at the same time, I want to be honest with him. Telling Dante about Henry is opening a Pandora's box. I can't predict what will come of it.

Henry considers. "He *is* my dad? For sure?"

"Yes. He definitely is."

"Okay, then," Henry shrugs.

I sigh, releasing my shoulders from their tense position. That part is done, at least.

When Henry was little, he used to ask me questions about his father: *What's his favorite color? Does he have a dog? What does he look like?*

Now he asks me a different sort of question.

"Why doesn't he know about me?"

"It's complicated," I say. "You know I was very, very young when I had you. Your father was young, too. We were in different places then. Now…now we're older. Things have changed."

How much have they changed? Which things are different, and which have stayed the same?

I hope the answer is that Dante changed, and I changed, but the way we feel about each other has endured…

I'm afraid. Afraid that when I tell Dante the truth tonight, that will be the end of any chance we had of rekindling our relationship.

All I can really hope for is that he can love Henry despite it all. Because Henry deserves that, even if I don't.

34
DANTE

I tell Callum my theory that Du Pont was aiming for him, not Yafeu Solomon. Aida doesn't like that idea one bit. But Callum looks relieved to at least know who's been taking shots at him.

"You think he wants revenge for Jack Du Pont?" He frowns.

"Yeah, I think maybe he does. He was overseas when Jack was killed—so who knows what version of the story he was told by their family? They don't know what really happened themselves. When he looked into it, it probably appeared like we were covering it up. Like we might have been responsible."

"I am responsible," Callum says quietly.

"That's not true—" Aida tries to say, but he interrupts her.

"Yes, it is. Jack worked for me. I brought him to that ransom drop knowing it was dangerous, knowing it was probably a trap, knowing we were outnumbered and at a tactical disadvantage."

"Jack knew that, too," Aida says firmly. "He went along willingly."

Callum just shakes his head, not willing to forgive himself for getting his friend killed.

"So what now?" Aida asks me.

"You two need to lie low," I tell them. "You can't give Du Pont another chance to take a shot at you. That means no public appearances and especially no planned events. You give this guy advanced notice of where you're going, and the next time, he won't miss."

"It was only dumb luck he missed last time," Callum says darkly.

"Yes, you're welcome," Aida says. "For once your wife's clumsiness paid off."

She's trying to make a joke like she usually would, but her face looks strained and pale. Her hand is pressed against the side of her belly, like she feels a pain there.

"I don't want to wait for him to find me again," Callum says. "Let's track this fucker down and put an end to this."

"I've got an idea of where he might be," I tell Cal. "But I don't think you should come with me. Stay with Aida. Stay out of sight. We don't want to tip him off just yet that we know who he is. Let him think you're hiding out."

Callum scowls. I can tell he doesn't like the idea of hiding. He wants to take action just as much as I do. Probably more.

But Aida is clinging to his arm. She definitely doesn't want him stepping foot out of the house.

"Please, Cal," she begs, looking up at him.

Aida never begs for anything.

Callum looks as surprised as I am.

"Please," she says again.

"Fine," he agrees reluctantly. "I'll stay put for now. But call me the minute you find anything, Dante."

"I will."

I'm acting like I don't want to bring Cal along so we can lull Du Pont into a false sense of security. But the truth is, I want to keep him safe. If Aida were to lose her husband right before the baby was born, it would destroy her. For the sake of my little sister, I have to protect Callum, whether he likes it or not.

I'd like to take Nero along with me, but he's working on the hard drive I stole from Kenwood's house. Even though I don't think Kenwood hired Du Pont anymore, I still want Nero to crack the encryption so we can see what kind of shit Kenwood has been secretly recording inside his house.

Instead, I call Seb as I'm climbing into my SUV. He picks up after two rings.

"Hey, big brother."

"Hey. You free this afternoon?"

"Depends. What's on the menu?"

"Exploratory mission."

"Long drive?"

"Less than an hour."

"All right. Come pick me up—I'll text you the address."

Seb sends me an address I don't recognize. It turns out to be a fancy condo building in the Loop. I wait in the car, and he comes down five minutes later, looking flushed and slightly out of breath.

"What the hell were you doing?" I ask him.

He grins. "What do you think?"

"You got some girlfriend living there?"

"Somebody else's girlfriend who gets lonely from time to time."

"For fuck's sake—you taking lessons from Nero?"

Seb shrugs. "He's settled into monogamy. Aida's about to have a baby. And you're perpetually boring—so somebody's got to have a little fun."

He buckles his seat belt and flips on the music.

I know he's joking around, but he doesn't actually look like he's having that much fun.

Seb's been in a rough state the past year or two, since his leg got fucked up. He's been bouncing around, sometimes helping us with work, sometimes disappearing for days or even weeks while he drinks, parties, and does who the fuck knows what else. Apparently bangs girls who are already in a relationship.

He's unshaven today, messy-haired, his shirt looking like it hasn't been washed. Dark circles under his eyes. I had hoped he'd latch on to this South Shore project like Nero did, and it would give him something different to focus on. But Seb has never been as interested in the family business as the rest of us.

Still, he's useful for a job like today.

I had Nero look up all the properties owned by various members of the Du Pont family. There were three within a two-hour drive of Chicago. One was a little house in Evanston owned by MaryAnne Du Pont, now MaryAnne Ghery. Since she's a schoolteacher with three small children, I crossed that one off the list. The second was an apartment downtown owned by Charles Du Pont. That's a definite possibility. Charles Du Pont is only distantly related to Christian, but he's an older man who seems to live alone, so he could be hosting his third cousin. But the third place is the one I'll be checking out first.

It's a country estate outside of Rockford. It's actually owned by Irene Whittier, who's even more distantly connected to Christian than Charles Du Pont. But Callum pointed it out to me on the list. He said Jack used to visit the estate in the summer, to ride dirt bikes out in the hills and help his great-aunt Irene exercise the horses. Jack never mentioned if his cousin Christian used to go there, too. But it seems possible, since both were the same age and about equally related to Irene.

It takes Seb and me an hour and a half to drive there. It's funny how different everything looks once you get outside the city. Sometimes I don't leave Chicago for months at a time. I forget how flat the rest of the state is. In the city, the high-rises are like mountains, creating a sense of structure and direction, no matter where you are. You can always tell which way you're facing based off the river, the lake, and the buildings. Out here, you only have the sun for a guide. The roads and fields look the same in almost any direction.

The Whittier estate is large and beautiful but extremely run-down. The closer we get to the main house, the more obvious the chipped paint and broken shutters become. I don't see any other cars parked out front. Most of the windows look dark.

"What do you want to do?" Seb asks, eyeing those windows

nervously. I'm sure he's thinking the same thing I am—that we're not keen to get out of the car if Christian might be up in one of those rooms, rifle at the ready.

"Stay in the car," I tell him. "Watch out for me."

"All right," Seb says, his eyes on those windows.

I climb out of the Escalade, feeling exposed in the empty front yard.

The paving stones are cracked, and the yard is full of weeds. I feel a little better once I'm in the portico, sheltered from above at least.

I knock on the door, then ring the bell. There's a long wait, during which I hear a couple of dogs barking in the house.

At last, footsteps shuffle toward the door. I've got my gun in my hand, inside my jacket, in case I need it. When an old woman opens the door, I release the trigger and drop my hands to my sides.

"What do you want?" the woman demands.

She's stoop-shouldered and broad-faced, dressed in a man's cardigan and rubber boots. Her hair is so thin that I can see the pink scalp underneath. She's carrying a bucket of seed mix, and her boots are crusted with mud—it looks like she was feeding chickens out back when I rang the bell.

"Sorry to disturb you, ma'am," I say. "I was wondering if I could speak to Christian."

She squints up at me like I'm insane. "Christian?" she squawks. "Why in the hell would you come here looking for Christian?"

"I thought he might be staying with you," I say calmly.

"You thought wrong."

She goes to shut the door, but I stop it easily with the toe of my boot.

"Are you sure you haven't seen him?" I ask, trying to keep my tone polite.

"I haven't seen Christian in eight years. *Not* that it's any of your damn business, whoever you are. And not that I'd tell you if I had."

She peers up at me suspiciously. She might be old and frail, but she's sharp enough to know that a friend of Christian wouldn't come knocking unannounced.

Still, I think she's telling the truth. Her outrage at being bothered seems genuine enough.

I release the door. "Thank you for your time."

"'*Thank you*,' he says." She shakes her head. "As if I had a choice!"

With that, she slams the door in my face.

I'm not offended. I like ornery old ladies. They've lost the desire to hide how they actually feel about things, and I respect the honesty.

Irene is right to mistrust me. I've got no goodwill toward her grand-nephew. In fact, I have a hard time picturing a face-to-face meeting between the two of us where both walk away alive.

I've got to find him sooner than ever now because Irene might call him, if she's got his number. It won't take him long to figure out who the giant on her doorstep was.

I'm about to head back to the Escalade when I have one more idea. I text Seb:

One second. I'm gonna check around the back of the property.

Without waiting for him to respond, I cut around the side of the house. The property isn't fenced, so it's easy to cross Irene's grounds. However, I'm mindful of the dogs I heard barking in the house. I don't know if there are more prowling around, and I don't want to have to choose between shooting an innocent dog or losing a chunk of my leg.

Irene's grounds are mostly untended—several open fields, an old horse paddock that looks like it hasn't been used in years, a tumble-down barn, and a few wooded lots.

I'm about to turn back to the car when I see what I was looking for, way out on the edge of the grounds: a tiny cabin. Large estates usually have a house like that for the groundskeeper—out of sight of the main house but close enough to watch over the bulk of the property.

This one looks as untended and overgrown as the rest of the grounds. But I'm still going to look. It would be the perfect place to hide if you wanted to stay at your great-aunt's house without actually being bothered by that aunt.

Irene is too old to come tramping all the way over here. Christian could stay for months without her noticing.

As I get closer, I see a rear-access road winding up to the cabin. You could drive right up and park without being noticed. There's no vehicle around at the moment, but I think I see fresh tracks in the mud next to the cabin.

I approach the hut warily, looking for cameras. Looking for trip wires, too. We had plenty of those in Iraq. The insurgents used fishing line, transparent and set up at shin level. Almost impossible to see until you blundered right through it and set off an incendiary device. Or one of those damn bounding mines—you trip it, and the propelling charge launches the body of the mine three feet in the air, where it explodes, spraying fragments in all directions at just the right height to rip open your guts.

Yeah, we didn't love those.

We carried around Silly String to spray the area. The string would hang suspended on the trip wires without detonating the bombs. But I don't have any Silly String right now. So I just watch where the fuck I'm walking, carefully picking my way through the overgrown grass.

As soon as I get to the cabin door, I become certain that Christian has been here. I can see the arcing line through the dust where the front door swung open. I check all around the frame for booby traps, then turn the knob and step inside.

It's not locked. I doubt Christian expected us to figure out his identity, let alone where he was staying.

I can smell his soap, over the mildew and dust. He's been washing up at the sink. And sleeping in the cot in the corner. The bed is neatly made: the corners pulled tight and the blanket tucked in all around, military style. I'd recognize that technique anywhere— six inches between the top edge of the blanket and sheet, four inches of folded material, four inches from pillow to fold.

The cabin's been swept clean, and a single plate, mug, and fork sit drying next to the sink.

There's no TV or stereo—just an old cabinet against one wall, with a couple of moldy books and a battered teddy bear high on the top shelf.

I'm not interested in any of that. I'm drawn straight to the neat stacks of paper next to the bed. The folders and clippings are set atop an upside-down crate. I scoop them up, flipping through the pages one by one.

Chicago library welcomes Imogen Griffin as newest board member...

Fergus and Imogen Griffin are pleased to announce the engagement of their eldest son Callum, to Aida Gallo, daughter of Enzo and the late Gianna Gallo...

Callum Griffin voted in as alderman of 43rd ward...

Alderman's bodyguard slain in cemetery...

Dante Gallo arrested for murder of Walton miller...

Jack du Pont, son of Horace and Elena du Pont, was laid to rest at Rosehill cemetery on...

Shooting at Harris theater...

Gallo construction announces massive redevelopment project on south shore...

Old South Works Steel Plant rezoned for commercial and residential real estate...

Anti-trafficking rally hosted by freedom foundation to be held at Grant Park. Speakers will include...

I scan the headlines, the clipped articles, and the screenshots printed off social media. It forms a timeline of the Griffins and the Gallos over the past two years. A few things are missing—for instance, Christian apparently didn't link our families to the break-in at the Alliance vault, which was written about in the papers but only briefly, since the bank manager was careful to keep secret the more interesting details of the theft. And of course, nobody in the press knows who the thieves were.

The clippings mention the shooting of *Bratva* boss Kolya Kristoff at the ballet but not the kidnapping of Nessa Griffin that preceded it. The Griffins never made that information public. They always knew they'd have to get their daughter back on their own.

I'm sure Christian knows more than what he has here. To prove that point, the final paper in the pile includes a list of names:

Mikolaj Wilk
Marcel Jankowski
Andrei Wozniak
Kolya Kristoff (Russian boss)
Ilya Yahontov
Callum Griffin
Dante Gallo
Nero Gallo

All people who were present in the cemetery the night Jack died.

I don't know where Christian got that information. So I don't know if he's aware of who actually killed Jack. It was Marcel Jankowski who cut his throat, on Mikolaj's orders. But unless one of the people on that list has talked to Du Pont, he probably doesn't know if it was the Polish Mafia, the *Bratva*, myself, or my brother who struck the killing blow. I assume he knows that Cal wouldn't do it, but he obviously blames him anyway.

I'm so absorbed in the papers that I almost forget I'm in Du

Pont's cabin and he could come back any second. I almost jump out of my skin when the door abruptly opens.

"It's just me!" Seb says impatiently, shaking his shaggy hair out of his eyes. "What the fuck are you doing?"

"What are *you* doing?"

"I drove the car around so you wouldn't have to walk back."

"Oh," I say. "Thanks."

"What's all that?" He nods at the papers.

"Stalker clippings," I tell him. "Du Pont has been researching all of us."

"Oh yeah?" Seb grins. "Did he get my game against Duke where I scored forty-two points?"

"No." I shake my head. "You're not in here at all."

"Well, that's some bullshit."

I know he's joking but only sort of.

"Isn't he supposed to pin those all over the walls, connected by red string?" Seb says.

"Nah, he's the tidy type." I shuffle the papers together again so I can put them back where I found them.

"You can say that again." Seb eyes the tightly made bed. "Nothing lying around except that old bear."

He goes over to the shelf to pick it up.

"Don't touch anything!" I bark.

Too late—Seb has already taken it off the shelf. Most people wouldn't be able to reach up there without a stepladder, but Seb doesn't even have to tiptoe.

"It's heavy." He frowns. "Dante…I think it's a whattayacallit…"

I already realize even before he says it.

It's a nanny cam.

Seb points the bear at me. A little red light flickers behind the glassy left eye.

The camera is live. Someone's watching us right now.

"Put that back," I say quietly.

"He already saw us—"

"*Shh!*"

I hear a near-silent hissing noise. The sound of an aerosol releasing as chemical components mix.

"*Run!*" I shout to Seb.

We race for the door, reaching the splintered frame at the same moment. I shove him out ahead of me. Right as my hands meet his back, a force like a thunderclap hits me from behind. It throws me out of the cabin. Like a log caught in a flash flood, I slam into Seb, and we both go flying. We tumble down into dry grass while the cabin becomes a raging fireball behind us.

"FUCK!" Seb grimaces, clutching his leg. He came down hard on his bad knee.

"You okay?" I say, rolling over.

He groans something in reply, but I can't hear it because my ears are ringing. I'm gonna be deaf by forty if I keep this up.

"What?" I yell.

"I said are *you* okay?" Seb shouts back, staring at me wide-eyed.

I look down at myself. I've got a shard of wood the size of a pencil sticking out of my right bicep. As I move, I feel more pieces of wood and metal embedded in my back.

"God damn it."

I grab Seb and throw his arm around my shoulder, helping to hoist him up.

"I'm okay," he protests, but I can tell he's favoring his good leg.

"Let's get out of here. I'm sure that old bird's calling the cops."

Seb and I hobble back toward the SUV. I'm heartily glad he drove it over here because neither of us could run all the way back across the property at the moment. Also, if he hadn't come in and picked up that bear, I wouldn't have noticed the camera or heard the bomb activating. First thing I would have known about it was the whole place exploding around my ears.

Too many close calls. I can feel my luck running out.

As we climb into the car, Seb says, "You better go to the hospital."

"What time is it?"

"Five forty-two."

I'm all too aware that the last time something blew up in close proximity to me, I was late to meet Simone.

That's not happening again. Not even if the whole city goes up in flames.

"We'll just stop at a store," I tell Seb.

"What kind of store?"

I grimace. "One with pliers and alcohol."

35
SIMONE

I wait for Dante out in front of the hotel. I'm so nervous, I feel like I'm going to throw up.

I spent over an hour getting ready. The pathetic part of me hopes that if I look beautiful enough, he might forgive me. I know it's ridiculous, but when you spend your whole life trading off your looks, what else can you turn to in your most desperate moment?

I would do anything to go back in time and change the decisions I made.

But that's impossible. All I can do now is tell Dante the truth. The whole, entire, ugly truth.

I left Henry with my parents. They're playing board games.

I got Henry all ready for bed before I left, in clean pajamas, teeth brushed.

"Where are you going?" he asked, eyeing my dress, heels, and earrings.

"I've got to go out for a couple of hours," I told him.

"Are you going to see *him*? My father?"

I hesitated, then answered honestly: "Yes."

"I want to come with you," Henry said at once.

"You can't."

"Why not?"

"I have to have…an adult conversation with him. Just the two of us. But I think—I hope—you'll be able to meet him soon."

"I already met him," Henry said, his voice muffled by the toothbrush.

"I mean, meet him properly."

Henry spat into the sink, looking cross. "I want to come with you now."

"You can't," I said again, more firmly that time. Then I kissed him on the cheek, smoothing his hair. "Please be good for Grandma and Grandpa."

"I always am."

As I walked toward the elevators, I heard the room door crack open behind me. Henry poked his head out in the hall. I shot a look at him, and he retreated into the room, slamming the door behind him.

I hope he doesn't say anything to my parents about Dante, but at this point, it hardly matters. I know they want to keep Henry a secret from the Gallos. But that's not their decision anymore.

Dante pulls up in front of the hotel. He's driving a vintage convertible—probably one of Nero's—and he looks freshly showered. There are a couple of folded blankets in his back seat, the kind you lay out on the ground for a picnic or a nighttime visit to the beach. He dressed up and made plans for us, like it's a date. My heart clenches in my chest.

He jumps out to open the car door for me. I see he's moving stiffly, like his back is sore. Still, he pulls the door open, stepping aside to let me get in.

As he climbs back in the driver's side, I notice his right ear is bright red, and so is the back of his neck, like he got a nasty sunburn, despite the fact it's fall. A white bandage covers his bicep, only half-concealed by the sleeve of his T-shirt.

"What happened to you?" I cry.

"Noth—"

He was about to say, *Nothing*, before he stopped himself. He doesn't want to lie to me.

"I found out who's been shooting at us," he says. "His name is Christian Du Pont."

"Who's that?" I'm mystified. "Did Kenwood hire him?"

"No." Dante shakes his head. "Actually, he wasn't shooting at your father at all. It was Callum he wanted. And possibly me, too—I'm still figuring that part out."

"What?" This makes no sense to me.

"It's a long story." Dante sighs. "Basically, he blames the Griffins and the Gallos for the death of his cousin. And he's not exactly wrong."

"Did you find him today?"

"No. I found where he was staying. Found his little stalker journal. But then the whole place, uh, sort of blew up."

"WHAT?"

Dante winces. I know this is exactly the kind of thing he doesn't want to tell me. But, unlike me, he's never shied away from the truth about who he is and what he does.

"Are you okay?" I ask him, trying to recover my calm.

"Yes. Completely okay."

That probably isn't true, but he's trying to make me feel better. My heart is going a million miles a minute. This isn't how I expected to start our conversation.

"Anyway," Dante says, "I can tell you all about it over dinner."

"Actually—" I swallow hard. "Maybe we could just...go for a walk or something."

I don't want to be around other people for this. I don't want anyone to overhear us.

"Oh...sure," Dante says. "There's a park about a block down the street..."

"Perfect."

"I'll pull the car over here."

He parks alongside the curb, and then we climb back out again.

I'm not really dressed for walking. God, I really didn't think this through. I'm wearing strappy sandals and a black cocktail dress with a light blazer over the top. The air is chilly now that the sun has gone down. I wrap my arms around myself, shivering a little.

"Hold on," Dante says. He jogs back to the car, grabs his leather jacket out of the back seat, and puts it around my shoulders. "Better?"

I nod miserably. I don't want Dante to be kind to me right now. I can't stand it.

He can sense my nerves. He can tell something's wrong. As we turn into the park, he says, "So what did you want to talk about? Is it about your job? Because I could—"

"No," I interrupt. "It's not that."

"What, then?"

His huge frame walks heavily alongside me, each step audible on the paved path. I can feel his body heat even through the leather jacket wrapped around my shoulders. When I glance over at him, his black eyes are fixed on me with surprising gentleness.

I can't do it.

But I have to do it.

"Dante," I say, my voice shaking. "I love you…"

No, that's wrong, I can't start like that. It's manipulative.

He's about to respond in kind, but I cut him off.

"No, wait, just listen—I've done something. Something awful."

He's watching me. Waiting. He thinks that whatever I've done, it doesn't matter. He's probably picturing violence or theft or betrayal, something he's familiar with from his world. Something he would perceive as forgivable.

As always happens when I'm stressed, my senses become heightened. I can smell his cologne, his aftershave, his soap and deodorant, even the pomade in his hair. Under that, his skin and his breath and that hint of raw testosterone he produces in excess of a normal man.

These scents don't clash—they blend to make what, to me, is the epitome of masculine fragrance.

Besides that, I smell the dry, smoky scent of the crushed leaves under our feet, the raw pinesap in the air, and the car exhaust from the roads surrounding the park. Even the slight tang of lake water.

I feel the cool breeze on my face, the loose curls dancing around my cheeks, and the leather jacket heavy on my shoulders.

I hear the noise of traffic, of other people walking and talking in the park, though none very close to us, and the leaves crunching as we walk, and Dante's heavy tread.

All those things become a jumble in my brain, making it hard for me to think. I have to dissociate so I can get through this. I feel like I'm watching myself walk down the path. I feel like I'm hearing my voice speak, without any control over the words coming out of my mouth:

"When I left nine years ago…it's because I was pregnant."

The words come tumbling out so quickly that they slur together.

Dante falls utterly silent. Either because he doesn't quite understand me or because he's in shock.

I can't look at him. I have to keep my eyes on the pavement so I can finish what I have to say.

"I had the baby in London. Your baby. That was Henry. He's not my sister's—he never was. She helped me raise him. But he's your son."

Now I steal a glance at him.

The expression on his face is horrifying. It strangles the rest of the words I intended to say, cutting them off like a hand around my throat.

Dante's eyes are black pits in a pale face. His cheeks, his lips, his jaw, all are rigid with shock and fury.

I have to keep going. I have to finish while I have the chance.

"I hid him from you. And I'm so sor—"

"*Don't,*" he snarls.

I skitter back from him, stumbling on my heels. It's just one word, but it's saturated with hatred. He doesn't want me to apologize. He sounds like he'll kill me if I try.

Dante stands there, his shoulders hunched, his fists clenched at his sides. He's breathing slowly and deeply. He looks like he wants to pick up boulders and hurl them, uproot entire trees and break them over his knee.

I wondered, deep down, if he suspected Henry might be his son...

Now I see he had no idea. He never even considered it.

He never imagined I could hide something like that from him.

I'm terrified to speak another word. The silence is unbearable. The longer it goes on, the worse it feels.

"Dante..." I squeak.

His eyes dart up to me, his teeth bared and his nostrils flared. "HOW COULD YOU?" he roars.

That's it. It's too much for me. I turn on my heel, and I run away from him as fast as I can. I run back out of the park and down the sidewalk the block and a half back to the hotel.

I'm in heels, and Dante is faster than me—if he wanted to catch me, he could. But he doesn't chase me. Probably because he knows if he did, he might rip me apart with his bare hands.

I push through the doors of the hotel and run to the bathrooms. I lock myself in a stall and slump down on the tile floor, sobbing into my hands.

I've done something that can never be put right.

I broke Dante's heart nine years ago, and now I've done it all over again.

He was willing to forgive me for leaving. But this...he could never forgive this. I should have known from the start. I should never have let us get close all over again.

I cry and cry until my whole body aches. My eyes are swollen shut. I can hardly breathe from the mucus in my throat.

I wish I could stay in this bathroom forever. I can't deal with the mess I've made. It's too much. It's too awful.

Unfortunately, that's not an option.

So I pull myself off the floor, still shaking and weak. I go over to the sink, and I splash my face with cold water until the swelling goes down a little. Then I dry my eyes with one of the fancy folded hand towels in the basket, and I try to take a deep breath that doesn't end in another shuddering sob.

Finally, I'm ready to go back upstairs.

I take the elevator up, dreading making small talk with my parents. I have to say good night to them. And maybe put Henry to bed, if he hasn't gone already.

I go into my parents' suite, thinking they might still be playing board games with Henry.

The Ticket to Ride board is all folded, back in the box along with all the tiny plastic pieces. Mama is drinking a mug of tea, while my father sits on the couch, a biography open on his lap.

"How was dinner?" Mama asks. "That was fast."

"Yes," I say numbly. "Did Henry go to sleep already?"

"He did." She nods, taking a sip of her tea. "He didn't want to play anymore after you left. Said he was tired and went right to bed."

"I hope he's not getting sick," Tata says, turning the page of his book.

Henry never goes to bed early if he can help it. He must have been angry that I didn't let him come with me. I hope he wasn't crying in the other suite, too far away for my parents to hear him.

"I'll go check on him," I say. "Thank you for watching him."

"He's such a good boy." Mama smiles up at me.

"Good night, little one," Tata says.

"Good night."

I go through the adjoining door to our suite. Henry and I have our own separate bedrooms—I'm trying to give him his privacy, now that he's getting older.

Still, I tiptoe over to his room and crack the door, not wanting to wake him if he really is sleeping but feeling the need to check on him all the same.

His bed is a jumble of pillows and blankets. It's hard to spot him in all the mess. I open the door a little wider.

I don't see his curls or his long legs hanging out from under the blanket.

Heart in my mouth, I step all the way into the room and stride over to the bed. I pull the blanket back.

Empty. The bed is empty.

I try to hold back the panic, but it's impossible. I run wildly through the little suite, checking my room, the bathroom, and the couch in the sitting room, in case he fell asleep somewhere odd.

Losing all control, I yell, "*HENRY!*" several times.

My father comes into the suite, looking around in confusion.

"Simone, what—"

"Where is he? Did he come back into your suite?"

It takes too long, way too long, for my parents to understand. My mother keeps saying we should check all the rooms, even though I tell her I've already done that. My father says, "Maybe he was hungry? He might have gone downstairs looking for food?"

"Call the front desk!" I shout at them. "Call the police!"

I run down the hall to Carly's room, pounding on her door. Then I remember I gave her the night off—she probably went out for dinner or to see a movie.

I try to call her just in case. No answer.

I run to the ice machine, the stairwell, the elevators. I sprint down to the main lobby and check the commissary like my father suggested, praying I'll find Henry perusing the chocolate bars and chips. He does love sweets.

The only person in the commissary is an exhausted-looking businessman, trying to make an unenthusiastic choice between a banana and an apple.

"Have you seen a boy?" I ask him. "Nine years old? Curly hair? Wearing pajamas?"

The businessman shakes his head, startled by my wild shouting.

I run all the way outside the hotel, and I look up and down the busy city street, wondering if Henry would have come out here. He knows he's not allowed to wander around by himself, especially not at night. But if he was angry that I didn't bring him along to see Dante...

I hesitate on the corner, next to a white painter's van.

Is that what happened? Did Henry come downstairs to try to get another look at his father? Did he follow us...maybe all the way to the park?

The back of the painter's van opens.

I step aside to get out of the way, still dazed and looking in the direction of the park. Wondering if I should run over there or if I should call Dante instead.

At that moment, a cloth bag drops over my head. It's so sudden that I don't understand what's happening—I rip and pull at the cloth, trying to tear it off my face. Meanwhile, arms close around me, and I'm lifted off my feet. I shriek and struggle, but it's no use. In two seconds, I've been tossed in the back of the van.

36
DANTE

I'VE NEVER BEEN BLINDSIDED LIKE THAT IN MY LIFE.

Simone's confession was a four-hundred-pound linebacker, flattening me out of nowhere. I feel like I'm lying on the turf, gasping for breath, my whole head exploding.

Never, not for a second, did I think Simone might be pregnant with my child. We only had unprotected sex that one time at the museum. She was a virgin—I didn't even consider it.

But now that the idea is in my head, so many things are falling into place.

How she got sick those last few weeks we were together. How she seemed increasingly anxious about my job. How she demanded to meet up that night, and her horror when I arrived, bruised and bloodied and reeking of gasoline...

She was going to tell me that I was about to be a father. And then I showed up looking like the least fatherly person on the planet. Like the last man you'd ever want around your child.

I understand now.

I understand...but I'm not okay with it. Not one fucking bit.

She flew across the Atlantic. She disappeared out of my life without another word. She carried my baby for nine months, gave birth, and then RAISED MY FUCKING SON WITHOUT EVER TELLING ME HE EXISTED!

I'm so angry at her that I can't even think about it without going into a blackout state.

When Simone ran away from me in the park, I didn't try to chase her. I knew it was better for her to get away before I said or did something I'd regret.

I wasn't going to lay a hand on her—I'd never do that.

But if some stranger had walked up to me asking the time, I definitely might have murdered *them*.

I could never hurt Simone.

Even now, filled with bitterness and fury, I know that to be true.

And I am bitter. I'm as deeply, wretchedly bitter as a whole barrel of quinine. I'm soaking in it, pickling in it.

She stole our baby. She raised him on the other side of the world. I never saw him grow in her belly. I never saw him learn to crawl or walk. I never heard his first words. And most of all, I never got to raise him. Never got to teach him, help him, care for him. Instill in him a sense of his culture, his family, his heritage, from my side.

Instead, he was raised by Simone and Yafeu fucking Solomon, whom I still hate. Yafeu got his revenge on me, and I didn't even know it. I tried to take his daughter from him, and he stole my son instead.

I stalk back and forth in the park, radiating so much rage that people jump out of my way on the paths.

It's not enough. I need to vent some other way.

So I stomp back to my car, still pulled up in front of the hotel, and jump into the open convertible. There's a pile of blankets in the back seat—I planned to take Simone for a drive out to the dunes later. I thought we'd sit on the sand and look at the stars.

What a fucking fool I was.

I roar away from the curb, speeding recklessly down the road. Usually, I drive carefully—not today. Nothing but cold wind in my face can dash away the heat burning behind my eyes.

She betrayed me. That's why I'm so angry. I was willing to accept that Simone left me. I could forgive her for that. All the pain it caused me could be washed away by having her back again.

But this…nothing can give me those nine years back with my son.

Fucking hell, I barely looked at him!

He was right there next to me in the hotel room, and I hardly gave him a moment's thought.

I try to remember now.

I know he was tall, slim. He had curly hair and big dark eyes. A lot like Seb when he was little, actually.

Picturing his face, I feel the first stab of something other than anger. A fragile flutter of anticipation.

My son was handsome. He had an intelligent expression. He looked strong and capable.

I could meet him now, meet him properly.

That must be why Simone told me about him.

She didn't have to—I had no idea. She could have kept pretending he was her nephew.

I remember asking her about that at the Heritage House event. She turned red and hesitated before she answered. GOD DAMN IT! How could I have been so stupid? There must have been a hundred hints of what was going on, from nine years ago up until today.

If I had gone to London, I would have found out. I would have seen Simone pregnant. Instead, I stayed in Chicago, sulking.

I thought about chasing after her. Hundreds of times. I even bought a plane ticket once.

But I never went. Because of pride.

I told myself she didn't want me, that I couldn't make her change her mind.

I never considered that there might be another reason she left. Something outside the two of us.

Now I feel something else: a jolt of sympathy.

Because I realize how sick and scared she must have been. She was eighteen years old. Barely an adult.

I think of how much I've changed since then. I was impulsive, reckless, a poor decision-maker. Can I blame her if she made a bad choice, too?

If it even was a bad choice.

I think of all the stupid things I did over those nine years—all the conflict and bloodshed, all the mistakes I made…

Simone raised our son in Europe, away from all of that. He was healthy, happy, and safe.

I'm not glad she did it—I can't be.

But…I understand why.

I picture her standing in the park, shaking with fear of the thing she had to tell me. Why was she so scared? Because she thought I'd hurt her? Because she thought I'd steal her son?

No. If those were the reasons, she wouldn't have told me at all.

She told me…because she loves me. Because she wants me to know Henry after all these years and for him to know me. And because…I think…I hope…because she wants to be with me. She wants us to be a family, like we always should have been.

I'm driving down the freeway at a hundred miles an hour, barely having to weave through traffic because it's getting late and there aren't many cars on the road.

I've been driving toward the South Shore development without even realizing it. And now I know the reason why—not to see the high-rises or the empty construction equipment my workers have abandoned for the night.

I want to see her face.

I drive up to the billboard right as it flips from the ad for Cola to the one for perfume.

Simone's face hits me like a slap.

She's beautiful. Dreamy. And sad. Yes, she's sad, I know it. Because all those years, she longed for me, just like I did for her.

We were two halves of a heart, torn apart, bleeding and aching to be stitched back together again.

She loves me. And I love her. I can't stop loving her.

No matter what she's done to me, no matter what she might do in the future, I can never stop. I would cut off my hands for this woman. Strip the flesh off my bones for her. I can't live without her, and I don't want to try.

Forgiving her isn't optional. I have to do it. I can't exist without it.

Because I can't exist without her. I tried and I tried. It will never work. I'll get down on my fucking knees and crawl across glass for her.

As soon as I realize this, the anger seeps out of me. My chest is burning but not with fury.

It's love. I fucking love her. I always have and I always will.

I'm parked in front of the billboard. The dark night is silent all around me.

Until someone sits up in my back seat.

I shout and spin around, reaching automatically for the gun under the seat.

Then I see it's a boy.

My boy.

It's Henry.

He looks at me nervously, trying to flatten his curls with one hand. He bites his bottom lip with the unmistakable appearance of a kid who knows he's in trouble.

He's wearing flannel pajamas, navy blue with red piping. I can't stop staring at him.

I must have been fucking blind before. He's got Simone's smooth luminescent bronze skin. His curls are a little looser and a little darker. His face is longer, not square like hers.

In fact, it's just the shape that Seb's was at that age. He's got long lashes like Nero had, and Aida. But the actual color of his eyes... they're dark, dark brown. Almost black.

Just like mine.

I'm frozen in place, looking at him. Silent. Totally unable to speak.

"I…I hid in the back seat," he explains unnecessarily. "Sorry," he adds, wincing.

"It's okay."

Those are the first words I've spoken to my son.

His eyes dart away from me and back again. I can tell he's as curious to look at me as I am at him, but he's scared.

"It's all right," I say again, trying to reassure him. I don't really know how to talk to a kid. I had younger siblings, but that was different, and it was a long time ago.

"I wanted to meet you," he says.

"Me, too," I assure him. Then, as gently as I can, I say, "Does your mom know where you are?"

He shakes his head, looking guiltier than ever. "I snuck out," he admits.

He's honest. I'm glad to see that.

"We should call her," I say.

I hit the number on my phone. It rings several times, then switches over to voicemail. No response from Simone.

She's still upset over the way I reacted. She must not have noticed Henry's missing. She's probably crying somewhere.

I'm about to text her, but Henry interrupts me.

"How come you never came to visit me?"

I hesitate. I don't know what Simone told him. I could have discussed this with her, if I'd stayed calm instead of losing my temper. "What did your mom say?"

"She said you were far away."

"That's true. I was in the army for a while—did you she tell you that?"

Henry shakes his head.

"I went to Iraq. You know where that is?"

"Yes," he says. "I like geography. I learned a song about the hundred and ninety-five countries."

"They eat kebabs in Iraq. You know, meat skewered on a stick. Lamb or beef, sometimes fish or chicken. That was good, better than the barracks food. They had this stew called *qeema*, too."

"I don't like soup." Henry wrinkles his nose.

"I don't like soup either. But stew, if it's good and thick, that can be a real meal. I bet you get hungry, a big kid like you."

"Yeah, all the time."

"I was that way, too. Always growing. Are you hungry now?"

Henry nods, his eyes bright.

"What's your favorite food?"

"Ice cream."

I start the car engine again.

"I bet there's someplace open that serves ice cream…"

My phone starts buzzing next to me. I see Simone's name, and I pick it up, thinking she noticed my call or saw that Henry was missing. I'm planning to tell her that he's with me, he's safe.

"Simone—" I start.

A male voice replies instead. "Dante Gallo."

It's a smooth voice. Almost pleasant. Still, it sends a sick electric pulse across my skin.

I know who it is, though I've never heard his voice before. "Christian Du Pont," I say.

He lets a little hiss of air, halfway between annoyance and a laugh. "Very good."

He already knows I've figured out his name because he saw me in his little cabin.

I'm the one flooded with a nasty sense of shock.

Du Pont called me on Simone's phone. That means he has her phone. And he probably has Simone as well.

"Where's Simone?" I demand.

"Right here with me," he says softly.

"Let me talk to her."

"No…I don't think so…" he replies lazily.

My brain is racing, and so is my heart. I'm trying to stay calm, trying not to antagonize him. My voice is like a steel cable stretched to the breaking point.

"Don't you fucking hurt her," I growl.

Du Pont gives that huffing laugh again, louder this time. "She's a true beauty. Even more than her pictures. That surprised me."

I'm gripping the phone so hard, I'm afraid I'm going to shatter it in my hand. Henry is watching me, wide-eyed. He can't hear the other side of the conversation, but my expression is enough to terrify him.

"What do you want?" I ask.

"That's an interesting question," Du Pont says. I can't see him, but he sounds pensive, like he's leaning back in a chair, smoking a cigar, or just looking up at the ceiling. "What I actually want is impossible. You can't bring someone back from the dead, after all. So I have to look at other options. Other things that might make me feel just a little bit better…"

"Simone has nothing to do with this!" I snap.

Du Pont doesn't respond to my anger. He stays perfectly calm.

"I don't think that's true, Dante. You know, when I came here, I had a simple and specific purpose. Revenge. I planned to do it cleanly. Callum Griffin, Mikolaj Wilk, and Marcel Jankowski. Kolya Kristoff deserved to die as well, of course, but Fergus Griffin had already taken care of that. So I intended to work my way down the list and be done with it. But you got in my way."

"I didn't even know who you were trying to hit at the rally," I tell him.

"That's what's so interesting about fate, isn't it, Dante?" Du Pont hisses. "I knew all about you in Iraq, even before I ended up in a unit with your spotter. You were a hero to those boys. To me, too, when I first got there. I wanted to meet you. A couple of times, it almost happened. One night we were both at the al-Taji base, close enough that I could see your back, sitting in front of the fire. But something always intervened to keep us apart. And after a while, I started to think it was better that way. Because I wanted to beat your record. I thought it would be so much more fun if the first time we met face-to-face, I could tell you that. Then you went home, and I thought, 'Perfect. Now I know exactly what number I have to beat.'"

I'm in agony listening to this bullshit. I don't want to hear about this ridiculous military rivalry between us that existed only in his head. I want to know where Simone is right now. I need to hear her voice to know she's safe. But I'm clinging to every shred of patience I can muster, so I don't antagonize this psychopath more than I already have.

"Then they sent me back," Du Pont says, an edge of bitterness in his voice. "And I never hit that number."

I already know he wasn't "sent back." He was discharged for being a nutjob. But I doubt he's going to acknowledge that, and I certainly don't need to bring it up.

"I thought that was the end of our parallel paths." He sighs. "Until Jack died."

"You know *I* didn't kill him," I say. Not because I give a fuck what Du Pont thinks about it but because I don't want him taking it out on Simone.

"I know exactly what happened!" Du Pont spits. "Though it took me months to get the real story. You all covered your asses, kept your own names out of the papers. Let them write about Jack like he was a fucking criminal like the rest of you. When he *wasn't!*"

"He was Callum's bodyguard," I say, not asserting one way or another if that likewise made Jack part of the Irish Mafia or only an employee. "They were friends."

"*Friends,*" Du Pont sneers. "Do you drive your friends around like a servant? Do you open doors for them? Those Irish fucks treated him like a dog, when our family has ten times the pedigree of theirs."

There's no point arguing with him. I know Cal cared about Jack. He was devastated and guilty for months after Jack's death. It took him a long time to forgive Miko, even after Mikolaj married Cal's sister. Callum probably wouldn't ever have forgiven him, if Mikolaj hadn't saved Nessa's life.

But none of those things are going to make Du Pont any less angry at our families. We walked away from that battle with our families intact. Christian didn't.

"What do you want?" I repeat, trying to get him back on track. I don't give a shit about his grudge. I only care about Simone.

"It's not what I want," Du Pont says in a calmer tone. "It's what fate has decreed. It's brought us together again, Dante. It's making us face off against each other, just like we did in Iraq."

Following the musings of a madman is exhausting. I never knew Du Pont in Iraq. But he thinks we had some kind of rivalry. Like Nero guessed, it appears he wants to reignite it here and now. He wants the showdown he was denied.

"That's what you want?" I say. "A competition?"

"It seems the fairest way to resolve our conflict," Du Pont says dreamily. "Tomorrow morning, at 7:00 a.m., I'm going to release the beautiful Simone into the wild. I'm going to hunt her like a deer. And I'm going to put a bullet in her heart. I've told you the time, and I'll text you the place. You'll have your chance to try to stop me. We'll see whose bullet finds its mark first."

This is not at all what I thought he was going to say. My hand trembles around the phone. I would give anything to be able to reach through the space between us, to tear out Du Pont's throat.

"I'm not fucking playing games with you!" I shout. "If you put one fucking finger on her, I'll eviscerate every last Du Pont on this fucking planet, starting with that old bitch Irene! I'll track you down and rip your spine out, you—"

He's already hung up the phone. I'm shouting at nothing.

Actually, I'm shouting at my son, who's been watching me this whole time with his big dark eyes, his hands clenching the blanket still lying across his lap in the back seat.

I'm shaking with rage; I can't help it.

That lunatic has Simone. He wants to shoot her right in front of me tomorrow morning.

"Is someone gonna hurt Mom?" Henry whispers.

"No! No one's going to hurt her. I'm going to get her and bring her back. I promise you, Henry."

It's the first promise I've ever made to him.

I'll keep it or die trying.

37
SIMONE

I'm lying in the back of the painter's van with my arms zip-tied behind me.

It's extremely uncomfortable because Du Pont isn't driving carefully. Several times when he's taken corners too fast, I've gone rolling over, slamming into the wheel well or the ladders, buckets, and bags he's keeping back here.

He's taped my mouth, but I wouldn't talk to him anyway. It's irritating enough listening to him hum while he drives. His humming is atonal and repetitive. Sometimes he taps the steering wheel with his long fingers, not exactly in beat with the humming.

It stinks like paint and other chemicals back here. I'm trying to breathe slowly and not cry because if my nose gets stuffy again, I'm afraid I'm going to suffocate with this tape over my mouth.

I heard Du Pont's conversation with Dante. He wanted me to hear it.

It seems like some kind of sick joke. I can't believe he actually intends to let me loose, just to shoot me.

I don't understand why he's doing this. I didn't have any part in his cousin's death. I wasn't even in the same country at the time.

Though, of course, that's not why he kidnapped me.

He wants to torment Dante.

And he thinks the best way to do that is through me.

He doesn't know we just had a fight. Thank god for that. My body shakes as I realize that if he knew about the fight, if he knew what we were talking about…he would have kidnapped Henry instead. He doesn't know Henry is Dante's son. That's the only thing I can be grateful for right now. The only thing helping me to hang on to a semblance of calm.

I don't actually know where Henry is…but I have to believe he's safe, either with Dante or somewhere in the hotel, in which case he'll find his way back to my parents again. Wherever he is, it's better than the back of this van.

God, I've got to get out of this. I can't let this psychopath kill me. Henry needs me. He's so young, still. He's already lost Serwa; he can't lose me, too.

I look around wildly for something I can grab. Something I can use to escape. A knife, a box cutter, anything.

There's nothing. Just paint-splattered tarps and the duffel bags that I can't hope to unzip without Du Pont noticing.

Then he takes another corner, and I hear a rattling. A screw rolling around on the bare metal floor of the van.

It's difficult to reach it. I try to squirm in that direction an inch at a time so Du Pont doesn't see. I have to back toward the screw so I can grab it in my hands. Meanwhile, it keeps rolling away again, right when I'm about to reach it.

Du Pont starts fiddling with the radio. I take the opportunity to push against the wheel well with my feet, shoving myself back in the direction of the screw. My fingers skate over it, numb from being twisted behind me and bound too tightly with the zip ties. I grab the screw, drop it, then grab it again. I clutch it tight in my fist, glancing nervously up at Du Pont to make sure he didn't notice.

He finds his station and sits back in his seat with a sigh of satisfaction. Billy Joel pours out of the radio, loud and eerily cheerful. Du Pont starts to hum along, still off-key.

I grip the screw between my thumb and fingers. Twisting my hand the best I can within the bounds of the zip tie, I start to saw at the edge of the plastic, slowly and quietly.

38
DANTE

I take Henry back to my house. We drive up to the ancient Victorian, surrounded by trees that have mostly lost their leaves, the grass so thickly carpeted that you can barely see green between the drifts of red and brown.

The house looks creepy in the dark. The old woodwork has darkened with age, and the leaded glass barely shows the light shining from inside. There aren't many lights burning anyway—only the one in our housekeeper's room and my father's.

"Do you live here?" Henry asks nervously.

"Yes. So does your grandfather."

"Grandpa Yafeu?" He frowns.

"No, your other grandfather. His name is Enzo."

I drive into the underground garage. It smells of oil and gasoline, which aren't unpleasant scents under the right circumstances. At least down here, it's brightly lit and clean. Nero has always been tidy, if nothing else.

Henry looks around at all the cars and motorcycles. "Are these all yours?"

"Mostly my brother's. He likes to fix them up. See that one over there? It's sixty years old. Still beautiful, though."

"It looks funny," Henry says, looking at the bubbly headlights and boatlike length of the old T-bird.

"Yeah," I agree. "It does."

I take Henry upstairs into the kitchen. I'm surprised to see my father sitting at the little wooden table, drinking a mug of tea. He looks equally surprised that I've appeared with a child at my side.

"Hello, Son," he says, in his deep, rasping voice.

"Papa, this is Henry," I say.

"Hello, Henry."

"Hi," Henry says shyly.

"Do you want some tea or cocoa?" Papa says. "I think Greta has the kind with marshmallows…"

"I like marshmallows," Henry says.

"Let me find it."

Papa gets up from the table, shuffling around the kitchen, searching the cupboards. He never cooks anything himself, so he doesn't know where Greta keeps anything.

He's wearing a clean, pressed dressing robe over striped pajamas. His slippers are leather, likewise clean and new. My father never let himself go physically, no matter how destroyed he was after my mother died. He still put on his dress shirts with the French cuffs and the cuff links, his three-piece suits and his oxfords. He gets his hair cut every two weeks, and he spends thirty minutes shaving every morning.

The only parts of him that grew wild are his thick gray eyebrows, which hang heavily over his beetle-black eyes.

He was a big man, once—not as big as me, but physically imposing. He's shrunk over the past five years. Lost weight and height. He's as intelligent as ever, though. I've seen him beat Nero at chess, and that's not easy to do.

He finds the cocoa, then heats milk in a saucepan on the stove. We have a microwave, but he's never trusted it.

"Where did you come from, boy?" Papa asks Henry, not unkindly.

"We were living in Los Angeles for a while," Henry says. "Before that, we were in Spain."

"Who's *we*?"

"Simone is his mother," I tell Papa.

Papa pauses in the act of spooning cocoa into a mug. His eyes meet mine. He looks over at Henry, more carefully this time. I see his gaze combing over Henry's height, his hair, his eyes, the way he slouches in his chair at the little kitchen table.

"Is that right?" my father says softly.

"Yes." I nod. "That's right."

Papa pours the hot milk into the mug and stirs. He carries it over to Henry, taking the seat across from him.

"I've known your mother a long time, boy," he says. "I always liked her."

"She's famous," Henry says, sipping his cocoa. The foamy milk leaves a little mustache over his top lip. That makes him look especially like Simone—a very specific and precious memory I have of her, from a long time ago. I press my thumb and index finger into the inner corners of my eyes, turning away from him for a moment and breathing deep.

"She's a very beautiful woman." Papa nods. "I was married to a beautiful woman myself, a long time ago."

"Papa," I say. "I have to go out again. Can you take care of Henry? He can sleep in my room."

"I can." My father nods. "He doesn't look tired, though. Henry, are you tired?"

Henry shakes his head.

"What do you like to do for fun?"

"Do you have any board games?" Henry asks eagerly.

"I have a chessboard. Have you ever played chess?"

He shakes his head.

"I'll teach you. After we finish our drinks."

I step into the living room, out of sight of Henry and my father. For the hundredth time, I check my phone to see if Du Pont has texted me yet. Nothing. No missed calls either.

It's almost midnight. In seven hours I'm supposed to meet Du Pont god knows where, to stop him from killing the woman I love. And I don't have a fucking clue how I'm going to do that.

My phone rings in my hand, startling me so badly, I almost drop it.

"Yes?" I bark.

"You sound stressed, Deuce," a drawling voice says.

"Fucking hell, Raylan!" I cry, inarticulate with surprise.

"I got your message."

I don't stop to explain—I rush right in.

"I need to know everything you know about Christian Du Pont. He's a fucking psychopath. He—"

Raylan interrupts me. "Why don't I just tell you in person?"

"What do you mean?"

"I caught a transport into Chicago. We're on the tarmac right now. You can come pick me up, or I can take a cab."

"You're here? Right now?"

"You better believe it."

My whole body goes limp with relief.

I don't know what the fuck we're going to do. But if anyone can help me, it's Long Shot.

"Stay there," I say. "I'm coming to pick you up right now."

———

I pick Raylan up at O'Hare. He's unshaven, his hair so long that it's over his collar, his clothes and skin both filthy. He grins when he sees me, his teeth and eyes white against the dust.

"Sorry," he says. "I meant to shower somewhere along the way."

I hug him, not giving a fuck about the dirt, which puffs up in a cloud as I slap his back. "I can't tell you how much I appreciate this."

Raylan shrugs it off like it's nothing for him to have flown halfway across the world to help me out. "It's been too long, Deuce," he says.

It's funny seeing Raylan with his same old duffel slung over his shoulder, wearing his torn-up cargo pants and a battered pair of boots that I hope to god aren't the same ones we were issued in the field. His country-boy drawl is the same, and the grin that flashes across his face.

He looks a little older, though. He was just a kid when he worked as my spotter, freshly enlisted, barely over twenty. Now he's got the lines at the corners of his eyes that you only get from squinting in bright desert sun, and he's deeply tanned under the dirt. He's got a lot more tattoos, too. More than the military would have allowed.

He's not in the army anymore. He works for a mercenary group called the Black Knights. Sometimes they're employed by the army as private military contractors. Other times he disappears for months at a time on murkier missions that skirt the line between legal and illegal operations.

I don't give a fuck what he's been doing. All I care about is that he looks as sharp as ever—fit and practiced. I need a trained soldier at my side for this. My brothers always have my back, no matter what. But they don't know battlefield tactics. That's what I'll be facing in Christian Du Pont, not a gangster. A tactician. A soldier.

"You got your rifle in there?" I nod toward his duffel.

"Of course," Raylan says. "A couple of other goodies for us, too."

He throws his bag in the back of my SUV and climbs in the passenger seat.

"Goddamn," he says, sinking into the soft leather. "I haven't sat on anything but canvas or steel in a month."

"Probably haven't had any AC either," I say, turning up the air.

"You got that right." He sighs, tilting up the vent to hit his face.

"So," I say, once we're back on the road. "Tell me what you know about Du Pont."

"He got transferred into my unit about eight months after you went home," Raylan says. "Seemed all right at first. He wasn't exactly popular, but nobody disliked him. He was quiet. Read a lot. Didn't drink, so some of the other guys thought he was a bit of a stick. He knew his shit, though. He was accurate as hell—and hungry. He wanted to go out early and stay out late. Wanted to rack up his numbers. It was obvious he was competitive. And after a while, I could tell he was competitive with you, specifically. 'Cause he'd ask about you. Ask how many hits you'd gotten in a week or a month. What was the most you'd done in a day. You were kind of a legend by then. You know how army time is—six months is like six years, and stories get crazier every time they're told."

I nod, uncomfortable. I never liked any of that shit. I didn't like the attention, and I didn't want to be treated like some kind of hero. To me it was a job.

"Anyway, it started to get weird. If we hit all our targets, he'd start looking for someone else to shoot. He'd say, 'What do you think about those men down in the market? You think that one has a gun under his clothes?' Plus, he didn't like the Iraqi police or their ERD teams. We were supposed to be working with them, driving the militants out of Mosul. Each team had a segment of the Old City to clear. We were supposed to create escape routes for civilians to get out.

"Once we started closing in on the insurgents, we had them cornered by the al-Nuri mosque. They were using some of the civilians as shields. So the snipers were supposed to pick them off, out of the crowd. Du Pont shot four of the ones we knew were ISIS. But he hit six civilians, too. And I knew how accurate he was. There was no fucking way that all six were an accident. One was a pregnant woman, not even standing close to anybody else.

"Then, when the civilians started to run, we tried to guide them out through a gate on the west side. All of a sudden, the gate just fucking exploded. Whole thing collapsed, burying a dozen people, including a bunch of the ERD team. Du Pont said there must have been a grenade or a mine there. But it blew right as he took a shot over by the gate. I think he planted the bomb himself, and then I think he fucking set it off with that shot. Couldn't prove it, though. We were on opposite sides of the perch, and I didn't actually see what he was doing.

"There was an inquest. He was on notice. For a while he was careful. He got paired with a different spotter. And that guy was a piece of shit, too. His name was Porter. If Du Pont was still fucking around, Porter was covering up for him. They'd go off to their assigned position, and then they'd come back hours later, and what they said they were doing never quite matched up with what we'd seen them doing.

"Finally, a girl got attacked—"

"What girl?" I interrupt.

"A local girl. She worked for us as a translator. We found her body burned with gasoline in an empty house. Dress pulled up around her waist. Couldn't prove it was Porter and Du Pont who did it—but that was the last nail in the coffin. They both got the boot. Barely escaped court-martial. Discharged and sent back stateside. We were all relieved to see them go. I left the army and went private contractor a few months after."

I nod. It's about what I expected, reading Du Pont's file.

I fill Raylan in on what's been happening here. The rally, the shot at the restaurant, and what Du Pont said when he called me on Simone's phone. As I talk, it starts to rain—fat droplets spattering against the windshield and breaking apart.

"Wait…" Raylan sneaks a look at me. "Are you talking about your girl from way back?"

I once told Raylan a very brief, highly edited version of what happened between Simone and me. But Raylan is a sneaky fucker. He uses that Southern charm and casual manner to get all kinds of information out of you, bit by bit, when he's got all the time in the world at his disposal. I'm guessing he formed a fairly accurate picture of the situation, over time.

Now he's trying to hide his smile and his amazement to hear that Simone and I have reconciled. Sort of.

"I thought you were looking slightly less miserable than usual," Raylan says. "The one that got away is back again…"

"She was," I say gruffly. "Now she's with that murdering piece of shit."

"We'll find her," Raylan says seriously. "Don't worry, Deuce."

But I am worried. Very fucking worried. "He's smart, you said…"

"Yeah," Raylan admits. "Very fucking smart."

"He'll have the advantage, wherever he wants to meet."

"Yup. But there's two of us and only one of him."

I think about that. Think how to best use it to our advantage.

"Let me see what you brought in that bag," I say.

39

SIMONE

BEFORE I CAN SAW THROUGH THE ZIP TIE WITH THE SCREW, DU Pont turns down a long gravel road, which bounces me around in the back of the van like the last kernel in a popcorn machine. I think every inch of my body is going to be bruised by the time we stop. I cling tight to the screw with my sweaty fist, not wanting to lose it.

I can't see out the back of the windowless van, but I know we've been driving in a straight line down some highway for hours, and now we've turned off onto this side road that definitely isn't paved. We must be in the middle of nowhere.

At last, the van rolls to a stop, and Du Pont gets out. I hear his crunching footsteps coming around the side of the van. He opens the back doors, seizes me by the ankle, and hauls me out.

He sets me down outside the van, barefoot on the gravel. One of my strappy sandals came off while he was driving, and I kicked off the other, thinking bare feet were better than heels. The rough stones poke my feet, and the ground feels cold. It's still night, but the sky is beginning to get that gray hue that shows dawn isn't far off.

Du Pont looks me over, expressionless. He has a strange sort of face. Not bad looking—in fact, in many ways, he should be handsome. He's got a lean, symmetrical face. A straight nose, thin lips, blue eyes. But there's a fire in his eyes that reminds me of preachers, and zealots, and people who bring up conspiracy theories whenever they've had a drink or two.

"Thirsty?" he says.

His voice is like his face. Low, soft, almost pleasant. But fizzling with a strange energy.

Dante's voice, while rough enough to send shivers over my skin, always has the ring of honesty. You know he means what he says. Du Pont is the opposite—I don't trust anything that comes out of his mouth.

Like this offer of water. I don't want to drink anything he gives me—it could be drugged or poisoned. But my mouth is parched from all the crying I did in the bathroom right before Du Pont grabbed me. My head is throbbing, and I really do desperately need a drink.

Du Pont can tell, without me saying anything.

"Come on," he urges. "Can't have you passing out."

He uncaps a water bottle and approaches me. Without meaning to, I shuffle backward over the rough path, not wanting him to get so close to me.

Du Pont smirks, grabbing me by the shoulder and holding the water bottle to my lips. He watches as I take a few hesitant gulps. Some of the water leaks out and runs down the sides of my mouth, down my chin, dripping onto my bare chest and down the front of my dress.

Du Pont just watches, making no move to help mop it up. "Better?" he says.

The water tastes heavenly, despite being lukewarm from the long drive in the van. But I don't want to give him the satisfaction of relief or gratitude.

Du Pont turns around and closes the van doors. He's pulled the van into a little offshoot between the trees—not a road but a cubby of sorts. Now he's tugging something over the whole van. It looks almost like a big fishing net, covered in leaves and moss. He throws a couple of branches on top, and the van becomes camouflaged, enough that you'd drive right past it without noticing.

While Du Pont is fucking around with the net, I've got the screw out, and I'm madly sawing at the last bit of plastic holding the zip tie together. Finally, it snaps. The second it does, I sprint off down the road. I'm running full out, ignoring the rough ground cutting my feet. With my hands free, I pump my arms, using the full length of my legs, not allowing myself to notice how stiff and sore I am from the long ride in the back of the van.

I'm a good runner. I regularly do eight miles on the treadmill. I'm fast, and I can go a long time.

And right now, I'm fueled by the adrenaline coursing through my veins like battery acid. I might be running faster than I ever have in my life.

I can't waste a second looking back, but I think I'm getting away. I don't hear anything behind me. Maybe Du Pont is trying to clear off the van so he can turn it around to chase after me. As soon as I hear the engine, I'm going to leave the road and run into the woods.

That's what I'm thinking when he slams into me.

He tackles me to the ground, taking out my knees and wrapping me in his arms so we crash together, my arms already pinned to my sides and my legs trapped between his.

It's almost gentle, the way he takes me down. He makes sure I don't hit my head or skin my face raw.

I don't know how the fuck he caught up to me like that—silently, without me even knowing he was closing in. He leapt on me like a lion, overpowering me instantly.

I shriek and struggle, trying to wrench my way out of his arms. It's impossible. They're locked around me like steel. I start to sob, because I realize that's how it's going to be when he lets me loose. He's faster and stronger. He's going to kill me so quickly that I won't even see it coming.

I can smell his aftershave and the light scent of his sweat. I hate it. I hate being this close to him. I hate being touched by him.

Du Pont doesn't seem to mind it at all. He lies there, holding me as tightly and tenderly as a lover, until I stop struggling. Then he stands, hauling me up, too.

"Don't do that again," he says. "Or I won't be so gentle next time."

He pushes me back down the path, forcing me to walk ahead of him. We trudge along. It seems to take forever just to reach the place where the van is hidden. Then he keeps me walking, over several miles of stony ground. The road turns into a path. The path becomes steep and winding.

Eventually, we come to a cabin. It looks like it was cozy and woodsy once—made of logs, with tight, even shingles over the roof. There's a little porch out front, with a single window next to the door. I see a water pump standing in the yard.

Du Pont pushes me inside.

"Sit." He points to a dusty old couch.

I sit down on it.

Du Pont picks up a large metal tub and a kettle, then goes outside for a second. While he's gone, I look wildly around for something useful. A knife or a gun, or even a heavy paperweight. There's nothing—the cabin is practically empty. Thick dust blankets every surface. Cobwebs hang across the window and rafters. It's obvious that no one has been here in a long time.

I can hear the pump working next to the house.

Du Pont returns, lugging the metal tub and kettle. He sets the tub down in the middle of the floor and the kettle on the hopper. Then he strikes a match, setting a fire inside the grate.

I can feel the heat spreading from the hopper almost at once. It makes me realize I was shivering on the couch, my arms wrapped tight around my body. I'm only wearing the skimpy cocktail dress, nothing else, and it's cold out here in the woods.

Du Pont leans against the wall, his arms crossed, watching me.

He's silent and still.

I don't like the look of the metal tub full of water. I'm afraid he's going to use it to torture me—holding my head under the water until I tell him whatever he wants to know.

Instead, Du Pont waits for the kettle to boil, and then he dumps it into the cold water in the tub, warming it. He pours in some powdered soap, swishing it around with his hand to mix it in.

"Get in," he says.

I stare at him.

"Wh-what?"

"Get in the tub. Wash yourself," he orders.

He holds out a washcloth, threadbare but reasonably clean.

I don't want to get in the tub. But I know he can force me to do it if I refuse.

I walk over to the tub, planning to wash my face and hands.

"Take off your clothes," he barks.

I pause beside the tub, my stomach churning.

Slowly, I reach behind me and unzip the dress. I slip it off, stepping out of it. Then I take off my underwear, too.

Du Pont watches me, his eyes bright but face totally still.

I step into the tub. It's too small for me to sit, so I have to stand.

"Wash yourself," Du Pont orders again, holding out the washcloth.

I take the cloth. I dip it into the water and start using it to soap down my arms.

"Slower," Du Pont says.

Gritting my teeth, I slowly wash my arms, shoulders, chest, belly, and legs.

Du Pont instructs me how to do it. He tells me to wash between my fingers and toes, between my thighs, even the bottom of my feet. The water is reasonably warm, and the soap smells fresh and clean, like laundry detergent. But it's incredibly uncomfortable doing this under his eye, especially because I'm still shivering, standing out of the water, and my nipples are hard as glass.

Just when I'm hoping it's over, Du Pont tells me to turn around. He takes the cloth, and he starts washing my back.

The tenderness with which he scrubs me is utterly disturbing. The cloth slides lightly over my skin, making my flesh crawl. At least he doesn't touch me with his hands—only the washcloth.

He slides the cloth down between my ass cheeks, and I jerk away from him, jumping out of the tub.

"Don't touch me!" I snap. "If you try to...if you try to do anything to me, I'll fight you. I'll bite you and claw you and hit you, and I know you're stronger than me, but I'm not going to stop. You'll have to kill me right now and spoil all your psycho plans."

Du Pont looks amused. "I'm not going to hurt you, Simone," he says in a bored tone. "You're exactly right. That would spoil all the fun. I want you in your best condition for the hunt."

I don't know how he can say those words with such a calm, pleasant expression on his face. His thin lips are turned up at the corners in a hint of a smile.

"Get dressed," he says. "Then you can have something to eat."

He holds out a dress to me. Not the one I was wearing before—this one is light cotton, loose and soft. It's pure white. I shudder as I pull it over my head. I know why he chose this—it will be like a white flag in the woods. Giving away my position wherever I go.

Du Pont takes a loaf of French bread out of his duffel bag. He tears it in two, holding out half to me.

"Eat."

40
DANTE

At 4:40 a.m., my phone buzzes with a text message from Simone. It's not really from Simone, of course.

It's a pin, sending me a location.

A spot in the Wisconsin woods, two hours and twenty-eight minutes from where I'm currently located.

Raylan and I start speeding in that direction immediately.

I have to go ten over the limit or faster. Otherwise we won't make it there by 7:00 a.m.

"Watch out for cops," I say to Raylan, through gritted teeth. I don't have a second to spare for getting pulled over.

"How do you want to do this?" Raylan asks me.

"We have to triangulate. Try to figure out his location. Then close in on him from two sides."

"You don't know what he's got set up. He could have traps. Mines. Other people."

"I don't think there's anyone else." I shake my head. "You said he didn't have friends in the army. I doubt he has any now. The hotel room above the rally, and the shooting at the restaurant…that was one person. Same with his little shack outside his aunt's house."

"One person on their own ground still has the advantage," Raylan says.

I know he's right.

"If you see Simone, you get her out of there," I tell Raylan. "Don't wait for me."

"Yeah, likewise," Raylan says. "Though I really don't want to get shot by Du Pont. He was such a little creep. It would be embarrassing, you know?"

I snort. "I'll keep that in mind."

"Now, if it was a bear or a wolf that got me..." Raylan says, looking around at the woods on either side of the road. "That would be cool, at least."

"There are no wolves in Wisconsin."

"Oh, there damn well are, my friend. Big gray wolves. Not as big as the ones in Alaska, but still twice the size of a husky."

We crossed over the border into the other state about a half hour ago. I know it's probably mostly in my head, but the woods look thicker and darker here, more menacing. I don't know this area. I don't know what Du Pont has planned.

All I know is that he's determined to use Simone to hurt me.

He couldn't have picked a better target.

When I was in the army, I was never afraid. I was too unhappy for that. I didn't want to die, but I also didn't care that much if I did.

Now, for the first time, I have a vision of a possible future. Me, Simone, and Henry. Living in Chicago or living in Europe, I don't give a fuck which. All I care about is that the three of us could be together.

Nothing is more important to me than the idea of us together in the same room, as a family. I haven't experienced that, not for a moment. I won't let Du Pont take that away from me.

I have to see Simone. I have to tell her I forgive her. And most of all, I have to save her.

If I have to choose...if only one of us makes it out of this...it's going to be her.

Raylan and I are speeding closer to the pin. The closer we get, the less we talk. We've already run over our potential strategies. We won't know exactly what to do until we get there, until we see what the fuck Du Pont is up to.

For now, all we can do is mentally prepare ourselves.

It's 6:22. The edges of the sky are beginning to turn deep purple instead of black. It'll be sunrise, soon.

As we drive on, the sky lightens a little more.

Thank god it stopped raining. The ground is still wet and muddy, though. The pavement is dark with silvery patches of standing water.

At last we come to the place where the map tells us to turn right. We're leaving the empty two-lane highway, turning onto a winding dirt road leading into the woods. The pin looks to be about eight miles up.

I'm on edge as we slowly creep up the rough road. The road becomes fainter and fainter as we go, so rocky that I wouldn't be able to drive up it at all in a normal car. Luckily, I brought the Escalade. It bumps and jolts us but never bottoms out.

Raylan and I are watching for anything in the road, tense in case someone ambushes us from the close-pressing woods on either side. There's not much we can do to prevent that. We have to keep moving forward.

When we're about a mile from the pin, I stop the car. It's 6:41.

"Better get out here," I say to Raylan. "The pin is a mile that way." I point northeast.

There's no cell service out here. Raylan won't be able to call me or to follow the map. I lost connection a mile back, and I'm just going off memory now.

"I'll hoof it," Raylan promises me. "I might even beat you there, with how rough the road is."

"I doubt it." I laugh.

"Just try me."

He throws his duffel over his back. He's got his Dragunov rifle in there, along with one of my old guns. A couple of smoke grenades, rope, a bowie knife, and some old clothes of mine.

"See you soon, Deuce," he says.

"See ya, Long Shot."

We didn't call Raylan that because he could shoot from a distance, though he certainly can. We called him that because he's the eternal optimist—always thinking he can get the job done, whether there's a real chance or not.

That's why he's come along with me on this suicide mission. He believes we can grab her and get out alive. I hope he's right for once.

I watch Raylan disappear into the woods, and then I keep driving up the winding road. Eventually, it disappears entirely, the trees and bushes crowding in so close and the path becoming so steep that I have to abandon the SUV and continue on foot. I've got my own rifle over my shoulder, and a knife in my belt. Extra ammo packs, and a light Kevlar vest under my shirt.

It's damn cold. The air is wet from the rain, and my feet sink silently in the spongy ground. The only sound is from the last droplets dripping from the trees.

At five minutes to seven, I come to a log cabin. There's a pump out front. No light shines from the single window. I'm about to approach, when I see an arrow scratched in the dirt, pointing east into the woods. Directions from Du Pont.

I go east, but not directly along the path of the arrow. I skirt around, heading in the same direction by my own path. I'm not going to walk willingly into Du Pont's trap. Not out in the open.

The sun is rising, tinting the sky orange through the tall pines. I can see the light, but I don't feel any warmth from it yet. Only jogging through the woods is keeping me warm.

After another half mile, I come to the top of a ridge. Down below, I see an open meadow. The grass is yellowed and dry, thick with morning mist. Sunlight is just starting to extend across the open ground.

At exactly 7:00 a.m., a shot rings out.

My heart clenches in my chest. For a second I think Du Pont

shot Simone exactly at seven—that he brought me all the way out here just so I could hear it myself, without any chance of saving her.

Then I see what looks like a white bird flying across the field. It's Simone—running as fast as she can, her long legs whipping back and forth under her skirt.

I want to call out to her, but she's too far away to hear. And I don't want to draw attention to her or to myself. Instead, I look around for any sign of Du Pont, terrified that any moment I'll hear another shot, and Simone will drop.

Thinking the same thing, she starts to run in a zigzag.

"That's right," I mutter under my breath. "Don't make it easy for him."

Then, even better, she comes to a thick stand of grass and drops out of sight.

"Good girl," I breathe.

I head down the ridge, trying to circle around to where Simone might be going, while watching for any sign of Du Pont.

41

SIMONE

CHRISTIAN DU PONT DRAGS ME DOWN TO THE EDGE OF A MEADOW. I'm still barefoot, now wearing the white cotton dress and nothing else.

I'm freezing. The cold seems to leach out of the ground, into my feet, and then up my legs. Soon my toes are so numb, I can barely feel them. The bottoms of my feet, already scratched from my run down the road, are punctured by twigs, pine needles, and stones. The numbness is almost a blessing.

The sun is starting to come up. I'm glad I won't be fleeing through the woods in the dark, at least. Though maybe that would have been better. The light will make it easier for Du Pont to see me. He's got his rifle slung over his back, plus several handguns on his person, a huge wicked-looking knife, and god knows what else.

He's changed his clothes, too—he's wearing some weird shaggy brown suit now: a onesie that covers him head to toe, with a hood hanging down his back.

His skin looks pale and blotchy in the early-morning light. His eyes glitter at me like two chips of ice.

I have nothing. No weapons. Not even a coat.

"You think this is fair sport?" I say to him. "You're geared up like G.I. Joe, and I'm empty-handed?"

"Don't worry," Du Pont says softly. "You have your champion."

He positions me at the edge of the meadow. "All right," he says. "Go."

I turn to face him, my arms crossed over my chest. "What if I refuse?"

He pulls one of the handguns out of his belt, cocks it, and points it directly at my chest.

"That would be a very bad idea."

"You'll just shoot me right now?"

"I could shoot you in the palm," he says, as casually as you might order a drink at a restaurant. "You can still run with half your hand blown off."

Reflexively, I clasp my hands together.

"Get going," he hisses. "Three…Two…"

I turn and flee.

Before I've taken two steps, I hear the gun explode behind me, and I think that's it, he's already shot me in the back. Then I realize I'm still running, so he must have fired up in the air instead.

I sprint across the meadow, the dry grass whipping my legs.

A cloud of gnats rises as I disturb their rest, and a startled bird flies off in the opposite direction. My chest is burning, and I can taste blood in my mouth. I'm running hard, the cold morning air burning my lungs.

I can't see much on either side of me because of the fog. I have no idea what Du Pont can see. I'm cognizant that at any second, I might feel a blinding flash of pain and then nothingness, if he's already taken aim at my head.

Well…I'm not going to make this easy for him. I start darting back and forth, hoping that will make it harder for him to track me. Knowing I'm probably not fast enough to avoid his scope.

Then I come to a place where the grass is thick and wet and marshy, almost chest high. I drop into it and start to crawl, hoping he can't see me in here, that he won't be certain which direction I've gone.

I find a wet channel in the grass, almost a stream. I wedge myself into it, hoping I can crawl along it without shaking the grass.

It's freezing cold and muddy. I'm getting mud all over my arms and the front of the dress.

That gives me an idea.

This dress is a white banner, drawing attention to me everywhere I go.

I remember how Du Pont camouflaged the van with a net, leaves, and branches.

I strip off the dress so I'm naked again. I wad it up and hide it in the mud. Then I keep crawling. While I crawl, I deliberately get as muddy as possible. I smear dirt in my hair and on my skin.

I'm coming to the edge of the meadow. I look for the deepest, darkest, thickest brush. Somewhere I can hide. Somewhere I can move unseen.

I'll have to get out of this channel and run across open ground. I know as soon as I break cover, Du Pont might shoot me. But if I stay where I am, he's sure to track me down. He saw where I dropped. He knows I haven't moved far.

I take three deep breaths to steady my racing heart.

Then I burst up from the grass and run toward the woods. I drop and slide under the bushes like a baseball player sliding into home plate. Right as I drop, a bullet whistles over my head, embedding itself in the trunk of an elm.

I lie still in the thick brush, gasping for breath. Waiting for more bullets.

None come. He missed me. And he can't see me now.

But I'm sure he's already chasing me.

I wait thirty more seconds, catching my breath. Then I jump up and start running again.

42

DANTE

When Simone breaks cover, my natural inclination is to watch and see where she runs. But I force myself to look in the opposite direction, to search for Du Pont instead. Sure enough, I see a muzzle flash over on the far side of the meadow as he fires at her.

I shoulder my rifle, searching for him through the scope. I know where he shot from. I just have to find him.

I can't see anything. I'm looking, looking, my eyes straining for the slightest motion. Then I spot not a figure but a shape. The motherfucker is wearing a ghillie suit. It's brown and shaggy, blending in perfectly with the dark, wet woods.

I fire at him, a fraction of a second too late. I didn't have his exact position. I missed.

He's melted away into the woods, circling around to where Simone went down. He's closer to her than I am. He'll get there faster.

I sprint around the opposite side of the meadow, praying he didn't hit her with that shot, praying she can keep away from him a little longer.

As I'm running, I'm jumping over logs and brush, pushing my way through the forest where there isn't any path. I'm trying to be quiet, but I've got to be fast, too.

What I'm not doing is paying attention.

As I run through the woods, I hit something that feels tense and springy. Before I know what's happening, a massive log comes swinging down at me, hitting me on the head and shoulder. It throws me through the air, slamming me into a pine.

It's so sudden that I hardly know what's happening. I black out for a second, coming around to a ringing in my ears and hot wet blood running down the side of my neck.

My right arm hangs down, unresponsive. That fucking log dislocated my shoulder.

It was a deadfall. The kind of trap you set for deer or even cougars. I blundered right into it.

This scares me for two reasons—one, Du Pont just fucked up my firing hand. And two, if there's one trap, there could be more. Du Pont could be driving Simone right into them.

I've got to fix my arm. I'll be useless without it.

I've never dislocated my shoulder before, but I've seen it happen to other people. I know I've got to pop it back into the socket.

Grabbing my limp, flopping wrist in my other hand, I pull my arm forward and up in a hard, jerking motion. Even though I'm trying to stay quiet, I can't help the roar of pain that comes out of me. My shoulder feels like it's been doused in gasoline and set ablaze.

Just as abruptly, as it pops back into place, the pain dissipates. It doesn't feel good—the joint throbs with every heartbeat. But I can move my right hand again.

I have to find my rifle. It went flying when the log hit me. I find it a dozen feet away, spattered with mud, and I check to make sure the barrel is clear of debris. Then I sling it over my shoulder and start jogging again, more carefully now, looking out for other snares.

I hope Raylan's okay. I haven't seen any sign of him yet.

I'm coming around to the spot where Simone left the meadow. I slow, scanning the brush with my scope. I'm looking for her, and also for Du Pont. When you're searching for somebody you know is camouflaged, you don't look for color, or pattern, or individual features like a face or hands. What you look for is a shape. The rounded shape of shoulders and back.

I look for motion, too. But it's difficult because the last leaves clinging to the trees are rustling dryly, the branches are moving in the breeze, and the trunks of the thin, spindly saplings are scratching together. There are birds and squirrels chirping and squeaking, creating echoing noise that bounces around in the confined space.

I see a flock of starlings atop a lightning-blasted pine.

As I approach, the birds look down at me warily, stirring on their perches.

That gives me an idea.

I run at them, swinging my arms in the air.

The whole flock soars into the air, circling and whirling as a single mass. They fly over the trees, turning one way and another, looking for somewhere safe to come down.

As I watch, they take a hard turn away from a spot in the woods off to the north. They avoid it as one mind, heading in the opposite direction and coming down in another lonely, empty tree instead.

The birds saw something on the ground. Or more accurately, someone...

I turn to the north and start running again.

43
SIMONE

Run, or hide?

That's the question.

I sprint through the woods, branches and thorns scratching at my bare skin.

I don't know how to run without leaving a trail. I'm sure I'm smearing mud and blood everywhere I go, leaving footprints and broken branches in my wake. I don't know how to avoid it.

If I hide, Du Pont will follow my trail, then shoot me.

If I keep running, he'll see me or hear me.

At least the air is warming just a little. I'm no longer giving out clouds of breath every time I exhale.

I hear something that sounds like a groan, way off in the woods. I don't know if it's animal or human. At this point, I'd prefer an animal.

On the other side of me, much closer, I hear a sharp snap, like a person treading on a twig.

Immediately, I drop behind the closest tree, huddled as small as I can get, listening.

At first I hear nothing. Just long silence, with the slight hissing of a breeze in the trees.

Then I hear someone moving, over on my right side. It's obvious they're trying to move slowly and quietly, but I hear them all the same. My senses always get stronger when I'm stressed.

On the light breeze, I catch the unmistakable scent of Du Pont's aftershave.

He's very, very close.

It's torture hiding behind this tree. Part of me thinks he's already spotted me, and he's closing in. The other part of me believes that my only hope is to stay perfectly still while he passes by.

I close my eyes. I keep my mouth shut. Covered in mud, I'm almost exactly the color of the bark and the soft, loamy ground. Only my white teeth and eyes would give me away.

I barely breathe. I will my heart to beat quietly.

More silent than a whisper, I hear him passing by on my right-hand side.

Slowly, so very slowly, I creep around the trunk of the tree, to keep the bulk of the tree between me and him. And then I peer around the edge of the bark.

He looks monstrous. He's pulled up his hood so he's covered head to toe in that shaggy brown suit, like a bear that's learned to walk on its hind legs. He moves in a slow, creeping way, his head sweeping left to right, looking for me. I see the glint of his rifle, barrel up at the ready.

I'm behind him now. I'm waiting for him to keep going so I can run in the opposite direction. Instead, he stops exactly where he is. He takes cover behind a fallen tree, thick with green moss and white toadstools. I follow his gaze upward to the top of the ridge.

There's a figure up there. He's lying prone on the ridge, rifle set up in front of him. I can only see the top of his shoulder, or maybe it's his head. It's difficult to tell at this distance. All I know for sure is that he's dressed in dark clothes, and he's big. It's got to be Dante.

I watch Du Pont raise his rifle up, aiming at the figure. His finger curls around the trigger.

"DANTE, LOOK OUT!" I scream.

Too late. Du Pont fires. The figure tumbles back off the top of the ridge, hit dead-on.

Du Pont is already wheeling around in my direction. I'm running away as fast as I can, through the thickest stands of trees, hoping they'll provide some cover.

I hear another shot and then a popping sound, followed by hissing. I throw a look back over my shoulder. A sheet of smoke rises in the air, thick and pale gray. The smoke is between me and Du Pont. Or at least I think it is—I don't have a good sense of direction. I have no idea where I am relative to the meadow or the cabin or the van. I'm completely lost.

I keep running, tears streaming down my cheeks, hoping against hope that Du Pont's shot only caught Dante on the shoulder, that Dante is still alive.

I reach a small stretch of ground that's open and leafy, and I sprint across it, trying to get back under the cover of trees. As I'm running, the ground gives way beneath my feet. I'm plunging.

My arms pinwheel, reaching for something, anything. I grab a tree root and hang on to it with both hands, two of my fingernails tearing off at the quick.

I'm dangling over empty space, barely clinging to the root. Trying not to scream, I look down into a deep pit.

Oh my god. It's some kind of trap. I can't see the bottom. I don't know how deep it is or what's down there. But I know it's far enough that I'll probably break my leg if I lose my grip on this root. Plus I'll be stuck down there. No getting out. Du Pont will be able to track me down at his leisure.

I have to pull myself back up.

I'm clinging to the root, which is thin and slippery with mud. I try to haul myself back up, but my hands slide, and I almost lose my grip entirely.

My hands are freezing cold and numb. My whole body is aching—scratched, bruised, shivering.

I want to cry. I want to give up. But I can't.

Tightening my grip, I pull myself up a few inches, then a few more. I dig my bare toes into the side of the pit to give myself purchase. As I get closer to the top, I try to grab the muddy edge of the pit. A chunk of crumbling dirt comes off in my hand, grit raining down in my face, blinding me. I spit the dirt out of my mouth and try again.

44
DANTE

I RUN NORTH TOWARD THE SPOT THE STARLINGS AVOIDED. I KNOW there's a human there.

As I approach, I bring my scope up to my shoulder and scan the area. I see what looks like a figure lying prone on top of the ridge, and I grin. I recognize my old rifle. Raylan found us.

The figure isn't Raylan—it's my clothes, stuffed with branches and leaves, positioned to look like a person. It's a decoy. Raylan is trying to draw Du Pont in. Which means that he's got to be close by, waiting for Du Pont to show himself.

I take my own position, forming the third side of a triangle. The decoy is the point—Raylan and I are the other two corners. Hopefully, Du Pont will walk right into the middle.

The woods are silent. No birdsong or chirping frogs. There are too many people around. The animals know we're here.

I slow my breathing, scanning the woods through my scope.

Then I hear a sound that makes my blood freeze. Simone's scream: "DANTE, LOOK OUT!"

A rifle fires. The dummy tumbles off the top of the ridge.

I swing my barrel around, searching for the shooter or for Simone.

Raylan spots her first—he's closer to her. She's running away through the woods, naked and covered in mud.

Raylan grabs his smoke grenade, pulls the pin, and flings it down behind her. It detonates, throwing up a screen of smoke, shielding her from Du Pont.

Unfortunately, it also shields Du Pont from me. And it leaves Raylan wide open.

I hear Du Pont's rifle shot echo through the trees. Then a grunt that has to be Raylan. A body falls down the ridge, rolling over as it goes. Raylan was wearing a vest, same as me, but a vest won't stop a high-caliber bullet. It only slows it down a little.

I'm torn between the need to check on Raylan and the need to follow Simone.

Really, there's no choice—my feet are already turning in Simone's direction, and I'm running after her, determined to get to her before Du Pont can.

I hear a shriek and splintering branches. *Fuck.* Another trap. I'm running full out, my shoulder throbbing like a drum, my heart thudding so loud that I can hear it in my ears.

Branches whip at my face as I crash through the trees, sprinting toward that scream.

I reach a clearing and see Du Pont standing at the edge of a pit, his rifle raised, pointed down at Simone. She's is clinging to the soft, crumbling ground, looking up into Du Pont's face with an expression of pure terror.

He's already got his gun pointed right at her. If I shoot him in the head or the back, he may jerk the trigger and kill her.

No time to think. No time to aim.

I raise my rifle, without even using the scope. I point and shoot.

Du Pont's trigger finger explodes in a mist of blood.

Snarling with rage, he wheels toward me.

I shoot him three more times in the chest.

He's frozen in place, his teeth bared, his eyes bulging.

Then he topples over, tumbling into the pit.

I run to Simone, grabbing her by the wrists. I pull her up out of the hole, wrapping her in my arms and pressing her against my chest.

"Dante!" she sobs. "You're alive!"

I kiss her everywhere. Her hands, her forehead, her cheeks, her lips. She's covered in mud, and I don't give a shit. I strip off my shirt and put it on her naked body—it's so big on her that it hangs down almost to her knees. I take off my boots and put my thick wool socks over her bloody, battered feet. Then I scoop her up in my arms and carry her.

She lays her head against my chest, shivering so hard that I can barely hold her at first, then slowly relaxing and sinking into the warmth of my body.

I carry her back the way we came, back to where Raylan fell.

"I'm so sorry." Simone sobs.

"Don't you ever be sorry," I tell her, my voice thick with all the things I've wanted to say to her all this time. "I love you, Simone. I have *always* loved you, and I *will* always love you. I'm never going to stop. Wherever you go, whatever you do, you have my heart in your hands."

"I love you so much," she cries, her voice cracking. "I can't believe you found me…"

"I'll always keep you safe," I promise her.

"Is Henry—"

"He's safe, too. He's with my father."

She turns her face against my chest and cries harder than ever, with relief this time.

I carry her all the way back to the ridge.

I'm full of relief that Simone is safe. But the closer we get to Raylan, the sicker I feel, worrying that I'm going to find my friend's body. Worrying that he sacrificed himself to save the woman I love.

I find the spot where he fell, and I set Simone down so I can look around, over ground that's rough and muddy, where the leaves are churned up, and I can see a streak of dark blood.

"Oh, there you are," a wry voice says. "'Bout time. I almost finished my sudoku."

I whirl around.

Long Shot is propped against a tree, holding his hand to his side. I can see blood seeping through the cracks between his fingers.

"Raylan!" I shout, running over to him.

"Relax," he says. "I'm not dying. It just fucking hurts."

Du Pont's bullet has torn out a chunk of his side, even through the Kevlar vest. The hip of his jeans is soaked with blood, but he's made a kind of compress out of moss, and it does look like the bleeding has slowed.

Tying the compress on with the remains of Raylan's shirt, I haul him up. Simone helps support him from the other side.

"I've got him," I tell her.

"No, it's okay," Simone says, serious and determined. "I can help."

Supporting Raylan between us, we start walking back out of the woods.

Raylan is pale, but he looks over at Simone with curiosity.

"Nice to finally meet you. I can't say Deuce told me a lot about you because, as you know, he's not a man of many words. But when we managed to get him drunk once in a blue moon..."

"Watch it," I warn him. "I can still leave you out here for the wolves."

Simone shakes her head at me.

"Thank you," she says to Raylan, sincerely.

He says, "Deuce didn't tell me much, but he said enough for me to know you were a girl worth saving."

He squints at me. "You did kill Du Pont, didn't you?"

"Yeah." I nod.

"Good." Raylan winces. "I never liked that guy. Did I tell you he used to eat his peas one at a time? I should have known then he was nuts."

45
SIMONE

Dante drives Raylan and me directly to the nearest hospital. It's a tiny clinic in Sarasota, where the only other patient is a kid with a broken arm. He looks thrilled to have some kind of entertainment at hand, besides his own aching arm. The staff members are a lot more suspicious. They separate me from the two men, asking a barrage of questions that make it clear they don't believe Raylan's story of being shot in a hunting accident.

They let me use the shower at least. I stand under the hot spray for forty minutes, watching dirt, twigs, leaves, and blood swirl down the drain. I start crying again, seeing the cuts and welts all over my body, remembering the feeling of fleeing for my life.

But I also remember what it felt like to have Dante's arms wrapped around me as he lifted me into the air, then pressed me against his chest. I've never felt a more powerful sensation of relief, gratitude, and safety.

Dante's arms are the safest place in the world. The only place I've truly felt secure.

I would face any danger, as long as he was with me.

Once I'm clean, and the doctor has stitched up the worst of the cuts on my feet and legs, the hospital lends me a pair of scrubs to wear. They're soft and faded from a hundred washings, and quite honestly, they're the most comfortable thing I've ever worn.

It takes longer for them to sew up the wound in Raylan's side. They have to put a couple of pints of blood in his arm, and Dante and I check into the only motel in the town so Raylan can rest and recover overnight.

The motel room is tiny, last decorated in 1982 most likely, with wood-paneled walls, mustard-yellow drapes, and a scratchy wool blanket.

To me, it's the best hotel I've ever stayed in because I'm staying there with Dante. We eat at the kitschy little family restaurant next door, both of us ordering double stacks of pancakes and bacon, which turn out to be surprisingly delicious.

Then we go back to our room, and Dante throws me down on the creaky, lumpy bed that groans alarmingly under our combined weight.

I look up into Dante's face—into his fierce black eyes.

"I'm sorry," I tell him again. "I should have told you about Henry."

"I should have come to London," Dante says seriously. "I should have never let you go so easily. I should have tracked you down that year, or the one after, or the one after that. I was prideful and bitter. I was a fucking fool."

"I'll never lie to you again," I promise him.

"I'll never fail to find you."

He kisses me. His lips are rough and warm. His huge, heavy arms envelop me completely.

He moves his hands down my body, gently squeezing and massaging the aching muscles of my neck, shoulders, chest, and back. He finds every tight and knotted place, and he presses out the stress and pain of the past twenty-four hours. His hands are so warm and strong that they force out trauma from my flesh, leaving a deep, contented pleasure in its place.

My body has been in so much pain that it seems impossible that I could become aroused again. But as his palms brush over my breasts, my nipples respond to his touch. A warm flush spreads from my breasts down to my belly.

Dante takes my breast in his mouth. He sucks gently on the nipple, lapping at it with his tongue. He trails his tongue all the way down my navel, to the little patch of skin right below my belly button.

The skin is tight, but if you look closely, there are a few silvery lines, the ghostly remnants of the stretch marks I got in the final month of my pregnancy.

"I never noticed those before," Dante says. His voice is soft, with a tone of wonder, not anger. "I bet you were the most beautiful pregnant woman."

"If you wanted..." My voice catches in my throat. "Maybe I could be again..."

Dante looks up at me, his hand tightening around mine. "Do you mean that?" he says huskily.

I nod, tears pricking at my eyes. "I'm not on the pill. In fact..." Mentally, I count back through the days since my last period. "Now could be a good time."

Dante presses his face against my pussy and inhales my scent. Even with his dark, dark irises, I can see his pupils dilate with lust. "You do smell fucking phenomenal..."

He runs his thumb down the slit between my pussy lips, feeling my slick wetness. My pussy is thrumming with anticipation, my clit already swollen and sensitive, even though he's barely touched me yet. My heart is thumping, and I feel that anxious anticipation, the desire coiled inside me like a spring.

I can smell Dante's skin, even when he's down between my legs. His scent is intoxicating, enticing, irresistible...

My body wants him. Craves him. Needs him.

I'm sure it's true...I'm fertile right now. Ovulating. Biologically driven to mate with this man who is the biggest, strongest, and most ferocious one I've ever seen.

"Come inside me," I beg him. "Make a baby with me, Dante."

His eyes are black pools of lust. He rips off his shirt, revealing those thick slabs of muscle on his chest, shoulders, and biceps. The dark hair on his chest arouses me, as do his tattoos and even the scrapes and cuts from our time in the woods. Evidence of what this man did for me, risking his life to save me.

He unbuttons his jeans, dropping them down his hips, revealing that heavy, thick cock, which springs up already fully hard and seeking the warmth and wetness between my legs.

He grips the base of it, positioning it at my entrance. Then he drives into me in one long, firm thrust.

I'm so wet that his cock slides all the way in, all the way to the base. We're pressed together, face-to-face, chest to chest. Dante supports himself on the thick pillars of his arms, pinning me to the bed. Clenching his ass cheeks, he drives his cock into me again and again.

I wrap my legs around his hips, my ankles linked behind his legs. I grind my clit against him with every thrust. It's so swollen and sensitive that each thrust sends a wave of pleasure pouring over me.

"Come inside me," I beg him again. "Get me pregnant."

Dante wraps me in his arms and fucks me harder, driven wild by my request. "You want my baby? You want to carry my child?"

"Please," I moan.

That's all it takes. My desire for his seed makes him explode inside me. I feel his cock pulsing as he shoots rope after rope of cum deep inside my pussy, right at the entrance of the cervix.

The twitching of his cock and the sensation of his thick hot come brings me to orgasm as well. My pussy clenches around him, squeezing and contracting, drawing his cum deeper, all the way into my womb.

Dante kisses me deeply, wildly, erotically.

I kiss him back, certain his seed will take hold.

We're going to make another baby. Intentionally, this time.

And Dante will be with me every step of the way.

46
DANTE

Once Raylan is feeling better, we drive back to Chicago.

I go straight to the Griffins' mansion on the lake. I want to talk to Callum and my sister, to tell them Du Pont is gone. They don't have to worry anymore.

But when Simone and I get there, only Riona is sitting in the kitchen, looking tense and expectant. She jumps up as we come in.

"There you are!" she says, relieved.

"Where is everyone?" I ask her.

"At the hospital. Aida's having the baby."

"Oh." A wave of relief washes over me, followed by concern. "Is she all right? Was it early?" I'm worried she went into labor too soon because of stress.

"It's fine," Riona assures me. "She's full-term. Cal's been texting me updates. It should be any time now."

Riona opens the briefcase sitting on the breakfast nook table and takes out Kenwood's hard drive.

"Nero left this for you. He said, and I quote, 'You won't believe the shit on here.'"

I take the hard drive, turning it over in my hands. It feels heavy and fraught with all the awful information contained in its metal shell.

"What are you going to do with it?" Simone asks me.

I know what she's worried about. She thinks I'm going to use it to blackmail Kenwood or his fancy friends.

I look her right in the eye.

"No deals," I promise her. "Kenwood's going to jail, if I can make that happen."

"Thank you," Simone says, in an exhausted tone.

Riona goes over to Simone and rests her hand gently on her shoulder.

"Are *you* all right?" she asks. "You need a drink?"

"God, yes," Simone says. Then she stops herself. "Actually, just water if you don't mind."

Simone's amber-colored eyes meet mine, and a surge of warmth passes between us. I know she's being extra careful, just in case. In case a fragile little zygote might be taking hold inside her right now.

"I could use a drink," Raylan says, in his smooth Southern drawl. I see him eyeing Riona, taking in her clear, creamy skin, her bright green eyes, and her high ponytail of flame-colored hair.

Riona narrows her eyes at him. "You look like a scotch might kill you."

"I do a lot of things that might kill me." Raylan laughs.

"Do you think that's impressive?" Riona sniffs, tilting up her chin in disdain.

"Nah." Raylan grins. "Just the truth."

"The liquor cabinet is over there." Riona points. She was willing to mix a drink for Simone, but not some bedraggled stranger.

I'd like to warn her that coldness to Raylan is the wrong course of action if she wants to get rid of him. The higher she builds those walls, the more he's gonna want to batter right through them. That's the nature of Long Shot—he loves an impossible challenge.

On the other hand, I'm in the best mood I've experienced in nine years. I'd actually enjoy the entertainment.

Raylan strolls over to the liquor cabinet, taking down a bottle of Johnnie Walker scotch. He's a bourbon man usually, so I know he grabbed that one just to annoy Riona. "What's your poison, counselor? Let me mix you a drink."

"No, thank you," Riona says sternly.

"Let me guess…" He pretends to look her up and down, though I saw him do that already. "I put you as a gin and tonic girl."

A light flush comes into her cheeks. That's exactly right, though I don't know how Raylan guessed it.

"I suppose Dante told you that," she says.

"He never even mentioned you," Raylan says. "Guess he's not as good a friend to me as I thought."

"How do you know I'm a lawyer, then?" Riona demands, catching the hole in his statement.

"Well…" Raylan takes down two tumblers and fills them with ice. "You've got the navy suit, Souliers heels, and an Akrivia watch. All stealth wealth, because you want to put your colleagues in their place, but you don't want to piss off the judge by showing him you make more money than he does. The no-nonsense hair and the unisex cologne send a nice little 'fuck off' to anybody who tries to sexualize you in the workplace. And then you've got your two-hole punch and your notary stamp over there in your briefcase."

Riona's eyes dart over to her briefcase, open in the breakfast nook, though turned at such an angle that I don't know how Raylan managed to peek inside it.

He's grinning at Riona, thoroughly pleased with himself. She's not happy at all.

He hands her the gin and tonic, garnished with a twist of lime.

"Very astute," Riona says coldly. "But you missed one thing."

"What's that?" Raylan says.

"I fucking hate lime."

Riona upends her gin over the sink, dumping it out. Then she sets down her glass and flounces out of the room.

Raylan looks over at Simone and me, grinning. "I think she likes me."

An hour later, the littlest Griffin comes into the world. He's small, furiously angry, and blessed with a thatch of dark curly hair very like his mother's. When he opens his eyes, they're as blue as Callum's.

While Enzo, Fergus, and Imogen are meeting their grandson, I'm having a reunion of my own in the waiting room.

My father brought Henry to the hospital with him. Henry's wearing an old Tupac T-shirt that once belonged to Nero, and his hair looks freshly washed. He runs over to Simone and hugs her like he hasn't seen her in years.

Simone wraps her arms around our son, and I hug them both. It's our first time together as a family. What I feel in this moment can't be put into words. All I can say is that everything I suffered was worth it. More than worth it. I'd do it again a thousand times, just to hold Simone and Henry against my chest.

There's no joy without pain. The greater the pain, the greater the joy. At least for me.

All three of us are crying. I'm not ashamed for my son to see my tears. It's proof that I loved him all this time. Part of that hole in my heart was from him, even before I knew he existed.

After a while, Nessa Griffin pokes her head into the room, calling to us.

"Come see the baby!" she says, smiling her gentle smile.

We file into the hospital room. Aida looks sweaty and tired but thoroughly pleased with herself. "Look what I made!"

I look down at the infant in his bassinette, tightly swaddled in hospital linens. He's still frowning, though he's been subdued for the moment.

"What's his name?" I ask Aida.

"We still haven't agreed on one," Callum says. He looks exasperated but too happy about the baby to actually be mad.

"Nothing felt right," Aida says serenely. She's not worried. Much like Long Shot, my sister always believes things will turn out in the end.

"What about Matteo?" my father says, suggesting a family name.

"Or Cian," Fergus says, probably doing the same.

"I like Miles," Henry says quietly.

Aida perks up. "Miles Griffin?" She considers for a minute. "I like that."

"And you're all right with Griffin as the last name?" Callum says, willing to accede to any first name, as long as he gets the last one.

"It sounds good together," Aida agrees.

Henry flushes with pleasure. He touches the baby gently on the cheek.

I put my arm around Simone, resting my chin on the top of her head.

Aida smiles at us. She looks almost as pleased to see us here together as she is to have successfully brought her son into the world.

"Good to have you back, Simone," she says.

47

SIMONE

IT'S SPRINGTIME AGAIN. A LITTLE TOO EARLY IN THE SPRING TO BE sitting out in the park, but I'm always hot now, so it doesn't matter.

Dante and Henry are keeping warm on the basketball court. Dante's showing Henry how to shield the ball with his body as he drives to the hoop. Henry tries to imitate his father, failing twice, before he successfully makes it past and shoots his shot. The ball spins around the rim, then falls in.

"Nice!" Dante shouts, clapping Henry on the back.

As if in response, I feel the baby turn over inside me, her little feet now pressed firmly against my side. She kicks her heels, sending ripples across my belly. I press my hand on the other side of my flesh, feeling her feet tap against my palm.

I got pregnant that day at the motel, just like I knew I would.

When I told him, Dante swept me up in his arms with a new gentleness. Even though I hadn't started to show yet, he lifted my shirt and kissed my stomach a hundred times.

He's come to every doctor's appointment with me. Made midnight runs for orange juice and a particular kind of Parmesan cheese I've been craving.

I'm flushed with energy. I've been filled with a mad creative spirit, stronger than any I've felt before. I don't know if it's the pregnancy or being with Dante, but ideas flow through my brain all day long. I've filled sketchbook after sketchbook with designs.

After the baby is born, I'm going to start my own fashion line. Dante's already helping me find a warehouse where we can manufacture the clothing right in Chicago.

He goes with me to pick out textiles, asking me what I love about each one. Asking me to teach him why particular colors and shades pair well together.

"I like seeing them through your eyes," he tells me.

I carry my daughter along as a silent passenger on this journey. Someday soon I'll show her all these things, like I show them to Dante and Henry. She'll join us, and our little family will be complete.

My feelings about this pregnancy could not be more different than the last time. There's no fear or worry. Just a deep sense of anticipation.

But my feelings for the baby are the same as for Henry—I love her already. With all my heart.

"I hope she's exactly like you," Dante says.

I hope she's better than me—prettier, smarter, kinder. But most of all, I hope she finds her perfect match someday. I hope they tumble into her life like Dante did into mine.

Because I know better than anyone that no amount of beauty and brains, or fame and success, can make up for a hole in your heart.

That hole is healed now. My heart is full. Full to overflowing.

I never knew there was so much happiness in the world.

PATREON

Want to see uncensored NSFW art and stories too hot for the printed page? Check out my Patreon:

BRUTAL BIRTHRIGHT

Callum & Aida

Miko & Nessa

Nero & Camille

Dante & Simone

Raylan & Riona

Sebastian & Yelena

ABOUT THE AUTHOR

Sophie Lark writes intelligent and powerful characters who are allowed to be flawed. She lives in the mountain west with her husband and three children.

The Love Lark Letter: geni.us/lark-letter
The Love Lark Reader Group: geni.us/love-larks
Website: sophielark.com
Instagram: @Sophie_Lark_Author
TikTok: @sophielarkauthor
Exclusive Content: patreon.com/sophielark
Complete Works: geni.us/lark-amazon
Book Playlists: geni.us/lark-spotify